BLOODSTAINS

•

•

•

Jeff Mudgett

BLOODSTAINS

Second Edition

ISBN # 978-0-615-40326-7

Copyright # TXu001632665 / 2009-04-10

Cover design: Cindy Hill

Interior design: Kimberly Martin

Special thanks to Kim Estes, Kelly Davis, and most of all, Melissa Mudgett.

Fiction-- based on a true story.

Printed in the United States by ECPrinting.com & Justin Kulinski.

BLOODSTAINS

•

•

•

●

[signature]

10/28/17

INTRODUCTION

There are no vampires, werewolves, or mummies between these pages. They weren't necessary. For in the words of Joseph Conrad, "Men alone are quite capable of every wickedness." Bloodstains is the story of a real monster: my Great-Great-Grandfather, Herman Webster Mudgett. History knows him as the infamous serial killer, Dr. H.H. Holmes. One of the most evil men to ever roam this planet. You will come to know him as wickedness personified. His blood stains my soul.

Not for the faint of heart, Bloodstains is a psychological battle between an unfortunate soul and the spirit of a terrible monster. A contest with evil things that live down in deep, damp, dark graves. Things eager to be dug up to finally have their chance to tell the truth. Bloodstains gives them that opportunity and you the chance to hear them speak.

To accurately portray such an experience would be difficult for a Hemingway, let alone a first time author. Therefore, be patient with my sometimes struggling writing. Remember, there were no ghostwriters involved in the creation of Bloodstains- just a ghost.

Before you begin in earnest, do me a favor and set the stage. Read the PROLOGUE, close the book, and stare into the monster's eyes on the front cover for as long as you possibly can. Holmes will take it from there by properly introducing himself.

PROLOGUE

Before midnight, and between trains, the station is quiet. The Englewood stop, just south of Chicago, stays that way until about twenty minutes before every arrival. Then the station slowly comes to life.

The terminal consists of a large flat sided two-story building that buttresses a long wooden platform. A nondescript thing, the station's only colors are its drab coverings and the foliage of planted trees. Oftentimes, like tonight, the crisp wind off the lake crystallizes the night, freezing those waiting and making the station seem not of this world. Dreary and dismal, even by the light of day, none come here unless they have business. Only the ignorant come here alone and in the dark.

Amidst the shadows, a fine and courtly figure watches from the second floor window in the workroom loft, anticipating the train and the soon to be disembarking passengers. At this ungodly hour, with none of the usual daylight hustle, the station is perfectly suited to his needs.

Two miles from the station the day's last northbound train approaches, the locomotive's flood the only light strong enough to pierce the misty night. Inside the train, a conductor, his day near done, makes his way down the center aisle announcing, "Next stop Englewood & 63rd!" He glides through the ten cars and wakes the departing passengers giving them just enough time to disembark before the train shortly resumes its way to Chicago.

Oh yes, he remembers hurrying back from nine, *the young lady in seven*. Squinting at the seat numbers swimming before his weary eyes, he finds her and lightly touches the soft shoulder. "Young lady, your destination," he offers in a subdued voice, her beauty and charm having motivated his fatherly concerns. She is strikingly lovely – almost unapproachably so even for one such as himself. Dressed formally, her layered clothes, hat and stitched boots radiate femininity.

Smiling sweetly, she stretches while awakening and murmurs, "Why, thank you, sir. We seem to have arrived so quickly. It's as if the entire trip was a dream." She brushes the loose strands of her hair back under her hat, gathers her things and peers out the window. Englewood seems so cold and dark. She wishes she had taken her mother's advice and bought the more expensive ticket for the earlier train.

At the station the bell above the main entrance doors rings, muffled by the wet air, announcing the arrival of the midnight train. Heavy boots parade across the platform sending a shower of rocky dust down through the cracks to the earth below, as personnel ready the accommodations for arrival. From the inky darkness the train's huge mass of steel is a relentless force of gushing wind and sound as it emerges through the fog, only to be lost again amidst its own huge white puffs of pressurized steam that cloud the station in heavy mist. Within seconds of stopping, passengers emerge from the train, shivering in the cold, and quickly dispersing towards their final destinations. Had anyone been paying attention they would have noticed a distinguished gentleman, dressed all in black, purposefully moving across the stand. He is visible for seconds before disappearing back into the shadows.

With the discerning eye of a jungle cat hidden amongst jungle trees, the shadowy one keeps his distance. Tonight's offering is once again sparse. Those that are available are hardly worth the effort.

Moments before he is ready to give up he spots her, a striking young lady with a beautiful smile and a lively spring to her step. He watches her collect her bag and walk down the sidewalk through a small group of passengers, heading, he's sure, towards the hotel the conductor was paid to advise her to seek out.

His eyes stay fixated upon the young lady. Her beauty cannot be hidden, even by this bleak night on the devil's own platform. Blood surges through his veins-- he must know this one.

He moves deftly to ensure that she is guided in the proper direction. Noticing him for the first time, she looks up and their eyes lock and she is startled by how unusual his are. They are blue as the sea and so in contrast with his blinding white complexion. She has no choice but to blush scarlet as her gaze falls to her feet. Having given her enough, he falls back and short-cuts to where he knows she is destined for: the structure he designed, constructed, and has operated for the past two years. The place known around town as The Castle.

A few steps later the dark bulk of a medieval looking hotel looms in front of her. The front wall rises from the moat-like sidewalk, while high above, a row of perfectly balanced bay windows angle down almost as if aimed at her and her alone.

She pauses to admire the architecture, taking in the remarkable construction. The building's turreted roof and exotic cornices steal her breath away. Artistically on the wall is the advertisement: "World's Fair Hotel." With Jackson Park and the World's Fair only a short carriage trip due east, the Castle is kept open twenty-four hours a day. The hotel always has a vacancy for the young, the attractive and the unattached female.

Entering, she finds her lodging pleasantly warm and smelling of fragrance. She is awestruck by the imposing semi-hexagonal entranceway and the columns of cut glass windows. Her mesmerized reaction has been scripted down to the slightest intake of breath. Nothing has been left to chance.

The valet rushes to take her bag, at the same time directing her to the uniformed manager behind the front desk.

"May I help you, young lady?" the manager asks, having been instructed minutes before her arrival on what to expect and provide her.

"Why, yes, yes, you may. A room for one night, please. I'm here to seek employment at the Fair," she joyously rambles, already comfortable in such a homey place.

"Of course," he replies, having heard the same hundreds of times before. The manager provides her with the Doctor's favorite room, the one in which privacy is guaranteed. "Excuse me, Miss, we have a service reserved especially for those young ladies seeking employment at the Fair. Would you like us to notify your family as to your whereabouts? We can have a notice delivered within two days."

"How thoughtful! Let me give you my mother's address." She scribbles on a note card which she hands over to the manager with a smile.

In turn the manager slides her room key across the counter. The young lady grasps the key and heads for the stairs. The manager smirks as he glances at the address and her naïve admission. He files the note, its actual sinister purpose to arise soon thereafter.

Color coded gas jets, gorgeous frescoed stucco craftsmanship and black and white diamond adorned flooring direct her up the swooping stairway to her room, her baggage delivered immediately behind her. Despite being intrigued by the room's European décor, the young lady, exhausted by her travels, quickly blows out her candles and climbs into the big bed within minutes of changing her clothes. From a peephole beside a picture hanging on the wall, she is watched, her observer waiting for the perfect moment to proceed. When the moment arises she never realizes or suspects a thing, only enjoying her delightful dream begun minutes before by an undetectable stream of chloroform gas seeping in from an outlet under her bed. When, where, how, even if, she awakens is now a matter to be decided by the Doctor - her new master.

She 'dreams' of two men entering her room through a secret panel in the wall, who then escort her down the long hallway to a hidden chute which she is lowered into and gently dropped away. They know this merchandise demands the utmost care. She plummets some forty feet but lands softly accompanied by a cushioned *whoosh*. Her new accommodations are quite different. Eerie shadows play across the cold concrete walls as belching furnaces announce their evil purpose. Images of candlelit death and torture surround her.

What could have fostered such a horrible nightmare? She woozily asks herself.

Still dreaming, or so she hopes, she is stripped of her clothes by two different men, placed upon a steel gurney, and restrained by leather straps secured to her ankles, wrists and forehead. Assistants rush to and fro preparing, she guesses, a surgery, in what seems a hospital operating room.

When she is ready, he arrives, once the shadowy figure, now the surgeon, and donning his apron, inspects her body for any imperfections which might disqualify her. Finding none, he determines her to be of exceptional quality, in fact, perfect. Deciding to proceed immediately, he prepares to take from her what he needs, but this time, rare indeed, he elects to ensure that she survives the procedure. It seems her elegance has piqued his interest. Even so, and without further delay, he begins. His steady hand and razor-sharp scalpel going to work. His soft hums fill the huge room.

During the procedure he periodically turns to the small writing desk alongside the operating table to find his favorite leather-bound volume. His bloody hand sets down the scalpel and cracks open the book, the previous experiments' bloody remnants snapping open almost in final protest, as they give way one more time. There in the stained margin is the fountain pen the doctor uses to record his surgical observations. Back and forth, pen to knife, knife to pen… his unmistakable penmanship detailing her surgery, his planned use for her, and his new treasure's life to come.

CHAPTER 1

"**P**ops wanted you to have these," my father said, keeping one eye on the dog while looking for a place to set down the two old boxes he was carrying. Like so much of his father's stuff, both boxes were military surplus. My grandfather, Bert-- Dad called him Pops-- had died a few years ago. To me, Bert was the old man in the bowler hat that lived with Grandma.

"Settle," I told the dog. The fact that the dog knew my father didn't matter; he would have attacked him were it not for the order. A big German shepherd, Rex had materialized out of the blue one day, snarling and snapping at everyone except me. No one touched him, but I fed him, and in return he guarded my world.

"Shoulda put that dog down years ago," my father said after stacking the boxes in the corner.

I continued grinding away with the lathe on the brass fishing reel in my hands. The brilliant golden sparks splashed across the floor, giving us both something to concentrate on rather than each other and the reason he was here.

"I forgot I had the boxes," he added above the noise of the lathe.

To tell the truth, I didn't give a damn what was inside the boxes-- they were from Bert; the one I hated.

Burn in hell old man.

Outside Navy jets circled overhead as young ensigns conducted touch and go landings adding their luxurious overwhelming sound to the night. Despite not having flown in over twenty years Dad still wore the dark brown leather flight jacket he was issued at flight school. It was adorned with colorful squadron insignias and softened from the countless salt-sprayed sunsets the coat had endured on the decks of the aircraft carriers he had served on with distinction. The jacket smelled of jet fuel, gunpowder and cigarettes. He wore the coat a lot. It gathered deserved attention wherever he went.

My father had been a strict disciplinarian and big on the respect small boys should afford their fathers. The motto I lived by was: "Children are to be seen and not heard." When I was four years old I already knew how tempered steel was made-- out of disrespectful flesh. I used to go get the stick for him when I had one coming.

He'd grown up the same way.

Time had changed us both in each other's eyes. We were now that thing all strong fathers and independent sons eventually become, having reassessed one another after years of so-called "time-out." There was no back-down in either of us.

Most times our conversations amounted to three or four short sentences. That 'rule' kept arguments to a minimum. Today we were both working overtime as our competitive natures churned over this gift. Inside I reveled in the knowledge that his father, the one who meant nothing to me, had finally broken down and tried to clear the slate by gifting me with something, even if the thought was long overdue and after he was gone.

Half-laughing, never looking up, "He left something for me?"

"Your mother thinks this was his way of saying sorry. You're the only one he even mentioned."

"I didn't think he had anything," I said, "At least nothing worth caring about."

Bert had been a quiet man. A very quiet, stoic man. In the thirty some years we knew each other-- if you could describe our relationship as in any way knowing-- he uttered two full sentences in my general direction. One was for me to, "Duck your goddamn head!", as my grandmother was teaching me to ride one of her Tennessee Walkers in the corral. The horse was massive, standing sixteen hands. A California oak with a heavy low limb threatened to decapitate me each time we passed under it. I was hanging on for dear life and mimicking the horse's dip each time we got close. After yelling at me and seeing that grandma wasn't going to alter our course, he proceeded into the work shed, grabbed his axe, walked out into the corral, and started swinging with a vengeance, terrifying all of us, including the stallion. Ten minutes later the twenty foot branch came down with a loud crash. He didn't say another word, just walked off to God knows where. Grandma stood there half in shock. My hands were locked into the horse's mane in terror.

That was Bert.

As a child I used to intentionally call Bert "Uncle" instead of Grandpa, with that twist of the knife only a child can inflict on an adult. My cut used to infuriate my father and earn me a whipping every time. It was worth it. They both knew my insult was a ten year old boy's way of telling his grandfather to kiss his ass. I never called him grandpa. He didn't deserve the honor.

Bert's funeral lasted about thirty minutes and the reading of the will about two. Not one tear was shed by anyone in the family. At least that's what they told me. I hadn't gone. The putting down of Grandma's last thoroughbred had been more emotional.

We didn't cry at things like funerals. Mudgetts resided in a Darwinian world of fact and logic that necessitated rebelling against everything which already was. We had no sympathy for the weak. To us, life was nothing more than chance, made up of seemingly endless sequences of a roll of the dice. When the time was over the dead were just so many molecules to be recycled by the planet we resided upon.

I remember puzzling over my lack of emotion when a child. Was there something wrong with me that didn't allow the tears common decency demanded? Instead, in its place was that subdued shade of gray guilt and my inevitable judgment of weakness for those so afflicted. Their crying afterward seemed only irrelevant advertising for that most useless of human produce-- pity. Further self-inspection always left a filthy taste in my mouth, as if I needed to feel guilt for the way I was born, regardless of my lack of choice. For the sake of those around me, I learned to fake the emotions that always failed to materialize in my gut.

The people close to me knew I was different. They showed this realization all over their faces, like the way our pastor would stand watch over me every Sunday when I was a small boy. His sermons always seemed directed at me.

"Mom, why is he watching me like that?" I asked her one Sunday. "We're not the only ones here."

"I don't know dear, follow the sermon," she said, holding my hand a little tighter.

After a while I learned to accept the stares and obvious refusals of others to stand too close to me.

At twenty one I finally gave up trying to figure it all out, accepted my differences, and escaped.

Fishing was how it was done. The long periods of quiet contemplation peppered with brief bursts of excitement was how I managed the nagging mystery that was my life. Didn't matter where, with whom, or how much every journey cost, just that each happened. Whether with salmon eggs for trout in the High Sierras as a toddler, silver spoons for Bonita in San Diego Bay as a growing boy, Japanese feathers for Yellowfin tuna off the coast of Mexico, or with three pound live bait for the biggest marlin in the world off Pinas Bay, Panama, fishing was my heaven.

When old enough, I'd pack my gear and head off to sort my life out as best I could. On the way, I'd turn and ask the demons sitting on my shoulders what about me attracted them so. For forty years they refused to answer. So I resigned myself to their company for the rest of my life-- except, that is, when fishing. For the instant that first jig was cast at some whirl on the surface they'd vanish, leaving me alone to enjoy the day.

They always came back.

"What are they?" indicating the boxes, finally unable to resist. "You looked?" Of course he had. His discomfort at being on the other end of that question, his father having died and left him nothing, not even a thought, was obvious. Even his titanium toughness was working overtime with this sleight of dead hand.

"They're what are left of the only thing he enjoyed in his entire life… fishing," my father managed to say, his face blank. "He knew you liked to fish too."

"Great." Both of us recognizing how ridiculous it was for a father to have to explain to his son that his grandfather knew he liked to fish.

Still following orders, my father continued, "The tackle boxes meant a lot to him. They were off-limits to your uncle and me when we were kids. Messing with them carried an ass-whipping." He leaned back for effect, hands hidden away in the pockets of his now civilian style khaki trousers. Sparks still flying, I kept working away on the fishing reel.

Dad went on to explain that despite Bert having died almost six years ago, he had forbidden his bequeathal of the boxes to me until after grandmother died. The boxes were the sole personal items in his last will and testament. The fact that his entire will consisted of just five sentences surprised no one in the family. This was just him. The snub, if accurately called that, bothered no one, or if it did there was little outward display of emotion over his lack of words. So while the rest of the family wrangled, as all good families do today, over the proceeds of my grandmother's considerable fortune, none thought to question or even inspect the old boxes they assumed were filled with red and white cork bobbers and perhaps an old whetting stone or two.

"There's a letter to you in the big one. Read it, but doesn't make much sense," Dad said, talking over his shoulder and shaking off the obvious affront to and from the grave as he walked back out the gate. Mission accomplished. Nothing more was needed.

Halfway out to his car he turned, "By the way, I just remembered, your mother wants you and Susan to join us for dinner."

"Tell Mom we'll be there."

Without another word he slid into his truck and drove away.

At dinner, neither of us discussed the boxes. The only one who touched delicately on the subject was Mom.

"The boxes were his way of asking you to go fishing, honey."

We both nodded, knowing she would never understand the truth about Bert. After all, she wasn't a real Mudgett.

That night the boxes and their contents were already just another pile of clutter in my overflowing garage.

CHAPTER 2

The first time the name Herman Mudgett came up was at a family dinner four or five years before Bert died. With few exceptions, the entire Mudgett family-- brothers, sisters, cousins, aunts, uncles, everybody was there, having driven in from all corners of California. The table was full of this and that and all of us eager to eat, drink and hear the latest about General Robert E. Lee from the eccentric one ... Grandma.

You see Grandma, bless her soul, was adamant that our family were direct descendants of the Civil War General. Despite not having one scintilla of evidence to prove her claim, Grandma refused to give up, spending large amounts of money hiring professionals to track the matter down. She wanted her theory proven and then broadcast to the entire world.

Years before, she had even talked my mother into naming me Jeffrey *Lee* Mudgett.

The issue never failed to infuriate Bert, but no matter how loudly he yelled or how softly he begged, he couldn't get her to stop. And when she wouldn't he took his anger out on those around him.

The issue came to a head at that family dinner.

Seems the professionals had recently notified her that it was time to give up and move on, that she was just plain wrong. And their finding was much worse than that. Instead of General Lee our ancestor was one Herman Webster Mudgett, better known as H. H. Holmes. He was my Great-Great-Grandfather on my father's side and he had been found guilty of murder and hanged by the neck until dead almost one hundred years ago.

Grandma, to her credit, came clean and fessed up. Embarrassed, but willing to accept reality, she handled her disappointment rather well. She hardly batted an eye telling us the truth, while at the same time dishing out her famous chicken dumplings. To be honest, most of us didn't care who we were descended from but the opportunity to tease Grandma over this criminal was just too tempting. To add fat to the fire, the rogue shared the same name as my grandmother's favorite dachshund, Herman-- the one we all hated. The dog was a mean, heartless cur which had bitten all of us once or twice. The laughter over this coincidence was epic.

While all this was going on, alcohol flowing, Bert sat at the head of the table offering nothing. Probably planning his next fishing trip up the Sacramento River... alone.

My brother, Bob, Grandma's closest confidant and the only one of us beside her who had read the experts' search results, jumped into the mix with details about this man Herman Mudgett.

"Well, seems they left out quite a bit about dear old Herman. I spent most of last week looking him up at school," he slowly said, pausing even, giving the matter time to sink in.

I could feel another good laugh coming at Grandma's expense. Bob's sarcastic wit was legendary.

"What did you find, sweetheart?" she asked.

But instead of teasing, he was solemn, "It wasn't pretty."

The laughter around the table died away as Bob divulged for the next hour that our direct ancestor had been anything but common. Herman Mudgett had been a celebrity, notorious for his misdeeds, and as much a part of nineteenth century Americana as the Civil War, the railroads and the Gold Rush. He was Mr. Hyde and Dracula rolled up into one convenient ball, bouncing up after all these years right onto our front porch. In the blink of an eye we had all gone from being related to General Robert E. Lee to having the distinct lineage of a Jack the Ripper.

The family, all in all, took the news rather well, except that is for the old man. Bert sat quite, not uttering one syllable the entire time my brother talked. Right before our eyes, he receded into a gray haze, retreating into the deep hollow of his past and what I would come to learn was a denial of this previously private horror. From his actions, or lack of them, it was obvious that Bert had known the truth about this man and for more than sixty years hadn't divulged a single word of the story to any of us. Not even to his wife.

My grandmother, who was clearly shocked that the man she had shared the majority of her life with had been unable or unwilling to confide this horrible fact, his deepest secret, to her, sat staring at him. Averting her glare, Bert's face grew redder and redder under her attention. You could see both their minds working, now ignoring my brother's continued words. Then all at once she erupted in a mass of questions, demanding to know everything. Her voice growing louder and louder until at the end she was literally screaming at Bert in front of us all. This had never happened before. Even so, he wouldn't budge, refusing to answer any of her questions, his silence infuriating her even more. I remember wondering at the time whether she would have married him had she known the truth.

Well, as any good family would have done under similar circumstances, we began to rationalize.

"Who cares, he's dead and buried, bones in a grave," I said. "What's for dessert?"

The nods went round the table. Even Grandma calmed down enough to offer one or two mechanized mannerisms. Everyone was in agreement, everyone except Bert.

Exploding in anger, and rigid as steel, he stood up, catapulting his chair back into the wall behind him with sufficient force that the crash knocked the family portrait down onto the floor. With that crash he slammed his fist down on the table, demanding complete and utter silence. Everyone in the room eerily obeyed.

Having our complete attention, he said, "No one will *ever* mention my grandfather in this house *ever* again."

He circled the table with his eyes, demanding silent acknowledgment from each of us before stopping at me. I will never forget the icy stare he gave me, his eyes slamming into me like silver bullets. The stares intensity actually hurting. My grandmother, quizzically, looked back and forth between him and me while tracing his stare until he finally broke and stormed out of the room.

What the heck is going on, I remember asking myself, and *how the hell does this crap involve me?*

That was all he ever said about the matter, and true to his demand, we respected his wishes and Herman was never brought up again in his presence. No one even called that damn dog by its name when Bert was around.

A short time thereafter, for the second time in his life, Bert was diagnosed with cancer. The disease was incurable, or so the doctors said. Beaten by disease, time and destiny, which despite his best efforts he had been unable to escape, he slid away into a deeper, darker, lonesome tunnel, the one we all thought at the time was of his own making.

He died, the same way he lived, unloved.

CHAPTER 3

The morning after with my second cup of coffee in hand, and Bert's words echoing in my head, I walked out to the back patio where the engulfing shade of the whistling spruces always seemed to set me at ease. My special place to contemplate the vagaries of life.

Our house sat high on a narrow peninsula overlooking San Francisco and San Pablo Bay. Riding the updrafts created by the cliffs, great flocks of sea birds would wheel over the house. Below and to the east the Sacramento River ran out into the delta in great organized parades of energy within natural chaos. Bridges built during the Great Depression stretched here and there, making previously insurmountable obstacles nothing more than temporary inconveniences. Often times our view was so clear you could see the Sierras from the porch. Often, and in the blink of an eye, the fog would roll in, making everything all but invisible. Then with another snap of some great finger, the wind would come up, blowing so hard it was difficult to maintain your footing, but leaving the air so clean and fresh that every breath was startling. Susan and I loved where we lived.

As beautiful as the view was that morning, my thoughts were dominated by Bert's icy stare while ignoring everyone else at the table. He hadn't looked, really looked at me once my entire life— so why then? It was almost as if he had been trying to warn me of something.

Weird thoughts began bubbling to the surface. Strange new sensations wedged themselves between the boundaries of what my life had been for forty years and what my existence had become in just thirty minutes at Grandma's table. I couldn't shake the feeling that something had come alive; an eager thing with a multitude of new instincts. In an instant my differences had been given a name, a name that could no longer simply be written-off as another Mudgett eccentricity. Being "a chip off the old block" meant something now, something not even I could deny.

No matter how many times I told myself that none of this was important, all this talk about long-dead supposedly evil relatives, I couldn't shake the feeling that somehow my destiny hung in the balance-- the one 'Uncle' Bert had kept hidden from me my entire life.

That night I quit fishing.

CHAPTER 4

From then on, I read anything I could get my hands on concerning Herman Mudgett. Researching H. H. Holmes became an obsession. I now understood the need of those early explorers driven to search their entire lives for some legendary pot of gold.

The sheer mass of written material was overwhelming. Unfortunately, generalization dominated most of the work. I tried to limit myself to the more scholarly reports, but soon learned that the sheer number of comments, and their outlandish nature, made logic almost impossible:

". . . the alleged greatest criminal of the world."

". . . It is not possible to find in the annals of criminal jurisprudence a more deliberate and cold blooded villain than the central figure in this story."

The 1896 report from The Chicago Times-Herald: "To parallel such a career one must go back to past ages and to the time of the Borgias or Brinvilliers, and even these were not such human monsters as Holmes seems to have been. He is a prodigy of wickedness, a human demon, a being so unthinkable that no novelist would dare to invent such a character."

And the 1896 Chicago Journal: "The nerve, the calculation and the audacity of the man were unparalleled. Murder was his natural bent. Sometimes, he killed from sheer greed of gain; oftener, as he himself confessed, to gratify an inhuman thirst for blood. Not one of his crimes was the outcome of a sudden burst of fury--'hot blood,' as the codes say. All were deliberate; planned and concluded with consummate skill."

He was the first killer ever given the label "serial." He was also America's first killer classified as psychopathic. In addition to these scientific characterizations, judging by the raw numbers of victims involved, he was also most likely the most prolific murderer of all time.

The monster had even written his own book. His memoirs were first published by a Philadelphia newspaper and ran as a series on their front page in the days leading up to his hanging on May 7, 1896. These words were believed to be the last ones written by a man preparing to meet his maker. They offered me the only first-person perspective with which to study my ancestor.

Holmes used this worldwide platform to explain his claimed innocent upbringing to a nation hungry for anything from the killer:

"Come with me, if you will, to a tiny, quiet New England village, nestling among the picturesquely rugged hills of New Hampshire. This little hamlet has for over a century been known as Gilmanton Academy. So called in honor of an institution of learning of that name, founded there by a few sturdy, self-denying and God-fearing men, over a hundred years ago, (approx. 1796), who could they now leave their silent resting places in the churchyard nearby, and again wander for an hour through these quiet streets, would, with the exception of new faces, see little change."

These words delivered his message with the texture and dexterity of a stiletto at the throats of his young victims. Their author, the supposed master of the whispered hypnotic word, was just months from having been convicted for murder and sentenced to death by hanging. Writing without the faintest glimmer of guilt or regret, he seemed focused on a future plan, as impossible as that appeared at the time, possibly to create public sympathy for his appeal, or, maybe to render his past less horrendous after his demise.

He describes the beginnings of a life filled with hope and peaceful coexistence.

"Here in the year 1861, I, Herman W. Mudgett, the author of these pages, was born. That the first years of my life were different from those of any other ordinary country bred boy, I have no reason to think. That I was well trained by loving and religious parents, I know, and any deviations in my after life from the straight and narrow way of rectitude are not attributable to the

want of a tender mother's prayers or a father's control, emphasized, when necessary, by the liberal use of the rod wielded by no sparing hand."

Had I been unprepared, these words could have been the biography of a trustworthy young man destined for greatness in medicine. Instead they are the words of someone so sinister as to make experts develop new names and characterizations for his evil, as Holmes had made the old ones obsolete.

My research, separate and apart from his words, revealed a child growing up within a strong family environment. But environment had little effect on Herman. Legend has it that his after school activities were bizarre to say the least. While other children were playing with balls and toys, Herman enjoyed the time he spent in graveyards. As a matter of fact, no graveyard was safe from his despoiling, as he sought fresh corpses purely for entertainment. He apparently maintained a schedule of recent burials, knowing the normal time humans needed to get over their attentive compassion for the dead, so that he could dig the still fresh dead up for his play. The knowledge of anatomy he gained from these corpses would later provide him with the speed and dexterity with which he could perform dissection following murder… and avoid capture. This expertise would save his life numerous times.

As he matured past adolescence, his knowledge grew to include the commercial potential of the bounty his unique hobby yielded. He paid his college tuition by selling organs and skeletons to medical schools. Money notwithstanding, he soon grew bored with the staleness of the deceased.

"H. H.", as he preferred to be called by his closest friends, appears to have killed his first woman before he was ten years old, and his first adult male shortly thereafter. Five may have been done away with before he was thirteen, including his best friend. He never looked back, building a momentum that eventually reached a crescendo of ten murders in one week.

His talent and modus operandi was to charm and manipulate his way through the physical and financial lives of others, leaving nothing behind but shattered families, befuddled police forces and a clueless society at large. He was the best there ever was at what he knew he was born to accomplish: the creation of fear, intense pain, and finally death.

To the world Herman was a model citizen and the pride of his church and school. He was a bright student graduating with honors. He had an insatiable thirst for knowledge, especially the sciences. He was a good looking young man who at the age of eighteen married Clara Lovering, the pretty daughter of a well-to-do citizen from Tilton, New York.

Herman played the part of the faithful and loving husband, teaching school for a year before enrolling as a student at the University of Vermont in Burlington. Clara worked to support the family while her husband studied. After one year in Vermont, he transferred to the University of Michigan at Ann Arbor in order to study medicine. His own words again:

"After having paid my college fees, bought my books and other articles necessary for my second year in college, I found myself hundreds of miles away from friends and relatives and with about $60 in money with nine months of hard study before me, allowing but little time for outside work if I wished to keep up in my studies with the other members of my class.

The remainder of my medical course differed very little from the first few years; filled perhaps more completely with hard work and study, and almost wholly devoid of pleasure and recreation. At last, however, in June, 1884, our examinations were passed, our suspense was ended and I left Ann Arbor with my diploma, a good theoretical knowledge of medicine, but with no practical knowledge of life and of business. After taking a vacation of less than one week in my old New Hampshire home, I went to Portland, Maine, and engaged with a large business firm of that city to represent them in Northern New York in the sale of their products; my prime object being to find some favorable location in this way where I could become a practitioner (of medicine)."

Taken at face value, the musings of this ambitious, credible young man, who without the financial support of his immediate family but with the strength of his convictions, pursued a higher education at one of

America's most prestigious institutions in order to obtain a medical degree and become a successful practitioner are indeed admirable. Unfortunately, these quotations from Holmes fail to tell the whole story. While he was at Ann Arbor he utilized his acquired skills at grave robbing to build a business that consisted of stealing fresh bodies from graveyards, substituting them for the living holders of life insurance policies and collecting the proceeds of those policies. He soon began profiting many thousands of dollars from these life insurance swindles, a business he continued for decades after. He became fabulously wealthy.

After graduating with his doctorate, Holmes began the practice of medicine in a suburb outside of New York. He soon grew bored. Not just with his occupation, but also the small town, his wife, even his first child. He deserted all for the big city of Chicago.

When he arrived in Chicago fresh off the train, the world before him was a whirlwind of opportunity. What he found and immediately loved was an environment well-suited to his predilections. I tried to imagine the relish with which he must have emerged from that train. He would have been dressed meticulously and groomed to perfection with blue eyes sparkling in apparent innocence-- the perfect camouflaged predator. How could any of his victims have possibly prevented their fate?

Holmes possessed considerable attributes that he used to his advantage. The *Chicago Tribune* called him "about the smoothest and best all-around swindler that ever struck this town." He also moved with the grace and the debonairness of a prince. His physique was athletic and his face, dominated by those eyes, belonged on the stages of New York and Paris. He was often described as delicate and refined, but his strength, when he decided to reveal it, was as quick and fatal as a black panther's.

His sole distinguishing feature, besides his striking appearance, was a disfigured little finger on his left hand. I was never able to discern the cause of the disfigurement or whether the oddity was a birth defect. He apparently never discussed the disfigurement with anyone, at least none who survived the discussion.

During his murder trial reporters called attention to his habit of rubbing the same finger between the thumb and forefinger of his opposite hand. He often did so while staring at the judge or jury foreman after an unfavorable ruling was passed down. Holmes drew even more attention to the finger by adorning the misshapen pinky with an incredible ruby stoned gold ring. Legend had it he often boasted taking the ring off the finger of one of the mayors of New York City. When I checked, there was no evidence to verify the alleged theft.

Finger or not, most women thought him the most charming man they had ever met. His looks, magnetic personality and his license as a physician made him irresistible to even the most chaste and resolute of women. They flocked to him. Holmes took full advantage of their attraction.

Holmes was promiscuous to the core. My research revealed that most of the young women he employed during his years in the Englewood area of Chicago were his mistresses at one time or another. Some stayed with him for years, even after learning of the others and determining his true nature. One can only surmise the fate of short-time lovers. The Tribune noted that Holmes had ruined the lives of at least two hundred "pretty young girls," had six wives and twenty-five children scattered around the country. Amazingly enough, as one of the Chicago dailies attested to at the time of Holmes's trial, "When the world marveled and continues to do so today at the enormity of his crimes, the surviving wives of this monster refused to believe the charges made against him and patiently await the hour of his vindication." There was little doubt that his sexual propensities bordered on the enormous.

Once he singled a woman out, he would apply his practiced methods and soon possess her, not as a normal lover but as a near slave. As an expert at seduction Holmes was without equal. Those few that were capable of resistance and refused his charms, he simply hypnotized.

He was a master at the art of hypnosis, rivaling the later guru Rasputin. He realized at a very young age that most humans could be made susceptible to his suggestions and to their own subconscious natures. He never stopped perfecting the talent. While practicing the art he spoke very slowly, as slowly as he possibly could while still being understood, leaving long pauses while projecting a voice both dominant and demanding... yet gentle. He was always in control of conversations. The substance of his communications was positive and uplifting, while underneath his motives were as cold as ice. The only thing he did better than broadcasting his own message was to listen, the secret of all great hypnotists, making sure he understood each response so that he could apply it to his next sequence, therefore ensuring his purposes.

His brooding eyes were especially haunting. This fact was reported by almost every reporter in attendance at his trial. He would shift his eyes high and into the corner of the socket so that each dark pupil was half obscured by lid. He then focused with the intensity of a sniper on the eyes of his intended victim. No man or woman, no matter how strong or brave, could hold his stare. These eyes were the stiletto that signified his intent to kill and none survived them. All who tried to call the devil's bluff paid a terrible price.

Elevated claims of superior intellect within the pages of a novel are often nothing more than hyperbole and flair intended to sell copies. These are not. Holmes' intellect can be traced and proven, utilizing the transcripts of his trial in Philadelphia over one hundred years ago. There, in perhaps the greatest public display ever of his remarkable prowess, Holmes took over for his lawyers and argued his own case. His magical and mysterious performance, in the words of one journalist, "kept the onlookers spellbound."

Holmes's aptitude at trial, despite his having never practiced or even studied law, became a topic of discussion among the legal authorities of the time and have even been used as examples by law schools across the country teaching moot court to the nation's future litigators. According to the *Philadelphia Inquirer*, "In some points, the keenest lawyer could not have beaten him in his thrusts and parries."

I imagined him, sitting at trial, awaiting his turn to present evidence and cross-examine witnesses. I saw his condescending all-knowing smirk at his opponents and witnesses. How he must have enjoyed himself amongst the hubbub and attention from around the world.

Even at the end, he played the room like a gifted actor. The only emotions he displayed were those he needed for some hidden purpose or plan. To put it all into perspective, he had just been sentenced to death by hanging. Despite that icy fact, the rendering of that judgment produced little emotion in the man everyone suspected would break down into tears and beg for a continuance, appeal, or just mercy.

Instead, following the jury's verdict of guilty, he calmly wrote in the margin of his newspaper the name of the foreman and one other disfavored member of the jury. Plans of retribution blossomed in his head for these unfortunates who had merely given their all in the interest of justice, believing that the judicial and law enforcement systems would protect their lives by keeping this monster, alive and dead, under control. God bless their souls. These citizens would soon become the victims, as would many others, of the unexplainable Holmes' Curse. The same one which would dominate America for years following his execution. How misguided their confidence was, assuming themselves impervious to his now infamous ability to carry a grudge.

His prison memoirs are replete with further evidence of his tenacity and single-mindedness. Reading his words, I was almost able to picture just what a lecture by my relative would have been like:

"I proceeded to burn him alive by saturating his clothing with benzene and igniting it with a match. So horrible was this torture that in writing of it I have been tempted to attribute his death to some humane means—not with a wish to spare myself, but for fear that it will not be believed that one could be so heartless and depraved, but such a course would be useless, for by excursion, the authorities have determined for me that his death could only have occurred in this manner, and to now make a misstatement of the facts would only serve to draw out additional criticism from them. The least I can do is to spare my reader a recital of the victim's cries for mercy, his prayers and finally, his plea

for a more speedy termination of his sufferings, all of which upon me had no effect."

I pictured myself within his clutches, tied and constrained at his mercy, struggling to understand his logic and depravity all the while waiting for the unimaginable to occur! What terror his many victims must have experienced in the final moments of their lives-- the shortness of breath, the accelerating pulse, the dilating pupils, their minds racing with the possibility of hopeful escape. How he must have teased those most obvious in their desire to live.

The more I learned about the beast, the more I came to believe that he may have indeed belonged to another species-- that he may indeed have been born pure evil. But how could I prove such a revolutionary concept? I knew that if I pressed criminologists and psychologists to better define Holmes they would all fall back on the same old worn out characterizations that I was slowly coming to realize were inadequate for Holmes.

But not everyone failed to appreciate his evil, especially those who came into personal contact with the doctor. One was the learned judge who presided over his trial and charged the jury that convicted Holmes. He remarked, "Truth is stranger than fiction, and if [this] story is true, it is the most wonderful exhibition of the power of mind over mind I have ever seen, and stranger than any novel I have ever read."

Even more to the point was a vivid piece of evidence I found concerning how best to characterize Holmes. These words were from a sentence written by the man himself.

"For one month and six days thereafter I took no human life. That duration left me needy."

I can't remember how many times I reread these words, their directness setting a foundation for comprehension. Whether the statement was made with pride or disappointment, I couldn't tell, but I rather suspect the latter. Or perhaps just another lie. What I did realize was that when one applied this length of time, thirty-six days, to the number of years he lived beyond adolescence, the conclusions reached by the experts as to the total number of victims he dispatched quickly turned rather ridiculously low.

I tried to recall a novel or a movie that came close to portraying a similar being. The Silence of the Lambs and Hannibal Lecter came to mind. But even that horrible make-believe character was inadequate for comparison purposes. Factually my Great-great-grandfather was *the* monster, the one against whom all others should be measured. He was the most horrible, evil man-- performing his own crimes rather than ordering another in a uniform to accomplish them-- to have ever walked upon our good earth. How could anyone who knew the facts argue differently?

Worst of all, my knowledge of this man included that part of me I could no longer deny. I owed my existence to conscious decisions this evil thing had made. More even than that, were he not the monster he was, I would probably never have lived.

One question began to dominate my life. What was I if he was the living example of evil?

CHAPTER 5

Were I to look back on all that's happened since, I really couldn't say what caused me to get out of my chair in front of the television that night, walk out the back door with Rex close at my heels and head straight for the boxes. Perhaps this reaction was the slightest glimmer of a connection with my long dead grandfather. Maybe a sliver of guilt for having ignored his illness and funeral. Possibly my decision was motivated by a growing feeling of emptiness creeping over my own rapidly disappearing life. Or maybe I just couldn't sleep.

Whatever the cause, I remember sitting down on the cold white concrete floor of my garage and without further ado tearing away the cardboard, opening the gray, dust covered lids and turning each box over with a steely crash. The scattered contents spreading out before me in an almost animated symmetry. Sixty years of fishing history representing his many treks up the Sacramento River, were now at my feet. In that instant the boxes and their contents became very interesting. Bert's stuff taking on a life all their own, shining with an intensity I wouldn't have thought possible just minutes before. All his goodies so elaborate. Here were reds, blues, varnished woods and polished metals creating a bright spectrum as diverse as anything I could recall seeing in quite a while. This was the time capsule of a suddenly complex man.

For the first time in my life, we - my grandfather and I - were communicating.

The fishing reels were as good as new, the hooks on his lures as sharp and shiny as the day they were bought at the corner tackle store in Martinez. There were even two handmade lures that more resembled pieces of jewelry a man would present his wife rather than a lunker. A knife, wrenches, a gaff, etc., the assortment astounded me. They looked to be the only things he might have ever truly cared about.

The types of lures he used made it obvious that the only fish he was interested in was the Striped Bass. Transplanted from the east coast, 'Stripers' reached sixty pounds and were renowned for their fight. Bert was reported to have been damn good with Stripers, but there weren't any photographs to prove his prowess.

Grandma had told me once or twice about his fishing, also that the mere act was therapeutic for Bert. That his trips were always preceded by massive migraines, the pain so severe that the old man would hide away in his darkened bedroom until life was bearable again. No one was allowed to make a sound when an attack was occurring. As soon as he was able, Bert would desert the family and civilization for two or three days at a time; oftentimes once or twice a month. When he returned there were neither stories, nor fillets to eat-- just him home again, the same as always, but no doubt calmer.

He refused discussion concerning his trips. The question of whether the trips were actually used for fishing never crossed anyone's mind.

Digging through the items, I came across the letter my father had mentioned earlier. The single piece of paper was at the top of the pile. The words were simple, yet somehow complex:

Jeffrey,

> *I enjoyed fishing. Fishing allowed me the chance to stay away from that which tormented me. When luck ran out, Port Costa, the spot across the river from your school, always brought me peace of mind. Take the little I have to give and seek out your own sanctuary from that which pursues you.*

The final moments are what define a man.

Bert.

These words, more than he spoke to me my entire life, were as cryptic as one would have expected, had I been expecting anything at all. I had no clue what they meant, other than the wandering sentiments of a terminally ill, heavily medicated man perhaps showing guilt for his lack of love. When he wrote the note he was dying from a brain tumor causing him excruciating pain. Despite this, he never gave up, cried or begged anyone for anything. Not for help, and certainly not for forgiveness. This letter was all that he gave back.

Don't ask me why, this wasn't my way, but I carefully refolded the letter making sure each crease was just so, and carefully placed it into my shirt pocket. As I did, a strange sense of calm settled over me. That cool allowed me to better survey his things scattered on the floor, the prized possessions of a man lost in a world of solitude. They were his treasures. Maybe they deserved some respect.

So for twenty or thirty more minutes, when my new found sentiment ran out, I sorted through Bert's stuff. About then, my normal skepticism came back with a vengeance, realizing this 'gift' might have been nothing more than his last attempt at humor, possibly to get even for all those times me calling him uncle. Sitting there, I could almost hear him laughing-off my never having gone fishing with him. If that were the case, it *was* funny in a rough Mudgett sort of way.

Satisfied with my effort, it was time to repackage the items, close the boxes and place them high up on the shelves-- away from all things day-to-day, and shut this, his real tomb for good.

"Well, let's just leave this at that and call the whole thing a good ending," I said to Rex, who, head on paws had been watching the entire time.

Laying the boxes over, I began sweeping the stuff back into their old tin and wood coffins. What would have taken him hours to categorize and compartmentalize took me seconds. Filled to the brim, I rolled both over on their bottoms, shaking them back and forth, rattling them away, in order to settle the contents out enough to be able to close the lids.

For some strange reason, the second box, the oldest and heaviest of the two, refused to stay upright and twice toppled over with a loud bang on the concrete floor, both times re-scattering the contents. Lifting it high over my head to better see, there didn't anything irregular enough in the box's shape to account for this bizarre movement.

"Too much wine and not enough coffee," I rationalized and blamed myself for the two spills.

Trying again, what struck me was the obvious separation between my hands while one was on the inside and the other on the outside over the bottom. There was space where there should only have been a floor to the box. There was also weight–– a weight far heavier than that of an empty wooden ammo box. Out of nowhere and for no apparent reason, my nerves began screaming 'caution,' as if telling me to slow down and back up.

Rex, looking straight into the box, sensing something too, was growling, his pelt razor-backed, and fangs bared

"Easy does it, boy." He wouldn't stop.

Trembling with excitement my fingers traced the outline of what was, no doubt about it, a false bottom.

There seemed also to be a latch, sunken and hidden, but certainly a latch. *Could this be what Bert had wanted me to see?*

Waves of adrenaline washed over me, and as I peered over the edge, the latch released of its own accord and the entire works sprang open with an energy from who or what knows where. As the bottom opened the space released a sound like a vacuum does when opened to the atmosphere, like something escaping from a cell to once again breathe the free air we all take for granted.

Two books and a map tumbled out onto the floor. The dog went crazy.

"Rex!" I yelled, trying to get the dog to cease his painful barking. "Down!" he wouldn't stop. This lack of obedience wasn't like him at all.

Gathering myself, I stood up and backed away from the boxes and books and tried to calmly survey what was in front of me.

Taking a deep breath, I said out loud to us both, "Christ, they're two old books and a stinking map of California. What's there to be afraid of?"

It all seemed harmless enough. Rex didn't agree.

The map seemed the safest place to start. Unfolding the almost parchment feeling paper, I laid what looked like a poster over on the work bench and smoothed the edges while running my hands back and forth. The map had been published by the California Fish & Game to depict the Sacramento River and California Delta system. The details emphasized shoreline. Very detailed in its depictions of routes to and from secluded entrances to inlets and bays, this was the type of map a man would use who enjoyed fishing from shore rather than from a boat. On the margins, in the crisp handwriting I knew to be Bert's, were thirty-two separate numbered notations concerning particular locations he had visited while on his forays. A few were nothing more than nonsensical sentence fragments that seemed more poetry than fishing advice. Others were precise in the extreme, explaining the exact location of the spot he fished from on that particular trip and the results he obtained. Each note was dated: one all the way back to the 1940s, while the last entry was dated October 7, 1960.

In the five minutes I spent looking the map over, I grew satisfied that the document belonged with the lures. Not stopping to wonder why it wasn't, I refolded the big map and threw the paper back into the box with the fishing gear, writing this off as just another one of his idiosyncrasies and prepared myself to move on to the main event— the two books.

How like him to do this to me. Not one word of explanation as to what they were or what he intended me to do with them or of how he had come to be in possession of the books in the first place. I cursed him while at the same time accepting his eerie gift, or condemnation, whatever the case eventually turned out to be.

They were more than just two old books. That much was obvious. They had the look of diaries to them. The older one looked to be over a century old and was very elaborate, looking like it belonged behind paneled glass within a museum to be kept free and safe from prying amateurish fingers in order to reduce unnecessary wear-- and maybe innocent victims. The other was at most fifty or sixty years old and seemed the normal diary any of us could have purchased at the corner book store.

Too excited to notice the concrete tearing at my knees after all this time, I ran my hands over the leather cover, as if a first time lover, trying to find a clue from the many cracks and crevasses. Finding nothing, I rapped the surface with my knuckles to determine texture and depth… and maybe to find the courage to open the book. Failing, I instead caressed the spine, up and down, at least twenty times, stroking and each time I did a spooky sound emerged, almost moan-like as if begging me to open a cage. Unexplainably, each time I reached over the corner, the cover of the newer book would catch my shirt sleeve, dragging and then itself opening the book. Yet when I looked to discover the culprit, there was nothing to physically justify the snag.

How strange.

I took the older book in both hands and bent the rectangle, gently at first, then with all my might. The book's spine was extremely pliable, and had the feel of large reptile cartilage and hide, possibly crocodile. Flip turning the top pages between my thumb and index finger, each page rattled away like the hard raspy purr of a big cat, the twirling pages also serving to fan my unexplainably sweating forehead in the cold confines of my new found laboratory.

It was time.

I had run out of things to test to use as an excuse for delaying opening the book any longer and discovering the true contents inside. Finally finding the courage, I opened the book only to recoil in disgust as a musty smell, akin to ammonia, exploded out from the book and up into both my nostrils. The sensation the smell caused was like hard horseradish as the substance drives up into your sinuses straight through to your soon to be burning brain.

Blinking, eyes watering, trying to read as hard as I could, the most apparent thing was that the inside front cover was blank, that is, except for the very flamboyant signature of one H. H. Holmes.

CHAPTER 6

There was no introduction, just the monster's signature at the bottom right corner of the otherwise blank page. The signature was actually quite elegant, as different from a normal doctor's signature as one could possibly imagine.

The next page was filled from top to bottom in what looked to be the same hand as the signature. The prose started off explaining that the author was rewriting a number of entries, from memory, because of an incident he'd experienced with his grandfather. Seems he'd received a hearty punishment from the man after learning that the small boy was writing down each day's lesson. There was no date on the page. Neither was there a description of the content of the lessons.

After he finished administering my punishment, grandfather demanded that I retrieve all written information I had drafted about our times together and the lessons he was providing me. When I had, he gathered all into a pile and burnt them before me until they were nothing but a pile of ashes. He then explained that his grandfather had forced him to do the same when he was a boy. I vowed to never do the same again, but immediately after he left the house that day, I rewrote all the entries I could remember and endeavored to myself to do a far better job in the future hiding my work from any and all eyes, especially grandfathers.

Not ready to begin reading in earnest, I stopped at the end of the page. This was too much too fast. I needed a more general understanding of the nature of both books before beginning reading them page by page. I didn't want to continue with content until knowing my way, so to speak, around both books.

Turning the older volume over in my hands, I watched amazed as each page separated and turned with an unbelievable ease, never once sticking to another yet cracking as if to alert the reader to text on both sides. Raising the book over my head so that the volume was under the hard halogen light on the ceiling, the high quality of the paper fully concealed the text of the next. There was no see through. Despite my lack of expertise authenticating anything documents, there seemed little doubt this parchment-like material was the real thing.

"Incredible," I said, still using Rex as my never argumentative sounding board, and reached over to find my untouched coffee, waiting where I had left the mug, now as cold as the water from the right side of the tap. Right then Susan made her fourth attempt for me to come in and eat. Sensing my focus, she finally gave up, going on to bed alone. Sleep was no longer one of my immediate necessities.

I turned back to the inside front cover, where the name "H. H. Holmes," demanded my attention. The words were signed in big flowing letters. Curious, I flipped the book over to the inside back cover. Instead of more writing what jumped out at me was that ten pages were ripped out from the back of the book. I checked the other and sure enough the same thing. There was nothing obvious to indicate why these pages had been removed. Despite the lost pages there was writing on the back inside cover of the oldest book. A simple, and hurriedly scribbled list of names.

At first glance the list resembled the same genealogical listing the professionals had compiled for Grandma. The names were organized in chronological order. Recognizing some of the names, and upon closer inspection, I was shocked to see that the list was a compilation of my direct ancestors, entirely composed of Mudgett males!

There were eight names that seemed drawn out with the same hand but all in different ink. Messy edits littered the page, as new names, apparently from time to time, had been added to the list and then, for some reason, crossed out. Notations describing personal characteristics accompanied each name. The varying types and tone of ink made it evident that the list had been compiled over an extended period of time, possibly decades. Herman Webster Mudgett was the name in the middle of the list. I didn't recognize any of the names above him, but did all those below his.

Chills ran up and down my spine at seeing the last name at the bottom of the list. The name was Jeffrey Lee Mudgett— mine!

Catching my breath, there were three names before Herman's and four names after. Most of those had a line through them. Two of those had also been circled, I guessed sometime before having been lined-out. Again, both times the circle and line-out were done in different inks. One of those names was Bertram Mudgett.

There were three circled names that were not lined through. One was of Herman himself. The second name, Scribner Mudgett, was at least two generations before Herman. Alongside Scribner's name was an arrow pointing upward to another name with notation: Thomas Mudge. I made note to check the names with my brother. The last name to be circled without a line through it was mine: Jeffrey Lee Mudgett in full. My name was the only one that was without a notation of any kind next to the notation.

This had to be a joke of some kind, or some sort of mistake. After all, Holmes was hanged until dead 61 years before I was born! *How could he have even known my name?* This whole thing was nothing but a fraud. What else could you call the impossible?

Hoax or not, the fact that my name was mentioned in this book for the time being robbed me of the ability to concentrate on anything else. My brain swirled with endless possibilities. Maybe Bert added my name? That seemed the most logical explanation, except that the handwriting in which my name appeared seemed to be identical to that for those added before Bert was also born.

Why was Bert's name included on a list that also contained the mass murderer's name? Was this mere ancestry? That had to be the answer-- trying my damndest to convince myself of that, and failing miserably. Nothing helped. Whatever this was, every rational explanation I came up with only served to raise more questions.

For the life of me, I couldn't stop. Why was mine circled? The only thing that made any sense was that being a circled name on this list meant you were being considered for something-- a position of some sort. The

names that were lined through, having been stricken, were for some reason no longer under consideration. Those that were circled remained a
possibility, but for what?

The only one who might be able to answer questions about our lineage was Bob, so I ran in, not caring about the hour, and called my brother.
Excited, yelling into the phone, "You still have the…"

"Hold on, bro, hang on. What's got into you all of a sudden?" he said.
"This isn't like you at all. By the way, do you have any idea what time it
is?"

"I need that stuff, you know that work, that lineage line Grandma
gave you from those guys she hired?" I'd already decided that the existence
of the books would remain confidential, at least until I'd come up with
something concrete.

"Sure, it's sitting on my desk, hold on while I go grab the file." A couple minutes later he was back on. "Ok. Shoot."

"What's the name of Grandpa's great-great-grandfather?" Both of us
doing the mental gymnastics necessary to run that lineage calculation,
"And run a check on a Scribner Mudgett."

"What do you need to know that shit for?" he asked, laughing. "You
still hung up on the old sicko Herman?"

"Yeah, kind of."

The line went silent for a few minutes. Finally returning, he said,
"You know, this is a little more complicated than I first thought. Give me
some time to sort through this mess and figure it out. I'll get back to you."
And with that the line went dead.

He called back in an hour, telling me that our ancestors had come to
America from Wales and Scribner was Bert's great-grandfather and my
great-great-great-great-grandfather.

"Let me know if you need anything else." and he hung up again. It
was, after all, three in the morning.

I ran the name through an internet search site, and right off the bat
came up with the fact that the man may have been one of the original
pilgrims at Roanoke. That line went dead also-- historically speaking that

is. The Lost Colony of Roanoke, as the disaster came to be known, was
the location of the most mysterious dead-end in American history, circa
1585. It seems Sir Francis Drake had left fifteen men there upon his return to England. They were never heard from again. No one, and I mean
no one, knew what had really happened there. Now for the first time, one
of its possible inhabitants, and not from the relief expedition, was being
identified as an ancestor to a thriving line of descendants. If his blood
were alive in my veins, he by definition would have had to have survived
any massacre or sickness. Even more puzzling was the fact that his descendants were on a list that contained America's first 'serial killer'. Was
it possible that Holmes hadn't been the first and Roanoke not such an
insolvable mystery after all? As I would learn with time, Mudgett names
from this list would begin surfacing quite often and at the site of many a
historical mystery, especially those involving foul play.

The same list my name was on.

Well, there it was, and right in my face. What every one of us dreams
of while watching Indiana Jones on a cinematic crusade to rescue humanity from some imagined evil-- a mystery that gives one's life purpose. I
don't know how I knew, just did, that these books and their contents were
the beginning of a journey as perilous as any I'd ever heard of, but where
to start? Despite constantly reminding myself that this was somehow just
a hoax, I couldn't help the growing feeling that with each turn of a page
my life was going to change.

At the same time a part of me was pleading to put the books back
into their secret hiding place, fill both boxes with concrete, take a two
hour boat ride and throw them overboard into the deepest part of the
ocean. But I couldn't, not for all *that* tea in China. I was far too excited.

Suddenly everything around me felt different. The garage seemed,
for lack of a better word, haunted. Surrounding me was that eerie sensation of being watched, as if strange eyes were reading right along with me.
I couldn't shake it off. The feeling became so overpowering that at one
point I even walked the perimeter of the garage and entire front yard.

There was nothing, just me all alone and by myself, but that sense of foreboding wouldn't stop.

"Get a hold of yourself," again out loud, "treat this the same way you would a case at law. Break the matter down piece by piece and come up with a rational unemotional explanation about the books' makeup and true author."

And so I did.

***

Assuming the author was indeed Holmes, the first page of the older diary looked to have been written about 1867 when Holmes would have been six years old. Eager to determine the possible life span of the man, I grabbed the second volume and turned to the last entry: it was dated September 14, 1960. If that date were to be believed, the man would have been 99 years old, give or take, at the time of this last entry and his presumed death, that is, if the two were indeed related. That age alone seemed to throw veracity out the window. Very few human beings lived that long, and no one in the family had, at least none I was aware of.

Mysteriously, that last entry had been written while the author said he was living in the San Francisco Bay Area. I was three years old in 1960; also living in the Bay Area. Without appreciating the significance of that yet, I moved on.

The writing style demonstrated a keen ability to communicate. Each item was described down to the finest detail, particularly the reactions and mannerisms of his victims. The handwriting was crisp and clean, almost professional in a stenographic sort of way. The author's educational background was apparent, the grammar perfect and the composition excellent. Logic was stressed throughout, as if the author was a scientist. Each page of the diary was signed apparently to dispel doubt for judgment one day.

Every page following the first chapter was also dated.

Dates, that's what I needed to hone in on, I told myself, the dates he used describing his experiences in relation to those of known historical significance. I flipped through both trying to find any obvious ones. There were hundreds! Holmes' diary was an American, no, a world history book. The issues contained in the diaries included some of the most significant historical events of the past century.

The diary described a voyage Holmes said he took to the continent the fall of 1888. There was something about that year that intrigued me. I couldn't get the date out of my head. Backing up and skimming that section, there were seven, maybe eight pages about that time period. Not much at all. They described his search, as horrendous as his description seemed, for pristine ovaries to supply his experiments with materials. The entries said the search had occurred in London. Puzzled, I referred to an English treatise on the 19th Century and was stunned to see that 1888 was the year of Jack the Ripper!

Remembering another book on the subject, I ran into my library and standing at the shelves, too excited to sit back down, reviewed my yellow highlights. Most noteworthy was the fact that after the book was published the English author had been widely rebuked for arguing that the Ripper had been an American doctor. She further stated she had evidence proving this doctor, a surgeon as well, was in London the fall of 1888 selling skeletons to the University of London Medical School. Buttressing those arguments were statements by Scotland Yard stating they possessed evidence possibly establishing a mid-western American doctor as a prime suspect. Fascinated, but skeptical that my relative was the one, I forced myself to put all that aside until later so as to continue with my general search through the diaries for overall veracity.

There were hundreds of entries detailing the doctor's time while inside the basement of his Chicago Castle of horror and death. He wrote of being dressed in hard leather to escape the predatory effect of the acids and embalming fluids he practically swam in. The pages flew through his contemplation of the mysteries of life... and death, each segment delineating the most basic of human emotions, reaching conclusions unique to this horrific man. Particular components of his many theses were provided by individual victims, selected due to their unique characteristics. Oftentimes, when dissatisfied with the results, he would discard whatever was left and begin again-- with a new victim. Many of his conversations with his victims were repeated line by line. The dialogue of life and death. He talked of teaching them their true and final natures, or so he said, making them admit to things they had probably refused to tell even their mothers or religious counselors. When they were of no more use to him, the method of extermination utilized was discussed down to the most clinical detail.

The books discussed much of our history. For example his trial in 1895 and subsequent supposed execution in 1896, the Great Earthquake and Fire of San Francisco in 1906, bullfights in Spain and Mexico, the "co-direction" of a well-known Hollywood movie in the Roaring Twenties where the murder scene, watched over the years by hundreds of millions worldwide, was anything but role playing and most stunning, two nights a guest in the Lincoln Bedroom, as well as supposedly chatting with FDR in the Oval Office.

Wait a minute. Hold on. The White House?

Sure enough, the author went into quite a bit of detail about his alleged host and the exact accommodations of the Lincoln Bedroom. Retrieving my coffee table book of the White House, with pictures of the bedroom, I compared the photographs with the words. The similarities were striking. While there, Holmes discussed privately debating with the President about world affairs.

None of this is true. It can't be!

The diary mentioned horrible tales of experimentation in Argentina during the 1950s with ex-Nazis and of reminiscing with those war criminals about the results of their 'experiments' over drinks. He mentioned the camaraderie he shared with these doctors and of being disappointed he hadn't had the run of the concentration camps during the war.

The sheer weight of these "tall tales" began piling up. He discussed an illicit affair with a much too young daughter of Seattle's biggest lumber magnate that ended tragically for her and mysteriously for the region. On and on they went, so many in fact they made me begin to think them too numerous, too fantastic, to have been made up. Who would have the courage, no, the audacity to have even imagined these atrocities? The entries turned some of the most accepted historical events on their collective ears. If just half of them were proven true, history would have to be rewritten. *They can't be true.* But one thing was for certain-- it would have been impossible, with technology being what it was at the time, to falsify these historically correct events at the same time they were occurring, especially considering there was no television or internet, hardly even radio at many of the times.

Don't stop digging, I pounded on myself. He was hanged until dead in the nineteenth century. If you stay focused, you'll discover the chink in the armor which will prove the falsity you're looking for. There is something here, perhaps something small, but will nonetheless reveal enough to enable one to throw the whole thing out. Something this talented novelist overlooked while preparing this fantastic piece of fiction. So instead of accepting any more of the fascinating descriptions, I turned toward solving the question of just how much of this material could be trusted.

Holmes was reported by the national media to have been the greatest liar that ever lived. But while this fact was comforting, this conclusion offered little in aid. For if Holmes were indeed the author what would he have gained by writing lies in his own unpublished private diaries? Lying to the world was one thing, through the media, but to himself in his own diary? That just didn't make any sense. Or was he creating a 'diary' to cover his own tracks after allowing his earlier tracks to be discovered? But what would have been the good in that, for after all, these books had remained confidential for decades, if not a full century? The 'all lies' answer lost even more credence when I forced myself to accept how much trouble this man had gone to in order to maintain the confidentiality of our family's secret.

So where in this mass of butchered history was my best chance at solving the grand riddle?

Then it came to me-- San Francisco was my best shot. Having worked downtown in the financial district as a young lawyer, my intimate knowledge of the area provided me with the best off-hand chance of detecting any bald faced lies. Skipping to that section, I read for hours. To my utter amazement I was forced to admit his description of San Francisco before The Quake was both geographically and historically precise. Apparently he *had* lived and 'worked' there. In fact, with these words, I was forced to admit The City came to life with a vibrancy reminiscent of Jack London or Richard Henry Dana:

Tall ships at anchor in the Bay, their hulls rocking in the waves of the passing ferries from Yerba Buena, carrying visitors from the East Bay, moved with a rhythm that tranquilized all that watched them. Talk of industry filled the air on Market Street, gradually changing to the days' menus at the great hotels located further inland and farther up the steep hills: The Fairmont, and my favorite, and greatest of them all, The Palace. I made sure to dine at all of them as many times as funds allowed.

The smell of perfume wafted through the air, carried along by the finest clothes from Paris, London and New York adorning the most beautiful women in the world. Money overflowed from every pocket passed on the street. Fifty years after the gold rush, San Francisco was indeed the richest city in the world.

Holmes cherished the rich clientele of the elegant hotels on Nob Hill. He stayed at one whenever he enjoyed the city. There the bars were the liveliest and the cuisine the most superb. These hotels were reserved for the rich and famous. They were perfect for Holmes. The impenetrable image the rich always projected stimulated him to greater heights and the wives and mistresses these captains of industry possessed made for the most delicious of prey.

These pages were the notes of a man with a purpose. He was a carnivore surveying his hunting grounds as a lion would have, resting high over the savannah, watching the herds of prey and contemplating his next strike. Escape routes were identified: the shadows of alleys, the locations of police stations, the beat of security and most importantly, access to clean exits to avoid detection and apprehension after kidnap or murder. Just as important was the author's desire to confuse and confound law enforcement officials into believing that the victim was simply missing of their own volition. He remarked that he had grown tired of escaping one step ahead of the law, every few years having to establish a new office in another city where he wasn't recognized. He often lamented that one day he would run out of great cities to conduct his adventures, unless of course he could start all over again with a new persona.

His modus operandi for selecting a victim was simple-- he would charm her as the philanthropic good doctor, gaining her trust over time, then having her divulge innocent details while categorizing the minutest pieces of her everyday life. Within days, her normal defense mechanisms would be at their lowest point, she having accepted him as her new confidant, true good friend, even potential lover. Once Holmes felt confident, or when he simply grew tired of the play, the game would be accelerated, but not before each potential trouble spot was eliminated. His focus then moved onto the most important decision-- the best location for her demise. The place would be selected for its clear benefit as the one where a woman would decide to voluntarily disappear, unhappy with life due to a poor marriage or oppressive family environment. If done right, his actions were nearly always undetectable.

The San Francisco portions intensified three or four days before "The Quake." To the author, there seemed something in the air, for the City felt charged. He wrote of premonitions. Uncharacteristically, his writing became sloppy while he described the people's unusually hurried pace, as if they too could sense the coming disaster. That charge seemed to motivate him further and, incredible as it may seem to us as latter day observers, to greater depths of depravity.

His description of the quake and utilization of the resulting anarchy was graphic. *Chaos ensued, as the earthquake had first frightened, but the fires now terrified. Civil disorder prevailed to an extent that I was free to op-erate without concern and each of my gatherings was conducted in the open without fear of detection or regard for the disposal of waste.*

As a young man I had read much about the aftermath of the Great Earthquake in San Francisco, but knew little about the unrest that ran rampant as authorities poured all available assets into extinguishing the fires that raged-- but not the criminals. By necessity, martial law was de-clared to quell the rampant crime. Many suspects were shot on sight.

Holmes continued:

On two occasions, police interrupted me while I was in the process of ex-tracting perishables, but were soon off and away as I excused my actions by demonstrating medical credentials and further demanding that they immedi-ately set off to arrange emergency lifesaving equipment. Of course, I finished before they returned, but often afterwards hastened to think whether they ever discovered my true character or initial intent.

His stories about the city hadn't moved me any closer to exposing the fraud. There weren't any obvious errors regarding the author's apparently accurate recollection of a well-documented historical event. Giving up on that angle for the time being, I returned to the beginning of the oldest book and the chapters about his childhood. The earliest entries discussed his ever increasing intensity and the evolution of himself as a unique child. These intrigued me greatly. As much as I hated to admit it, even to my-self, some of his conditions seemed familiar.

The burning began again. For as far back as I can remember this has been a part of me, almost as if waiting for the right moment. Growing older, I have begun to grasp at least some of the significance. Along with the burnings come the cravings and desires that seem to make me so different from my friends.

Natural instincts have begun to emerge. I used some today, or should I say they utilized me, to resolve an argument with my friend Andrew over something as minor as the ownership to a piece of candy. Imagine that, over a piece of candy. I took the last piece from a bundle we had been feasting upon for over two hours, despite his having previously proclaimed that same piece as his own. Enraged at my actions, he locked me into some form of wrestling hold he was familiar with from the lessons his father had been giving him and his two older brothers. The lock threatened my very oxygen, leaving me weak and flustered. Then I, in an alteration I had felt before but not in this proportion, became white calm enabling me to coolly assess the situation. Instinctually, my left hand extended up below his shoulder while the right rolled over on top of his arm as both simultaneously applied pressure to counteract and offset his energy while at the same time allowing the thumb of my lower hand to pierce the muscle of the arm which threatened my airway. The sudden strength I now found at my disposal was amazing to behold. His screams filled the air, causing me to quickly release the hold upon him before serious damage ensued.

Andrew asked, "Herman, where did you learn to do that?" trying to rub the soreness away while defeated far past any retaliatory thought.

I shrugged, as desirous of ascertaining these same facts as he. More than the method used, what intrigued me most was my vivid recollection of each moment. Incredibly slow so as to be far removed from real life, and his complete obedience to my silent demand for him to release me.

For the next three days I attempted to recreate the same maneuvers, all without success, the instinct seeming to have vanished, leaving me to surmise that my sudden ability had only materialized under surreal conditions involving stress and at a time when most needed to ensure my survival. I needed to learn how to recreate these same instincts whenever I desired them. But how?

Those early entries haunted me with their portrayal of his eagerness to learn a dark side. This was something more appropriate to a supernatural thriller, not real life. No one was born with instincts or powers - not like this. If true - *God I'd grown tired of having to remind myself of that same caveat* - he must have been either taught technique, or to the extreme, was born genetically different.

For the next four months the boy's writings revealed his work treating the human beings around him as nothing more than lab rats. The most illuminating passages were those involving his admittedly beloved mother. While not violent, they stretched the boundaries of maternal respect, while she, at the same time, morphed from mother to puppet and finally slave. Over time, she excused his chores and voluntarily took care of all small things necessary for his everyday life. He was not yet eight years old.

Herman continued growing into his true self. *I enjoyed watching the light fade from her eyes, once she substituted the pain with the knowledge that I hadn't been teasing after all. Close to her end, I had second thoughts allowing her to live, but only after obtaining her promise to assist in the future during my most strenuous efforts.*

This entry was dated when Holmes would have been ten years old. The page depicted a day after school when he stopped off at a neighbor's house on the way home.

His words at this young an age reached out and grabbed me by the throat. Was it possible that an adolescent could act and then later write about such an incident like this? I hoped not, praying that his real talents were as a much older storyteller. The grand liar the journalists all described.

CHAPTER 7

I was exhausted. There was too much here to absorb in a hundred sittings let alone one. Sore eyes begging, I closed the garage doors and set the books aside, ready to head into the house for some much needed sleep. But my plans didn't work out that way. While closing the second diary, a name caught my attention that stopped me dead in my tracks. The name was very familiar to me. Hoping I had read the note wrong, my hands shook rereading the name. I hadn't. The woman's name was indeed Rachael. My mother's name was Rachael.

The section described a woman and her small child. Apparently, the main character did them no harm, but shadowed them for days, watching her while assessing the baby boy. The baby's name was Jeff.

The monster had followed my mother and me for days when I was but three years old!

Careful not to be noticed by either, he began by ensuring that the woman and child were who he thought they were. He followed them to the store, to my grandparent's house, even to church! The audacity of the man-- the monster entered our House of God to watch me inside apparently to see the reactions of the patrons to my face.

Experts like to say anyone who has hiked through deep mountain forest has been unknowingly watched by cougars. The experience is described as the unknown terror of having been stalked, contemplated, even strategized over. Then passed over and allowed to continue, to live, but forever ignorant of the precariousness of life at the moment and forever thereafter.

Just like that big cat, he waited each night outside our house while we slept. At least that's what the books said.

The contents of the diaries had now suddenly taken on a completely different perspective. The now maybe not-so-long-dead ancestor had changed from historical fiction to first-hand threat.

He watched me as a child!

Wait a minute, the New York Times had written of his execution and immediate burial on their front page. Their reporters had claimed to have watched him twitch hanging by the rope in final life... and then verified his certified death.

This was a lie.

Balanced again, I read on, but was immediately shocked again to find him describing my physical qualities as a small boy, almost as if he were reviewing my qualifications for an upcoming event. He mentioned my stance, my strength, my coordination. He even described created special situations allowing him to observe my reaction to certain stimuli. The texture of my flesh, muscular makeup and reaction to pain were next. I was three years old for Christ's sake!

How close had he come to me and my mother? He answered that next by writing he'd touched us both trying to ascertain the level of my temper at mere prodding and poking. He received none, endearing me to him further and then immediately apologized to my mother for the inconvenience.

The final page was a debate, an actual pro and con, about his estimation of my character. My character to do what?

He didn't answer that one, but I had apparently passed with flying colors. His last comment about me was simply:

"Yes, the boy will do nicely," then, "I expect much of him." The author's words seemingly implying I had little choice in the matter. The words more resembled a father's after seeing his boy pitch a no-hitter at Little League. A dad puffed up with pride and eager to tell the whole world that his boy had accomplished such an amazing feat and that great things awaited him.

In the twenty minutes I took reading these pages much of that which was unanswered over the first forty years of my life began to fall into place. Answers were being generated to too many of the questions my mind had debated over ever since I was a boy... those sometimes shocking things that periodically bumped around late at night in my head. Before the books, I would tell myself, "No, don't go there, they're nothing but silly thoughts, just nightmares. All men have them." Now I wasn't so sure.

No matter how hard I tried to convince myself that I had nothing to do with any of this, I couldn't wash away the suddenly personal aspect to this thing. And what if I had failed his tests? My mind turned somersaults assuming we would have been put down in order to sanctify his line. Holmes never allowed loose ends.

I went into the bathroom and threw cold water on my face. Looking up, I saw myself for the first time since finding the books. The image brought me up short. Heaven help me, but I had no idea whose pale face was staring back at me. My features were more distinct, all edge and angle, more purposeful than I could ever remember them being before. The face in the mirror reminded me of a condemned man's in a movie.

Running back to the garage, why I don't know, I slammed the book shut, but then, as if to signify the coming fight, the anomaly happened. The closed book's cover, flat on the deck, caught again on my shirt sleeve. Knowing this hitch was more than just a catch, and now afraid, I jerked my arm free, the snag dragging the book open to a page near the very end. Despite fearing, perhaps half knowing, what I might find, I couldn't resist reading the page. The content and tone was different from the others. Instead of describing his day or an event that had piqued his interest, this one was a note from the author to the one reading the book. While not mentioning me by name, there wasn't any doubt who the note was meant for. Me. His words began by precisely describing what I had felt upon first finding the books, my initial doubts and the small changes that had occurred as I slowly began to find my place within the pages. His descriptions of my feelings were terrifyingly accurate.

The note further advised the reader to put the books aside and seek help. He actually said, and I quote, "to seek help", and to do so without further delay. The words warned that this was a matter of life and death. *Whose death? Mine?*

What was clear was the choice he was giving me-- to either continue down my rabbit hole, or run away from some sort of impending destiny.

Ignorant, I turned away from the warning, believing myself stronger than all this silliness. Supernatural things were a figment of man's sometimes ridiculous imagination. There were no such things as spirits, curses, the devil and pure evil.

So in the coming days I kept reading, but while doing so, one thought continued playing over and over again in my head-- the image was of me marching down a long corridor, in the cowardly lion's footsteps, to see a Wizard.

CHAPTER 8

Horrible nightmares began after finding the books. They were painful things and unlike anything I'd ever experienced before in my entire life. The dreams seemed directed, narrated, as if on a Hollywood movie set. They progressed in an orderly fashion. I couldn't shake the feeling they were being used to show me things. When they scared me awake, and at first they always did, I was left out of breath and in a sweat. If I did get back to sleep, the dreams would recommence exactly where they had left off. A good night's sleep became a thing of the past.

Each dream grew more complicated, each nights chosen subject more complex. The narrator within them changed as well. At first the 'he' was a strange, dark, blurry object that used primitive gestures to communicate, but over time he became more vivid, more human-like, eventually taking the shape of a tall, lean, well-proportioned man. Soon nothing about him was out of place, everything just so. Timeless, he began resembling the perfect Holmes of history.

During the dreams he would read my mind, responding to my thoughts and questions in long drawn-out explanations in regal tones. Well spoken, his vocabulary was immense. My reiterations would often take me days, repeating his words, before fully comprehending his intended message. He seemed intent on teaching me about my true self-- the one he said had been kept hidden from me my entire life.

The dreams often consisted of him asking me a series of vague questions so as to, or so he said, draw forth my primitive ego so long hidden in sub-consciousness. The ones we all expect to hear in a psychiatrist's office. They often went something like this:

"Can you guess what it is I want from you, my boy?"

I hadn't verbally asked him anything, but had indeed pondered this very question. I would later come to understand that these simple questions without answers were just his way of ensuring that I traced my deepest perception back to the original foundations I had always run from.

"*Why nothing,*" he voiced slow as molasses, "*Nothing at all, my boy, only that one day you embrace the core of our being, that obscure instinctual force that separates us from the rest.*"

I had no idea what he meant, not yet anyway.

The repeated "*my boy,*" as if expressing ownership, roared through me like a freight train. The words choked me, and I fought back with all my strength. Nothing seemed to work. Sensing my resistance, he would simply nod at me, the way a father does when he wants to communicate that discipline is coming to a son who has disappointed him, or God forbid, dared to disobey.

He punished my 'disobedience' by torturing me with terror, often too horrible for words, in the dreams.

Watching me struggle he would grow silent for an extended period of time as he seemed to attempt what must have been for him the closest he had ever come to expressing love, often just moaning, "*Hmmmmmm,*" in that slow, specific fashion that all who had known him said made them a slave to his next suggestion. His actions were reminiscent of his nationally reported muttering of, "*Ahemmmm,*" at his trial following the jury's verdict.

Then he would ask me, "*Now that you mention this, my boy, I do have something I would like to ask you.*" Once again, I hadn't said a word.

He paused, giving himself time to process my thoughts with that intense transfixing gaze of his. Then he let me have it right between the eyes:

"*Jeffrey, do you believe in a god? No, no, not necessarily that one. As a matter of fact, don't trouble yourself with any one in particular, for any or all of them will do,*" he said laughing, his eyes shifting away from me as if looking to see if we had the audience he obviously wanted. *"As a matter of fact, just pick one, any of them, there's been an endless supply. Try to believe in him or her with all your heart. For to understand me, you need to believe in him. Set yourself into that timeless equation. It's always worked before, that unavoidable human neurosis that so ably serves my purposes and will one day serve yours."*

I was too afraid to answer his question about a god, instead trying with all my might to inhibit all thought. He took my silence as a negative. Besides, he knew the question was about a subject I had no experience answering.

"Good, but do not despair—for neither did I, believe in one that is, at your age," he said, treating me as if I were a thirteen year old boy. *"But let me give you some advice, Jeffrey--"*

Raising his hand to stop me from interrupting, he actually sighed before saying, *"--it makes no sense to believe in me and not one of them as well. Seek balance in your beliefs. Good and bad."* Grinning, he let the words settle before beginning again. *"Perhaps... perhaps it would be better if you do, believe in one, I mean, before I return for our next meeting together."* Apparently satisfied with our progress, he added, *"Yes, Jeffrey, I can see I need to give you more time."*

And with that he was gone, for a while anyway.

As the dreams intensified, so did our relationship within them, almost as if he wanted us to grow closer, like a grandfather and his grandson. The one I never had.

He would read to me for hours, only interrupting himself by pushing dreams with which he showed me things, evil things I didn't know existed. He forced me to consider issues too horrible for a normal human being to even contemplate, let alone perform. Over time, as much as I hated to admit, they grew less horrible; not only in content but also how they affected me.

I began waking without the shortness of breath the first dreams caused. This *new* condition terrified me more than the dreams themselves. Determined to remain human, I fought as hard as I could to stay terrified. Nothing seemed to work. There was no doubt about it - he was changing the way I perceived things. Evil things.

As long as I did what I was told during a dream he stayed civil. But if I refused anything he suggested, they all ended the same way.

I would be flat on my back, constricted in too small a space, my feet jammed against the far wall, my arms forced tight against my ribs, my neck bent sideways in order to fit. Sweat would be rolling down my chin, collecting in a muddy mass of pungent dirt upon my chest. The very next cognizant moment would be punctuated by a mound of wet earth hitting me across my face and wide open mouth, the smell so foul as to force me to stop breathing through my nose in order to avoid vomiting within the confined space. Over and over again the dirt would hit me forcing me further and further down. Sharp protrusions at my back cut into me, making me scream out in agony through the earth on my face.

In each dream the sudden recognition of where I was would come to me with the same terrible freshness—as if each was the very first time. Of course! I was being buried alive inside a coffin designed for one, but now containing two. The pain in my back was due to the skeleton of the previous occupant. As the shoveling continued I grew more and more aware of my new surroundings, my new home, yet each thought continued to be interrupted by the constant, familiar scrape of dirt and spontaneous impact of another shovel full of earth.

Before long, the dirt was piled high enough until I could no longer see my shoes. All sound growing more and more muted as the foul decay filled my nostrils and covered my ears.

Then, just before all vision was lost, there he would be again.

He would be standing at the edge peering down at me in order to witness my discomfort. His clothes, obviously not his, were baggy dark linens that hung down past his elbows and knees. They appeared to be

the uniform of a larger police officer or prison guard. They were stained
with the same dirt I was being buried with. He said nothing, just looking
down, while shaking his head displaying his obvious disappointment in
me.

His face would be my last image as the lid slammed shut with a horrendous crash that echoed for an excruciating period of time before claus-
trophobia overwhelmed everything there was. I kicked and screamed like
an infant child. When the fit was over and I was near calm again, I forced
myself to contemplate the lid, now close enough to tickle my nose and
hinder the blinking of my eyelids.

Next, with no warning whatsoever, my vision and perspective would
be altered. I would find myself looking down at the old wood casket sunk
deep into the earth. The box looked just like the one I had been impris-
oned within. Within moments the realization would hit me. Yes, I was
watching myself being buried alive! Then, just like that, him apparently
thinking I'd been given enough freedom-- I'd be slammed back down inside the box first person singular. It was as if he wanted me to see what it
looked like doing the burying instead of being buried. Well his plan
worked - I wanted to be the one on top-- the one doing the shoveling.

Who wouldn't have?

Back down in the hole my entire body was crushed, piniored between the casket lid and my new old friend below me. My pupils pulled
from my eyes in search of the faintest glimmer of light within the darkest
dark ever experienced. Gasping for air, my lips were forced up against the
silky lining on the bottom of the lid. The taste was sickening. Outside my
coffin, a strange staccato began drumming down upon the casket. It
didn't take me long to figure out the sound was from renewed shoveling,
and dirt landing upon the lid, but this time at a much faster pace. The
shoveling would go on forever.

When all seemed lost, I would awaken in a sweat covered crash of
horrendous coughing, sitting up in bed, immediately searching my person
for dirt… and of course, never finding any. Breathing normally again, my
relief at finding myself alive was immense.

I'd tell myself, *they're nothing but dreams, albeit terrible ones, but still just dreams! Everyone has them.* Trying to talk myself out of their severity did no good. My entire day was soon dominated by the thought of them. Holmes' dreams were erasing the rest of my life.

Amidst all this, the strangest thing began to occur. I started feeling empty without one, one of his dreams that is, and heaven help me, started looking forward to falling asleep-- actually craving the terror of his gruesome games. Funny thing was, he had predicted the change would happen, saying I'd grow addicted to the energy they offered, like a drug, I'd soon need his 'injection' to live. He finished with, "The rest is only a matter of time.

CHAPTER 9

Proving the handwriting false seemed the most obvious place to start and the sooner the better if I were to have any chance of resuming my old life, the one before Dad had delivered those damn boxes. I missed fishing.

Besides, how ridiculous to even consider believing one single word until the source was authenticated. A handwriting analysis was the best, most decisive chance there was for me to prove the diaries were junk. Because if they hadn't been written by the monster, well, who the hell cared?

Well as it turned out, authentication proved to be a lot harder than I first thought. The procedure to prove a deceased's authorship requires possession of a verified sample of the suspect's hand to compare with the item in question, and a certified expert qualified to make an accurate comparison of both.

Holmes had been hanged by the State of Pennsylvania in 1896, at least that's what the court records, newspapers and history books all said. The hanging was reported to have been conducted in front of hundreds of observers, prison officials and law enforcement personnel. His death certificate had been signed by the warden of the prison where the execution was allegedly performed. To believe he authored both diaries was to consider all that an illusion and quite possibly the greatest vanishing act of all time, not to mention perhaps the most monumental mistake our government had ever committed, especially when you take into account Holmes' victims to follow. No one, not even the genius Holmes was reported to have been, could have pulled this, perhaps the greatest con of all time, off.

Of course he could have authored the first book and not the second. Hell, the second diary could have been drafted by one of his servants following Holmes' final orders before his death. He reportedly had a rather sick sense of humor and was certainly capable of just such a last morbid joke. He had the money and quotient of fear to have seen these acts carried out even many years after his death. The possibilities were endless, assuming the illusion was even his doing in the first place. My only choice was to break everything down into the smallest possible components, then piece by piece eliminate each one as I proved the greater mass incorrect. Once pieces started falling by the wayside, the rest would soon follow and a valid conclusion about the diaries would make itself apparent.

There were three separate and distinct issues to be sorted out. First, whether the author of the volume written before the supposed execution and the author of the volume written after the same event were the same man. Second, whether Holmes had written either one of the books. Finally, if Holmes had indeed written both.

Aside from his printed memoir, I was unaware of any other handwriting samples by Holmes that could be positively identified in order to compare the separate samples. I dug through family files and old boxes for weeks, having little luck except for two professional black and white photographs of Holmes taken in preparation for his wedding to Clara Lovering. While providing none of the samples I was after, the pictures were captivating, giving me my first good look at the man's young face.

Then I remembered something that had jumped up and bit me while researching the newspaper articles. The articles went on and on about Holmes sitting in his prison cell, writing his memoirs while awaiting his hanging. Those memoirs were in his own hand; as he obviously had no typewriter, having been watched by prison guards and newspaper reporters as he scribed away for days. His words had been the sensation of an entire nation, if not the world. Everyone had waited for the weekly release of the latest entry from Holmes. When he finished them, he sold the works for an incredible amount of money. I knew it was possible, if not likely, that samples of the handwritten versions still existed, but where would the originals have been kept after they were printed for the hungry nation to read? It just wasn't feasible that something that valuable would have been simply discarded and destroyed.

During the trial, hundreds of dailies were printed every morning. Of those, two were the most critical. I went back to the relevant copies of the Philadelphia Examiner and New York Times, both containing artists' renderings of Holmes laboring at the small writing desk within the jail cell at Moyamensing Prison. The articles described the work he performed at his prison desk in intricate detail. Most importantly, they both showed him writing by hand.

The memoirs' authenticity was beyond reproach. Here was my standard to gauge the validity of the diaries! But where was this cipher now?

After weeks looking, I came across a potentially promising lead. Following the trial a judge had ordered a review of the memoirs before he granted permission for Holmes to release the work to the publishing house that had agreed to purchase them. Following that review of the original, the judge then released the manuscript for copying. The Federal Government requested copies as well. At that point, for unknown reasons, the trail of the originals stopped cold. However, I knew that once the Federal Government obtained possession of something like this, they were ruthlessly reluctant to ever give their copy up. The memoirs would have been archived away in some dusty backroom, bundled and shelved, the entire world forever ignorant of what they once were. I knew they still existed. It was just a question of putting in the time and energy to find their final resting place. These samples were all that would be needed to either prove or disprove the validity of the diaries-- period, case closed.

The one place with the foresight to have maintained these treasures in their original condition, was the Library of Congress in Washington, D. C. But before heading off on what might be a wild goose chase spent sifting through the millions of pieces of similar material stored in that library, there was one piece of the pie that if done right might first eliminate the need to visit the Library of Congress at all. My first obstacle would be to establish that the two diaries were written by the same man.

If they weren't, while not 100% conclusive, chances were Holmes had been properly executed and the diaries were, or at least one of them was, and the critical one at that, a fraud.

For the first time since finding the books, I had direction and purpose. My efforts to delegitimize the diaries, and ultimately the monster, began to take shape.

CHAPTER 10

By telephone I hired world-renowned forensic handwriting expert William Roberts to determine if the handwriting in the diary before the execution was the same as the writing in the diary dated after his "death." To my unpracticed eye, the samples before and after appeared to be the same, but I knew there were swindlers who could recreate handwriting to such a degree that their work would pass inspection by all except the most sophisticated technicians. The determination needed to be made by an expert. From my days at the practice of law, I knew Roberts was renowned as the best there was and after some minor haggling over price, he agreed to inspect the samples.

I made copies of the least sinister material from both diaries to supply Roberts with what I hoped was enough text to conduct an accurate review. And on a long-shot, copied the April 10th, 1896, Philadelphia Inquirer which was said to have run Holmes' handwritten confession on its Sunday front page. While doubtful, at this point, anything was worth a try.

I was adamant this material wasn't going on the internet, so we scheduled a personal consultation about the samples. The samples were then delivered to him by certified courier one week prior to my arrival, giving him ample time for inspection.

Roberts took only three days before texting me to report that he had reached a conclusion: somewhat. I flew cross-country ASAP to meet over coffee at his New York condominium, which also served as his place of business.

Walking into his office, I was puzzled to find the room dark and cold. Cave-like, huge blinds hung down over the large windows canceling out what must have been picturesque views of downtown. Roberts, wearing that big city has-been look, moved out from behind his desk, looking tired from what I guessed had been an all-nighter. He was tall with a very long, hard, tanned face, and graying hair that needed a trim. His clothes and the watch he was wearing both shouted money. The room smelled of cheap scotch.

After some introductory feeling-out, he sat back down and I went right to the point, asking, "How confident are you regarding the materials I supplied you with?"

He leaned back in his chair and said, "There is nothing I would like more than to be able to pronounce without the slightest doubt that both were written by the same hand. . ." He handed me a copy of the copy I'd given him, ". . . but I'm afraid to say I cannot." He worked his pipe with good effect before continuing. "What I can say is that there is a seventy-five to eighty percent probability that the handwriting is from the same hand, however, there were some minor discrepancies. I cannot be sure whether these were caused by age, a changing hand or may in fact amount to the clues of a fraud. I need more material, and... I need more time. In the meantime, if you'd like, I can go over the relevant points that make my opinion obvious."

Staying quiet, but growing angrier by the second at his indecisiveness, considering how much he had cost and I had traveled, I silently considered where to go next after so soft an 'expert's' opinion.

Unsure, I finally just let go, "Let's cut the crap, Roberts. I'm not asking you to take the stand providing expert testimony. Climb out on the limb for once in your life. Is the handwriting the same, or isn't it?"

He sighed before giving in, "Yeah, they're the same, but like I said, I'd need more time and better samples before I could swear to this conclusion in court, which is where 99% of what I do ends up."

I repeated that this one wouldn't.

He went on. "The newspaper material is similar to both samples in the diaries, but once again, I'll need more, something directly from the hand and not reprinted."

So there it was. In layman's terms, the best expert in the business was of the opinion that the two diaries were *probably* written by the same man, but that he couldn't stand up in court and swear to that fact. Seems my quest wasn't going to be solved so easily after all. To be fair, I'd pretty much known that all along anyway.

Giving me time to consider his opinion and my options, he continued puffing away, then added, "Before we go any further, may I state that I have never had the opportunity in all my years to inspect material such as this. The content is horrific. May I ask you its origin and how you came to be in possession of this horror?"

In full lawyer mode, "I'm sorry, but I'm unable to divulge that information, at least not right now," I answered.

Despite the air-conditioned room, Roberts seemed out of breath, obviously losing the battle to maintain his professional cool. I knew exactly how he felt. "One more thing, Mr. Mudgett. May I take the liberty of inquiring as to what your relationship, same name and all, is to the alleged author?"

Ignoring his irrelevant question, I instead silently asked myself what was I going to do when he read the rest, if even the most benign of the material had bothered this professional so much, a man whose very business was dealing in murder? How was the 'for mature audiences only' material going to affect him?

"Mr. Roberts… let me warn you that the next sample you are about to analyze will be even more troubling than the last. The material may even go so far as to affect your concept of what evil is. I will only allow you to read this material in my presence. There will be no copies or samples taken. The content will be kept in strictest confidence. Can you accept these conditions and the unpredictable influences these materials may have upon your life?"

I had practiced this short speech on the flight over. The legalities of what we were getting into, way over both our heads, mandated the formality.

Roberts was clearly troubled, but he was also hooked. The professional within this man could no more turn down the opportunity to read more Holmes material than he could have refused his first kiss or alcoholic drink. All that was needed now was to make sure he understood that his New York Old Club style concerning the contents would not be tolerated in any way. They could not be shared with cronies over a gin and tonic.

"I see... and of course, Mr. Mudgett." He stared at the second diary as I pulled the volume from my briefcase. "When can we start?" he eagerly asked.

Mid-way to handing him the book, I pulled back and for the umpteenth time second-guessed my decision to include him further. Could he be trusted? He seemed so dangerously eager. Did he, no, *could he*, realize what this might mean? Realizing there were answers to my questions, in the end, I gave the diary to him. I had no other choice.

He examined the binding, just like I had, flipping the book over and over before opening it. Skimming through the pages, he stopped, heaven knows where, and began to read. Within minutes, his face went pale. He handed the book back to me almost as if he were afraid to go on.

"So much more than I expected. Is it real?"

I laughed. "That's exactly why I'm here, Mr. Roberts. Tomorrow I have an appointment at the Library of Congress, Rare Book Division. I'll be back in New York as soon as I locate original samples for you to compare with the writing from both books. As soon as I do, you need to get right to work. Agreed?"

He nodded yes, his raised eyebrows probably indicating him contemplating what he had gotten himself into, this deal about and maybe with the devil, but he was way past backing out, no matter what the cause or excuse. Right now he just needed me to leave so he could have another drink. Oftentimes the best at what they do pay a stiff price.

"With the kind of samples you're talking about, verified handwriting samples that is, I'm almost positive I'll be able to give you a definitive thumbs up or down. When do you expect to have those comparison samples to me?" he asked.

"Like I told you, let's plan tomorrow, but two or three day's tops."

Rising to leave his office, his last words seemed I owed him more. I couldn't shake the feeling that somehow this innocent man's life might now be in jeopardy. Roberts was either part of a team about to solve an astounding historical mystery or privy to an elaborate, possibly illegal, fraud. Either way, someone or something probably wouldn't appreciate his involvement, maybe even me, but truth was I needed him as much as he wanted to be a part of it all.

So I, with some guilt, kept my mouth shut.

Walking down his hallway to the elevator, I couldn't help thinking the best there was had just informed me that were he provided with adequate samples from verified works of Holmes, matching the writing in these diaries, there was a much better than even chance that an innocent man had been hung in the doctor's place over a century ago.

CHAPTER 11

As if graphic nightmares weren't enough, whispers began to invade my waking world, and at the most bizarre times. Impatient, the voice could no longer wait for my dreams to converse. Anyone seeing me during those first few days would have thought me crazy, watching me suddenly stopping without notice, turning circles looking about as if trying to determine the identity of some invisible conversationalist. They would have seen me, doing whatever it was I was doing, suddenly breaking out talking to myself, full volume, as if a real companion were standing no more than two feet away. Insanity personified is what they probably would have thought.

The voice was soon with me everywhere. Beside me at my computer, driving with me to work, etc. We began chatting life up. It/he even commenting on my dress, grooming and eating habits. He was there for all of it. We even conversed with each other as I read about him. Yes, at some point I gave up arguing with myself about whom or what the energy was, finally admitting, somewhere deep down inside, this was all just about me. I shudder to think what a tape recording of my musing might have revealed to interested professionals.

The voice would often start, rather innocuously, like this:

Let us not be amiss this fine morning, my delightful boy, he would whisper then laugh.

Can I reward your long wait with something truly exciting? At which point he would commence telling me about an amazing historical event, scientific discovery or horrendous example of torture and death. Or he would point something out I'd missed in his book, some nuance he was rather proud of. Growing strangely accustomed, I even took to asking him about something I'd just read that was over my head. He would always respond and often in a forthright scholarly manner. Sadly enough, I began counting on his answers.

He adored chatting about philosophy. *"You need not feel your silly guilt, Jeffrey, certainly not from desiring to live the instincts you were born with. The human race created the concept of guilt to equalize what they couldn't possess. Cease your search, that worthless thing all men do their entire lives while hiding from themselves, for you have found your freedoms."*

While he talked, a new image of myself began sprouting in my head, taking on a life of its own, possibly evolving from a thing of Herman's making.

"Happiness equals instinct, Jeffrey. I mimicked no one, or thing, or god. Nothing was forbidden me, and if proclaimed to be, I destroyed it. Destroying weakness promotes our species. Spit on virtue. Tell me, what is wrong with killing? The things we vilify occur every day in nature. We celebrate them! I ask you - is life good? If so, tell me how, and for what good reason? You can't, because our existence lacks rationality. Life is misery relived over and over again and those fortunate who came into contact with me, I did a favor for."

In the back of my mind, I knew the voice wasn't, couldn't be real. The only viable explanation had to be that there was something wrong with my mind-- perhaps the initial stages of mental illness. That had to be why. But how do you account for an illusion so real, so brilliant and so sympathetic to your own concerns?

"I am real, my son, as will you be soon enough."

I began taking Holmes for granted.

CHAPTER 12

On the plane to D. C., and later that night in the hotel, I prepared for the next day by going over any third-party written material I'd been able to get my hands on that had analyzed the Holmes memoirs. My reading didn't take long to recognize a recurring theme running through them all: the Holmes' piece was illogical and lacked coherency. Holmes was said to have rambled in the fashion of a deranged psychotic. All, and I do mean all, reasoned that his final attempt at emotional authenticity was due to the fact that *his own death* was staring him in the face. There was universal agreement that this man, so despised, had broken down and revealed the coward he truly was.

I knew this wasn't the case. The man they portrayed wasn't the one I knew the monster to be. Horrible? Yes. Evil? Without a doubt, but a coward? Not a chance. He'd never been afraid of anything his entire life. Quite to the contrary, he was reported to have been addicted to dangerous situations. He thrived on them. I was convinced their erroneous interpretations were precisely what Holmes intended in order to obscure some greater purpose. My now overwhelming obligation was to learn what that purpose was.

Wiping the slate clean, I reread the same material, but this time while assuming he was planning an escape at the same time he was writing the autobiography. What other purpose could he have been hiding while in prison awaiting execution? I picked through the excerpts used by later writers to illustrate Holmes' insanity. My reason being that these sections would have been the ones Holmes put the most work into in order to camouflage his actual intent. With this frame of mind, after just two pages, his memoirs began to come alive.

His writing was powerful, overflowing with charismatic, seductive capabilities as hypnotic as his spoken word was said to have been. He was verbose when required and to the point when circumstances necessitated. Holmes knew when to let a reader imagine and create for themselves the angle he was after. He was masterful at spinning a web then enticing the next ignorant victim into the trap. The same way he physically trapped victims, his writings trapped news reporters and historians alike, but this time on paper.

The book teased with tales of a predator following the great herds through huge cities camouflaged by sickness and misfortune. He scoffed at law enforcement tactics and techniques, even hinting as to the exact moment of his upcoming escape from prison by boasting that he would walk out in broad daylight to observe his own hanging from the front row of the gallery. His verbosity did indeed appear ridiculous, perhaps even insane… to the naïve.

The book further chilled with a curse on those and theirs who were unwise enough to have either insulted or inconvenienced him during his brief incarceration and ended with the threat that he would go on as an immortal to haunt the earth forever. By doing so, he successfully planted the seeds of his insanity within the nation's newspapers.

I compared the published memoirs to the diaries. The diary entries before the incarceration were succinct, quite brilliant really, as were the ones immediately after. The standard I had come to expect from Holmes. Yet, the prison memoir intended for publication was composed in such a way as to leave all who read the work believing he was indeed off his rocker. Was there any doubt that these words, written after he was condemned to death, were anything but a tool?

My guess was that he needed the book to set the stage for the ultimate substitution of some kind. Holmes knew that a switch alone wasn't enough. He needed the closure an official declaration of insanity would provide. Without it he could never be sure that all involved were satisfied. Unless satisfied, Holmes knew that eventually some interested soul would check the available evidence to verify final proof of his death unless the matter was deemed unnecessary. How much easier to write a book, be labeled a crazy coward, and never have to look back over his shoulder ever again.

***

At first light, and even from a distance, the Library of Congress was breathtaking. An overwhelming place, energy seemed to radiate down from the huge structure, causing the hairs stood on the back of my neck to stand as I realized this building was filled with answers to some of the greatest questions to have ever faced mankind. Stepping from the cab, steaming coffee in one hand, briefcase in the other, prepared to do battle, I fell in love with the grand building on the long walk up to the entrance. I was awestruck.

In the entrance, double sided stairs led to a perfectly balanced interior. Huge columns dominated everything within shadow's throw. Classic Greek and Roman statues watched over the central room, holding the light of knowledge above everyone present.

As everyone new does, I felt small and out of place, especially knowing I was there for far more than most who entered this grand place.

The tainted material I was hoping to find didn't belong in this grand arena … the thing that waited for me inside, kept safe here by all that is supposed to be good, was evil. Perhaps I didn't belong here either.

My discomfort must have been apparent. A librarian approached me offering assistance, and after twice affirming my specific request with higher officials, she informed me that the Rare Book Division was expecting me.

What followed was a seemingly endless identification process. Once that was completed, I was required to check in the one diary I had brought with me for comparison purposes. Thankfully, they had no idea what they held in their hands. After some debate they allowed me to take the volume inside with me. This process was followed by an hour long wait before another staff member led me down a hallway to a much

smaller room. Alone and behind closed doors I waited while they re-
trieved the book they claimed Holmes wrote in his jail cell more than one
hundred and seven years ago. Kept locked away from prying eyes, records
showed that the book had been inspected five times in the last fifty years.
To match the surgical character of the room, the technician brought out
clean white gloves for me to wear the entire time handling the book. The
keepers seemed reluctant to allow me time with this treasure. They never
took their eyes off me the entire time the book and I were in the room.
Overhead cameras swiveled mimicking my every move.

My initial plan was of course to gather any Holmes handwriting samples I could find. The primary hope was that his original handwritten
memoirs were here having been stored away forever. Anticipating this
breakthrough, my breath caught as the package was brought out and un-
wrapped.

My hands shook and my heart pounded opening the cover.

In that instant I knew it wasn't to be. The original copy was just that-
- a copy of the first printing. That print offered nothing to Roberts and
me. My hopes dashed, disappointed, I sat back and considered one last
option, one more chance. In the diary, Holmes had written about a visit
he'd made to the Library in 1952 to retrieve some information he needed
for undisclosed reasons. He mentioned scribbling on two of the pages in
the margins with pencil. If true, I needed to find those pages and obtain
permission to copy them without gathering undue attention which might
shut down the entire plan. There was no time to waste.

I soon found the two pages but was again disappointed to see that
either Holmes or an attentive attendant had erased them from the margins. The indents, however, were still visible. Stepping outside, I called
Roberts and informed him of the situation.

"Copy the pages, I can work with the indents."

So I stuck to the plan and began the process of seeking permission to
copy them.

While the administrative wheels slowly turned, I found myself admiring the bastard again, drawn to the original printing in such a way that

one would have thought I had never read a copy before. Waiting, time flew, as I finished half the book. Hours later, without yet having gained permission, I called it a day, determined to return in the morning.

That second morning I was soon immersed again. Proceeding, I reminded myself not to fall into the same trap that duped the researchers before me. *This was not, not, the monster's last attempt to set the record straight by admitting to his crimes before final judgment.* Nothing could have been further from the truth. He had used these words to lay the foundation for his getaway-- the undisclosed escape from prison that required the taking of more innocent lives in order to further his malignant purposes for decades to come.

Pressed for time, I skipped over irrelevant sections trying to identify portions also included in the diary... and quickly found one. The words followed Holmes on what, for him, was an un-extraordinary day.

In 1891 I associated myself in business with a young Englishman, whose name I am more than willing to publish to the world, but I am advised it could not be published on my unsupported statement, who by his own admission, had been guilty of all other forms of wrongdoing, save murder, and presumably of that as well. To manipulate certain real estate securities we held so as to have them secure us a good commercial rating was an easy matter for him and he was equally able to interest certain English capitalists in patents so that for a time it seemed that in the near future our greatest concern would be how to dispose of the money that seemed about to be showered upon us. By an unforeseen occurrence our rating was destroyed and it became necessary to at once raise a large sum of money and this was done by my partner enticing to Chicago a wealthy banker named Rodgers from North Wisconsin town in such a manner that he could have left no intelligence with whom his business was to be. To cause him to go in the Castle and within the secret room under the pretense that our patents were there was easily brought about, more so than to force him to sign checks and drafts for seventy thousand dollars, which we had prepared. At first he refused to do so, stating that his liberty that we offered him in exchange would be useless to him without his money, that he was too old to again hope to make another fortune: finally by alternately starving him and nauseating him with the gas he was made to sign the securities, all of which we converted into money and by my partner's skill as a forger in such a manner as to leave no trace of their having passed through our hands. I waited with much curiosity to see what propositions my partner would advance for the disposal of our prisoner, as I well knew he, no more than I, contemplated giving him his liberty. My partner evidently waited with equal expectancy for me to suggest what should be done, and I finally made preparations to allow him to leave the building, thus forcing him to suggest that he be killed.

The contrast between these words and the ones in his private diary illuminated the true purpose behind his 'partner's' assistance in obtaining the highlighted funds. Poor unfortunate soul that he was, the man never realized that his death was nothing more than a cog in the wheel, planned from the first moment Holmes was made aware of his usefulness to the project. As it turned out, the Englishman ended up being disposed of right alongside the banker. Two weeks later, Holmes utilized the same technique on another banker, this one from New Jersey. The total net for the three weeks' work amounted to almost $135,000, an enormous sum in the nineteenth century, but nothing extraordinary for Holmes.

I made further comparisons, reading the following episode in the memoirs.

The first taking of human life that is attributed to me is the case of Dr. Leacock of New Baltimore, Mich., a friend and former schoolmate.

Holmes neither agreed nor disagreed with the 'attribution.' For good reason-- according to the diary he had taken life on at least ten occasions prior to this occurrence.

I knew his life was insured for a large sum and after enticing him to Chicago I killed him by giving him an overwhelming dose of Laudanum. My subsequently taking his dead body from place to place in and about Grand Rapids, Michigan, as has been an often-printed heretofore, and the risk and excitement attendant upon the collection of the forty-thousand dollars of insurance were very significant matters compared with the torturing thought that I had taken human life. This will be understood that before my constant wrong-doing, I had become wholly deaf to the promptings of conscience.

This was the line often quoted by those looking for medical confirmation to establish a why and wherefore to the evil before them. Decades after, the same line was used to define the condition known as psychopathic, and later sociopathic. Criminal defendants would soon learn to use this "Holmes" tactic in presenting the defense of criminal insanity.

Holmes joked about the line in the diary:

My conscience is as strong as that of a mother with child, the difference being mine learned to do what it was told.

What a checkmate, I thought, to all the experts' explanations for the cause of Holmes' evil.

Prior to his death, which occurred in 1886, I begged to be believed in stating that I had never sinned so heavily either by thought or deed. Later, like the man-eating tiger of the tropical jungle, whose appetite for blood has once been aroused, I roamed about the world seeking whom I could destroy. Think of the awful list that follows. Twenty seven lives, men and women, young girls and innocent children, plotted out by one monster's hand, and you, my reader of a tender and delicate nature, will do well to read no further, for I will in no way spare myself, and he who reads to the end, if he be charitable, will, in the words of the District Attorney at my trial-- the same one who would suffer a horrible death months after the hanging-- when the evidence of all these many crimes had been collected and placed before him by his trusty assistants, exclaim: "God help such a man! "If uncharitable or only just will he not rather say: "May he be utterly damned." And that it is almost sufficient to cause one to doubt the wisdom of Providence that such a man should have so long been allowed to live. If so I earnestly pray that this condemnation and censure may not extend to those whose only crime has been that they knew and trusted, aye in some instances, loved me, and who today are more deserving of the world's compassion than censure.

I must have read this section ten times before finally recognizing that this paragraph was absolutely one of those he used to lay the framework for escape. This was also his favorite; the one that must have given him the heartiest laugh when he thought of the reactions these words garnered amongst his now loyal readers.

The big bad wolf came to mind, *"The better to know you with, my dear."*

He admitted to multiple murders in the memoirs. How odd for a man to use an admission that he had murdered twenty-seven human beings as an aid to escape instead of the more normal proclamation of innocence. What could he possibly have thought to gain using this unusual strategy? The search for sympathy also puzzled me. Was this the so-called junkyard dog persona? No, that couldn't be his intention either, as he often waxed eloquently about how good his parents were to him as a child.

Could these words have been intended to foster a leniency that suited his purposes? That seemed impossible at so late a stage, especially when he had just admitted to being the first 'serial killer' in American history. Had he been attempting to hypnotize his readers on paper? That seemed rather far-fetched, even for a mind as brilliant as his.

Perhaps not, farfetched, that is.

I went back and looked at the comments of the guards again, the ones who expressed their sympathy for him after he had been found guilty and, more importantly, *after* he had admitted in writing that he had tortured and killed scores of innocent human beings. The same guards, who were by their very natures some of the most difficult creatures to con, swindle or build emotional relationships with in the entire world. But Holmes had done so. How could this anomaly be explained?

So overwhelming was this spellbinding comparison of material that I completely lost track of time and had to be interrupted and asked to leave at closing time, again, having spent the entire day trying to decipher meaning. What had started as a search for handwriting samples had evolved into much more. The keepers couldn't tear me away. *You must be the first to truly understand the doctor*, I repeatedly told myself, while also recognizing just how dangerous this acquisition of unique knowledge might end up being.

The next day was miraculously more of the same. *My second victim was a Dr. Russell, a tenant in the Chicago building recently renamed "The Castle." During a controversy concerning the nonpayment of rent due me, I struck him to the floor with a heavy chair, when he with one cry for help, ending in a groan of anguish, ceased to breath. This quarrel and death occurred in a small outer office, and as soon as I realized that my blow had been a fatal one and I had recovered somewhat from the horror of having still another victim's blood upon my hands, I was forced to look about for some safe means of concealing the crime.*

Dr. Russell's death had been testified to at the trial by a witness that had once worked for Holmes. The testimony was a lie, apparently previously coached by Holmes. The doctor had needed the incriminating testimony to be heard. From the diary it was clear that Doctor Russell's death had not been caused by the blow from a chair, but rather the penetration of the 'needle', as Holmes privately referred to the weapon. The needle was the sharp, pick-like object favored by Holmes. He inserted sharp the point below the victim's skull at the back of the neck, resulting in a quick death with almost no sound or attention-calling flailing about by the stricken. The method used had nothing to do with alleviating the victim's pain, but rather the control such a death afforded Holmes, and also so he could avoid any damage to the skeleton. A damaged skeleton was worthless to Holmes, but if pristine, the result was worth as much as $2,000 to the nation's medical schools. When in need of quick cash, Holmes often turned to the production of skeletons. One expert believed Holmes went on to provide over fifty percent of the skeletons exhibited at the Universities across the nation.

While on the difficult subject of disposing of bodies, Holmes discussed his business associate, Benjamin Pitezel.

In short, in this writing, in each instance when the manner of the disposal of their remains is not otherwise specified, it will be understood that they were turned over to him.

It will be understood that from the first hour of our acquaintance, Benjamin Pitezel, even before I knew he had a family who would later afford me additional victims for the gratification of my bloodthirstiness, I intended to kill him, and all my subsequent care of him and his, as well as my apparent trust in him by placing in his name large amounts of property, were steps taken to gain his confidence and that of his family so when time was ripe they would the more readily fall into my hands... [Y]et so it is, and it furnishes a very striking illustration of the vagaries in which the human mind will, under certain circumstances, indulge; in comparison with which the seeking of buried treasure at the rainbow's end, the delusions of the exponents of perpetual motion or the dreams of the haschisch fiend are sanity itself... [N]othing would at the present time give me so much satisfaction as to know that her, Pitezel's wife, body had been properly buried, and I would be willing to give up the few remaining days I have to live if by so doing this could be accomplished, for, because of her spotless life before she knew me, because of the large amount of money I defrauded her of, because I killed her sister and brother, because not being satisfied with all this, I endeavored after my arrest to blacken her good name by charging her with the death of her sister, and later with the instigation of the murder of the three Pitezel children, endeavoring to have it believed that her motive for so doing was to afford an avenue of escape for herself if ever apprehended for her sister's death, by pointing to her as a wholesale murderess, and, therefore, presumably guilty of the sister's death as well; for all these reasons this is without exception the saddest and most heinous of any of my crimes.

Has any man ever done more harm to one family than the monster did to the Pitezel's? At the time I thought not, but would later learn that their familial fate was not uncommon for acquaintances of the doctor.

The memoirs concluded with this:

It would now seem a very fitting time for me to express regret or remorse in this, which I intend to be my last public utterance for these irreparable short-comings. To do so with the expectation of even one person who has read this confession to the end, believing that in my depraved nature there is room for such feelings, is I fear, to expect more than would be granted. I can at least, and do refrain, from calling forth such a criticism by openly inviting it.

Quite fitting and no wonder the experts thought him crazy, further concluding that his memoirs were the sad ramblings of a condemned man concerned with meeting his maker. How wrong they were. The memoirs were, in my opinion, the finest first person accounting of the mind of a monster the world has ever been given the opportunity of examining... and then, as is so often the case with misunderstood treasures, proceeded to cast aside.

***

The officials at the Library of Congress initially refused my request for permission to make the copies. In fact, the authorities could not have been more adamant. But after extensive explanation, as much as I could, of the nature of my research, and reminding them of my relationship to the author, they finally acquiesced, providing me with the opportunity to make copies of two chapters. I hoped that by copying the surrounding chapters instead of just the two pages we were really interested in, less attention would be drawn to my actual purpose. I held my breath while they inspected those pages. The plan worked, as they noticed and said nothing.

Four hours later, with what hopefully was sufficient material, I was on the way back to New York. Roberts picked me up at the airport and weaving in and out of traffic, drove with one hand while holding the samples in the other, reading the entire way. The material around the samples mesmerized him.

"I could have used more, but this might be enough," he complained in the fashion I was growing accustomed too.

"Right," I said, "Coping these damn near took an Act of Congress. If you need more, you know where to go. Tell me something, what is it about making copies that sets them off so?"

"Copiers use a harsh light, a flash really, and technicians believe that the flash destroys micro fibers which over time tears down the page," he said while never once looking over until we arrived at his office. He was out of the car in a flash, without even locking the doors, and took off, giving me barely enough time to catch up and jam my hand between the closing doors of the elevator so I could ride up with him.

Upstairs, he left me alone out in the kitchen while he inspected the two copies in his back room-- something about working better alone. My bet was he liked to drink while he worked. Thirty minutes later he walked out wearing the biggest smile I'd seen in quite a while.

"These are close to a perfect match," he said. "But again, there are strange discrepancies,"-- I was growing comfortable with his expert talk -- "that are either the result of physiological changes in the same author's body and musculature or the most elaborate attempt at writing fraud I have ever been privileged to examine. That being said, I'd almost stake my reputation that the handwriting is a match."

Still confused, "Which ones match, Roberts?"

"All three are the same-- the copies, the first diary and the second diary," he replied.

For quite some time neither one of us said a word, both of us wanting to let the gravity of the moment sink in. Roberts finally broke the ice, "Where do we go from here?"

To be honest, I wasn't sure.

In the end, we made plans to meet, but only after he'd had enough time to eliminate the issues he had alluded to. With more time he said he could— and all of them. Leaving, I could hear him telling his secretary on the cell-phone to schedule him a flight tomorrow to Washington D. C. Roberts was on board.

Flying home, the books never left my sight. They had a different look and feel to them now. In three days they had gone from interesting literary tripe to perhaps two of the most valuable books in the world… ones that might one day stand written history on its ear.

That old saying about assuming making an ass out of you and me had been proven correct again. Doing so was never going to happen again, not with me, at least not where Holmes was concerned.

Three weeks later, Roberts called telling me he was prepared to swear on a stack of bibles the books were Holmes'.

CHAPTER 13

With the first piece of hard evidence in hand, the next step would be to verify the existence of the concrete grave Holmes was said to be entombed within. One of the more bizarre aspects of the Holmes legend was the report that following the hanging, he'd been buried inside ten feet of concrete after placement in a casket that was itself also filled with concrete. Historically, I'd never heard of anything even remotely similar... or more a potential clue for debunking the Holmes myth and finding out what really happened.

I wasn't so much interested in identifying the body entombed within the concrete, as I was already fairly certain the cadaver wasn't Holmes, as much as I wanted to verify the existence of the concrete at or near the spot the reports all mentioned. If the concrete wasn't there, ten feet down, odds were that the legend was a lie and many of the Holmes' stories manipulated make believe.

This part of the journey needed an extra pair of hands, someone who would reliably cover my back when the stakes were high. I had just the guy in mind and so called my old friend and dependable buddy, Kim. We had known each other for thirty years, having played college ball together and then served alongside each other aboard our first ship. He was an engineer extraordinaire and the best I'd ever seen at applying technology to practical problems. Over the years, his ingenuity and expert testimony had saved many of my clients from going to jail.

"You remember that favor you owe me?" I asked after calling him late one night.

"I thought it was the other way around," he replied.

"I need your help Kim." We never used each other's first names, preferring locker-room insults... unless in an emergency.

"Where to this time?"

"Philadelphia."

"I'll be there day after tomorrow," and the phone went dead. I knew Kim would already be clearing space on his busy slate. That was the kind of friend he was.

After some emails back and forth between us concerning the equipment we would need, he went off in search of electronics while I made sure all the preliminaries to pull this thing off were lined up.

The next day, flying east again, reading, always reading, I began to second-guess the effectiveness of the judicial system that existed in the late nineteenth century. Could that system, or an entire nation for that matter, have been foolish enough to believe this man, this Doctor of Death, was so concerned about the condition of his corpse after hanging to have agreed to his diabolical requests concerning concrete tombs? This was beginning to look more and more like the con I'd begun feeling in my bones.

If anyone realized that life wasn't about the body we carried but instead the identity of our soul, it was Holmes. What eventually happened to his body after death would have been the last thing on the doctor's mind. No, there had been another motive for the concrete sarcophagus in that twisted brain of his. Whatever the fraud, the judicial system had bought his story lock, stock and casket filled with concrete barrel.

For that reason, the ten feet of concrete interested me the most. Sure, finding out who was actually buried within the mass was important, but determining that fact would take more time, tons of cash, impact statements, even court orders. Not to mention that opening the block up would have required jack hammers and back hoes. There was no way Kim and I could attack that much concrete in secret. Besides, I had the feeling that once the lid was off this whole thing, pun intended, the government would be the one digging up the gravesite and breaking through the tons of concrete in order to disprove my story. How could they not, particularly if the family of the one I suspected was within the concrete still existed?

The man down there had worked for our government. He was owed respect and had been given none. Gears would begin turning. Formal apologies would be in order, not to mention reparations with over one hundred years of interest tacked on. We were talking tens of millions of dollars.

First up was determining if the remains were Holmes or not... the easy part. Encircled within so much concrete, the remains would probably be in pristine condition-- perhaps eerily so. Identification sans DNA might even be possible.

But that was the government's problem. All I needed right now was to find the gravesite and positively ultrasound the concrete to verify the legend. That kind of stuff was right up Kim's alley.

Holy Cross Cemetery was easy to locate; out in the open between MacDade Boulevard and Union Avenue in Yeadon, Pennsylvania. Yeadon is small town Americana and about as different from metropolis Philadelphia as possibly can be. Holy Cross serves as the final resting place for an odd assortment of famous and infamous individuals, including organized crime bosses, politicians, and even a famous professional boxer.

With permission, Kim and I visited the cemetery early the next morning, entering through iron gates bulwarked by mortar casings that gave the place an air one would expect of such a place. At first glance, the cemetery was where we all see ourselves finally resting. The gate was adorned by a simple sign that read, HOLY CROSS. The staff was professional and the site well-maintained. The detailed map the cemetery provided visitors pointed out each individual's position, except, of course, the one we were interested in.

We made our way around the grounds, paying particular attention to older sites and those unadorned with headstones. Reports had alerted us that Holmes' grave was barren. One of the more recent books on Holmes had discussed the author and his partners visiting the site to view the grave. They were unable to identify Holmes' grave, but noted several without headstones. The author assumed one of those sites was where Holmes was laid to rest. We checked off each of those sites unsuccessfully. We also looked for larger double sites that could have accommodated the extra space necessary to support the requirements. By dimension alone, we were able to eliminate every site but four. We earmarked those in order to find them in the dark when we returned with the equipment. On our way out that afternoon we saw nothing to indicate the presence of motion detection devices or burglar alarms on the grounds.

That night was moonless dark and cold as ice. With the clock pointing straight up, we prepared for the unexpected, but I experienced none of the goose bumps that had riddled me at the library. And why would they? Holmes wasn't here.

As he always did, Kim led the way.

"Hold this until I get over," Kim said, handing me the device he had flown out with all the way from the other coast. The ultrasound device was long and cumbersome, weighing almost thirty pounds. As I was considering the technology he was scurrying over the high back wall. He moved with an aplomb that made me think Kim was more practiced in such nocturnal excursions than he ever let on. Instead of waiting a suitable time for him to get ready, as he was expecting, I flipped the device over as soon as he disappeared, knowing that his hands were the best in any business and would catch the machine no matter what. He did.

From behind the wall between us, I heard him harshly whisper, "Jesus, you jerk! This thing costs six grand. How'd you know I was ready?"

"Did you ever drop a pass that counted?"

Nothing but silence, then, "Asshole."

I smiled knowing he was wide-awake now for sure.

When I was over the wall I held the small flashlight in my teeth and noted the first possible site we had marked that morning on the map. The first grave was about two hundred feet to the north. The compass on my wrist gave us our line. Two minutes later Kim was hooked up and scanning. Within three minutes we had crossed number one off the list.

Five minutes later, number two was eliminated. There were only two left.

Number three was covered by an eerie old oak tree. One of those ancient looking majestic ones, with large symmetrical limbs reaching as if in reverence towards the sky. The tree must have been at least eighty feet high. The roots were probably ten, possibly fifteen feet under the surface. The placement of the casket here would have been impossible, unless, unless that is, had the tree grown this large in the time after the burial, and if the oak had been planted afterwards, was such healthy growth by the tree, standing on so much concrete and not earth, at all likely?

This possibility seemed implausible, so without waiting to see electronically if there was anything underneath the tree I crossed three off the list and was halfway to the last site when the voice spoke for the first time in days. *Your friend has discovered something interesting, Jeffrey.* I turned noticing Kim was no longer behind me. Running back, fearing the worst, I found him focused on his readings, right under the tree and obviously within the oak's huge root system.

"Come on, man," I said, "This tree's too old. The grave can't be here."

"Hold on," Kim said, "Something's here, alright. Five, six, no ten feet deep! Yep, this is where he is, and there's no doubt about it." Kim kept playing with the settings on the instrument panel while I began questioning my knowledge of trees out loud.

"How old's a tree this big anyway? Do they get this big in a hundred years?"

"I don't have the slightest idea, but I do know this: something massive is registering on the machine."

Letting him concentrate, I questioned if the cemetery would have allowed a tree to grow over one of the sites, that is, if current management even knew the site was here. I didn't have the slightest idea.

Moving around behind Kim, we both watched the small digital screen in his hand. With headphones, Kim listened to the sound bouncing off what was below.

"We're talking concrete," Kim said. "Concrete's the only thing besides steel that produces a signature this strong. This one's big."

With my foot I dragged off a boundary marking the size of the grave had Holmes' instructions been followed. I told Kim, "Follow the line and map-out the limits."

Pretty soon we had a rectangle roughly equivalent to the dimensions ordered dug and filled with concrete. Kim was right-- this was pay dirt. The tree must have matured in the time since the burial. This also explained why his grave was "lost" in so many subsequent literary pieces about our devil.

Rubbing my hand over the rough bark of the oaks trunk, I looked down and was once again run through by shivers. My mind flashed on an image of a huge hand-like root system, individual fingers splayed, locking the concrete tomb within their suddenly supernatural grasp, forever and always a secret, just the way *he* would have wanted his ultimate con maintained. Had Holmes planned this part too?

In the excitement of finding what we'd come for, I'd forgotten to keep an eye out. As we were finishing recording the final bit of data on the last side of the box, two floodlights burst on with an intensity so bright the light hurt. We couldn't see a damn thing, but had no trouble hearing what emerged from behind the glare.

"Place the device on the ground and put your hands up. You two gentleman are under arrest for trespass." The next thing I felt was the strong arm of the law spinning me around, pulling my arms back behind me and cuffing my wrists together. I watched them do the same to Kim. As our eyes grew accustomed to the light, we could make out two police officers. I looked for, but couldn't make out-- although I knew they were back there somewhere-- the cemetery interests. Both Kim and I were experienced enough to keep our mouths shut, having first met as teenagers in the back of a squad car after an altercation in a Vallejo bar.

"How many times is it gonna take before you Holmes idiots give up on this concrete grave stuff?" the one officer asked. "Besides, there's never going to be an exhumation of this site, not while I'm alive, anyway."

He was wasting his breath, but he couldn't have known we weren't there to dig. We were the first of the "Holmes idiots" that weren't looking for Holmes, instead only verification of the concrete as evidence supporting the real story and not the legend.

The unidentified man below my feet had been played to perfection by Holmes. I felt sorry for his bad luck at having been in the wrong place at the wrong time.

We had what we'd come for and without anything more to gain by opening this can of worms any further, I took one last sorrowful look back at the grave before, and in my best legalese, telling the officers, "My name is Mudgett. My driver's license is in my wallet. The man in that grave is my relative. By law I have the right to be here to visit and pay my respects. I was unaware that the grounds were closed at night. I apologize for that oversight. This man is my friend."

They knew I was correct. By the time we reached the front gate the cuffs were off. As we walked out they told us we were from now on unwelcome and would require a court order before being allowed to enter again. I thanked them for that. The cops then escorted us to our hotel and let us know, in no uncertain terms, we were to be gone by noon. I remember thinking at the time, very old west like.

We were off by eight.

CHAPTER 14

Mankind has held steadfastly to the belief that, no matter our underpinnings, we are all captains of our own destinies and what matters most are the choices we make determining the paths we follow. While true that those same choices are influenced by environmental factors and the many experiences we grow up within, they remain, for the most part, especially for the strong, solely ours. In other words, our futures are not determined at birth.

That's what I used to believe before the books, anyway.

As a young boy Holmes suffered a traumatic experience that would have made a dramatic impression on any life. His written words recreating that event are not for the faint of heart. They shatter a comprehension of the human condition while opening eyes to the unimaginable. In the fifteen or so pages Holmes takes retelling the tale, he succeeds in putting all of mankind on trial.

At six years of age, I was called to our church by the one those around me called 'the good Priest', the same man who had baptized my infancy and whom stood next to me throughout my adolescence. My mother treated him with the reverence reserved for a holy man and his word was never questioned in our house or the small towns he provided service to.

Two days before, he had specifically requested that I be there that day alone. Our family followed his orders to the letter. Neither my mother nor father had any idea what he intended for me that day.

Before the appointed time, my mother prepared me for my appointment, bathing, trimming and finally dressing me in my Sunday best. Her last gesture was to lick her hand and run it over my hair for presentation. Her glowing smile let me know she was proud of her clean-cut, well-raised, young boy.

As I left the house, I could see that my family was filled with some trepidation over the reason for this strange request. I alone knew why he wanted me there and that his desires were indeed forbidden. Of that I had little doubt. The father and I knew one another better than most. For two years his eyes had never left me. His attraction was obvious even to this young boy as he found me irresistible in some confusing way.

The walk to church from our house was two towns over and six miles long. I knew each step by heart, having given my father company when we used the distance every Monday to train his mules. Two hours after leaving my house, having climbed the high stone steps, I pushed on the iron rings on the huge oak doors of the church, applying my entire weight against the sudden strange resistance. For the first time, there seemed something reluctant to let me in. As the cold handles gave way and folded open, the doors seemed to give up their internal fight and burst away from my tiny fingers, as if repulsed magnetically. I was surprised that my small frame was capable of generating such force. Both doors slammed into their stops so heavily that the two stone statues of angels, inside both doors, wobbled, almost collapsing, barely avoiding making what would have been a terrible mess on the marble floor. I can still recall the echo the doors crash created, barreling down the pews and then bouncing back, like waves in the sea, two or three times. That explosion of sound and near calamity, in a place normally reserved for deference and utter silence, provided me with the most entertainment I had experienced in quite sometime.

The wide open doors allowed the wind entry, the hellacious hot summer breeze blowing through the open arch and extinguishing near every candle that served as illumination for the always-dark interior. Now darker than normal, shadows dominated the interior causing the huge space to come alive in long languid motions, stretching from the tall stained glass windows behind the pipe organ in brightly colored rays. My eyes adjusted to the darkness and false light of the place I had already decided was of no use to me in my life to come.

Walking down the pews, my footsteps clicked on the shining stone floor before I settled into the second row. I was the only follower there.

"Herman!" the father bellowed in the same deep accusatory tone he might have used on another occasion to say, "You are heathen!"

"Yes, Father. Mother told me you had summoned me."

He walked in long strides directly toward me, his eyes never leaving my person. His black gown hung down off his shoulders all the way to the floor. From fifty feet away, I could see the perspiration gathering upon his forehead, creating the sheen of fear and excitement in what I would come to learn was some form of self-denial. Whatever it was, I knew his sweat was from more than just the heat, as I watched his clasped hands wringing out their own reluctance.

"Good day, my son, Herman," settling his right hand upon the back of my neck, utterly controlling me, then, not even waiting for a reply, immediately pulling me up and forcefully directing me to the room at the side of the gold painted altar.

We walked together in lock step, soldiers in a war against I knew not what. He filled the air around me with the stench of his perspiration, musty and stifling, evidence of dangerous things to come, and used his strength to prevent me from running away. I would learn to love that smell in the years to come, for the smell told so much about the next victim and his or her ability to fight back against the destiny I had selected for them. As we entered the room, his hand tightened with the same heavy grip he had used on me that first time my mother had permitted me to be alone with him. Painful, his strong hands were indeed painful. As I would for the rest of my life, I craved more, not less.

The fact that I did not try to escape, as he had apparently expected me to do, obviously surprised him so much that he was unable to produce the words to express his present emotion. Instead, Father Benjamin simply growled, and that growl rumbled deeply across my shoulders as if he were the lion with the

impala's throat between his fangs. He quickly closed the door behind us, lock-
ing us both into the tiny compartment made for only one man... and God.

There were no more words between us. They were unnecessary. Instead,
he lifted me half up on the solid oak stand, face down and pulled off my trou-
sers, leaving my mother's sown dinner jacket with tie in place. His hot wet
breath pelted my neck with foaming specs of saliva. I heard the robe of God's
so-called disciple fall to the stone floors and felt what I knew not what at my
young body. A sudden pain seared through my flesh and soul as if the molten
liquid from a volcano. I refused to scream or protest, not willing to give him
that degree of satisfaction. Besides, my silence made no difference, for he made
noise enough for both of us, again and again. I memorized each sound, every
movement, and the colors all around me, as if time had stopped for this one
moment in this sacred place. I would remember this foul act for the rest of my
life, but never once would I recreate it.

My torture was over in a matter of seconds.

He pushed me away, as if the thing he had wanted more than life itself
just moments ago had now become vile and sinister. How strange I remember
thinking, for fervent desire to have so quickly changed to extreme repulsion.

One of the mysteries of man.

The book fell from my hands, the now obscene weight hitting the
floor at my bare feet. Well, there it was. Here was the very reason Holmes
had grown evil and all within the first twenty pages of the murderer's diaries. Although I still believed he had been born with a penchant for killing, I knew his choice had taken this defilement of his 'innocence' by
human garbage masquerading as righteousness to cement his later intentions. What small boy could have borne the scars of such a hateful event?
Who amongst us could have lived a normal life weighed down by this
tragedy? His character had been formed by cause, and not dealt from a
stack of evolutionary cards as the experts had opined.

Were that frocked man alive in front of me this instant, I would have
taken his neck between my hands and strangled the life from him... and

no one having witnessed would have thought me guilty. His foulness was the cause of the terrible murders Holmes would go on to commit. That priest was the murderer, not my ancestor, of the hundreds of young women that perished at the hands of the man he had in an instant ruined as a small boy.

This realization was like a tremendous weight being lifted from my shoulders. Suddenly, my weightlessness was as if I were Atlas being given the chance to hand off the earth and my burden to another— to be free. My worries about genetics being the sole guilty culprit evaporating before my eyes. For the first time since I discovered the diaries, I felt normal again, swimming in pure innocence.

"The evil has nothing to do with me!" I yelled at the sky above with the tenor of relief anyone would have felt if they, too, were given such a reprieve.

My character was my own!

The words Holmes used in his published memoirs, when he declared that he was born evil with the devil in him had been nothing but another ploy from the man who could no sooner tell the truth than genuinely sing Happy Birthday. How could I have been so naïve? There was no true nature that could have been passed onto me, only an evil created by perhaps the foulest thing that could happen to a young very malleable boy-- homosexual rape by a figure of immense societal position and fame-- his pastor.

Holmes was not my endowment of evil.

The fact that *reason* and *cause* could be stamped onto such an evil life felt satisfying in some bizarre fashion. I had nothing to worry about. My infancy had been as normal as they come, completely devoid of any such similar event. The only thing facing me now was the possible stigma of being a monster's descendant. *Ah, let them think what they will.* What others thought had never concerned me before and I wasn't about to let them now.

If I had stopped reading at that very instant and burned the books, my life might have returned to the same small place as before. But I couldn't... and destiny didn't.

When he was finished, I lay motionless upon the table, not having said one word the entire time, and waited until he walked off. Delirious, he seemed uncaring that I watched his every move, instead just wiping the perspiration from his head while trying to catch his breath. He looked neither sad, nor guilty, just finished. As if he were in a trance. Standing up, I carried my trousers out the room, past the altar and through the center of the empty vestibule. Watching me, he suddenly remembered where we were and what he had done and hurried after me. He caught me before I exited the now soiled doors, again painfully grasping my shoulder, and ordered my trousers back on before I exited.

As I complied, the blood ran down my fingers staining my pants. The red rays from the painted glass over the altar shot the length of the pews to mix with the red on my hand, which I twisted to and fro noting the differences. He watched with me. The blood's red was by far the brighter. The pain was gone.

Then, and I would never forget his words, he decreed, "Herman, our act today is between myself and thou. No other shall ever know. What we have done here is sacred. Do you understand?"

I turned and stared directly into his dark eyes. He had never seen mine before, not really seen them. No, those I saved for my best of friends. They now pierced his soul, causing him to lean back, away from his last attempted convert. I knew at that very moment he was asking himself how a six-year-old could hold the look of a grown man with none of the customary shyness, even after what just occurred.

I lifted my hand to his chest to feel his throbbing heart beating savagely beneath my infant's fingers. He literally shrank before my eyes. Seeing his soul, I watched the inconsistencies of his inhuman trail. With my hand I felt only fear from this less than common man. This was the same emotion I was to become expert in creating over the course of my lifetime, the rhythm of his heart forever etching itself in my mind. Over the coming months, his heartbeat would invade my dreams and thoughts time and time again, just as if my fingers had stayed put on his chest. His fear was my new found treasure.

What seemed a lifetime later, I answered his previous demand, "Don't concern yourself, Father, at least not yet."

My unexpected response seemed to settle him. Perhaps he thought my silence would require more threat or physical intimidation. His grip upon my person, still hard and threatening, began to soften.

We watched together, as I dragged my hand down his chest leaving his frock stained with my previously virginal blood.

At this point, my curiosity began to get the better of me. Where was the normal reaction any child in this position would have exhibited? There had been no terror, temper or tantrum, not even a crying to his mother.

I waited a moment more before formally introducing myself to the man I had known all my life. I did so with nothing more than a young boy's once innocent, beautiful smile. Can you imagine the turmoil raging in this man's mind witnessing that smile instead of the expected reaction from a just raped infant? In that instant, he knew his fate was in my hands, not the Lord's, and certainly not his own. I would never forget the feeling of power I experienced that very moment!

He meant no more to me now than the field mice under my bed, except that instead of dwelling on destruction and retribution, as would have been normal for all other boys not yet men, my mind worked over and over at how to master my new toy, to be able to use his vulnerability in my quest for perfect dominance. I knew his use to me would become obvious, after all, his true nature and character had only revealed itself minutes during his moans of weakness.

"Father," my voice dragging like a knife across a whetting stone, clicking metallically with each turn of the blade, "Did you enjoy my discomfort? Was I your first, or were the teachings I received today the normal Sunday school

curriculum for all your pupils?" my lack of outrage tacitly condoning his act, or so I wanted him to speculate.

This six year old boy was working angles in a fashion grown men would have found impossible!

This *thing* was courting the advantage he could garner by using the priest. Where did these pieces of strategy evolve from in the mind of a six year old? Astonished, I fell back on my safeguard: this was the work of a fictionalist, a liar, and had nothing to do with the truth and what actually occurred. He had rewritten this episode long after the original was destroyed. This was fiction!

The father's eyes turned this way and that, anywhere to avoid my stare. He retreated, suddenly adverse to my touch. He knew that his future depended on his next carefully chosen actions or words, for he was now accountable to his new master. I enjoyed his discomfort, his searching for relativity to replace his new reality.

There before the priest stood no ordinary child. I sagged in my chair as the evidence before me became overwhelmingly against the environmental cause I wanted, no needed, to prevail. His eyes, those alien things, were the evidence.

I set the book down and looked again at his picture and those eyes. H. H. Holmes was born with these eyes. He was born with the monster inside of him and the ability to project that power on those around him. No one schooled him in these supernatural tendencies. This rape had not taught him how to use these eyes. Nor had the event taught him to react so coldly, with clear and concise thought, to such terror.

He had been born a predator.

Without another word, he turned and moved back, while grasping the cross at his neck, desperation bursting forth from his terrified person. He already knew what was to be his ultimate fate and, at the same time, knew he was without a single avenue of escape from which to scream bloody murder to all his children about the devil he had discovered living in their midst. His fear and desperation were magic to me. Like a drug, I would later grow addicted to their effect.

Moving away, he hid from me behind the altar. As if that place would protect him from the entity he had awakened. He began to pray with eyes only half-closed, afraid to lose sight of me.

When he finished he muttered, "You may go now, my son," the knowledge of his now failed life causing tears to run down his cheeks.

Teasing my new pet, I taunted him. "You have no more guidance for me this sunny day before I return home and decide whether to report my lessons to my parents? No... well then at least tell me what I should believe in my last moments tonight before I fall asleep. Should I pray to the God you celebrate within these walls?"

Still crying, the father refused to answer.

I burst out with a young boy's high-pitched laughter, as if just having opened my favorite Christmas gift. My sharp chuckle resonated off the statues of saints who had watched the day's heresies without raising even one holy finger in my defense. Damn them all to hell. I demanded to know how they could have let their disciple perform such evil in this their holy place of worship.

In a matter of three pages I had been transformed from a sympathetic adult, hating the foul fake messenger of our holy God, into the sole human being who knew what had been set free that fateful day.

Was it possible to feel sorry for this priest?

"Father, that place you hide behind will not help you escape your responsibilities as one of my flock. For if anything here were able to protect you and redirect my new-found passion for your soon to be cries of agony, the same power would have never allowed me to walk through these doors in the first place. Good day."

With his stare upon my back I pushed through the big doors of his brand new ruins. My senses flooded with aggressiveness to all about me in a spirit of complete and utter defiance. The previous resentment to my own life evaporating in contemplation of the fun and games to come. I skipped home, singing to high heaven, suddenly with so much to look forward to and so many plans to make. For the first time in my young life, the huge void I had always felt being unable to love was now filled with the ability to hate. That made me smile. My young life was suddenly with purpose. I would set new standards of evil.

When I returned home that Sunday, my mother was instantly aware of a change in my character, but also of a presence, impossible to describe, that cleared the room ahead of me. Over the coming weeks, I practiced attempting to affect those closest to me with the intensity of my stare and newfound energy. My father was the only one who could hold my stare and soon took to marching me out to the woodshed whenever I pushed him too far with my testing. Everyone else, grown men included, submissively recoiled from my slightest glance.

He was already learning to scare with his eyes, and would soon be able to mesmerize. Years later he would learn to modulate the intensity of his gaze so that at its height, his stare could transfix a victim to near-unconsciousness. Later, at his trial for murder, the transcripts of the proceedings revealed the same. When he was permitted to stare at witnesses prior to their testimony, the witnesses were almost unanimously reluctance to argue anything even remotely contentious to Holmes. As a result, many refused to give direct testimony, even when the judge had ordered him not to stare at them during their testimony against him.

Two or three times a week, until he was fourteen years old and bored of the fun, Holmes would stop by the church on his way home after school. There, Father Benjamin would repeat to Holmes the confessions of the flock so that Holmes could obtain advantage over them as well. His real lessons and homework were the notes he took listening to his now slave repeat the sacred confessions. There were no secrets from the child. He used them all to his utmost influence.

Holmes used the father for other things as well. The man was the perfect specimen for determining the outer limits of pain and servitude his future victims could be put to. He made the most of the man's guilt and inability to confess his sin to another. He forced the entire spectrum of human emotion over the father's soul. Close to the very end, Holmes described Benjamin's final emotion as a 'love' for his owner, even as the boy's whip shredded his back to tatters.

From these early experiments, I would learn to never underestimate the dependency a slave develops for his master. While never completely understanding the nature of this devotion, I did learn to depend upon the addiction never failing me, even under the most trying of circumstances.

As Holmes promised, the father died a horrendous death. Predictably, given the killer's sadistic sense of humor and apropos, the method of killing was very similar to the conduct the man had inflicted upon the young boy, but to the extreme. After reading the horror once, I tore the pages from the book and burned them away from this earth forever.

CHAPTER 15

I lit my first cigarette in six years… and pulled, taking that first long drag all ex-ex-smokers know deep in their hearts and lungs. I held the heat contemplating what I'd just read, my hand shaking as both nerves and smoke settled in. The nicotine buzz settled first and with none of the usual accompanying guilt I'd expected. Lung cancer was the least of my worries right now. Time, I needed time to figure this out, and if a cigarette or a pack or two helped me to focus, they'd be staining my fingers for quite a while.

Concentrating on my smoke, trying to fall back, I thought, *how many times has a man been required to conduct his own interrogation as to righteousness? How often has the tortured also been the torturer? What had I done to deserve this?*

Strange urges begun to scour the bottom of my soul. Evil slimy things, before only nightmares, were now real life contemplations. Impossible to describe, they shifted my brain ninety degrees to the right and left when they hit. When they did, my mind felt as if that once imaginary place was now an anvil being slammed by the sledge of an ever more obviously futile search for sanity. Images popped into my head of demonic things, horrible beasts, flying off in pursuit of innocents after receiving their orders… from me!

Insanity, that's the only thing this can be.

This edge was slowly turning into a roaring inside that was now constantly stirring my blood. Holmes described that same kind of roar when he wrote of his time as a boy. *The power was an aphrodisiac. The embodiment of evil washing over my flesh and soaking into my bones.*

Those same kinds of thoughts were beginning to seduce me.

Trying anything to avoid further self-introspection, I looked out my windows and across the way. My neighbor's house was solid brick. Two rows of red roses delineated my yard from his. Sue's roses' perfect manicure broadcasting the difference with his just-let-them-go ones to the world. This morning the obviousness of it all angered me. The difference never had before. His yard was out of place, unkempt and smelled of neglect, causing my nostrils to flare. Ten years we'd lived here and I'd never noticed a damn thing about Bill's yard, but since the books, irritating things like these were beginning to metastasize at an alarming rate. My neighbor, who had never threatened a soul his entire life, was now the target of my new sensibilities-- and possible wrath.

Their house was the kind that locked in all sound. Nothing personal had ever emerged from behind those mortared walls. That was how the space between us used to be. Today, I could hear the irritating crackling of their fireplace-- burning, snapping, and the sound was grating on my nerves. This irksome noise demanded my attention. The sounds emitted by the conduct of their existence were now a claxon that denied me peace and quiet. I was ready to plow my way through their lives, leaving only shattered remnants in my wake unless they fixed what bothered me... immediately.

The solution seemed simple, the way *he* would have settled edgy nerves. Despite the logic, I wasn't ready for that, Holmes wasn't me, yet, and so forced the thoughts aside. But that answer wouldn't leave me alone. My privacy and solitude demanded a solution. Their inconsequential lives meant nothing to me, to say nothing of the lack of sympathy I now carried for anyone with the audacity to inconvenience me.

Whatever it is, the change is happening much too fast.

All at once, I was snapped out of my zone. "Jeff, did you see the Raider game?" Bill asked from his front porch with the same genuine vapidness that earmarked everything in his life. He'd been the same- inside basic normal- the entire time we'd been neighbors. This morning he was in his pajamas, his ass crack peeking out at me as he stooped to pick up his Monday paper. Don't ask me how but I'd known he'd been coming out before his front door even opened. Like I said, don't ask me how.

I stared him down.

Polite, inane chatter was out of the question this morning. Nothing involving his life was of the slightest interest to me… except that he now irritated me.

Long years we'd traded beers, and shared jokes, but now, he was nothing more than a bug to be squashed beneath my heel, a bug that before the books had meant something, at least as much as I cared about anyone. Hell, he had once invited us to his daughter's wedding for Christ's sake!

Bill seemed to sense my change in attitude. My new found intensity obviously frightening him. His head hung down, submissive-like. His hands were low, as if welded to his hips. He moved in short, worried steps, one right after the other and only in a direct line. There was no pride to him. He had never exhibited such nervousness around me before.

Without waiting any longer for an answer, giving me his back in retreat, he turned to re-enter his house, but not before saying, and only saying, "Whatever," attempting to salvage some of the masculinity we both realized he'd just given up.

This change isn't just me. I wasn't imagining it. Bill had seen and felt the energy as well.

Conversing with others was now a waste of time, except when serving my needs. They all existed only for me and when they did intrude on my solitary world, my bubbling anger was close to uncontrollable. I knew I had to slow this evolution down, and quickly, or something terrible was bound to happen.

The next morning I woke from the most intense sleep of my entire life. My normal routine would have been to fumble for my glasses in order to see enough to find the source of the loud clatter that roused me: the alarm clock. Today, after having put those lifetime inconveniences on, my vision refused to clear as my eyes normally did. Assuming they were the wrong ones I threw them down to fumble on the nightstand for the others, but was stopped cold in my tracks-- the clock was clear as a bell! In fact, my entire surroundings seemed so strange. Everything was different, even the headboard of the king-size bed that had been ours for eight years looked bizarre.

Then it came to me-- my vision was perfect. *Amazing!* For the first time in my life I had awoken to a crystallized world rather than the perpetual fog of bad eyesight.

After giving myself time to digest the miracle, I was almost hesitant to drink my first cup of coffee for fear of realigning the old circuitry in my head. The coffee, thank goodness, didn't change a thing.

What could have caused this?

Could this physiological change have resulted, chemically speaking that is, from the terrible smell which erupted when the books were first opened? That had to be it. Some kind of weird chemical reaction, whatever it was, had caused these unheard of alterations.

Walking outside, for the first time spectacle-less, the sky was empty and red, dawn having just broken as the brightest stars flickered and faded away. Looking up the road I watched a passing car, but in a strange falsetto of three dimensional displacements. I locked eyes with the driver until he could no longer maintain my gaze, even behind the steel and glass that separated us. His apprehension of my intensity was obvious. I hadn't the slightest normal impulse to look away. I couldn't recall looking at someone like that, with such cold, calculating rationality, in my entire life.

Back inside the house the phone rang. Without picking up I knew Susan was calling to check up on me. Due to recent fears for her safety, I'd insisted, and she'd agreed, to her spending nights at her mother's. Not trusting myself, I let the phone ring knowing we could make up later.

Was it possible to explain these physiological changes that were occurring to my body after reading two old books? Was it possible for my vision to have cleared in one night? Was there such a thing as reading people's minds through a stare? It seemed that long dormant instincts, having been rekindled, were re-energizing the sensory centers of my brain. Whatever was happening, one thing was for certain: my body and psyche were undergoing very real changes.

I recalled hearing something about this on late night radio-- the station with all the UFO kooks – while driving home. Most of the talk was centered on the development of brain tumors that radically altered brain waves and the thought patterns of the afflicted. The symptoms seemed similar. Those occurrences had been marked by unfortunate endings.

I made an appointment with a neurologist later that afternoon.

CHAPTER 16

The voice began 'lecturing' me about the natural sciences, repeatedly ridiculing mankind's need to believe in our races own innate goodness. He laughed at the concepts of salvation and redemption. Man's ignorance created hell to justify pain and suffering, he would whisper in my ear. Then in the same breath he would ask me that if it were possible for a man to be born evil, beyond the helping hand of God so to speak, had there ever been a need for a devil?

Life is evil because life is war, he preached. On and on he went, lecturing that our time here was all about either victory or defeat. He wouldn't stop, explaining how our species fights for the possessions of others, as ownership was in our inherent nature. When I argued, he would reply with questions, as in why it so easy for science to admire the predatory traits of carnivores, yet at the same time deny similar characteristics in humans, despite our acceptance of evolution as a whole?

Holmes' logic slowly began making more and more sense.

He continued, using his rape as evidence, knowing environmental factors were my last defense, that contemporary man had for the last century or more utilized sociobiology to discount the idea of pure evil as a sub-species. This theory postulated that factors play a large part in influencing the disposition toward perpetrating evil acts, including murder. In other words, terrible home lives, non-nurturing mothers and abusive fathers were responsible for fostering psychopathic natures. Yet, Holmes argued, this argument fails to explain the gender-specific differences in homicide: 88% of all murders are attributable to men.

How could that be true, he asked, if the sociobiological concept was correct? Women suffer from far more environmental factors than men do, yet nearly all serial killing is perpetrated by males. If one accepted this theory you would expect that psychopathic females would commit at least the same numbers of violent crimes as men do. However, most of these women avoid committing such conduct despite the fact they have the same opportunities to perpetrate murderous acts, especially with the availability of modern firearms.

He closed by informing me the choice was mine. That if I listened to him, did what I was told, he would ensure that I proudly left this world a more natural, i.e., wicked place, than I found it.

Science had also recently begun pushing the delicate subject of genetic evil. Emerging studies addressing this issue presented me with the best chance of determining whether the characteristics of Holmes, and those of my lineage before him, could have been passed down to me.

More specifically, could a group of genes define a possible serial killer? The new evidence appeared to be saying yes. An even greater question was: can this instinctive behavior lead to murder? Studies seemed to suggest in humans there were groups of cells that triggered preprogrammed motor acts, as in the cat's motor response to motion and immediate pursuit. There seemed little doubt that stereotypical motor patterns did create fixed action sequences in mammals, and with absolutely no training.

While not answering the most important question about violent behavior, this concept of an evolutionary evil and a biological factor toward aggressive conduct, was as plausible as any previously offered. For the first time, science was tentatively crossing the line Holmes had written so much about while conducting his experiments. His century old argument about a possible link between genetics and murder might not have been so far off base after all.

New methods being used to test and prove biological and genetic similarities were forcing scientists to admit evolution into the equation. Exploding medical technology and the MRI machines were resolving the mysteries of man's brain. With this imagery, science was now capable of accurately comparing the brain of a psychopath with that of a normal person's. These snapshots were showing that the brain of a psychopath not only functioned differently, but was also physically distinct as well. These two men had been born different. More amazing, higher levels of activity were being recorded in a psychopath's brain. These differences in brain activity related to the emotional reaction of psychopaths in their particular neural structures. Except that instead of applying genius to art or science, their brilliance was in the pursuit of evil. Science and medicine seemed on the verge of proving that morality might indeed involve a tangible neurological process.

The science of it all was now staring *me* straight in the face. Evil might be a living, breathing thing capable of being passed down through the generations like a family heirloom.

If so, Holmes' actions might have been produced by the genes he had been born with and were not the result of some mental illness as all the books claimed. He had possibly inherited these traits from his grandfather and passed them on to Bert, who in turn, might have passed them on to me.

With these new concepts to bounce off old facts, I raced back to the newspaper articles that described Holmes during his trial. Reading them again, the words now appeared from reporters describing another species of human being: "those reptilian eyes," "icy," "hypnotic," "riveting." And, "His looks were dazzling;" he had "natural sex appeal irresistible to the opposite sex", commanding "occult like followings, often bordering upon the possession of slaves, and seemingly happy to be so." He had an "uncanny ability to spot and utilize nurturing women and submissive males" that "transcend[ed] the bounds of traditional thought." And most disturbing, he displayed both a "complete lack of empathy" and a "total lack of fear," and on and on ad infinitum.

Our long lineage seemed almost to prove the once thought impossible possible: a killer being reproduced, not once, but a number of times and in accordance with a set rhythm. That line may have walked through my family at consistent intervals. These numbers now seemed ready to expect me to accept my place on that back page and continue the line with the same energy that was so proudly exhibited by Holmes.

No! I wanted out of the line, but how?

The logical explanation seemed to be the skips, the spaces that proved some on the list were either immune or strong enough to resist becoming another like Holmes. There were three skips. Those three had lived normal lives, lives dominated by family and duty. My father was skipped as was his grandfather, a politician who had ably presided as mayor over a small town on the east coast of the United States. While both exhibited many of our same aggressive characteristics, their lives were devoid of any crime. They were good, strong men. Holmes' father appeared to have been skipped as well.

The rhythm of those skips made Bert's life appear the key to mine. He had either figured out a way to defeat his destiny, or those solitary fishing trips were something far, far more sinister than the simple pursuit of another lunker.

But more critical than the nature of those trips was the reason why Holmes had finally lined out Bert's circled name in the diary. The secret to my continued existence was finding out why. Somehow I knew deciphering the spacing was my only chance.

CHAPTER 17

With every turn of the page, Holmes re-established his title as the world's foremost authority on terror. A crown he had worn in secret from that world, but now with so much pride for me.

My focus was on those chapters which appeared to have been drafted by a teacher for a student. They were easy to locate. Unlike the normal diary first person format, they were instructional, emphasizing dialogue and sensory familiarity. Understanding them - I knew - was critical to solving the entire mystery. Yet the deeper I went the further from the truth I seemed to be. The name *Oedipus Rex* kept popping up in my head.

The 'teachings' were dominated by his never-ending search for human secrets. Specifically, those emotional frailties that oftentimes revealed the most about our natures and man's rapaciousness. The chapters were experiments, but not in a laboratory sense. They were out in the field of everyday society. Holmes was fascinated in learning how the human mind worked under the most terrible of conditions, the very conditions that Holmes excelled in creating. He craved testing the limits of love and most often when that same love was forced to compete with horrible pain.

Holmes discounted what all the great teachers had surmised about the human condition. He refused to accept conclusions from fabricated environments. This is why, over and over again, his recounting began so similarly, with Holmes breaking and entering at night, waiting for his victim to peacefully awaken, conveniently restrained of course, then administering the pain or threat of pain that would cause, or not, the frailty he sought. Holmes was an expert at this staging of extreme life.

*Twice, once in Madrid and once in Mexico City, I was given the oppor-
tunity to observe man at war with nature in the pomp and pageantry of the
bullfight. For some unexplained reason my fascination with Latin culture was
without bounds and I took every opportunity I could to experience Latin life
to the fullest. Nowhere was this mix of romance, beauty, vulgarity and brutality more on display than the ceremonial execution of the magnificent bull.*

Holmes was fascinated with the Mexican and Spanish intelligentsia's
contemplation of death. He theorized for years about the love-hate relationship these two civilizations burdened each other with. The Span-
iards' obvious disappointment in Mexico's centuries-long refusal to
accept the "gift" they had been offered, and the Mexicans' self-hatred for
continuing to voluntarily wear their Spanish gold shackles as history's
finest slaves. But that hatred was set aside at the bullfights! Here both
civilizations joined in their immense love of the event.

The production of the bull fight amazed him, especially the celebra-
tion that followed the death of the animal. But the hypocrisy of the event
was what invigorated his intellectual interest most. He grew irritated at
the staged outcome of the so called fight and with the acclaim the matadors received afterwards. Maybe, down deep, his anger was created by the
fact that these killers were celebrated while Holmes was forced to lay low,
living the life of the fugitive, when he believed himself to be the greatest
choreographer of death that ever lived.

He discussed the bullfights many times, one event in particular.

*The bullfight may be the most misunderstood public celebrations of hei-
nous cruelty ever practiced, other than the games at ancient Rome's Coliseum,
but even so I will admit that bullfighting fascinated me. The entire event has
a biblical sense to it, a pagan blending of societal reformation, while the atmosphere is one of fiesta that oftentimes results with the mixture of alcohol and
blood. Beyond the pomp and circumstance, what emerges is a futile grasping
at the meaning of life and more so death and the undeniably guiltless pleasure
the crowd achieves at the expense of an innocent animal.*

Make no mistake about it; he felt no pity for the bull, or for those he murdered either, but was fascinated by the human ability to make sport of one and evil of the other so easily. The death that was heralded on a beautiful sunny afternoon before thousands of elites accompanied by their small children in Sunday best brought out his all in analysis and comparison, and compare he did, that master of human death, on that day and for many days thereafter.

The bull explodes from his pen at the side of the ring, a magnificent black silhouette of force. Each step vibrates with a mystical energy that runs up from the earth into the gut of each spectator, causing perspiration on everyone there. With his chest high horns out and legs blasting through the soft earth, he searches out any adversaries, for he is the ruler of all and afraid of nothing. He is the same bull as those that roamed the earth millions of years before. The primitive power he projects thrills everyone. He is the aphrodisiac of life.

The matadors strut out from below the arena and onto the sidelines in a hilarious show of false honor and courage. They are careful to remain safely ensconced from the perfect animal. The ridiculous clothes they wear to draw attention from the crowd are only dwarfed by the red cape used to confuse the animal's attention. The fight is delayed.

The men enter the ring, but only after the animal has been crippled by the picadors who sever his neck muscles, the same muscles that direct the speed and strength of his formerly deadly horns. While this is going on the men hide behind barriers awaiting the cuts of the horse-drawn picadors from their armored positions atop blindfolded mounts. After the stunned bull is bloodied and rendered a shadow of his former self, the celebrated ones emerge to prance and preen to the crowd in shows of orchestrated bravery. Then the fight begins.

The cheers from the throng at the sight of the bull being sliced and carved fostering intense pain in an animal already aware that he was fighting for his life intrigued Holmes the most. The way in which the animal was handicapped by the severing of the necessary muscles on the

animal's neck, the ones that presented the most danger to the partici-
pants, caused Holmes to chuckle in abject irony. The act also sets his
mind to work.

*Each act is choreographed, every turn, every thrust, every plea to the heart
rendered crowd. There is nothing left to chance except for the one in one thousand possibility that a matador slips and falls before, instantly transformed by
that mischance, a deity with hooves. By now the bull is exhausted and confused,
much the same way my victims are before the coup de grace is administered.
Blood streams down the bull's flanks as his tongue hangs a foot out of his mouth
in a desperate search for oxygen and water. He is offered nothing to replenish
his strength, but instead is subjected to the act of pantomime in the give and
take of the ring. Each matador's dance step is offered as flirtation to the mag-
nificently clad women in the stands and as wonder to their jealous male companions.*

*With ceremony, the sword of death is handed and sheathed beneath the
cape of the matador. He approaches his victim, each step a mirror of glamour
and previous practice, while the bull nervously waits, aware, yes, aware of his
pending fate. Maintaining his script, the lead plays out the final act until the
curtain is scheduled to come down with one thrust, but yet, all too many times
the final parry is a false one leading to more and more before the innocent beast
is finally and fully put down. And all to the cheers of the adoring crowd. Tragic
really, but all the more motivating for my own sport, and the intimate
knowledge I've gained about the lack of boundaries of our own human species.*

*When the 'fight' is over and the still warm bull dragged off by meat hooks
behind a mule team, the crowd, unable to scream their "oles" any longer, leave
satisfied, themselves exhausted from their adulation of the heroes. They carry
their favorite from the arena high upon their shoulders and serenade him down
the boulevard to his nearby home. As they do, I follow along with them, watching my own new favorite from the shadows parallel to the throng. His name
is, now was Jose Padillo and his blessed life of idolatry was about to take a
turn for the worse.*

Of all that day Jose was the best at inflicting pain while wearing his majestic expression of false duty. I imagined him as a young man in front of a mirror practicing these expressions while thrusting here and there, twirling on his toes. But I wondered whether he would be able to maintain them when the object was he, when he was the one in pain, fighting for his next breath while begging for mercy? Would he find these gestures as amusing as did his loyal throng? Yes, I would soon see whether that majestic manner he carried remained under reversed conditions. I pondered an excellent experiment, quite pleased with myself for imagining another unique foray in a world too empty of fulfilling mental exploration. Once I learned where he resided, I set off to gather the necessary tools for my next experiment.

What had first piqued my interest flipping through the pages now screamed for my utmost attention. Could this unrelated event, this testing of a stranger's passion for death, albeit that of an animal, be one of the keys I needed to begin understanding the mysteries involving my ancestor? Could these seemingly sympathetic words involving the torture and death of an innocent animal portray something good beneath the obvious layers of pure evil? Was it possible that something hidden had revealed itself?

I slid through the gated entranceway and unlocked iron doors, the same his courtesans had carried him through earlier up his stairs to place him onto his bed. Still in uniform, he had obviously quickly fallen into an exhausted wine-laden sleep. My unpracticed stealth left much to be desired, as on the way up I was forced to subdue one of his servants who discovered my intrusion and attempted to alert others of my presence. Once finally in his stateroom, and with the ease an inebriated victim always provided me, I rolled him onto his side and tied his hands behind him. He was also gagged to ensure silence for the time necessary to explain his predicament once he awoke and to set the stage for the rest of his short life. Finished, I settled down in the chair at the foot of his bed and waited patiently for him to gather energy sleeping for the ordeal that awaited the end of his last slumber.

Jose awoke one hour later but lay unexpectedly quiet, most likely contem-
plating his predicament. I stayed silent as well allowing his tension to build.
These were the times, when I gave my next subject the opportunity to contem-
plate their fate, that often proved the most fruitful. To his credit he did not
utter a sound.

I finally arose, stretching in the luxurious burst of energy I always felt
before proceeding in experiment and peered out his high window down onto
the still dark and quiet street below. Satisfied as to our privacy, I turned back
to my new friend.

"Mi hermano. Como estas?"I asked.

"Bien. Que pasa?"he mumbled around the gag.

"Mmmm. Todo mi amigo. Todo en tu mundo."

At that the celebrated Spanish temper erupted and he flew into a rage
while testing his bindings. He continued twisting and turning for some time,
only stopping when exhausted. When I approached him, he returned to his
chaotic antics. To settle him down I walked to the bed and stuck my thumb
into the nerve at the side of his neck, which, when done properly, creates an
exquisite pain. The application of the pain accomplished its purpose. He grew
respectful.

"Shhhh… silencio mi nuevo amigo! First let me tell you what it is we do
tonight. Most importantly, you will die, of that there is no doubt. But do not
be afraid, for I give you the same chance to exhibit your claimed hero's char-
acter that you gave the mighty bull. You may die a hero's death, as did the
animal yesterday afternoon, or you may experience the most horrible coward's
death you can possibly imagine. The choice is yours compadre as will be the
amount of pain I shall inflict upon you. Tu comprendes?"I asked.

He nodded.

"Bien. Before we begin, close your eyes, pray if you like, and accept that
your life is now complete and that only one more thing, the test of character I
just explained, remains. Do not waste any precious energy contemplating es-
cape or pleading for mercy. Give your all to showcasing your best just as you

demanded of the bull. Make these final moments' great memories for me and those I choose to share them with.

You have tasted the life of a celebrity, with accolades from the most influential and beautiful. You receive this grandeur from drawing the blood of another, albeit distinct, being. I need to know what it is to feel that same sucking of life in order to taste the needs that make up your grandiose existence."

His eyes wide in terror, muscles rigid as steel, the hopelessness of his situation overtook him. The eyes widening each time I mentioned the bull, obviously finding the comparison of his and the animal's status terrifying. The same reaction I witness each time I change the role of one previously in power to one deliciously helpless.

I released his gag. From his heart of darkness he spit at me, or tried as best he could from his dry mouth. I calmly raised my hand and traced his lips with my knife warning against any such further disrespect. Understanding, he nodded his head in respectful apology.

He was a small man, more diminutive than I would have imagined having watched him from high in the arena. However, his eyes revealed a serious intelligence that I welcomed as I waited patiently for him to accept his fate. I knew that his status as celebrity would make acceptance difficult in order for him to follow my instructions. Therefore each time he disobeyed I corrected any transgression utilizing pain.

When he had calmed sufficiently enough for us to proceed I cut the binds at his feet and assisted him to the other chair in the room, passing the stiletto across his throat, allowing him to recognize what further disrespectful conduct would result in. When in the chair I retied his arms, wrists up, to the arms of the chair.

"Jose escuchar. Yesterday you seemed to take such pleasure killing the bull. Tell me why you enjoyed killing him so much. Did you know this bull? Did you hate him for the infliction of past injuries or the possible goring of a family member by another of his species, or were you attempting to honor his bravery with a warrior's death?"

He paused to consider my questions and instead of answering honestly, gave the one response he felt might improve his chances. "Senor, the killing is only my job. This is how I feed my family!"

I laughed at his dishonest response, having watched firsthand his glee while performing the act. He lived to kill, just as I did. I recalled the lust written across his face while he performed. We both reveled at being the best at what we did.

Standing next to him, I very slowly asked him to carefully consider the following proposal. I informed him that I would kill him this morning, just like he had killed the bull, but like the bull, I was going to give him a chance to fight in order to possibly save his life and return to his family. To fight, I was going to equip him with a stiletto exactly like mine. At this glimmer of hope his interest rose while he listened intently as I informed him of the rules of the contest.

When I was finished, he asked if I was going to release him before the fight.

Yes, I responded, but only after placing you in the same condition to which the bull was subjected to before you demonstrated your immense bravery and skill to your tens of thousands of adoring spectators.

Stepping back I took the role of the picador. It was time for me to prepare my "toro" for his own so-called fair fight.

I surgically severed the critical tendons that connected his arms at the wrist to his hands, trying to be as professional as the picadors were slicing the bull's essential neck ligaments. After all, there were rules of decency to maintain. The blood flowed as he screamed out in pain. So much for the master of courage and pain, I thought, chuckling for both our benefits. Next, I released him from his ties and offered him the other razor-sharp knife to take with his once formidable grasp. He watched his blood spurting from the wound, making the knife slippery in his hand, before remembering me and concentrating on my then non-threatening lack of movement either towards or away from him. This was my time to perform to the crowd. We stood within three feet of each other.

As I suspected, there was nothing to the fight. He was a shadow of his former self, his physical inability dissipating before my eyes. His pain was unbearable. The loss of blood quickly rendered him impotent. Oh yes, he did indeed make two or three amateurish lunges at my torso, which I parlayed aside with tango-like movements, much like his at the arena. Pursuing my role to the maximum, I theatrically played the hero, kneeling at his face, inches from his blade and teased his body and soul as he had done the cursed animal. At one point I even turned my back to him and feigned the same yawn he had play-acted in front of the crestfallen bull. What bravery I exhibited as the master of life and death theatrics! And just as then, the response was nothing more than a tortured look of anguish from the victim. How he must have wished for the strength to attack, but he was nothing but meager, like the bull, as I knew he would be at this moment of truth.

Bored, but satisfied with the results of the experiment, I moved to end his life... slowly. I administered a purposefully faulty slash across his throat, inches from where a lethal cut needed to be, in order to play out to my imaginary crowd. Even so wounded, he stayed strong at heart. There were no tears or words to his God, as every last piece of resolve and energy was directed in obvious hatred at me, just as the animal had done him. Before he died to the imaginary cheers of my crowd, I severed his ear and bestowed this treasure upon myself. His last breath came watching me assess the treasured proof of my ability and his courage.

Walking from his room that morning before the servants were to arise I wondered had I allowed him to survive whether he would have returned to the ring, despite his first real lesson about courage and honor.

Probably yes, I told myself, for after all, he was only a man.

CHAPTER 18

What most men were allowed a lifetime to ponder, or to exist within blissful ignorance, was being forced at the speed of life down my throat. Almost as if I'd been born again, no not again, for the first time, my previous life a fog.

That morning, Susan, aware of my concern, came up behind me at the counter, looking over my shoulder at our joint reflection. "What's the matter babe?" she asked.

"Do I look any different to you, you know, over the past few months? My face feels harder. I hardly recognize myself anymore. My eyes are like drills, they go right through me when I'm shaving in the morning."

She reached up and stroked my cheek with her hand, her eyes as soft as ever. Knowing what I needed, she stayed quiet, letting me continue.

"People look differently at me now, almost as if they're terrified of me. You really can't see anything?"

"No, nothing at all, just the same man I fell in love with twenty-one years ago next month," and with that she kissed me on the side of my neck and left me to work it out myself.

Even loved, I remained convinced.

The voice started teasing me about God-- *He is only the postponement of life because of the fear of death. Trust me, my son.*

With all my might, I tried to resist him about this most important of all subjects. Nothing worked, in fact, he seemed to enjoy my attempt at refusal on this subject the most. Unable to withstand his teasing anymore, just as *he* said would happen, I began turning to God, any god that would listen. First quietly asking, and receiving nothing, then pleading, again nothing, and finally begging for help. Absolutely nothing was forthcoming. Not one word, nothing to compete with the now constant whispering of the one I had begun assuming was the dark brother.

Mary Shelley's words, those about Frankenstein, came to mind, 'Why did you form a monster so hideous that even you turned from me in disgust? God in pity made man beautiful and alluring, after his own image; but my form is a filthy type of yours, more horrid from its very resemblance. Satan had his companions, fellow-devils, to admire and encourage him; but I am solitary and detested."

Now I was the outcast, the one that ran outside and alone. I could feel that solitude on my skin. The filthy type who everyone was warned away from on Sunday mornings; the one to be feared; to be detested.

Not yet ready to give up, and as all strong men tested by evil do, I fought back, shouting unrecognizably skyward, "How could you have been involved in the creation of such an abomination? Foulness as to forever stain any other good you may have bestowed upon our world. Holmes was your choice!"

Interrupting, as he often did now, the voice added, *And in his own image! Ask him about that, Jeffrey.*

"Shut up ghost, this is between him and me," I yelled while pointing skyward.

In support of my case, I opened the second book to gather evidence to prove my argument. Where the book was opened to hardly mattered, for anywhere would do just fine. This time the page was Holmes' shorthand reminiscing of his slaying of the young newspaper reporter he had caught snooping around the Castle one night during the World's Fair. He subdued the man with the usual double dosage of charm and chloroform. Holmes' man carried the comatose victim down three levels where he was locked away for days with insufficient food and water, alone and in total darkness, accompanied only by his suspicions and knowing fears of the Doctor. Unfortunately he had failed to inform his superiors at the paper of his intended whereabouts. While the newspaper cub fretted below, Holmes reviewed the man's previous works, becoming quite intrigued at the youth's vigor in discovering then publicly revealing certain foundations of Chicago's underground. Thus, the Doctor decided to conduct his own 'interview.'

With minimal anesthesia he surgically removed, with minor loss of blood, the man's testicles. He then sutured and closed the wounds. He gave the man days to recover from the shock of the operation. The 'patient' was provided water but no food. On the fifth day, Holmes entered the room and found what he expected: an extremely frightened, sore and very hungry human being. Being the good host he was, Holmes fed the young man his own sautéed sexual organs, but only after having provided the man his choice-- starvation or the very familiar protein.

My tour de force offer of proof had left the opposition speechless. Nothing emerged from the sky above. Who, no what, could contest my direct evidence of the existence of such a monster?

Crestfallen, I remembered something I once read and had passed over as only so much gibberish. These words could no longer be disregarded, "The devil is the legacy of the widespread tendency to attribute the origin of evil to non-human influences."

He was here amongst us, and he was of me.

CHAPTER 19

He interrupted one night by insisting the book be put down so he could inform me of a particular insect that existed along the Amazon. Holmes said the bug was capable of performing a peculiar spectacle. It seems if cut in two, the separate pieces would immediately battle each other to the death. This sinister fight would take place nearly every time. The voice suggested we skip ahead forty or fifty pages and he would narrate the same fight, metaphorically speaking of course, that often occurred among human beings.

When we were there, he went silent, as if recalling a solemn occasion, then uttered, *"Jeffrey, let me show you the true nature of a human being when what we take for granted is suddenly eliminated."*

The passage began with Holmes touring the streets of Philadelphia, reminiscing about old acquaintances.

Walking down the boulevard late one night, I was struck by the vision of a woman of uncompromising beauty and elegance. Staring at her retreating form I was sure I had seen her before. Then that moment came to me. Her incredible likeness was of a gorgeous former lover I'd had in Chicago. Melody was her name and she was the daughter of Chicago's Senior Detective.

Coincidentally, I'd first seen Melody three years ago to the day. They were guests at the Castle. Perhaps "guests" is the wrong word. She and her father had been abducted on my orders by my man due to some rather tenuous circumstances.

One or two days before they were hosted, her father sent two officers by my place of business to investigate a number of disappearances. Both officers proved mannerly and extremely susceptible to my suggestions. However, despite my best efforts, their reports of "nothing unusual" apparently did not convince their superior officer. The next morning he took the matter upon himself and paid me a visit by dropping by unannounced.

Before many of my best customers he showed a complete lack of respect for a man of my position and character. I was left no choice but to accept his demands, ask him in and show him around the hotel and pharmacy. He even went so far as to inspect my living accommodations. To his obvious disappointment, not one item was out of place, as beforehand all corridors and passageways had been secured. After the normal chat, the same one I shared with law enforcement hundreds of times, he became antagonistic and for no apparent reason, insulted me quite harshly, even threatening physical harm and more than once.

The detective was a strong man, both physically and mentally, and proved resistant to my similar attempts at convincing him of my version of right and wrong. He left promising further investigation with a warrant for a more thorough, I think he called it, "intrusive" search of the premises.

He left me with little choice but to quickly cease operations that day in order to follow him home, where I hid in the darkness observing him and his family for two hours. Unexpectedly, his seventeen-year-old daughter left me enchanted. When clear, I ordered my assistant to slip into their pantry, while I waited outside and watched as he applied one of my patented medicines to their stew. The anesthesia soon left the family in various stages of unconsciousness. The wife was apparently one of those unfortunates who being allergic to this narcotic, suffered a seizure and died a rather violent death at the dinner table as we were gathering the unconscious detective and his daughter. This reaction occurred in perhaps two or three people per hundred. While unfortunate, her death was unimportant except that the location made disposal of her body away from the Castle more problematic. Hours later, we returned to the Castle with the father and daughter, securing them in the solitary room. As they remained unconscious, and with some haste, I was able to dress and make the second act of King Lear at the local theater enjoying a superb performance by a visiting group of actors.

Holmes designed the solitary room in the basement for just these kinds of encounters. The room had no windows and was constructed in such a way as to make the elimination of all incriminating evidence rather easy. A heavy table sat in the middle of the room directly over the large drain that accommodated heavy viscous materials. Upon the four walls hung surgical instruments, each in its own cubicle, arranged in progression to better facilitate the experiments and preparations for commercial vending of product. His tools were impeccably clean, as would be expected of any doctor's private surgical equipment. There were two chairs in the room. The one for the doctor was high backed with a bar to rest tired legs and feet. The other was a steel stool just high enough to not allow the users feet to touch the floor. This served the purpose of quickly creating fatigue and subconsciously preventing the user from focusing on anything other than the pain at hand. The stool was also angled forward making balance difficult, requiring the user's constant attention.

There were twenty small cubicles for candles in the room spaced to eliminate shadow from compromising the exactness of the labors. The sole door to the room was made of heavy iron and swung open only into the interior and just by key. There was no door handle. A door bell was situated at foot level enabling the doctor to request aid without using busy or messy hands. Everything had been thought of ahead of time to accommodate procedures, whether for surgery, torture, or both. Sound did not emanate from the room.

Holmes often left prisoners in solitary for days. He realized the effectiveness of simply allowing their own minds to torture themselves. He knew that worry soon destroyed resolve. The prisoner would often be starved. Holmes was an expert at what the bodies chemical reactions from deprivation could create. I can only imagine, the detective having investigated much of Holmes' activities, what the officer's first thoughts were upon awakening and realizing his predicament-- way down below ground level at the Castle.

When he was ready to begin, Holmes, dressed in frock, proceeded down the stairway into the basement.

The drug I used often left the patient confused and nauseated for hours afterwards. To speed the process I slapped the detective across the face a number of times before telling him, "My good man, it's time to wake up. Don't worry, that unsettled feeling you are experiencing is from the drugs I administered at your home with your dinner this evening. Your lack of comfort will soon pass, although I regret to inform you that your lovely wife was not so fortunate, bless her soul." The blindfolded detective reacted so violently to this news I felt it necessary to step back before continuing, "Ah yes, I see from your intense reaction to this news that the drug has lost much of its effect. Good, shall we begin?"

"You scoundrel! What is the meaning of this outrage? I demand that you release me at once!" he shouted. He was sweating profusely as if sick with heavy fever. His daughter was curled up into a ball sobbing in the corner.

He was unaware of her presence in the room. To remedy this I removed his blindfold.

"There now, can you see that we are joined here tonight by another? Do you recognize her?"

Hazy, the man shook his head trying to eliminate the last of the cob webs, his professional training kicking in, as he attempted to evaluate the totality of his circumstances. To accelerate this metamorphosis, I took her in both hands and walked her to him. She was soon close enough that all doubt was removed. I was behind her, our bodies touching. The shock upon his face as he recognized her was simply divine. These are the moments I lived for! His eyes darted back and forth from her eyes to my hands on her shoulders and my grinning persona above. I pulled her back against my chest, like a lover, and held up a hand as he prepared to speak.

"Detective, will you please excuse us for a few minutes, we have something to discuss in private."

Before he could reply, I led her off and out the door before allowing the heavy steel to slam for effect, the echo of its crash reverberating across the room. Once in the hallway where he couldn't see or hear us, I directed her to sit. She looked up at me as if expecting instructions, but I instead put my finger to my lips demanding she remain quiet. We had nothing to discuss, as no words were necessary to further this portion of the experiment. His fear of what I might say and do to her being quite sufficient.

After some time had passed we re-entered and I allowed her to return to her father. She collapsed onto his lap, crying incoherently. Perfect, just perfect! I knew his mind would be racing, trying to guess what had happened to her outside that could have caused this show of extreme emotion. From years of experience I knew that his imagination would proceed far beyond any ingenuity on my part.

"Your daughter is a very obedient child, sir. My dear tell your father exactly what I told you outside. There is no need for secrets here."

She rose from his lap and hugged him. Her tears ran down her cheek onto his face. He watched me smiling at them both. The moment was priceless.

When she said nothing, he pressed, "What did he tell you, Melody?"

"He didn't say anything Father, nothing I swear!" I knew his mind would be in turmoil at what he could not allow himself to believe. Heavy doubt would creep in, grinding away at years of love, and all in just seconds.

I pulled her from him back against me, and then stroked her gorgeous hair numerous times before directing her back into the corner. He watched my every move like a hawk.

"Why are we here?" he asked, casting his professional investigatory glance around the room before returning his eyes to mine again.

I laughed.

"Come now, my good man. You were here threatening me this afternoon. Don't you remember the insults you heaped upon me? Can our purpose now be a mystery to a man of your talent and intellect?" I laughed again. "Why detective, you are here to be punished for that intrusion into my life. Your daughter is here to ensure your punishment is complete. In the past I have found that good strong men like yourself are often able to accept and digest the punishments I heap on them, but none have ever been able to witness that

same punishment being transferred to a loved one. Your daughter is here to guarantee your pain and my satisfaction, perhaps even pleasure."

His shoulders actually sagged at this explanation. The horrible rumors and his suspicions about me were obviously true, that recognition registering over his entire face. He would soon find out that in actuality they were inadequate.

My footsteps squeaked on the damp floor as I turned from him and slowly approached the wall for an appliance. My surgical tools, shining, were perfectly maintained almost eager to wet their thirsty dry metallic teeth. I theatrically tested all options, as a lover would, running my hand sensuously over each, both prisoners never once taking their eyes off me, not even for a second.

Normally this exaggerated role playing on my part was unnecessary, as the commercial value of the specimens dominated the coming process. But this time was different. He had insulted me in my very home, applying his authority and power in a way that always infuriated me. This tonight was to be about my enjoyment and his coming realization of exactly who he had offended. This one I was looking very much forward to.

Having made my initial selection, I bent down, eye to eye, and showed him my choice of tool for him. The knife was a surgical saw, perhaps the most savage and painful surgical implement there is. For her, at the other end of the spectrum for pain, was my finest scalpel.

I placed the saw on his shoulder, almost as if a king bestowing knighthood and asked, "Tell me, detective, what would you do for me, what would you promise or give up in order to convince me to pardon your soon to be dead daughter"

He was unable to provide a solution. I repeated the question and this time when he remained silent I dragged the saw across the side of his head slicing his right ear almost in two. The intensely painful cut quickly covered his face in blood while his screams filled the room.

But still, as I was beginning to anticipate, he said nothing. I turned to his daughter.

"*My dear, come stand next to me. Disrobe for your father and I.*" *She looked at me as if in shock, then to him, silently pleading for guidance. She was unable to move.*

"*Come, come, and don't be shy, after all I am a doctor. Give me your hand and let us proceed.*" *Once offered, I took her hand and raised it to my lips, kissing her softly. While doing so I looked into that deep secret place all victims go in anticipation of terror. Lamb-like she shook, but dared not take her hand away, instead looking to her father for advice.*

Somewhat sorry for her I overlooked her failure to obey and began disrobing her myself. As each item was removed her beauty escalated captivating me even more. She was truly remarkable. I stopped for a moment to contemplate whether I really wanted to proceed with my plans to deform her. After all this was about his pain and she had nothing to do with why they were here. Realizing her emotion would do, I decided not to seriously harm her before resuming my action. When she was naked, I turned her to face him, her breasts full and proud and only inches from her father's face. A multitude of the most intense human emotions ran back and forth between them. My experiment was proceeding onto perfection!

With the gentle strength many women found irresistible, I pulled her to me trapping both her hands between us. Reaching around from behind her I cupped the bottom half of her breast in my left hand and began tracing the outline of her nipple with the razor-sharp blade of the scalpel in the other, barely cutting, just enough, and whispering the entire time in her ear that any unnecessary movements on her part would result in extreme pain.

The scalpel in the hand of an artist is as incredible an instrument as a concert violin. Consequently, her pain was minimal.

Her beauty, magnified by the hopelessness she now felt, and all in the presence of her once mighty father was another treat to behold.

The superficial circular cut now complete, we all watched as the line slowly filled with blood, turning into a fine red sphere around her nipple. Resting my chin on her shoulder I could see that her now permanently tattooed breast was more beautiful than ever.

The man, head back, every fiber strained to the maximum, roared in animal-like agony. His intensity and her own sudden complete realization of what had just occurred caused the girl to faint in my arms. His rage continued for an extended period of time. When he finally stopped, his head slumped in abject defeat. He closed his eyes unable to watch her any longer. Maybe for the first time since he was a child, he began crying. Setting her down, I bandaged the wound, stemming any further flow and loss of blood.

I then waited for him to gather himself, the entire time tracing the other nipple, in order not to cut this time, with the back of the scalpel's blade.

"Sir, the next time I ask you a question, answer immediately. Do you understand?" I went on coldly, as if only expressing my duty. "Your daughter has many beautiful attributes with which I can punish you with."

"God yes! Yes, I understand! Please let her go, let her live. I will tell you anything you want to know."

These were the common words of a tortured man. I had heard them countless times before. To be frank, his weak, almost pleading, rantings disappointed me, and all from a man who had projected such power earlier.

I lowered myself down to his level, my lips close to his ear. "I know. Our problem is that I want one and only one thing from you. I want your promise to cease all further investigations concerning my business affairs and me. How we go about ensuring that promise is difficult to foresee... perhaps if I give you sufficient time to consider options. Right now I have other more important things to attend to. While I am away for the next two hours, try to create a plausible scenario that will leave me satisfied as to your faithful compliance. Oh and by the way, and listen to me very carefully officer, if, when your daughter comes too, she attempts to untie your restraints I will repeat the same procedure on her other breast, only this time much deeper. Make sure you tell her the consequences of her actions, after all you are her father and by all accounts should be willing to do anything for her, including die. Do you agree and understand?" He nodded yes.

I looked at my watch, walked to the door and toed the bell notifying my servant. Before exiting I stopped and turned to the detective asking him if he loved his daughter. He of course answered yes. I asked him if he also loved life, and finally if he believed in an afterlife for them both.

Unconcerned with his response, I cut off his loud answer in the affirmative by closing the door shut behind me.

My concerned assistant caught up with me on the way upstairs and asked, "Doctor, should I ensure that the restraints are left untouched? You know of course that he will have her untie him." The danger the large detective presented to both of us, should he come free, concerning him greatly.

"No, Peter, let them be. Of course he will have her untie him. When I return from dinner, release some of the smoke into the room and observe them from the drain. When he is down, re-enter and restrain him again. Leave her untied."

The reality of this stark situation flabbergasted me. This law abiding innocent man was being forced to wrestle with evil, with the devil, and the fate of his daughter was the prize. Had this only been him, he could have sworn at the devil with the pride of the devout man who knows death is next. Swearing at the fiend while wearing the face of a true and noble human being. Of course, here, the looming terrible final moments of his child prevented that. Dignity no longer mattered, for every piece of his human engineering was now focused on protecting the life of his daughter. Whatever the means, whatever he was forced to commit, would be his final test.

When I returned, the first thing my assistant said was, "Doctor, you were right. She untied her father."

"Yes. And?"

"I did as you ordered. They have both been sedated and are now unconscious awaiting your return. I have left the room safe for you to enter. He has
been restrained again."

Two hours later, when they were again conscious, I entered with Peter
following behind me tying the strings of my surgical apron. Sensing that she
was once again going to be the object of my attention, the girl retreated, falling
to the hard floor behind her father.

Holding out my hand, I said, "Come to me my dear. Don't be afraid, at
least not yet. I have a very simple question for you. Before you answer I want
you to understand that if you lie to me your father will die. Do you understand?"

She nodded yes, her eyes upon me like the brilliant orbs of a fawn still alive
but in the jaws of a wolf. "My assistant informs me that you defied my order
about not untying your father. Breaking one of my rules comes with terrible
consequences. Before I begin let me make sure we all know exactly what happened. Did your father warn you what would occur were you to untie his restraints? Did he tell you that I told him I would disfigure you if he was to be
so foolish as to ask you to untie him, you the one he claims to love so much?"
Our eyes were locked, pulling out every ounce of her young innocence.

The officer could no longer stand our growing intimacy.

"Holmes how could you? You know I didn't tell her. You knew I
wouldn't!" the detective yelled, slamming up and down on his chair with
enough energy to lift it and him inches into the air. I waited with my hand
upon her shoulder as we both watched him, waiting for him to calm down. As
I expected, her attention left me and began focusing on him, first silently questioning and then aggressively demanding... now all on her own.

"Father, why didn't you tell me? How could you not have?"

His eyes, unable to look at her, instead burned with a vengeance at me, as
his understanding of my, no his, experiment cascaded over his entire being.
"Darling, can't you see what he is doing? Don't let him do this to us." He knew

he had not a moment to spare and eternity too regret. "He works us back and forth, distilling distrust to brew more agony."

Interrupting, I stepped between them, "My dear, please inform me if any of what I am about to say is incorrect." I paused, then, "While I was away, your father asked you to provide him the opportunity for freedom by releasing him from his bindings. When he asked you to do this, he failed to warn you of the consequences that such an act would result in should I discover your conduct. You now realize he had you perform this service for him at the risk of your own excruciating pain and grave injury, in fact, much more pain than you previously suffered." She stared at me, lingering on my every word. "I intentionally failed to inform you of my verbal warning to your father and of the consequences, for it was my intention to thus test your father's love for you."

I then gathered her in my arms and led her to my chair, sat her down and leaned in with my elbows on each arm rest, in effect surrounding her.

"Tell me how that makes you feel, my dear?"

Bursting into tears, she fell forward so that her head was on my chest. She was unable to look her father in the eyes.

"Can you provide me any possible explanation for why your father would forget to mention my warning before he had you risk life and limb? Could it be because he placed his own safety and potential freedom above your, his own daughter's, health and wellbeing? Could something that heinous be possible?"

"No, no, you filthy pig!" His screams actually shaking the concrete walls. "I wanted to save her. That was the only reason why! Don't listen to him, darling."

Truly intrigued, I let him finish, but she, dying to join the discussion, stepped away from me and walked over to him and said in a barely audible but highly edged tone, "Why didn't you tell me Father? Why didn't you let me decide my own fate? Had you, I would have risked my all for you anyway."

This was music to my ears! What a young woman she was. What a lady she would be when properly trained. One or two more steps were all that was now needed. So after retrieving my scalpel I walked to her and began gently combing her hair with the blade. The room was silent except for the heavy breathing of the condemned. For the first time since she had entered, she stood proud, almost defiant—- but not at me, at her father! Again I removed her blouse and lifted her perfect breast exposing the other nipple. Her father could not bear to look. She closed her eyes, but bless her heart, refused to cry in anticipation of what was to come. Her courage was a thing to behold.

But instead of following through with my promise I released her. Turning her back around to face me, away from her father, I told her so softly that only she could hear me: "No. Not this time, my sweet. You are forgiven, or should we say your father is forgiven. I spare you. After all, the mistake was his, wasn't it?" Then I kissed her on the lips. She never moved a muscle.

Psychologically, I knew that my relenting would forever connect her to me in ways much more powerful than her father's paternal bond. All that was needed now was time for the results too sink in. I signaled Peter my desire to depart again.

As I left them, I addressed her, ignoring him, "The same rules are in effect this time, but know that I will never forgive you again for any further misconduct. While I am gone, you have my permission to discuss this matter with your father. I suggest that you reach a clarification should another similar request occur." She nodded yes, in complete control of her own destiny now.

Holmes had proven another of his theories, demonstrating his ability to manipulate the grandest of human emotions. The two parts, as with the insect, had fought with each other at the very end when they should have only loved. How could something as evil as Holmes know so much about human frailties?

There wasn't enough oxygen in the room for me to breath.

Resuming my reading, the details of the officer's demise left me sick to my stomach for hours. Holmes, while doing his best to keep him conscious, dissected the man, all while lecturing to his assistant on what was and wasn't an essential body part. One at a time. I imagined myself there in the detective's place, kept conscious, the surgeon showing me my own organs, all while conducting a lecture as to which organs were essential to maintain life. Was there anything even conceivably worse?

CHAPTER 20

Grabbing the car keys late one night, I drove out without even bothering to close the garage, practically daring anyone stupid enough entry into my world. Safety from strangers no longer seemed important.

"Be my guest. Steal everything," I muttered.

I thought of the rough justice, entertaining in a sadistic sort of way, which would descend on the thief who stole the books. They would never know what hit them, perhaps only recognizing where they were going to end up after it was all too late.

If only some fool would do me the favor. Maybe the haunting voice came, and went, with the books.

My lack of focus caused the trip to the liquor store down the road from the house to take three hours. On any other night the trip would have taken me twenty minutes. I'd no idea where the time went; I only hoped I hadn't hurt anyone. Walking in the door, behind sunglasses to keep the glare from hurting my eyes, the place I'd known for years was strangely different.

"You all right?" the girl wearing her company logoed shirt behind the counter asked. She could see I wasn't myself. We had engaged in pleasant chit-chat for almost three years.

I looked up, but intentionally not into her eyes afraid of what she might see, answering, "Yeah I'm fine. A six pack of Bud and a pack of cigarettes please."

Waiting for her to return, it started again. My vision wobbling in and out. Trying anything I could to get it to stop, I punched the top of my thigh as hard as I could. The effect was almost as if I'd committed the act on someone else. There was no immediate pain. The only evidence would be the black and blue bruise tomorrow morning. However, the act did serve a purpose; my vision cleared and my voice settled.

I was awakened from my solitary debate by a sharp bang at the display counter to my left, followed by a jab like shove to my back.

"Move down, old man, we're tired of waiting." the culprit demanded in a practiced, Clint Eastwood-like whisper. He was a young tough, trying hard to impress his two buddies. Him being number one, they both stood back, watching, enjoyment written all over their eager faces.

I ignored him.

"Hey, asshole, didn't you hear me? I'm not going to tell you again." This time half-way yelling.

He was right of course in expecting me to comply with his reasonable request. I was taking too long. He was just unaware of what I was going through, or what I was becoming long before he had laid his young eyes on me. If he knew, I'm sure he would have waited his turn no matter how inconvenienced.

"No." I said. That's all. There was a part of me that wanted him to have a gun.

He flared up. He had to now in front of his friends, becoming animated like an adult video character, swelling his t-shirt so much that the lyrics were now recognizable-- The AC/DC Spring Tour.

Before he could make the expected stupid move, I spun around to face him and in an unrehearsed instant reflex reached out, as if programmed, and jabbed his Adams apple with my index finger, the thumb underneath the same finger for rigidity. I did this with the utmost confidence, as if practiced, although I'd never done anything similar before in my entire life.

Both his hands went straight to his injured throat. He began to choke and sputter, falling back into his buddies' arms. His eyes filled with water and went wide as the sun on a tropical sunset.

Everyone in the room was shocked by the suddenness of it all. Watching him, I pondered what I'd just done having never been trained in self-defense.

Did you see how easy that was, Jeffrey? The voice offered.

Fearless, I turned my back to the group and held up my hand at arm's length, turning my palm over two or three times in order to inspect my new found weapon. I sensed the kid closest to me posturing behind my back as if to make another foolish move, but stopped him in his tracks when I spun back around and held up that same finger. With the utmost respect he retreated.

I turned back to pay at my own pace.

Humiliated, they refused to wait their turn, threw down their merchandise and exited to their car. I followed them through the big double doors as they yelled the expected names and peeled off in the car daddy paid for.

Standing there considering what just happened, another of Shelley's prose ran through my mind, "Of what a strange nature is knowledge! It clings to the mind, when it has once seized on it, like a lichen on the rock. I wished sometimes to shake off all thought and feeling; but I learned that there was but one means to overcome the sensation of pain, and that was death--a state which I feared yet did not understand. I admired virtue and good feelings, and loved the gentle manners and amiable qualities of my cottagers; but I was shut out from the intercourse with them, except through means which I obtained by stealth."

I raced home no longer willing to take for granted these slack moments in my life. This schizophrenia, for it could only be that, was turning on and off, cycling, at an increasingly alarming rate.

These accelerating wobbles were leaving me unaccounted for.

CHAPTER 21

Months went by as my fall off into the deep end continued to accelerate. Making everything worse, there was no baseline for me to remember and live by, so I began living the wobbles.

The wide awake trances, for that's what they were, had grown in intensity and were now lasting minutes instead of seconds, in some cases for over an hour. Imagine being clueless about your whereabouts, your conduct even, for hours... and regularly so. I woke from one in the dead of night watching two strangers sleeping in their bed in a home I'd never seen before. Another driving home in what I could only guess was a stolen car.

After suffering one, I'd be sore all over, as if wrung through a wringer. Afterwards there was never anything to definitively indicate violence had occurred, but to tell the truth, I never put much effort into investigating the obvious evidence. I was afraid too.

Well, that's the way my life was before the big change.

One day, as if a circuit had been altered, with a wobble came not unconsciousness, but a change in perspective. Just like had a writer suddenly decided to go from first person to third in a novel, but only in this book the protagonist was me! When it happened, the entire world around me turned into a play to observe. But more than that, now it seemed I was aware of what others were even thinking. Their daily lives something for me to manipulate and play with. My day becoming something akin to a clicking of channels on a television set, except that the channels were in my head and the remote control in my hand.

They all started the same. Without warning a large electrical *snap* would occur, changing my world, actually allowing me to watch myself interacting with others in what I assumed was an out of body experience. The one watched was me, as if in a mirror, but also something quite apart from who I had ever been before. This me was different; out on a separate plane or dimension.

The first time I watched, amazed, I actually tried to reach out and touch myself, for lack of a better description, so tantalizing was the vision. But instead of intercepting mass, my hand ran through the body like some sort of synthetic substance. Even the air around me was different, having a liquid feel which pulsed in waves as I walked through the middle. The scenes were timeless. Colder, too, even during broad daylight everything felt frigid. Where was the warmth of the sun?

Tennyson had long ago tried to explain something similar in his own personal life as to what I was now experiencing, "All at once, out of the intensity of the consciousness of individuality, the individual itself seemed to dissolve and fade away into boundless being; and this not a confused state, but the clearest of the clearest, the surest of the surest, the weirdest of the weirdest, utterly beyond words." For the most part, he had explained where I was.

The worst part about this last drastic change was the sudden ability to maintain consciousness, or at least what I thought was consciousness. Before, the innocuous gaps had always given me the excuse of never-never land, for nothing that happened during a wobble was ever a result of a conscious decision on my part. They were just blank. Whatever happened during one of them wasn't my fault. How could they be? Now watching myself act came much closer to that forbidden line of intent.

Snap!

The heat pushed hard at her face, as if someone were trying to suffocate her with a pillow. Every breath required a supreme effort as she made her way alone down the street. Had there been a breeze, it would have only made things worse, serving to punctuate the blast furnace that is summer in Sacramento.

Deep in the business district, too deep for a woman of her obvious beauty to be alone this late at night, she cursed herself for refusing the offered escort home from Teddy, the bartender at the cafe where she sang. At the time, the offer had seemed honest enough, it was just easier to refuse that sort of thing especially after hours. Men, all men she believed, at least the ones she dealt with, always wanted more from her than what they admitted. Better straight home, alone, crawl into the big bed and forget another lost day.

She'd spent years trying to break into the ranks. Her voice was good, just not exceptional, a fact she was finally recognizing as the years progressed and her outings continued to grow more widely spaced apart. The talent scouts and agents that promised her the moon when she began had all slipped away once they came to grips with the fact that she was not going to trade a chance at a glimmering future for a night of false passion and lies. And she had refused the same promises over and over again for the last ten years. Life here was beginning to resemble the disappointment that she'd been warned of by her father when she first boarded the bus for the big city-- hard work, small paychecks and broken promises.

But that was before she'd met Bill. Since then, life's edges were once again developing the gleam that makes insurmountable obstacles a joy to challenge. Waking up in the morning was a pleasure again. Doing her laundry was an adventure in silliness. Singing at the club was thrilling and the future as rosy as the flowers he gave her for her thirty-first birthday. Today was even more magnificent: he had proposed! She had accepted his offer that morning right after sunrise. They even agreed to begin planning a wedding that spring, back home in front of her family and old friends. Life, with a kiss, a tear and a nod yes, was now so much better.

All she needed to do tonight was get home. An easy enough task on any given night, but tonight was different. Tonight, in the dark, Kathy was being stalked by a terror she and Bill could never have imagined in their worst nightmares.

The same eerie feeling had dogged her late last night on the way home, as if something were biding time waiting for the opportune moment to strike. The feeling that refused to let her be. Kathy by nature was as tough as any woman had a right to be, but this was different. This was more.

She knew she was being followed.

Concerned, she tried to make as little noise as possible, hurrying along in the wet caused by the hours-old summer rain, tracing the same steps she had made hundreds of times before. Her leather boots clicked on the old stones, each step stealing her breath as she fought the emotion that swept over her. The directness of her path and determined demeanor itself belied her obvious attempts at anonymity.

Now, for whatever reason, every noise, shift and shadow seemed to be somehow sinister. Six more blocks, a locked door, a hot shower and bed was all there was left to conquer. Right now they all seemed an eternity away.

She couldn't have known any better, but her efforts were feeble, silly even, against the strength and focus that pursued her. What little noise she made was enough for the predator to follow her every movement. Had she known how easy she was, how little work it took to follow her, she might as well have turned and asked for quarter, but little good that would have done, for the creature behind her cared nothing for the merits of either sympathy or mercy. These were the traits of humans, not monsters.

The neighborhood seemed to shrink with each passing step as he closed the distance between them. He sensed that she was picking up her pace, walking with more purpose. Faster, but not yet panicked enough to run. He followed waiting and searching for the perfect moment to set her forever at ease. Ahead of him, she turned at the corner, and he, with grace and stealth, crossed to her side of the street, neither feeling his feet touch stone nor making a splash as he moved through the puddles of hot rain. He was soon within striking distance, mere feet away.

This wasn't his first stalking of live prey. He'd been this close before. Those times, poised to strike, and kill, he had regained control of himself at the last moment. The battle between the little that was left of him and the hungry drive of his evolving psyche was building to a fever pitch. He knew that it was only a matter of time before he would be swallowed by the evil that had lain dormant within him for so long. Right now, the old he, and she were both running out of time.

Despite the battle that raged within him, he cared neither about her fear nor the sympathy that others might have felt for her. They were the byproducts of the chase, as they'd been for eons of time, to be set aside as so much nonsense that interfered with the hunt. She was only prey, made more attractive by her beauty, vitality and youth, but still just another victim. Her future meant nothing to him. He felt no guilt for what he was about to do. She existed only to serve his bloody purpose.

His needs had become unbearable these past weeks. At times he felt as if his very blood boiled with a drive to fulfill his destiny. Long forgotten and dormant instincts exploded within him as the strings of DNA at long last merged together to create the creature that he had always been but never recognized.

Power flowed through his body, energizing each muscle with the adrenaline necessary for the kill. He willed himself to be patient, to make sure that his first was performed with the respect that was demanded of him.

He was on edge, the edge familiar to every killer. He'd never felt so alive in his entire life.

Twice more she turned to see if her fear was warranted by an actual presence or whether the fear was just another episode of her childlike imagination run amuck. Her eyes, wide and darting, searched the shadows for the predator she was sure existed. Not quite running, her movements had become confused as her fear overfed her system with chemicals, chemicals that often made the task of the killer all the more simple.

At one point she stopped to ask a mounted policeman for help, telling him she thought she was being followed. The officer turned and rode to within feet of where he stood motionless, waiting next to a lamppost and trash receptacle. Only the horse picked up his presence. With ears raised high overhead the horse bucked with a sharp snort and jerk of long snout against the bridle, sensing the nearby danger.

Seeing nothing and ignoring the signs of his steed, the cop rode back to her and reported the negative she knew to be incorrect. Her instincts as pursued victim were now as strong and undeniable as were his as her pursuer. For an instant he was disgusted enough at this policeman's ignorance to consider changing his selection, but he quickly ruled against that. The cop was far too ordinary, too predictable to make anything noteworthy or memorable of his death.

Kathy continued on, turning to cast one more glance in his direction, and for the slightest moment he allowed her a brief glimpse of himself. He felt he owed her that much for the gifts she would provide him for years to come and for the calm her sacrifice would usher in over the turmoil of his soul.

If anything, she seemed more relaxed, maybe realizing that she was beyond help. Perhaps she had accepted her fate. While interesting to contemplate her possible acquiescence to mastery, he cared not. His first kill was at hand, the one necessary to take his place alongside those before him who had likewise succumbed to their reason for existence.

Feet from her, he admired his selection for immortality. She was beautiful and carried herself with a grace and dignity, even when in haste, that left him thrilled. Her long, black hair flowed like silk past her white blouse, ending just below the waist of her fitted jeans. The intoxicating eddies that were swirling in the wake she cut through the early morning fog only confirmed that which he had guessed: she was perfect. Like a long-seduced, no longer reluctant love, she was ready to be taken.

Ready, his fingers spread, exercising, stretching the skin and muscles as if willing claws to emerge. He reached forward to take her by nature's best handle - her hair. The silk slipped into the junction of each of his fingers as he gathered as much as he could to pull her back, helpless, exposing her most vulnerable parts. The scent of jasmine at her neck emerged from under her hair, causing him to erupt in an involuntary snarl. He took his time studying his new possession, the outright dominance unlike anything he had ever known before. When he was ready, he took the long, thin knife from his back pocket and extended the razor-sharp blade with the push of a button.

Both their times had come.

He turned her, so she could watch what was about to occur. He allowed her to look into his eyes. The fear that widened the pupils of her soon to be dead orbs retreated as she realized that she was powerless to escape. Her soul surrendering and body giving up, submissive in his hands. She relaxed within his arms, accepting her demise, even anticipating the final end, hoping that what he had planned for her would be short and painless.

Her life's energy balanced, he noted her nobility in accepting fate; none of the senseless begging that he had expected. He took the back of his hand, the one holding the knife, and rubbed the blade up and down her cheek, the sharp edge passing inches from her eye, and admired the smooth texture of her skin.

All that was before, in her mind, was now no more. Fleeting memories of those that had nurtured her as a child, loved her as young woman, and created her dreams of life thereafter flashed in intense light and then, just as quickly, faded into irrelevance. Her face went slack, as she gazed into the killer's eyes.

Moments from immortality, the channel changed back with the now familiar *snap*, and with it, from somewhere deep within, I struggled to latch onto what I used to be, and the desire to preserve my old soul. For the first time that night, the voice, recognizing his sudden loss of control, screamed with disdain at the interruption.

Do it now, right now, my boy, or I will be forced to take matters into my own hands!

Hearing his order, my mind was a boiling cauldron of struggling morality. I knew that were I to continue, I would be forever locked on this path that had been chosen for me.

During my debate of the horror within, she made not one sound, possibly sensing silence was her only chance to survive. She was right.

"No! No!" I yelled, as loud and painful as a roar, her ear inches away.

Startled, she emerged from her semi-comatose state, and screamed with me, shocked into yearning for life again, maybe remembering this morning's love. Her scream allowed me to feel the slightest speck of good returning, cancelling out his desires. Ordering my hand to unclasp, I let the hair flow through my fingers, releasing her. We both stared at the hand as the fingers continued clasping and unclasping, as if an automaton unwilling to confront emptiness.

Unrestrained, almost free again, she stood there frozen, afraid to run away, awaiting the next command.

Pointing the knife at her, I whispered, "Go. Go now goddamn you woman, or you'll be dead before you take your next breath!"

At that the woman gathered her blouse and in one hurried movement ran as fast as she could back in the direction of the policeman. I watched her recede into the darkness, her continuing life my night's trophy.

I knew my refusal to carry through would anger *him*.

It did.

CHAPTER 22

I regained consciousness in the back of a speeding ambulance, flanked by two paramedics performing CPR. Intravenous lines hung from liquid-filled balloons connected to the veins of both my arms with double-thick needles. The first sound that I recognized was the older medic shouting to the other that they "had me back," his perspiration dripping down on my face and neck as he pounded on my chest with incredible force, apparently having in the last seconds succeeded in restarting my heart. Besides the renewed energy that coursed through my chest, the only other thing I felt was the cold connection of the face mask that pumped oxygen straight into my still-inoperative lungs.

My system was in shock - there was no pain. That would come soon enough.

Twice more I seized while riding in the back of the same ambulance. The second time, my torso was bare, the medics having ripped the clothes from my chest before zapping me with high voltage electric paddles, my body flailing on the gurney as the surges overcame my muscle control. They later told me I'd been dead both times; the second time for five minutes.

Each time dead, then alive, living it, or dying it, had seemed merely a regaining of consciousness. There had been none of the screaming faceless things trying to drag me down with them into the infinite holes that so many of the 'revived' literary dead describe the experience as having. None of the pulling and pushing as some 'decision' was being made about my soul. There were no fields of eternal brown grass, flowing back and forth in a soft breeze you couldn't feel, while running your hand over the tops of the grass, actually feeling it tickle and then seeing a very tidy, well-maintained gravel walkway to where you weren't given the time to discover. No, none of any of that for me— just a black nothingness.

My next recollection was of the hospital emergency room, ICU, surrounded by beeping machines, concerned relatives, a true friend and those same irritating intravenous tubes leading to and from my body. A young intern monitored the screens behind my head for my vitals. He nodded at me twice, observed my pupils, nodded again, told me everything was going to be all right, and then, without further ado, left for another more serious patient who was bleeding rather profusely over the floor not twenty feet from me.

The room was a blur of motion, strange vibrations and obvious concerns. I carefully watched the entire thing, life suddenly more valuable, taking nothing for granted, and trying to capture each snapshot in order to somehow escape the compressing gravity of the scene. My efforts were of no use. Instead I focused on the pressure of my wife's hand and the smile of my good friend, who had followed the ambulance over to the hospital. Our smiles, the best I had under the circumstances, met as I realized I should have known he'd be there. My dad always told me that to judge a friend you only had to do one of two things: loan him a lot of money, or see what he'd do if you were bleeding. Well, I had my answer.

Within minutes, the shock long gone, the pain grew so intense nothing else mattered. Sheer agony. I yelled, "Give me something! Anything, just make this shit stop!"

Then, out of the blue, hurrying across the room was Sam. Sam was a highly regarded surgeon in Oakland, who had flown across the Bay by emergency helicopter when he heard the paramedics voice my particulars and name over the emergency radio. Sam and I had served six years together in the Navy Reserve. We were still best good friends.

Sam was the ship's doctor on the supply ship I'd served as cargo officer on. The ship had a compliment of assault troops who often returned with serious wounds after missions. It had been my responsibility to see to it the wounded were well delivered to the ship's hospital after having been flown in by emergency helicopter. In the process, I had watched him save countless lives. Over time, we had become buddies. Now he was here to do the same again, but this time for me.

Rushing into the room, he shouldered the intern aside and assumed all responsibility for my well-being. His first communication to me was the wink he was famous for with more than one of his injured combat crew when things had simmered down. His move always signified they'd made it by the skin of their teeth. Now the wink was my welcome home. Second was too order the nurse to give me a shot of morphine. First one, then when that one wasn't enough, another. They barely made a difference. The pain continued to throb.

I overheard Sam tell both Sue and Kelly that I'd suffered a Grand Mal seizure-- the worst kind of epileptic attack. I didn't have the slightest idea what a seizure was, let alone the names Sam was throwing about. In fact, I'd never spent a day in the hospital in my entire life other than to witness the birth of my son some twenty years before. But from that moment on, seizures and the possibility of dying from another Grand Mal would dominate my life, that is, at least, when Holmes wasn't.

You displeased me greatly, Jeffrey.

As they continued to work over me, the mental fog remained thick, running in painful waves from ear to ear, but I stayed cognitive enough to overhear my wife, in the hallway, explaining to Sam that she had been lying in bed next to me watching television while I was sleeping. Without warning, I began to make horrible, loud, almost demonic-like sounds. She told him my body actually lifted off inches into the air from the bed. At the same time the hair on her body straightened as if in response to some electrical or magnetic pulse generated by my condition. She described snapping sounds, as if bones were breaking within my body, accompanied by blood spurting from my mouth.

Sam explained that the snapping sounds had indeed been bones breaking. Three ribs along my back and numerous ligaments across my chest and rib cage had separated due to the incredible violence of the event. The blood was the result of biting my tongue nearly in half when my jaw clamped shut during the seizure.

He went on to explain that medical science defined a seizure as an electrical discharge that originates in the temporal lobe. The primary manifestation of a complex partial seizure begins with an alteration in the individual's state of consciousness. Sometimes, he continued, seizures result in a partial loss of consciousness, complete unconsciousness, or, as had mine, even death. In general terms, Sam concluded, I had suffered a disease of the central nervous system without having ever before exhibited any symptoms.

Mmmmm. Very interesting, incorrect, but very interesting. Don't you agree, Jeffrey? I told you what would occur should you disobey me.

Sam informed Sue that the same attack might never happen again, or might in the next ten minutes. There was no way of predicting another onset. Besides general care, Sam continued, there was really nothing else that could be done at the hospital to prevent another seizure. He felt it too early to prescribe preventative medicines just yet, as many patients only experience one such event and never have another return. Right now, he wanted to redo the sutures on my tongue, bandage my chest properly, monitor my condition for a few days, and then release me, all under close supervision of course. Sam did prescribe pain-killers and then announced that all we could do now was to wait and see.

I know exactly when another will happen again. The next time I decide the pain best for your own good.

After two days in intensive care I was released, but only after Sam insisted that Susan set up the guest room for him to stay in to watch over me for the next few nights. The peace of mind he gave me by being there was immeasurable. No other attacks or seizures occurred.

For the next four months, I underwent every medical test known to man, or so it seemed. Probes, electrodes, injections were applied to every square centimeter of my poor head. I had enumerable EEGs and MRIs to find, either electrically or visually, anything that might reveal a lesion or tumor on the temporal lobe. None surfaced. My neural "superhighway," which orchestrates the flow of information between my brain's two hemispheres, continued to check out.

Failing those attempts, the doctors tried to induce another seizure in order to chart the path of the electrical short circuit as the event was occurring, hopefully determining the origin of the problem. They even tracked a dye through my brain with what seemed a hundred machines connected at every appendage on my body. The whole thing was hell.

I am rather enjoying this myself.

Nothing obvious cropped up, although they did find something that caused them to request another test, one they normally saved as a last resort. They wanted my consent to inject radioactive isotopes into my blood. This would enable what they only described as a "very serious procedure."

The specialist who was brought in from Chicago explained they believed they had detected a very small tumor, so small, in fact, that they were having trouble associating the tumor with the seizure. This test, she explained, provided the medical team with the best chance of identifying the exact cause. Without it they were throwing darts. She wanted a waiver with informed consent and suggested we get a second opinion. She left that up to me, but only after suggesting that this was the only way I might once again enjoy a normal life should they be able to verify the tumor and successfully operate to remove the growth.

Sue called Sam. He drove down again.

Our conversation started off the way they always had. "The worst part about this whole thing… is having to look at your ugly face every time I turn around," I started off.

He flipped me off, then said laughing, "Where's the coffee you promised if I agreed to come down here and answer your stupid questions?"

"There's instant in the cupboard," I told him, knowing he being a Seattle boy would hate anything but the best. While he stirred I asked point blank, "Sam, what are the symptoms of a lesion or tumor?"

"Varied. They often amount to nothing more than migraines, but… and I don't want to alarm you more than you already are… they can also cause another episode like you had that night."

You will have another, a stronger one, if you should ever disobey me again.

I watched Sam's face for the slightest indication that he too had heard the voice interrupt our conversation. He hadn't noticed a thing.

"He can't hear them because they aren't real," I said below my breath.

"What was that?" Sam asked.

"Nothing, nothing at all.... just talking to myself."

Real or not, you will do as you're told, my son, or you will perish.

I hadn't told anyone about the voices yet. Sue was aware of strange behavior, but I had managed to keep the most severe changes private. There didn't seem any point in putting them off any longer.

"Sam, are these lesions capable of producing... Jesus Christ... oh, I might as well just come out and say it, strange noises, you know, voices? Would they explain freaking conversations with another person in my head?"

"Jeff, are you hearing voices?"

"No! Well not exactly... hell, let's just say hypothetically speaking... yes."

"Well yeah, I think so," he answered, sipping his coffee but suddenly never taking his eyes off me. "There have been similar reports, but little consensus about their cause or generation. Most generally attribute voices to some form of mental illness, but it's taken a long time for modern medicine to get there. Decades ago the kinds of voices you're talking about were often referred to as evidence of demonic possession, a possession that required an exorcist to alleviate. These days medical science refuses to admit their actual presence, preferring to refer to them as imagined. However, in my opinion, a lesion or tumor in the proper location *could* cause voices, perhaps even a vision or two."

Of course they can. You're experiencing one right now, are you not?

Well there it was, and right out in the open, and with an explanation I could live with-- for a while anyway. I had to be the only man in the history of modern medicine suddenly happy that a tumor might be attached to his brain, pumping away— like something out of the movie Alien. The alternative was worse.

"Partner, you've experienced possibly the most severe seizure me or any of my colleagues has ever heard of, at least one that anyone ever survived from. Luckily, our tests reveal that you haven't suffered permanent brain damage as a result of the event. Unfortunately, we are all reasonably certain, and I hate to say it, another such seizure would in all likelihood result in, at the very least, irreparable brain damage."

Strained silences dominated the rest of the conversation as his explanation slowly began to sink in. Apparently, there was a medical reason for what happened, at least that's what Sam seemed to be saying. But how could that be? Hearing voices, seeing visions, ok, but coming perilously close to committing murder? I couldn't buy that last part, it just wasn't me. Now, more difficult to swallow than ever, the professionals were telling me that the books and monster had nothing to do with any of this. My changes were all self-imposed.

My world was doing flip-flops.

"One more thing Sam... can one of these events change the way a man thinks or reacts to certain stimuli? I feel like a fool even asking this, it all seems so science fiction, but here goes anyway: I'm talking about values, morals, you know, good and bad, the way a person was brought up as a child; can they be altered in an instant?"

"Personally, no, I wouldn't go that far, but I couldn't rule out the physiological possibility of what you just described. Now I might surmise that it's possible for a tumor to alter the way a man's senses operate, perhaps affecting the creation of the brain's vital neurotransmitter dopamine. The way he sees, smells, etc. Possibly even his physical projection of power and energy."

He went on – "Come to think of it, there was a recent study, quite interesting actually, that I skimmed over, concerning an autopsy report performed on an executed murderer. A tumor, undetected prior to the procedure, was found on the left side of his brain. The author, a German scientist, was arguing that this man, who lived forty some years in peace and quiet, suddenly developed homicidal rages as a result of the changes this condition rendered in his brain. Prior to the crime, the man had complained to his family physician of black outs and unaccounted for gaps in time in which he had no idea where he had gone or what he had done. The scientist believed automatisms occurred that apparently caused conduct without volition. He further argued that the patient's afflicted behavior was impossible to differentiate from his normal willful conduct. If you want to read the paper, I'll get a copy for you tomorrow."

"Yes, if you wouldn't mind."

"No trouble at all."

"One more thing," Sam said, "This procedure they want to run on you is as serious as they get. The only way I'd agree to it, if I were you, is if *the* end might be in sight if you said no and you should have said yes. You understand what I'm telling you?"

"Roger. By the way, I know you and I never do the sappy shit, ever, but this time, thanks Sam, and for all you've done."

We shook hands, leaving it there, except that as he walked out I noticed the peculiar long slow look he gave looking back over his shoulder at me. Men like Sam didn't do things like that unless they thought the look necessary.

Calling the specialist, I agreed to the procedure. She ran the test two days later. The results showed the growth they had suspected, but the tumor hadn't the mass to justify surgery, at least that's what I told them after they spent three hours trying to talk me into the operation. Instead, we agreed to continue closely monitoring the size.

Drugs became a part of my life. At six o'clock every morning I started taking five hundred milligrams of Dilantin to hopefully avoid another seizure and maybe, just maybe, silence the voice.

The medicine worked-- sort of. The strange sensations that the seizure had generated were controlled. But he wasn't. In fact, he laughed every time I took a pill. When he did I reminded myself the voice wasn't real, that the sensations were being created by the tumor inside my head. That did little good either. He just grew more adamant.

I knew the only way to fight back was to study the books harder. There was something I was missing.

CHAPTER 23

On two separate occasions, the authorities came within minutes of apprehending me during situations that would have been difficult to justify. Rather than spending the next few months looking over my shoulder, I made plans to spend time in Europe in order to give Chicago, which I left in capable hands, time to settle. Besides, I had always wanted to experience London.

***

The three words 'Jack the Ripper' stand out as perhaps the most feared phrase in the English language. Instantly recognizable by all, chills go up and down our spines whenever the mysterious killer is mentioned. Every year over a million people search the internet in order to quench a curiosity about the unknown murderer. Untold millions read the hundreds of books already published about the man. Images of flesh ripping slashings color our imaginations. Hollywood turns out another 'Jack' blockbuster every two or three years.

Gladstone bags, fog enshrouded carriages, the shrill yells of newspaper boys the morning after fill our cinematic consciousness. But more than that, Jack represents our greatest failure, for his memory remains a monument to society's inability to apprehend such a monster. Who he was will forever hold a grip on us until he is finally identified.

I, like many Americans, kept up with each new author's attempt to disclose the true identity of the world famous slasher. There were hundreds of theories. To be honest, I doubted them all. The mere mention of Jack the Ripper in some publication or periodical has always caused me to recede, recognizing the words as just another attempt at sensationalism. That old saying: "There are liars, damn liars and people who write books about Jack the Ripper," banged around inside my head with each new attempt.

As doubtful as I was, there was little question that Herman's material deserved, no demanded study. Could anyone argue that its author wasn't *the* authority on the subject? Besides, the very idea that Jack could have been an American intrigued me greatly.

***

Holmes left for Europe the fall of 1888. He arrived in London sometime in September. He stayed in England for approximately two to three weeks before returning to New York sometime prior to the New Year.

To Holmes, 1888 was just another year to operate within, another year to raise the tally and further his experiments in the medical sciences. He was twenty seven years old at the time and had already murdered dozens of women and the men foolish enough to have interfered. To him the murder of a downtrodden English prostitute would have been nothing more than an everyday occurrence, much like you or me going to the grocery store for a carton of milk. There was nothing special about them, and little to write about except that for the first time he began mentioning the specific organs he was seeking from selected victims. For what I had no idea.

There were only seven diary entries that could in any way be associated with the infamous murders in London. Those seven provided little in the way of evidence, in fact, they required quite a bit of conjecture on my part to connect Holmes to the Ripper murders. The entries were more concerned with his time in New York before the trip, his meetings with a physician in Wales, and a scientist in London about potential skeleton sales. Holmes never once mentioned the name "Jack" in the diary.

I remembered something that caught my eye after first learning Holmes was related. In a rather small and quite bizarre piece, Scotland Yard had expressed an interest in Holmes and an alleged trip they believed he, the American surgeon, might have made to London that same summer. For an organization as highly regarded as Scotland Yard to raise Holmes as a possible suspect threw a rather significant monkey wrench into the fraud angle. This was much like the FBI raising another suspect in the assassination of JFK— their query had to be taken seriously. Seems the Yard's investigation had established an American surgeon had either sold or attempted to sell skeletons to the University of London in 1888. Holmes did in fact mention having marketed skeletons in London that summer. These sales meetings were allegedly conducted close in time to when the Ripper murders were being committed.

But Scotland Yard needed more than mere skeleton sales to establish enough of a foundation to claim, let alone later prove, as considerable a political earthquake as the Ripper having been a Yankee. To do so they also needed to establish that an American doctor, (hopefully a surgeon), had indeed traveled to London in 1888, contacted medical schools offering merchandise and possessed the *modus operandi*, i.e., was a proven serial killer.

H. H. Holmes seemed to fit the bill on all counts.

***

Holmes boarded the train for New York three days after writing his note, with a planned stopover in Philadelphia. The liner was scheduled to leave for England in five days. Readying himself, telegraphs were sent to the appropriate medical schools in London, then across to the continent, alerting them of new business possibilities and requesting any special requirements that could be arranged in New York and transported across. Right away, two telegrams were forthcoming that detailed exact import requirements for Holmes to pursue and promises of enough money to pay for the entire trip twice-fold. Holmes allotted two days for each piece when he arrived in the Big Apple. He felt reasonably certain each requirement could be arranged in a city as large as New York.

His stop in Philadelphia was to catch up on some old business. An old friend and new fool had managed to forget a bargain the two had made a while back. Twenty-thousand dollars owed had a strange way of turning Holmes' friends into victims. Holmes spent two hours reacquainting his friend in the ways of business. Those two hours of intimate questioning provided Holmes with what was owed him and enough interest to pay for any luxuries he might desire on the trip. Holmes did not explain why he let his old friend live. Following that meeting, he immediately proceeded east.

Holmes rather preferred New York's summer heat. No matter the humidity, his clothes were always perfect, not a hair on his head out of place. Holmes was the epitome of cool, calm and collected.

Late in the afternoon the avenue was full of busy, hardworking people on their way home after work. Holmes walked southeast, making his way down toward the docks. He looked, with intent, down each side street, while at the same time broadcasting warmth and charm to each attractive by passer who caught his eye. Inside the warmth was a focused analysis in order to identify the next to meet his gruesome commercial requirements.

New York's high sided buildings provided superb shadows darkening the street and helping to disguise his presence. It was at these times that he worked the hardest, practicing his wares, luring each within his grasp, only to allow them to live another day having never recognized their closeness to death.

Bit by bit I became aware of the many nuances this city had to offer. At the same time, I fought to maintain self-control over the seductive nature of my new surroundings within this most compacted arena of humanity. However, I made note to remember, and fondly so, the minutia of New York in order to take full advantage upon my return from Europe.

There were four days to 'kill' before the ship left for Southampton. Holmes had not made any reservations for lodging while he was in the city. Neither did he have friends or acquaintances to call upon. None of this concerned him. As he had so many times in the past, he expected to locate his place of lodging at the same moment he identified his next victim. These two necessities were often found together. He rarely, if ever, paid rent for a room.

Wherever he walked, people watched in quiet admiration, drawn to his charm. He used their freely given attentiveness to best advantage. Holmes would tip his hat and offer his hand in that genuine gesture of assistance. Confused with his openness, women would blush, allowing him the moment to make introductions in a manner more suited to Sunday services rather than two passing strangers on the street of this metropolis. His introductions always included the slight touch of his hand to their arm. If he felt more necessary, the forwardness of this then outrageous conduct was instantly toned down with his doctor's eyes and classic decorum. Perhaps even an apology, another tip of his hat, and bow, offered with explanation that these actions had been quite unlike him and must have had something to do with the chemistry that passed back and forth between these two stars that had just collided. He was unbelievably forward for the time. He often followed with a line of French, setting everything at ease with apparent friendship and easy companionship, as if the two strangers had known each other for years.

He never said anything that frightened. That trait alone set him apart, dazzling the young ladies. They thought here finally was a man that cared what she thought, was interested in her day and listened, by Jove, to every word she said, and without the slightest inclination towards the obvious thing that attached itself to other men at these times, although he was quite the good looking gentleman they would later admit.

His needs were met, all of them, that first night in New York. As he passed the portals to one of the city's finest hotels, a bell rang above him in the lobby summoning the servant to carry the luggage of a stunning lady, covered in white, wearing a hat banded in flowers with a veil to keep the long extinguished sun away from her perfect features. Holmes stood back observing her every move, admiring her elegance and waiting for the right moment. He had begun the process of gathering the signals she gave off. In poker, professional gamblers call this work the "tell". The more he watched, the more she impressed him.

She carried herself with the haughty irritation of the very wealthy, perhaps being from one of the elite families this city is famous for. Watching her, I grew excited to a degree I had not experienced in quite some time. I imagined her attending to my every need, providing necessaries as well as ample entertainment during the time before the ship was to depart. I stood back and gathered some of her characteristics; the dress, her mannerisms, language, all of it, knowing that if I concentrated I would soon identify that one weakness every woman, this gorgeous one included, possesses. While this lady's might not be as obvious, I knew that with patience I would find her clue, and when I did, I would use that key to wrap her around my finger.

I imagined her obvious impatience - the servant late in responding — being all the more amusing to Holmes making her even easier to crave. He would have adored that haughtiness, so hard to find within Chicago's more industrial nature. This princess had been born to expect only the best and so took for granted the good fortune she had been afforded.

Between separate demands to servants, she looked up noticing Holmes staring at her. When he refused to look away as other men usually did, she flared in focused anger un-amused by his audacity. Still he refused to show deference, choosing instead to wear her down with his intimidating stare. She hated to admit such, but the man was powerful in some vague way. She was bored with the frailties other men showed the first moment she met them. Men had surrendered to her intimidating beauty her entire life. This one didn't and the fact that he refused to do so, stimulated her curiosity.

She noticed that he was dressed quite fashionably, unheard of in this city when compared to the Paris she preferred most. Holmes' clothes were smart but avoided the eccentricity that most rich men couldn't ever seem to resist. His features were balanced. The man's eyes, nose and ears were perfect. She always noticed the balance of a man's features, and why not? She expected the horse drawing her carriage to be balanced, so why should she expect anything less of her men?

Unable to wait another minute, Holmes stepped right up to her, bowed, offered his hand and asked, "May I be of some service, *my* lady?"

"No. No I am quite well cared for, thank... how dare you, Sir! You may not now or for that matter, ever, refer to me as yours!" her initial intrigue cancelled by his haughty forwardness.

Finally, here was a rare woman to excite me, Holmes thought.

He continued unabated, "Please," he said slowly, while at the same time taking her by the arm, causing her breath to catch and face to raise red as a rose, "...it would be my greatest honor if you would so allow me." Holmes knew that when this very act was done with courage, and proper pace, these seductive words were irresistible.

Her blush magnified with the impossibly smooth contact of his hand and smile. Shocked at her own involuntary submission to his airs, she tried in vain to restrain that never understood place deep within her that craved this strange thing. She failed. Had it been any other time with any other gentleman she would have immediately called out for aid, demanding the respect her place in society afforded her, but not this time. Instead, she let her gaze slide lower, waiting for him to hopefully accelerate their meeting.

Almost dancing, he led her out of the lobby and up the boulevard to what he guessed was her carriage. Weak in the knees, she couldn't remember the last time her heart had beat with such intensity. God, she thought, he has an aura about him, as if nothing could ever embarrass him, not even had he ever performed an act for which embarrassment would have been a possibility. She closed her eyes, trusting him, despite him having not earned that trust, drawn to him in a flood of emotion and, for so long nonexistent, an ache in her heart.

"*Mon enfant!*" Holmes exclaimed with just the right amount of emphasis, causing her barely perceptible sigh. His accent belonged across the ocean, certainly not here, she thought.

"What is it then that I may call you with?" he asked. He had intentionally not asked for her name, no nothing that trite, but instead the verb she would learn to respond to when he summoned her to his side. She had no idea how to answer, rather instead staying silent.

Watching her silence, he began to understand her. *She yearns to explore her dark side. For too long she has decided how and where love is to flourish. Life and love, as they have been defined, bore her. Her private fantasies are focused upon an elegant man of mystery.*

She moved closer to his side. *Calm yourself, girl,* she whispered to herself in a last gasp attempt at composure.

The entire lobby and street-side had stopped to watch this spectacle, the men unaccustomed to the bravado and the ladies drawn to the audacious charm being exhibited in their midst. His actions were enjoyed by all. Holmes never batted an eye to the obvious admiration of the crowd.

"Take my arm, my lady. Let us go. I will escort you to your carriage and we shall proceed home."

Holmes walked her to the curb, as if she had been his for years, and not mere minutes. The stalk was over. He fought to maintain even his demeanor and composure. One hour more and he would set himself free, but right now he needed to show restraint.

After the baggage was packed aboard the carriage, he led her inside and seated her, where at once, he cinched down upon her thigh with his right hand, invisible to the world, causing her to wince in pain, her expression obvious only to him. She looked up, assuming she had angered him and noticed the change of attitude the others had missed as he assumed complete control of her person. He took her closest hand and raised it to his lips, holding her there, staring into her eyes before kissing her. The two hands confused her, their results so different -- as he would the entire time she was to be with him. She would never be able to decide which hand she loved, no, needed more.

Before riding off, Holmes sent word to his servants that he would be auditioning new talent for the role of his lady and he would expect them ready to sail when the liner arrived.

Those few days, the killer would be more erotically entertained than he had been in ages. Years later, New York society, forever unable to locate the missing socialite in white, believed she had returned to the continent to live out the rest of her enchanted life. In fact, she was to remain in New York forever.

***

The ship rose then fell on the swell, the Atlantic spray slapping him across the face as he rode as far forward on the huge liner as he could. Holmes liked being the first to breathe the ship's air. He leaned out over the short stub of a bowsprit, the last holdover from the not so long gone days of sail, thirty feet over the wetness of it all, so that the only things he could see were the sea below and the sky above. The ship's bow steamed and smoked as they cut through the clear blue water on the way to Southampton. Porpoise played in the ship's wake, while sea birds glided feet from his face, riding the ship's updraft, hoping that flying fish would be scared enough by the ship to reveal themselves so that they could swoop down and harvest them before the tuna came up from below seeking the same meal. Holmes contemplated the life of those flying fish and their forced acceptance of the stakes, whether they recognized the danger or not.

Alone out over the sea, I enjoy contemplating the beauty that only I seem able to recognize as pure life and honest death play out below me. I marvel at the rawness of the struggle. Life is not evil, life is war. Every species, man included, fights for the space of another. Can there be anything more beautiful, more regal than life's struggles to survive certain death? In that final instant, life fulfills the promise, understood or not, that new beings first make with all in order to exist on this earth. When bloody and done, all is right again.

They had departed New York Harbor the evening before; Holmes having slept the entire time. When he was awakened by his servant, his clothes were already put away in perfect fashion. His man enjoyed the stateroom directly across the passageway from Holmes. He had served

Holmes for two years. Polishing and articulating fresh skeletons was his specialty. His anonymous work was featured at many medical schools around the world, as well as the greatest museums, including the Smithsonian in Washington D. C. Holmes often said that his servant's specimens were such masterpieces that they were capable of creating a chill if passed by too closely. The man was paid room and board for his services. He would have died for the doctor.

The ship they were passengers on was the Etruria. She was owned and operated by Cunard Steamship Company. She had been constructed in 1885 by Fairfield Shipbuilding & Engineering Company of Glasgow Scotland. Etruria was 7,718 tons with a waterline length of 501 feet, or 153 meters, with two great raked funnels towering overhead, each locked into place by a myriad of wires and cables. The ship had an incredible, at the time, top speed of 19.5 knots. She was perhaps the first true luxury liner constructed solely for the transatlantic passenger trade as a floating hotel and not another combination passenger/cargo ship. She carried nothing but passengers, their luggage, and the food and water necessary for the voyage, including plenty of champagne and caviar.

Her passenger accommodations were the utmost in luxury and "were notable for their well-articulated overall plan and layout, as well as for the added facilities and services they offered, along with the genuine sense of Grand Hotel bon vivant these types of ship had finally brought to the North Atlantic." Her interior was fashioned to demonstrate impeccable good taste and gracious elegance. Nothing had been left to chance. For the first time in the history of the maritime industry, a ship's accommodations had been designed with direct inside access to all facilities to minimize the impact that rough seas could and often did present upon the North Atlantic. Inside access also minimized the nuisance that the three smoke stacks presented from their constant expulsion of smoke and soot upon the outside areas of the ship. Ventilators provided fresh air to staterooms. The ship's reliance upon engines and propeller for propulsion, rather than sail, allowed a direct course to and from her destination, rather than the 'tacking' required for thousands of years, saving days from the duration of the transit.

Holmes' stateroom was spectacular, reserved for the likes of magnates and actors. John Jacob Astor would have felt at home in the same stateroom. The bathroom was ebony with an adjoining room for entourages or illicit rendezvous. The Victorian decorations added to the atmosphere. Stained glass windows and rich veneer paneling of the plush interiors dominated thought and conversation, but only for those willing to admit they had never partaken in something as incredible as this. Some of the first incandescent electric light illuminated this new world. All in all, Holmes was delighted to be a part of this new sea-going lifestyle which had succeeded in attracting the upper echelons and had now become the event in itself rather than just a mode of transportation. In other words, some just rode across the Atlantic, stayed the week the ship re-provisioned, only to return to New York as the entirety of their vacation. London was nothing more than a diversion while awaiting the second half of the main event.

The passengers dressed for dinner in the finest fashions; tuxedos with cummerbunds accompanying the most elegant long evening dresses, silk stockings and even dress pumps on the often unsteady ship. Each night proved to be a spectacle of the highest degree.

The entire passage, Holmes walked the Etruria's decks as if he owned her.

About four in the afternoon each day, Doctor Holmes would receive another invitation to dine at a different circular table of five or six to meet and introduce himself as the one all the ladies had swooned over, but always with the reserved air that allowed their husbands to relax believing Holmes to be harmless. Not once did they ever suspect the real focus of his attention during the long hours of his camaraderie and seemingly innocent flirtations. When the men retired to their "gentlemen's only" groups, Holmes stayed behind and entertained the ladies, capturing their attention with one of his soon to be famous impromptu piano recitals. Had the men only known his true intentions.

His favorite places aboard the liner were the smoking room where talk of politics ran unchecked until the wee hours of the morning, the music room where frustrated maidens and often angry ignored wives gathered to enjoy his special skills on the dance floor, and on deck with reclining chairs near the vestibule outside the ladies' salon.

The gossip rose to intense levels which facilitated eavesdropping. The things a studious gentleman could learn by listening to these almost happy maidens always amazed and astounded, my acute ears proving invaluable. Feigning sleep with a smoldering cigar at my side, allowed me to overhear then pry into the most incredible secrets. My book overflowed with the names and addresses of the wealthy whom I might one day visit upon my return to the United States.

Mid-voyage the diaries went blank, leaving me guessing as to what, if anything, had occurred the remaining few days of the voyage. When I checked, there was no record of any foul play or man overboard on the Etruria's or in Cunard's logbooks.

***

We disembarked in a single-file line, the oak and iron gangway offering solid footing as I made my way down from the ship onto the wharf. The cold English fog reminded me of San Francisco, cutting right through the thickest clothes to settle frigid in my bones. The dew clung to my skin and gathered in drips at the end of my nose and fingers. I felt right at home.

Alan followed close behind, tending to my four pieces of luggage. The first two pieces contained one month's worth of apparel and accoutrements. The third was filled to the brim with surgical equipment and containers for noteworthy specimens that might be marketable to the medical schools within easy distance from where I would be staying. The fourth contained two finely prepared and properly wrapped skeletons for sale, as well as other specimens that I had procured in New York and that were now eagerly awaited for by my two English customers. They would be delivered first thing tomorrow. I had wired ahead notifying them of the probable date, expressing my desire that cash be on hand.

Seven days had passed since my last specimen. The experiment and my condition required five samples per month.

With these words, the image of him as the evil genius, the mad scientist-- Doctor Jekyll and Mister Hyde-like-- rose to the forefront of my imagination. In time I would see just how inadequate that comparison was.

Holmes began discussing hormonal science. He went on about his scientific failures, growing increasingly frustrated with each new setback. Genius or not, it seems his efforts to procure the elixir of life from stolen female reproductive organs was for the time being unsuccessful. In 1888 he had begun the process of eliminating as many variables as he could in order to reduce potential contaminants. Holmes seemed convinced the source of the blood was the answer. He was sure the specimens he would obtain in England would make a significant difference.

He referenced other readings, one from an English scientist who he intended to meet with while in London. Holmes had earlier asked the same scientist about supplying him with fresh ovaries, 'packaging' them properly and shipping them to the United States in order for him to conduct his experiments. He offered considerable funds for each such delivered specimen. His requests had been refused. He wrote how disappointed he was by this and further considered contacting criminal types to fulfill his requirements. This approach was rejected due to its potential penal repercussions, not to mention the poor quality of the specimens he was sure he would receive. Holmes wrote how ridiculous the English must think him for requesting such specimens when fresh American ones were so close at hand.

This part of the 'Jack' diary intrigued me the most. Was it possible that modern man's greatest mystery had a scientific basis and motive? The English had once believed so. In a quote by Scotland Yard in the Agencies own book about Jack the Ripper, *Scotland Yard Investigates*, the authors said, ".... that the murderer was a medical maniac trying to find the elixir of life and was looking for the essential ingredient in the parts taken from the murdered bodies; that, like the witches in 'Macbeth', he spent the time over a bubbling caldron of the hell broth made from the gory ingredients looking for the charm."

This probably somewhat sarcastic quote when written was eerily similar to Holmes' description of his own activities. This was too right-on to be considered just another coincidence. But how had they known this part of the riddle and why had the Yard refused before now to divulge this critical information to the world? I didn't have an answer to either issue, not yet at least, but one thing was for sure-- circumstantial evidence was beginning to pile up at my feet and was slowly wearing away at my earlier skepticism.

Could the previously thought impossible be true?

If Holmes thought London beautiful he never mentioned his opinions in the diary. Reading through the section, I half expected to find him describing the bustling city like so many of the great historians had done during the period of time when London was the admitted center of the universe. Instead, his only general comments about London were centered around an event he had enjoyed in Philadelphia.

London seemed to dare a brave soul to take advantage of what nature provided. This city had been designed to showcase mankind's obvious glee in boasting of its strength while at the same time maintaining a 'noble' character. Monuments with statues depicting victories celebrating the death of hundreds of thousands bordered museums of sophisticated art and gentle civilization.

I laughed at this English ridiculousness, laughed so hard I cried. This reminded me of the last time I had laughed so strenuously. That was late one night. I was visited by two detectives concerning a body they found south of the tracks east of downtown Philadelphia. They neither arrested me nor placed me in custody, but proceeded to ask me a series of penetrating questions concerning my whereabouts during the window they had best deducted was the approximate time of death:

"Doctor Holmes, where were you last Sunday afternoon?" the shorter of the two asked. The other just crowded me, as he had been trained to do, encroaching into my space. Having experienced the same many times before, I just smiled, and maintained my soft persona. Besides, I hadn't killed this woman.

"Why, I was home enjoying the cookies my sweet neighbor baked. Why do you ask detective? Am I a suspect?"

Not answering directly, he continued, "Would you be willing to accompany us to the hospital to assist us inspecting the body?"

I could have refused, but decided to accompany them to alleviate my present boredom.

"But of course. Please be so kind as to first allow me to fill one prescription. The small boy and mother that you passed on the way up are in need of my assistance to fight a rather severe case of pneumonia. I'll be right with you."

Fifty minutes later we were downtown alongside the pathology table witnessing the autopsy of a Caucasian woman, approximately twenty years of age. She had been dead more than a week. I was familiar with the doctor performing the autopsy.

She was as gray as cold fish and smelled of one as well. The odor was strong enough that both seasoned detectives covered their mouths and nostrils making conversation difficult. The body had been located this morning by a group of passing school children, and the ever present barking dogs.

As I stepped to the table, I noticed both detectives carefully studying my eyes and facial features, hoping for that telltale weakening that gave away ninety percent of perpetrators when they were first forced to see their victims' changed appearance following death. To me, mine or not, this was a stroll in the park.

The doctor continued his cutting, immediately disappointing me with his lack of ability. He was making a mockery of autopsy science, by butchering the already butchered. I made note, to myself of course, to visit him one day, in private, to provide him with lessons in the proper usage of scalpel. He was an embarrassment to our profession.

When I had seen enough, I moaned aloud, shed my topcoat and shouldered through the bewildered onlookers and took the scalpel from the attending idiot and jokingly asked him, "Sir, may I see your license?" Unfortunately, the humor was lost upon those present, the circumstances being what they were, but I laughed aloud, mocking my now questionable compatriot.

The fool said nothing, instead falling back in humiliation and to watch my next act.

Removing the contaminated material he had left covering the relevant evidence, I proceeded to hold class and instructed those qualified in the determination of available facts one could glean from this corpse. All of them, facts that is, except for one peculiar abnormality: a wound so professional as to provide me with instant knowledge of who the perpetrator had been. Of course, I declined to reveal his identity. I would use this knowledge to my own benefit at a later date.

The cause of death was indeed homicide.

When I was finished, before the stunned gathering, I returned the scalpel to its subdued previous owner, calmly washed my soiled hands and arms, regained my coat, cap and of course, pipe, tipped my hat to the detectives and calmly walked out the front door, while stating, "Good day." The memory still brings a hardy chuckle.

I set the book aside for a moment to contemplate the Doctor's coolness. Normal psychopaths, if there was such a thing, didn't act like this. Holmes' blood was as cold as ice. He never lost his temper, always maintained his bearings, thus enabling him to stay one step ahead of his pursuers.

In my mind's eye I saw Holmes wandering London amidst a cacophony of sounds. Scores of horse drawn carriages lined up awaiting their next paying customer and all within half a mile of where he stood. The snorts, the squeaks, the stretching leather and the bangs all merging into one sound, deafening in its magnitude and the tradesmen hawking wares from their carts, trying to stay above it all while attracting commerce.

Huge crowds gathered at the slightest commotion, but with the modicum of civility and manners the British were renowned for. Everywhere he would have turned the people would have been dressed with class and dignity, as elegant gowns and the most expensive top-hats shadowed the finest pipes filled with the best tobacco. Sweet smoke filling the air rising above finely trimmed mustaches, and just enough beard should they desire to be identified as from the continent. Going as far as was necessary to demonstrate that "stiff upper lip" so widely discussed back in the States.

How quickly that renowned measure of civility would have changed as he walked away from the privileged and toward the slums.

Whitechapel was north of the Bank of England, the Royal Exchange and Mansion House, but only after crossing Bishopsgate Street. Here the grandeur of the previous walk would in the blink of an eye turn to the dreary Victorian scene of lore. The East End was a disgusting slum, overrun by vermin and disease, swamped in poverty and painted in misery. The streets were lined with paupers and all without even the barest minimum of medical attention. Row after row of nondescript dwellings-- darkly hidden behind a wall of smoke that rose from each and quickly fell in the fog to choke all passersby-- offered nothing to even the most curious tourist. Every dwelling was furnished by the poor occupants sitting on the steps down to the street. The same streets only wide enough for one horse drawn carriage at a time, provided cascading garbage did not prevent the passage.

Jack London later referred to the same area as the Abyss.

Holmes described that same Abyss in two sentences: *The East End was perfect. Mistakes would be overlooked, if they were noticed at all, and nebulous procedures could be practiced, even after pushing them to what would have been dangerous extremes in Chicago.*

The Abyss, due to its complete lack of law and order, was probably one of the few places in the world Holmes would have felt comfortable teaching his assistant the talents he would need to serve Holmes' needs when they returned to the States.

I assumed that was what Holmes was doing after reading the following entry in the diary:

While on the passage, my man studied the drawings I made of a female body, but those drawings were far different than the warm, wet, slippery experiments he was about to conduct, albeit under my supervision. He was taught the grayish-pink color of the ovaries when first removed, that their texture could either be smooth or an uneven puckered surface, etc. I made sure he was cognizant of the size of the organs involved, usually about an inch and a half in length, perhaps another inch in width and less than a half inch thick, weight minimal to almost nonexistent, at least to the senses of a man overflowing with fright and natural chemical stimulant. The uterus normally measured about three inches in length and two and one half inches in width, weighing no more than two ounces. Once I was convinced he was vaguely aware of what an ovary and uterus looked like, while surrounded by other female organs, we next discussed the exact location of the organs within the feminine cavity. Each is often differently located in individual specimens; therefore we based our most accurate references by delineating it in reference to the entire pelvic cavity. Gray was settled they lay largely symmetrical in the middle of the cavity, but inclined to one side or the other. Removal would be made through the severed abdominal wall. Since we were not concerned with loss of blood, my lessons were devoid of any securing of the uterine vessels or division of ligaments present.

I showed him how best to handle the organs with one hand while not damaging them for later experiment. After removal of the uterus, I found it simpler to then remove the ovary for packaging. These generalities were all good, but offered little experience for the circumstance he would be operating under. Mistakes would be made and I resigned myself to accepting, with all good patience, the less than satisfactory results that would by necessity occasionally occur.

He continued on about the training of his assistant.

It had taken me months to identify the most capable individual to carry out my orders. Alan emerged as both talented and dedicated. Before our trip I supervised him taking a female adult victim while in Chicago, though the surgery had been conducted indoors and not under the conditions which most certainly would be experienced in London.

During the exercises I taught him the best method of the insertion, twist and cut, so important to prevent excess damage thus reducing the commercial value of the organs we would be seeking. He was trained in the use of the eight inch surgeon's scalpel, the very same one I had employed for six years. This was the instrument of choice, but only after suitable time was spent becoming accustomed to its sometimes unwieldy nature. The eight-inch, when professionally modified and razor sharp, was easy to insert and near impossible to detect on one's person when well hidden. The drawback to the use of such a sharp penetrating blade was that mistakes were often magnified resulting in excess damage and severe blood loss. This condition, once created, could not be rectified or even minimized unless a competent surgeon was at hand.

The lessons included methods, rather simple really, of avoiding detection.

Alan was provided a metallic clicking device that I had purchased from a Philadelphia children's park months before. The sharp sound the device innocently produced carried for almost a mile and transcended all others. At first sight of police or significant interference, the clicker was to be sounded three times, followed by the compatriot's set routine of intentionally interfering with the progress of the closest policeman. We practiced the same movements many times while in Chicago. These procedures had proven quite effective.

The lessons concluded with instruction concerning obscuring incriminating evidence with sensational mutilation, thereby hiding the true purpose of the killing. The deeper and more horrendous the depredations, the more difficult it would be for the authorities to establish correct motive. The more ghastly the obscuring slashes, the less chance of apprehension, for Holmes knew the authorities and press would always latch onto the most sensational, often implausible, sometimes even the most ridiculous theory possible.

Let them think, I told him, the frenzied slashes are what make up who you are. Once commercial and scientific requirements are met, mutilate the remaining corpse to your heart's content. Adam smiled hearing my encouraging words.

Later:

Overall, his training has gone well. My man was now reasonably proficient, at least to such an extent that I was confident enough for him to proceed albeit with proper supervision. Accordingly, I ceased further teaching, not only because I was satisfied with his progress, but also because of the potential leverage the man was acquiring over me, difficult to deal with, should I later decide him incompetent. He would know too much. In London, that problem could be more easily resolved than later back home in Chicago.

***

As Holmes had himself just admitted, the accepted historical facts about Jack just didn't make any sense when I tried connecting them to the doctor. I knew that this technician of murder was not the amateur who had committed the coming Ripper slashings. Holmes had never exhibited these so obvious emotional characteristics before, and would never in the years to come. So why would he have felt them necessary in London?

The only explanation that made any sense was that the sensationalized slashings were how Holmes hid his real purpose; that his assistant had committed these killings while Holmes procured his real specimens elsewhere, perhaps cross-town.

The diaries soon confirmed this concept:

While my servant practiced, I made ready for procuring the specimen I was most interested in, for you see, I never intended utilizing the foul material we most assuredly were to acquire from the East End. The English specimen I needed was of higher quality. Clean and fresh, most assuredly uncontaminated by narcotic or alcohol.

I chastised myself for having been fooled by this obvious double-plot in the first place.

Upper End material was going to be far more difficult to procure than East End finds: difficult but not impossible. From past experience, I knew that the daughter of a socialite or wife of a soldier overseas would prove the easiest to put under my spell. Once identified, manipulating their private schedules was of utmost importance, specifically those factors allowing families and friends, authorities as well, to believe the victims responsible for their own extended tardiness. We would need sufficient time to cover the duration of the trip back, for were I to be made a suspect while on the ship, incarceration would be unavoidable.

His true motive had been right in front of me the entire time.

The flames my compatriot would spread on the East End, causing commotion and fervor, would provide me with the diversion I needed. His actions would engross that area while I performed the more delicate work. If done correctly, no one would suspect a thing.

Holmes had never been interested in the celebrated unfortunates that played such a huge roll in Ripper lore.

Two entries discussed murders committed by another.

Late one night we observed a murder. The killing was quick; one, or two cuts at most. The culprit appeared middle-aged, possibly intoxicated, and extremely emotional— perhaps an old lover. While the victim still breathed, a constable passed not twenty feet away from the scene, but oblivious to the entire matter. This experience was good for Alan, though it offered little in professional skills for him to emulate. What he did observe was the complete failure of law enforcement in responding to the crime, even after the expected screams and calls for aid following detection of the body. Response was indeed slow in coming, taking almost two hours and those who eventually arrived were disorganized and failed to preserve critical forensic information. I commented throughout, pointing out the differences between this and the more meticulous practices of stateside response. This unexpected event would later prove highly beneficial.

Later:

It seems there is another. The frenzy his killings are causing is unheard of. Crime in the East End had been moved to the front page of every periodical there is where a hundred possible suspects are speculated upon to the umpteenth degree. The failure of investigators to apprehend the killer angers the citizenry. Some of the quotes concerning evil supposedly never before witnessed on this earth are quite comical, "…a problem the like of which the world had never known…" However entertaining, the extra attention concerns me.

The "other" was never mentioned again in the diary.

Before this "other", Holmes had repeatedly expressed doubt that the planned antics of his assistant would be sufficient to draw enough attention away from his true interests. This worry tore at his mind. He even considered calling the entire enterprise off, fearing the sealing off of their planned escape routes through Liverpool. He decided to continue after witnessing the feeble London police and fervid English press to the killing he witnessed.

Police patrols were multiplied overnight. The crimes and ongoing investigation dominated everyday conversation. The mystery killer was soon being accredited with every act of foul play occurring within an area three times the size of that which any man could have possibly been responsible for.

***

Holmes did not elaborate further on the details of his expressed ob-
jective or about the two 'Ripper' killings that I came to eventually believe
his assistant committed. I was disappointed. More facts would have allowed me to better compare his descriptions with those so well memori-
alized by history. One more time I had to remind myself that these
killings meant nothing to him. To have expected him to race back to his
lodgings in order to accurately recall such minor crimes, when he rarely
did so stateside, was unrealistic.

While not describing the killing of his socialite, Holmes did note the
specimen's effect on his experiments.

*The uteri and cervix were, as I expected in one so young and well-cared
for, perfect and without crease, wrinkle or fold, to say nothing of abscess. I was
confident that this sample would provide me with enough data to make a conclusive determination about English hormones.*

When he continued writing, it was to mention more generalities.

*We waited two days before proceeding, the weather better suiting our pur-
poses. The temperature had dropped sufficiently so that it was possible to wear
two complete outfits, one over the other. This rather simple and often overlooked means of deception had in the past allowed me to escape detection a
multitude of times. This acts' effectiveness often set me to thinking why the
mind so focused on apparel and not the so much more permanent human
characteristics, such as skin tone, height, weight, etc. Whatever the reason, one
could almost always be certain of disappearing into eerie invisibility, never to
be seen again, by properly discarding the first layer of clothing immediately
after having committed the very crime. Once done, I often forced myself to turn
around and walk back up and into the initial crowd of onlookers, especially if
police were already present.*

*"Officer may I be of some assistance? I am a doctor of medicine." I would
ask.*

"Thank God, sir. By all means, do your best," the most common response.

*"And I will, now will you in all good haste obtain for me the assistance of
another medical professional? The situation is dire." At that they would run*

off. The Good Samaritan doctor would then proceed to act out the apparent services any similar doctor would have performed, despite my personal knowledge that this soul was long past revival.

By thus interjecting myself directly into the mix, I thereby disqualified myself from even the slightest mention of consideration by law enforcement, twice in fact, serving as an eye witness to another's being charged with my own heinous actions- quite amusing actually.

By all reports the weather that summer was dominated by a heavy all-encompassing fog that descended with a vengeance making good visibility near impossible and practically eliminating the smell of murder, a considerable factor most laymen are ignorant of. When coupled with the cramped gas-lit streets of the East End, the thick English fog made work far more comfortable for the doctor and his man.

The morning after, I was struck just how quickly English society became sensitive to the plight of these previously abhorred and disdained neighbors. Before the murders, each night scores died from natural causes. No one cared. For decades, these impoverished had suffered disease and famine in living conditions that few canines would have appreciated and nary a word from the ruling classes. But now, now that a killer was in the rich's near midst, all were focused upon the results, perhaps even fascinated, more so, that the same killer had but to walk only three miles to be amongst those that mattered. Quite odd, really, or maybe not.

We were scheduled to depart London, crossing the Channel for France the day after, but as a precaution I had been in contact with my agent to arrange passage with Liverpool shipping authorities on the next available transit to New York by liner. Should the Channel crossing prove too precarious we were prepared to cancel our continental exercises and instead head directly for home. By midday, I had not heard back from the agent and was becoming somewhat concerned that he may have reported our inquiries to the authorities. From past experience, I knew that ever narrowing restrictions almost always ended in incarceration and hence were to be avoided at all costs. I hoped there were no needless complications indeed, since I understood Paris to be lovely in the fall.

Pursuant to contingency plans, early the next morning I packed my own baggage, differentiating what was absolutely necessary from that which was not. With proper reward, my porter arranged to take early possession of my baggage, standing ready until word was given. He also arranged for rapid conveyance of my person in case of emergency.

Holmes' final note while in London was the most evidentiary-- *Early the next morning another victim had been identified and led to a suitable location. The space was behind a small house, cluttered with refuse and presenting perfect seclusion. The street was dark and strangely uninhabited for having so many tight dwellings in long rows huddled upon it. This one was particularly appealing due to its separation by a large fence that divided the two neighboring dwellings.*

As I suspected he would, my man overcame his previous problem with nausea due to the sight of so much blood. Calm and collected, he dispatched her with little problem, eliminating any unnecessary sound. Time was of the essence, as sunrise was rapidly approaching. He wasted no movement or effort, quickly arranging her body and making the necessary cuts to the abdomen. His cuts, I might add, were very professional. Those parts of the intestine that would interfere with his removal of the womb were severed and set aside to be utilized later for sensation. I doubt whether I could have performed the exercise with any more precision than that which was shown. When he signaled that all was ready, I made my way over to inspect the particular organs. They were, once again, heavy with abscess hence worthless for any scientific utility. I returned to my place of concealment to stand watch at the corner. Nothing unusual was observed. Eleven minutes had elapsed since the first cut, leaving only four remaining.

The last minutes were used creating the effect necessary to continue falsely directing investigators on their current incorrect track. The mutilation was done with a certain flair that I had not recognized before in the perpetrator. I filed this knowledge away for later utilization, but was quickly brought back to the present with the rather pronounced click-tick of the alarm alerting me that we were being intruded upon. We stood back and watched as a sole man approached, more attentive than was usual, noticed the crumpled remains, inspected them and proceeded off at a rapid pace, all without ever making a sound. His clandestine nature and actions indicated him as criminal. After his departure, we returned to our separate lodgings for suitable wash and disposal of evidence.

***

Herman left no clues as to whether he visited Paris that fall. When I checked the historical records for that city there was nothing abnormal which would have indicated a man of his 'talents' having visited. The returning passenger lists to New York did not include his name or any of the alibis he often used.

Neither had Holmes made any mention of the letters that mocked the police investigation and play such a huge part of the Ripper story both then and now. I wasn't surprised. That kind of foolish correspondence wasn't his style. Even if he were proved to be the Ripper, those letters would most likely have been someone else's, unless that is and quite possible, he had crafted them to serve him in another fashion, as he had done the memoirs while locked away in prison.

Factually, many issues point directly at Holmes. He *was* there in 1888 and he probably killed, after all, he did so everywhere else he stayed for that long an extended period of time. While in London, he visited medical schools to sell skeletons, the very same subject he was an expert at stateside. There are reports of an American doctor having done so. Holmes was a surgeon, capable of having conducted or of having trained another to do so, the extreme surgery performed on the victims and under the most trying of circumstances. He did disappear from Chicago during the period of time two Ripper murders were being conducted and the Ripper killings stopped abruptly when he returned to the USA. Separate witness accounts of the description of the suspect and Holmes' photographic likeness are strikingly similar, so much so as to be eye opening. BBC and London police profile composite drawings of the Ripper are near exact photocopies of Holmes' black and white photographs. Lastly, he was a convicted serial killer, with the appropriate modus operandi and was certainly capable of having been the Ripper, or, once again, of having directed his assistant to do so.

Despite this circumstantial evidence, I knew that for every question answered about Holmes being Jack, a hundred more would be generated; questions I couldn't answer. No one could. That was, after all, what 'Jack' *now* was all about-- a never ending debate rather than a final truth.

In any event, Holmes' proven acts in the states both before and after 1888 made what did or didn't happen in London pale by comparison. Jack the Ripper was the JV, a minor leaguer when compared to Holmes.

If Holmes was Jack, London's police officers had been up against the challenge of their lifetimes, and were completely unprepared for the instructional nature the monster made of that nightmare fall of 1888. Everything was intended as contrary *to be* contrary. Every action was designed to be misplaced. Every move was meant to motivate a member of the press to publish erroneous conclusions about the actual facts. The investigators never had a chance.

CHAPTER 24

From New York to San Francisco the case was touted as "The Trial of the Century." The proceedings captured the attention and imagination of the entire nation. Every newspaperman in the country clamored for the chance to cover the trial of the notorious H. H. Holmes in Philadelphia. A place in the gallery was the toughest ticket in the last hundred years and required a favor from the Mayor, the Judge or the Chief of Police. Two United States Senators were denied seats.

Every day, newspapers carried page after page of the trial's transcripts and daily interviews with experts and witnesses following their testimony and even cell-side chats with the evil doctor himself. When closing arguments were approaching, the collective country held its breath anticipating the verdict of the jury and the coming pronouncement of sentence by the judge. The only trial since then to compare with the Holmes trial's level of notoriety was the (approximately one century later) O. J. Simpson Trial.

The trial was well-documented. The decision and sentencing were analyzed *ad infinitum*. There have been umpteen well-written books about the Holmes Trial. Every five years or so another one is published. I read them all, but was looking for that something extra, so I concentrated on issues outside the case which might have gone unnoticed, possibly one containing a clue to the Holmes mystery *after* the trial. And find them I did!

Holmes was arrested in Boston on November 17, 1894, for conspiracy to defraud an insurance company. On September 12, 1895, he was indicted for the murder of Benjamin F. Pitezel and pled not guilty. The charge was never amended to include the suspected murders of the three Pitezel children.

The trial transcript is the most accurate recounting of anything involving the life of H. H. Holmes that has ever been published, recording every aspect of testimony given and arguments made even by Holmes himself. I poured over each page, trying to capture every possible nuance. Obviously, the subject matter is fascinating and amply illustrates his incredible intellect.

Holmes said very little about the trial in either of his works. By necessity all of it would have been from memory. The entries he did make were concerned with individuals who either raised his ire with their official duties or angered him with their testimony.

Much was made of the fact that Holmes lost his lawyers and was forced to conduct his own defense. From his private comments, Holmes enjoyed his time as counsel, while never seriously giving much thought to actually prevailing. He knew his guilt was obvious, the jury biased, and the odds of his being found innocent stacked against him. The nation wanted his blood and the only uncertainty was how long the jury would take returning once closing arguments were concluded, the press writing of wagers being taken across the country as to the hours, not days, the court would take handing down a verdict.

By all accounts Holmes performed brilliantly and did so despite the fact that his guilt was 'established' in the public's eyes long before opening arguments had commenced. According to the *Philadelphia Public Ledger*, "Holmes set about handling his own case with a readiness that would have done credit to the most experienced lawyer at the bar. He was cool and collected. Not once did he display the least sign of nervousness. Even when a decision of the court went against him he would accept graciously and make no complaint."

Holmes enjoyed the verbal jousting with opposing counsel, witnesses and the judge. Most of the formalities were nothing more than a game to Holmes, albeit one about his life and death. His later words regarding the *"lack of justice,"* as he called it, and in particular the failure of the government's burden of proof were far more illuminating of his true character and intellect than his false words commonly quoted by the many articles and books to follow.

Of vital interest was the weight afforded the verbal testimony the government's witnesses supposedly offered against me. Each of these witnesses had previously associated with me in some form of skullduggery or another. Four of them were willing and worthy students of my profession. Throughout their testimonies, their nervous conditions were entertaining, as well as educational to observe.

It soon became apparent that all direct testimony was the result of coaching at the hands of the district attorney's many assistants, as well as the undocumented rewards the government promised each in return for their testimony against me. Both questions and answers had been scripted in order to provide an easy roadmap for the jury. They had to be, for as I knew and the judge and jury did its best to overlook, there was no direct evidence by way of any condemning instruments, clothes, etc.

Nothing at all.

The government's attorney had, so my contacts told me, instructed each witness to look away from my eyes during cross-examination. This prohibition was easy to overcome. All I had to do was wait. Once our eyes did meet, the "truth" previously trumpeted by the district attorney fell apart and crumbled into irrelevancy and falsehood. Despite each and every witness's failure, none were afforded dismissal. I was to be guilty whether proper evidence was offered or not. Realizing this, I wasted little time being concerned with cross-examination, instead tracing the identity of each liar so that my visits to them after my freedom had been secured would be fruitful.

Two of the female witnesses, having fallen apart on the stand under my pressure, cried and reached out to hold my hand and beg forgiveness as they were walked away from the witness stand and out the portal. From their tears it was obvious they had been convinced of my mortality, but seeing me this close had changed their minds. Both seemed desirous of reconsidering the position they had placed themselves in by agreeing to assist the government. To be fair, I had already decided to forgive them their transgressions, but only after considerable and repeated lessons concerning my future expectations of loyalty. To the professionals that had convinced them to take this sinful path foregoing their loves, there would be no lessons, for their time upon this earth was limited.

He took no notes. Drawings depicted him at dock, leg crossed, one hand in coat pocket, head turned slightly in concentration, calmly assessing his opponents and the proof against him. He was perfectly groomed and pressed, as if the life at risk were some others and not his own. At one point Holmes and the judge had a spirited but educated discussion, during selection, concerning a juror's ability to render an impartial decision due to his having previously formed an opinion about the murderer from the newspapers that had roundly produced spin bordering on fiction instead of factual reports.

"Objection. Lack of impartiality," Holmes remarked with a wry spryness that surprised even the most practiced of the gallery.

The judge, looking him up and down, legendary temper bubbling, began to rise from his chair behind the bench, but thought better of it and settled back down to appraise Holmes over the reading glasses suspended low on his nose.

"Overruled," he said, with the sheepish grin observers had begun to recognize from his Honor. They could see he hated the defendant. The judge at some point had given up trying to hide his hatred. Holmes was overjoyed.

The joust was on.

"Your Honor, may I have the right to know why? The witness just admitted to having formed his opinion about me two days ago while reading the very same reporter's," Holmes calmly turned, raised his right hand and pointed at a gentleman busily scribbling away in the grandstand, "… who just so happens to be sitting three rows behind me at this instant… article in the *Philadelphia Ledger*."

Both were grinning, energized, the judge enjoying this as much as Holmes, as they went back and forth, working each other over. The judge, who knew this case was the pinnacle of his career, was the first to break legal position, explaining to the courtroom the sheer impossibility of finding any member to the jury who had not been previously exposed to the press reports about the alleged killer.

Citing two cases, one from the Philadelphia State Court and another from the United States Supreme Court, doing his utmost to convince the press of his legal knowledge, he turned back to Holmes, and finally rising from his bench, declared in a fashion that left little doubt about his own belief as to guilt and innocence, "You have no one to blame for that but yourself, Holmes!"

Then, recognizing what he had just done, gathered himself and sat back down but maintained his now famous raised eyebrows.

With a quiet calm display that washed over the entire courtroom, Holmes circled for the kill.

"Am I to believe that even you, *my* judge, have found it impossible to be impartial? If that is so, have you considered recusing yourself? Is that not the requirement of your profession and oath?"

The judge sat stunned and speechless behind his bench. Silence descended over the courtroom.

Round one to Holmes.

Seconds later, his Honor's dismay gave way to indignation. "My actions are reviewed at the highest levels for the slightest of imperfections. You have been entrusted as my defendant in this my courtroom and I will do my utmost to ensure your rights and liberties are guaranteed no matter how much I may feel personally that you are not entitled to any of them."

Holmes sat respectfully silent.

"Overruled. Move on, sir."

As some there later attested, Holmes respectfully did. His performance as his own attorney continued to hold an entire nation spellbound. The *Philadelphia Inquirer* reported, "Holmes was on the aggressive. It hardly seemed that he was a defendant…He was an orator, a prince at repartee, a lawyer, and a man fighting for his life all combined."

Some of his entries afterwards captivated my attention as a practicing trial lawyer:

The witness drawing most of my attention was the ex-police detective turned professional witness who testified against me at the trial. He was an excellent witness and offered many opinions, which I will be the first to admit, were all quite true. Yet he fulfilled his contract with a smirk that crossed all borders of dignity, repeatedly and sarcastically insulting me. The man was very confident of his eternal safety and my damnation. As a result, the man became my main entertainment when I needed time to refresh my mind from the exertions planning my escape was causing. He overlooked the fact that I now knew where he lived, him having testified to same, even the street address, no less. He even boasted while on the stand how proud he was of the fine wife and two beautiful young sons that made up his family. Yes, I would enjoy paying them a visit to discuss his insults and unprofessional conduct.

Despite Holmes' repeated and well-made objections to almost all offered evidence, the government made its case solely on the basis of circumstantial evidence. I could not locate one shred of direct evidence in the transcripts. Not one eyewitness stepped forth to say, "Yes. I saw Holmes do this to another human being." Nor was there one piece of physical evidence, such as a fingerprint, bloodstain, knife or scalpel, produced-- not a single one. From my own background, it was hard to imagine any case today proceeding on this lack of basic evidence. Hearsay, everything offered by the prosecution was hearsay, but in the end even that technicality proved sufficient.

Holmes' closing arguments against the flimsy nature of the evidence offered by the government, summed up, was this: "Because a woman was last seen having associated with the defendant, for no matter how short a period of time, and was not seen thereafter, no other 'evidence' being offered by the government, is it just to circumstantially convict a defendant of her murder?"

The judge and jury thought yes.

Holmes' private thoughts on the matter:

The judge and I argued for hours over the evidence presented by so-called experts and professional law enforcement. I understood the concept of circumstantial, but did not understand the limitless applications such a term could be given in order to make acceptable that which was unsubstantiated. Watching his Honor's eyes, I knew in his heart he felt the same way, but was constrained by the national attention and hence unable to provide his most honest assessments. I was very disappointed with his conduct.

Had the defendant been the slightest bit sympathetic, without the weight of public opinion crushing the judge and jury, I wondered if the judge, who by all accounts was a worthy and proper holder of the final gavel, would have been so liberal with the laws of evidence and life.

The words of the judge charging the jury, the most quoted of all those involving the trial of H. H. Holmes, perhaps bring home who and what Holmes was best of all. "Truth is stranger than fiction, and if Mrs. Pitezel's story is true, it is the most wonderful exhibition of the power of mind over mind I have ever seen, and stranger than any novel I have ever read." From this statement, there is little doubt his Honor understood Holmes, or at least that he knew Holmes was incomprehensible.

Three short hours later, the jury returned with a finding: "Guilty of murder in the first degree."

As the jury foreman, poor man that he was to become, read the decision, Holmes could be heard clearing his throat with a hearty, "Ahem." He was never seen to tremble, his lips never quivered and his incredible nerve never deserted him.

Shortly thereafter the judge sentenced him to be hanged by the neck until dead.

The next day the newspapers wrote that he could be seen scribbling on the periodicals he held in front of him as the jury foreman addressed the courtroom. Though they wanted to, they were unable to determine what his writings amounted to. The notes, as Holmes later described, were the details he needed to later identify each juror. He made a special request of the judge that each member be polled and recorded. This was his right under the system. When this process was completed, the press went on to write, "The most extraordinary case in the annals of American courts" was over.

Holmes remembered what happened this way:

The jury returned in under three hours. As they entered the courtroom through the etched wood door to the right of the judge's stand, each one made every effort to stand tall while looking me in the eye. I returned each stare. The jury foreman was the most obnoxious, attempting in some way to scar my soul before condemning me to death. What reason he had for this shallow attempt at courage, I have no idea, but I promised myself to never forget his face. The other members quickly sat down, seemingly aware of the consequences of their decision. His Honor requested that I rise to hear the findings. I did so without delay or disrespect. Without further ado and absent the faintest degree of suspense, the foreman read the guilty verdict.

Holmes was not concerned with the verdict. He was more focused on setting the stage for his escape and knew that he had not a second to spare, needing to utilize the built in dramatics of the moment to begin the process that would result in his freedom.

I needed all to believe that I was giving up my defense, accepting justice and that I was admitting my guilt. Rather than screaming like some crazed vermin, I sank back into my chair with abject disdain. Crying, the guards assisted me to my feet. I feigned weakness and caught myself by holding onto the arms of the bailiffs, who, bless their souls, took me carefully through the back doors of the courtroom, the doors reserved only for the condemned. Once the door closed behind me and the eyes of the world were sealed shut, I pulled myself up, shook them off and walked on ahead of the two guards to the wagon waiting to take me to prison. The morning's papers and the pathetic story they told of my final moments in court guaranteeing the first stage of the plan had been successfully carried out.

He kept at the game by filing an appeal. A three judge summarily rejecting his requests. Next he submitted the reprieve and request for pardon that he was entitled to. All these documents were reported on by the press as further proof of his weak character. Holmes even prepared his own emergency petition for a temporary respite from Governor Hastings, which was ready to be filed at a moment's notice should this finality become necessary. His explanation as to why the document might be necessary was more evidence of his genius.

The respite was as essential a part of my plan as was the ultimate substitution of the guard in my place upon the scaffold.

The legal document was necessary to counteract last minute contingencies. Consider if the substituted guard called in sick that final morning? Should such occur, I needed to be armed with a stop-all to allow myself another chance. The respite, as worded, was guaranteed to provide me with two weeks' time. As its legal basis, my associates had arranged grounds to disqualify a juror. That juror, married of course, had been visited by a very loyal employee of mine. She had ensured his cooperation and admission as to a personal characteristic that would have disqualified his participation as a member of the final jury. This was of course a fraud, but hoax was my ace in the hole. With respite in hand, sleep the last three nights was much easier. As things turned out, we never needed to petition its use.

As with so much of the Holmes story, the national press coverage provided me with the necessary background. The diary gave me the facts that made the real story work.

CHAPTER 25

Twenty-four hours a day prison guards sat in directly across from the maximum security cell watching Holmes through the steel bars. He was the only inmate given his own watch-- one guard for one prisoner. The guard sat with his back to a concrete wall. There was no door, window, or other cell opposite Holmes. The wall allowed that guard to watch his prisoner without having to worry about what was at his back. Holmes' guards were specially trained to monitor the conduct of the most dangerous human beings in the world. They were trained to notice anything, no matter how small or out of the ordinary. For this they were the highest paid guards in the prison system. They were maximum security for the maximum threat.

At the end of the cell block there is no sunlight, nor even the indirect light the other prisoners enjoy. Shadows play across the walls. For the others those dancing shadows would have been enough to create their intended psychological impact. To me they didn't make the slightest difference for I felt right at home, reminding me of the Castle basement. Shadow was my sunlight.

Vince Genoble was one of the four guards qualified to monitor the maximum security cell. Vince wasn't a big man but he was quick as a cat and strong as an ox. Vince's ability to maintain focus on his prisoner was unparalleled. He was the guard the warden turned to for the most difficult assignments.

Before this assignment Vince had been required to undergo a series of lectures pertaining to this particular prisoner. The lectures included Holmes' reported ability to cast spells over those closest to him, or those he needed to further his evil purposes. In particular, the guard was warned about the dangers of hypnosis. He was ordered not to converse with Holmes under any circumstances. Vince was also instructed to report any attempt Holmes made to communicate with him. Repeated attempts would result in the prisoner being restrained and muzzled.

"Fine by me," I imagined Vince saying to himself. He hadn't uttered four words to *any* of the worthless scum he had monitored over the years. He hated prisoners, without exception, and looked forward to the day when he would be promoted to the gallows detail. He couldn't wait until he was their last anything of everything.

Unfortunately, Vince's training only served to heighten his focus on this prisoner, which was exactly what Holmes was counting on. He knew that increased focus made for the easiest target. Holmes realized that the more attention he attracted from the guards, the simpler it would be for him to subjugate their subconscious minds. Should all go according to plan, and within four weeks, he would be secretly commanding their obedience.

Every day to beginning his watch Vince walked the two hundred yards of cells to the "D" block, where his chair and Holmes awaited. There he relieved Oscar and took his seat against the cold white concrete wall. Every day, while walking down that hallway, Vince reminded himself to avoid allowing Holmes to stare directly into his eyes-- absolutely not.

Through the vertical bars Holmes could see that each guard was well trained and vigilant. They did indeed watch his every move. The restrictions that had been imposed upon his ability to converse with the guards amused him greatly, although he was careful not to divulge the slightest trace of humor.

Years had passed since the last time anyone actually tested my intellect with an obstacle that required concentration on my part to overcome. This warden was proving a worthy adversary. Fortunately, my plan did not require great creativity, just proper management.

From day one I made sure I was the model prisoner, making every effort to maintain my appearance and decorum just as if I were attending a play in

New York City. My grooming was precise, even to the extent that my shoes were polished twice each week. All that was required was my will and, of course, proper capital. I had been allowed to keep the three hundred dollars I was arrested with and twice since the sentencing my outside men delivered me additional funds to continue my purchased favors.

My cell was sufficiently lighted for me to read and write twenty two hours a day. Two hours of sleep per day was all I required for my health.

The editor of the Philadelphia Enquirer talked the warden into allowing me a writing desk after I bargained with him for the publishing rights to my memoirs and written confession. Apparently he was required to donate to a "charity" of the warden's choosing and quite handsomely, or so I was told. I reported to the editor that I had begun writing the story on December 1894, so as to portray to the world my gathering guilt for the pain and sorrow I had caused. That was of course not true at all, but with that bargaining chip I was able to secure all I needed to transform my sparse prison cell into a functional and even comfortable base of operations.

The bargain with the *Philadelphia Enquirer* was for more than just material. Holmes had two objectives: to draw the guards under his influence and to leave a red herring for the outside world to rest confident in his demise so as to cover his tracks. He knew his escape would have to be camouflaged by direct evidence.

That's where his published memoirs came in.

The memoirs, to be released upon his execution, were the only sure way that the ruse would never be discovered. It was a necessary step to take. In his notes Holmes wrote of being absolutely certain that, was his escape ever discovered and a manhunt launched, he would eventually be captured and then shot on sight as retribution for the guard's death.

As the first who understood his true motives for writing the memoirs I could see that the lies he told in them were intended to create the impression that the trial and judgment had served to awaken him to his errors and that his evil ways were finally haunting him. Of course nothing could have been further from the truth.

The book set the stage for the weakness I needed to portray to those in positions of authority. I determined to finish the draft at any cost. In addition, the gross proceeds I would need to cover all costs of the escape were considerable. I estimated $15,000 in cash would be required, and later, after the accounting, that figure turned out to be considerably low. The book eventually made good on every item I counted on it for and quite surprisingly, turned a small profit.

Even as he worked tirelessly to finish the memoirs, Holmes enacted a careful plan to secure more and more control over his guards. There were a number of security measures he needed to overcome in order to succeed. The most critical of the restrictions was the ban on conversation. If he was to escape he was going to need to express his desires to each of the guards. Therefore, this one ban would require a piece-by-piece strategy to overcome. Carefully concocted, he gave himself three weeks' time before talking in open defiance of the prohibition would be necessary.

As strange as it seems, the first step was for Holmes to hum. That's all, just hum. He needed to hum a well-known song, a song that all the guards knew the words to. He would need to hum soft and low, breaking down the first strains of resistance to any forbidden noise, not yet words, emanating from his cell. Once they were accustomed to the rhythmic sounds of a song, he could slowly intersperse the notes with a combination of hum and slur, and once that was overlooked and accepted, well, then the rest would be easy. Holmes knew that if done right, before long, they would be singing right along with him.

Conversation would be easy after that first step.

The song he first hummed hour after hour was 'The Battle Hymn of the Republic.' The song was familiar to every guard in the prison and would thus be impossible for them to prevent from creeping into their subconscious minds.

Within two days he had interjected one or two words between the hummed notes. The first words he selected were the most innocuous and innocent he could think of.

"… Glory… glory… hallelujah…"

He repeated this exercise over and over, ten to fifteen hours each day. He was careful to do so without irritating or interrupting the coming trance-like state he knew would result with patience. And he never hummed while looking into the eyes of the guards, at least not for the first few days. No, that would have been interpreted as aggressive, setting back his plan at least a week. As he expected and before the guards even knew it, his noise had spellbound each to the point where they now looked forward to his 'entertainment' with a certain amount of glee, although each was extremely cautious not to show enjoyment. None of them ever mentioned the noise or their decision not to report the indiscretion to any of the others. Each believed this was their own private audience, only for them, with their new acquaintance.

Ahead of schedule by almost two full days, Holmes' voice could soon be heard down the cellblock, "Mine eyes have seen the glory of the coming of the Lord. He hath loosed the fateful lightning of his terrible swift sword." a complete violation of prison regulations and the warden's direct orders.

By the end of the second week, the guards were involuntarily humming along with him, "Our God is marching on." Three weeks after having sung along with Holmes, the guards were openly discussing him with their wives', including the assured injustices of his trial.

The progression continued until very soon the only time conversations ceased was when one of the guards alerted him that the warden was coming down for the weekly inspection of the block. Despite the various guards knowledge of this open transgression, Holmes was never punished or restrained for speaking in violation of the rule.

Holmes was accepted. Stage one was complete.

The next step would be to induce daydreams.

No escape would have been possible without Holmes gaining the ability to control the actions of his 'servants' through suggestion. His eyes were the key. His method was precise. He would slant his head to the side, gazing from the inside corner of the furthest eye and the outside corner of the closest, holding that position for as long as the effort took. His patience was legendary. This mysterious position made it nearly impossible for his victims to consider anything but the doctor's wishes. When 'locked in' he was well on his way to harnessing the mind of his intended target.

His special trick was to synchronize the power of his stare with the frequency of his deep, slow voice. Doing so, he would quickly be firmly in charge, acting the part of authority and causing the victim to flow to his infectious confidence and friendliness. He used the power of his awesome stage presence and wielded it ruthlessly to draw even the most doubtful individuals into his web.

From developed science we now know that what he was doing was bypassing the conscious critical mind of his victims, causing the subconscious mind to take over from this hypnotic trance. Holmes knew that the subconscious harbored many of the fears, imagination and secret beliefs of the human spirit. These were the fulcrums he needed to obtain willing subjects. Once he had secured control, Holmes would test his new subject to determine the degree of suggestibility each was prone to, for he knew that all responded differently. If satisfied, he would then suggest that they carry out basic innocent acts which served to lock them into a paternal respect for Holmes. With time he would progress until he was finally demanding they commit immoral acts. His goal was to retrain their mind so that the old morals of the subject would evaporate. Bad, once he had gained control, could be changed to good in his subject's eye with a wave of the doctor's hand.

Holmes would often, depending on the potential each victim demonstrated, take things a step further than even that, requiring criminal acts on his behalf. This ultimate condition was more often than not permanent, the patient remaining his until either death or Holmes' decision to release them. He was the walking definition of Svengali.

***

Confident his early efforts were successful, Holmes began focusing on the one prison guard he needed most.

"Not yet, my boy," he whispered as if talking to himself but within certain earshot of Vince. The familiarity he was projecting, however vague, was essential. Holmes had succeeded in wearing away the last of the man's hard edges. Vince was close to ready.

"Mr. Holmes what did you say? Is there something I can do or get for you?" Vince asked, lifted from his silence by the words sliding across the chamber, unsure of whether Holmes had been talking to himself or to him. This marked the first time he referred to or even thought of Holmes as "Mister."

Holmes' voice was becoming an elixir to the condemned young man. Holmes could sense the guard was taking a serious liking to him.

"No, my son, I'm just talking to myself, but thank you for your kindness and close attention."

With these words he pulled back; too much too fast could erase all progress. His plan required that he produce a stand-in, to take his place on the gallows-- the proverbial stool pigeon. Vince was the guard whose physical features most closely resembled his own. He was also the one most susceptible to hypnosis.

Their daily chit-chat continued to grow. What had once been only one-word acknowledgments were now full sentences. The first few conversations were guarded, whispered even, but were soon loud enough that they could be heard interacting two cells over. Holmes ensured that all the talk put Vince at ease consisting of material which was safe for the guard. Actually, Holmes had no interest in the guard's words. He could entertain himself for days by recalling word for word the great novels he'd once read. No, the talks with Vince had nothing to do with content, but with revealing to the killer the mannerisms of his new friend and of course to gain the guard's confidences. Holmes referred to these personality moments as 'beats'. He needed to know the rhythm of the guard's life so that he could repeat it himself under duress. Then he had to erase those beats from the guard's reactions so Vince could be made to emulate Holmes' own beats as he walked up to the gallows. Beats were critical to the success of the plan.

Their talks continued to progress, Holmes becoming Vince's first real listener in years. Holmes learned that following the Civil War, Vince's father had become a New York City policeman who had served with distinction for a number of years until dying late one night responding to a call on the South Side. Tragically, his body was never recovered. Vince felt his father was never given the respect he deserved for his meritorious service to the city.

Holmes 'surgically' reopened the wound.

With softening eye, he said, "Vince, my boy…" Holmes had taken to addressing the guard with paternalistic handles to soften the demanding requests he was later going to make. ."…they didn't mean their obvious affront to your father that way. He was one of many that were lost, part of the sheer numbers game that being a policeman in New York City involves." Making the man's father only a number cut him further to the core, forcing him even deeper under Holmes' influence.

Holmes sat, Freud-like, one leg crossed at an angle over the other, as if concentrating on every word. He knew that visuals were as important as his words right then.

Reacting to these words about his father, Vince rose off his chair racing to clutch the cell bars and said, "I don't care what they meant! My family was left out in the cold. We had no money, no food." His fingers turned red, clearly trying to bend the steel. Vince's eyes filled with tears, the first in years, which he wiped away in embarrassment with the back of his hand, but not before Holmes saw all he needed to know in order to dangle Vince from his rope.

"Vince, the system often forgets to provide aid for the needy. Perhaps they thought you were capable of supporting your father's family yourself."

With this one fell swoop Holmes turned their relationship into the doctor-patient rapport guaranteed to produce submission.

Vince was becoming my creature in every sense of the word. He was ac-
tuated by my slightest gestures, anticipating my wants and needs. He took to
leaving the bars of my prison cell unlocked and I was soon walking down the
hallway, though only when there were no other guards in attendance. One day
when one of the other guards, informed by a prisoner, questioned Vince about
my walks he did exactly what I instructed him to do, he lied. My bidding was
becoming his reason for living.

Using intimacy, Holmes began transcending barriers, reaching far
into Vince's vulnerable side. The farther he reached the easier hypnosis
would become enhancing his ability to direct the guard's everyday movements.

Away from the prison the guard began talking to his family and
friends, telling them he thought Holmes was innocent and that the execution was going to be a travesty of justice. His concern for Holmes began
to carry over onto the other guards. They all began to bestow special favors on the inmate. His food was upgraded from cell slop to the menu of
the guards. The 1895 *Chicago Tribune* quoted a guard as saying, "I like
that fellow, even if he is a rascal." While all this was going on, Holmes sat
back, directing, and with his all-knowing eye.

"Vincent, do you and your wife discuss my predicament?" Holmes
needed to redirect Vince's distrust in the system that had mishandled his
family and turn it to his benefit. "Do you and she discuss whether I am
guilty or not?"

"Yes, sir, almost every night during and after dinner," Vince humbly
replied. Upon hearing this Holmes shifted closer to the bars ready to
pounce upon the next vulnerability.

"What does she think about me, Vincent?"

The question was left purposefully vague, a tactic to draw out emotion and then trust. Once again it wasn't so much the answer that was
important as was the confidence with which the answer was given.

"She's worried about our friendship. She's afraid of my concern for
you, you being the killer and all," Vince said, his eyes leaving the doctor's

and falling to the floor in embarrassment. "She's threatened to report my sympathy for you to the warden unless I stop. I…I… threatened her with harm if she did."

"Very good, my son. Vince, do me a favor, won't you? Keep a close eye on her. We mustn't allow her irrational concerns to interfere with our… friendship… must we?" Holmes said with all deliberate pace.

On the defensive lest he lose any closeness with the doctor, his first confidant in years, Vince replied, "Don't worry Dr. Holmes. I wouldn't allow that to happen."

Holmes nodded thinking how much like a pet dog, eager to hunt with its master, Vince was turning out to be.

Delicately changing this critical subject, "Vince, I need a few things tomorrow. I'll leave you a list before the watch changes. But right now I'd appreciate some privacy, so would you be good enough to move your chair down the block so I can be alone for my nap?"

"But of course, Doctor Holmes," and did so in direct violation of every single one of the warden's orders.

***

The next step was to create conditions which would allow the necessary "changing" image of himself. In order to accomplish this mirage, Holmes needed to alter the perspective of anyone who might be present the day of the execution. The way the world thought of him had to be blurred and thrown into chaos. He needed for them to see in him that mystical monster they all thought of in the dark and knew by sight in their dreams.

What does the devil look like? Holmes would have chuckled while rubbing his palms together in his cell before going to work.

For the plan to succeed, the transformation needed to be convincing enough that five critical men were sold on the changes. The five were Vince, Frank the morning guard, the priest that would attend to Holmes the morning of the execution and the two reporters he would have previously given permission to interview and cover his walk to the gallows that morning.

The priest's belief in the transformation was of the utmost importance, for he was the one who would provide Holmes with the twenty minutes, the morning of the hanging, needed to apply makeup and change clothes with Vince.

The process requires a continual assault on all human senses. Their entire psyche must be convinced that my facial features are changing. Reality has little to do with the actual outcome. When twisted the proper way, the human mind is capable of seeing a normal man as the devil. Patience and a steel resolve is all that is needed, that and the aforementioned malleable human mind.

Despite everything to the contrary, the mind is far easier to convince than the naked eye. In fact, my altered appearance will only be achieved through my subjects' minds. The first step was requesting Vince to remove the looking glass from my cell. I explained this away as my own fear of the emerging devil under my skin. I repeatedly told my jailors that I could not bear to observe my reincarnation. In reality the final days' exercises would have been ruined with one inadvertent glance.

Holmes knew that the easiest way for him to convince the world that he was slowly being transformed into the devil was to let the nation's newspapers do the dirty work for him. The easy part-- they couldn't help themselves. Every morning there was another request for an interview from one of the nation's top periodicals. In each interview Holmes made sure to complain of pain and to describe the evolution of his features toward evil to an everyday less skeptical public.

To one reporter he revealed, "I am convinced that since my imprisonment I have changed woefully and gruesomely from what I was formerly in feature and figure. My features are assuming a pronounced satanical cast. I have become afflicted with that dread disease, rare but terrible, with which physicians are acquainted, but over which they have no control whatsoever. That disease is a malfunction or distortion of the osseous parts.... My head and face are gradually assuming an elongated shape. I believe fully that I am growing to resemble the devil, that the similitude is almost completed." This quote ran across most of the nation's front pages the very next day.

In another interview he said, "For the first time in ages I was allowed the opportunity to shave before a mirror. When I did and glimpsed my reflection I was shocked to see that the image was nothing of what I remembered I used to be. I screamed in abject terror, causing my guard to rush into my cell. When questioned even he admitted that my face was much changed from what it had appeared when I was first incarcerated." This soap opera fed the hungry public.

Holmes began insisting that interviews include an artist's rendition of his facial features. He demanded first right of refusal on any the newspaper intended for publication. I imagined him in his cell suggesting changes to the reporter's artist while at his side. Comparing those drawings today, side by side with real photographs of Holmes, they bear little resemblance to each other.

Holmes made sure to plant the thought of a transformation in the mind of each reporter and if they failed to report the change the next day they were refused another interview. Most did not need to be threatened. They could see the new Holmes for themselves, or thought they could. He was that good an actor.

Holmes lost a significant amount of weight after the judgment. By fasting he claimed to all to be ridding his body of the devil that possessed him. Not so. What he was actually doing was beginning the process of eliminating the baseline of his previous appearance. This new frailness created the clean easel to repaint the image he knew was necessary. As soon as his evolving emaciated features were mentioned in the papers, he turned 180 degrees and in secret from the press, began consuming huge quantities of food. The warden was all too happy but to comply, as Holmes' earlier refusal to eat had raised concern that more prolonged fasting might deprive justice, and country, of the execution of the century, thus the food was made plentifully available.

He began exercising in what everyone assumed was a crazy desire to renew his health. This part of the ploy seemed rather obvious to me. Who in their right mind would have thought it reasonable for a man awaiting his death in a matter of weeks to take up a rigorous regime of exercise? Yet, not one supervisor or physician questioned the activity, nor did researchers carefully review these actions afterwards. Lunacy, instead of some logical purposefulness, was just so much easier to assume. Once again, his laughter can still be heard on the grounds of the long-gone prison.

***

Changing *his* appearance to resemble the devil was not enough; he also needed to resemble Vince.

The two men were already of the same basic structure. Holmes had seen to that before selecting the guard, but they were in no way twins.

For his plan to work, Holmes needed to implant a new image of Vince in the minds of those that would be present on execution day. To do this, he called on another of his amazing talents-- artistry. He took to drawing pictures of those around him, most often Vince, altering those images, then suggesting those changes to his audience, so that the subconscious mind could accept the changes as real, even if nothing had actually changed. Vince found the attention complimentary while Holmes sketched his face as they talked. Being the talented artist he was, the images strikingly captured Vince's various facial expressions. Each drawing seemingly depicting something new about Vince, something fresh and revealing about his personality and reactions to various types of visual and mental stimulation.

These images needed to be published. Impossible, right? Hardly, as twice Holmes' drawings of Vince, represented as self-portraits, were printed in place of the media artist's rendition of Holmes in the next day's paper. No one ever suspected a thing, and certainly not the substitution. Both prints would come to be what the public visualized Holmes to look like. Those images were what Holmes wanted the spectators at the execution to bring with them, in their heads, to the gallows. The one image of Holmes with head covering, probably the most publicized of all renditions, and the most inaccurate representation of the criminal, was one of those two.

At night in his cell Holmes began the work of categorizing each sketch... and rehearsing.

Of even greater importance than my training of the selected guard to imitate my mannerisms, was the acting I would have to perform in order to resemble him. Vince had close friends and acquaintances at the prison who would notice the slightest inconsistency on the day in question, while any mistakes he made as me would be attributed as normal hysterics in the face of meeting my maker.

Our facial features were already remarkably similar though his had more length, hence my earlier efforts convincing those around me of the elongation of my own features. He was also more defined and ten pounds leaner. I set out at once to equalize the weight and in two weeks' time was reasonably close. I also began slowly shaving the heels off two pairs of my boots after lights out each night, sending the scraps out with the night bucket in the morning.

Holmes kept track of the impressions he made on his daily visitors about his transformation.

Afterwards I enjoyed reading the recounting of events describing my pitiful posture and thin stature. My once perfectly fitting clothes, expensively tailored by the best in New York were described by the Philadelphia Public Ledger the day after the execution as hanging loosely as if "made for another man."

Facial grooming was the easiest of all and actually presented Holmes with solutions to two rather difficult problems. He was scarred on his right cheek as the result of an altercation when administering chloroform to the husband of a young lady he was friendly with. Unfortunately for the doctor the use of the chemical was in its early stages and the quantity necessary remained a haphazard guess. If overdosed a premature death would often result causing perpetrators to minimize the dosage. As a result of just such an insufficient dosage, the man regained consciousness and attacked Holmes from behind, scratching him across the right cheek and leaving a considerable scar. Holmes hid the wound with an ample beard until some years later when Holmes perfected the composition of an almost undetectable form of makeup allowing him to shave the beard he had detested all along.

The most difficult components of my escape had still to be overcome. The most perplexing was the wearing of the hood from my cell to the gallows. The warden would insist on knowing my reasons for this unusual request. Fear, my request would have to be based upon my fear of death and the unknown. My admitted cowardice would provide me enough reason. Next was the necessary few minutes needed to change clothes with those of the guard. One prying eye during this period and the entire plot would fail. Lastly were the words I would be expected to speak before the final moments. While it would have been easier to insist Vince refuse the opportunity, no one would have believed H. H. Holmes had declined the opportunity to speak prior to the placing of the noose around his neck. Just as problematic were the issues raised by too long of a speech, thus providing listeners the chance to detect a different frequency or depth of voice. Therefore, something short and concise was necessary. I made note to prepare such a speech and to begin inducing Vince's memorization of the same tomorrow.

I would also be required to mimic Vince's voice for the approximately one hour needed while I departed the facilities after the hanging. For three days I practiced Vince's voice in conversation with the other two guards. Both mentioned noticing differences, while fully accepting my explanation of slight fever and throat infection.

Holmes continued selling the change in his appearance to anyone who would listen. He maintained interviews right up to the day before the hanging and the papers continued to print his offered fallacies to a hungry world. This interview ran nationally:

"I was thoroughly examined by four men of marked ability and by them pronounced as being both mentally and physically a normal and healthy man. Today I have every attribute of a degenerate, a moral idiot. Is it possible that the crimes, instead of being the result of these abnormal conditions, are in themselves the occasion of the degeneracy? Is it to be wondered at that since my arrest my days have been those of self-reproaching torture, and my nights of sleepless fear? I have commenced to assume the form and features of the Evil One himself."

These exclamations were always accompanied by an important caveat such as this:

"All criminologists who have examined me here seem to be unanimous in the opinions they have formed, although one inexplicable condition presents itself, viz.: that while committing the crimes these symptoms were not present, but commenced to develop after my arrest."

The *New York World* printed a study, before the execution, providing opinions from a phrenologist:

"In the meantime, Holmes sat in his waist-high enclosure, assiduously taking notes, while a professional phrenologist, John L. Capen, M. D., studied him from a short distance away. Dr. Capen was there as a representative of the *New York World*, and his analysis of Holmes's features appeared in the next day's edition.... Holmes, according to this specialist, was a man with a keen but intensely repulsive face: a face shaped like hatchet, like one of those old-fashioned hatchets... "The shape of the head is unusual, abnormal. The top of the head is flat, except for one sharp bump rising suddenly and sharply. It would be said to mean reverence by the usual phrenologist. But not reverence for human life--at all events, not in this case. The eyes are very big and wide open. They are blue. Great murderers, like great men in other walks of activity, have blue eyes. There are deep lines under the eyes that come from sleepless nights of troubled thought and helpless rage. Of the murderer's mouth not much can be seen, for the hair is as thick as the thickest fur. But one can see that the lips are very thin and the expression as cruel and cold as to be not human."

Everything was moving ahead according to plan.

Because of the nation's breathlessness concerning the upcoming execution and anticipated extermination of evil, Holmes, the celebrity prisoner, had unheard of influence. Perhaps the most amazing example of this was that the doctor was allowed to select the reporters he felt most worthy of covering the fateful day, as he had refused to provide any further interviews to any he had not pre-approved. He met with five before making his final choices.

Before any were even considered they had to agree to sit with me inside the cell and only while Vince was on duty. Two refused because of stated fears concerning their safety. Another reporter stormed out in a fit of anger after refusing to answer questions regarding his childhood. The last two reporters were eager to do anything required of them to have the opportunity to provide an eager nation with what it was clamoring for - news of my death – the more gruesome the better.

On the fateful day, these two reporters were the only media members allowed the opportunity of accompanying Holmes from his cell to the gallows. Hearst, as part of the publishing deal, agreed they were to be the only two within speaking distance of Holmes.

Even their reports were suspect. According to Holmes, he had carefully scripted both the day before the hanging. Their 'facts' were then recounted by hundreds of others across the nation. They carried his outright falsehoods and the depicted drama necessary for the escape. Reading them now side-by-side, their similarity and lack of variation is startling. The minor differences they contain are more than likely the result of that particular writer's style.

How could he have fooled them all getting away with such an elaborate plan? None of the media raised a single question about that admittedly peculiar day. None discussed the abnormalities that Holmes admitted couldn't be addressed. One glaring example was the wearing of the hood by the criminal from his cell to the gallows. Not one publication questioned or even reported this glaring fact, instead reporting only what he insisted be included. Another glaring example was the inaccurate reporting of the number of people in the cell with Holmes one hour prior to the proceeding. Had this number been accurately depicted the plan would have disintegrated. These types of inaccuracies were passed on without comment or question because Holmes had ordered it so in return for selected media's rights to his last comments.

The autopsy, or lack of one, was the most amazing aspect proving Holmes' control of the prison and media system.

I am amused at how easy it was to convince the press that my concerns over the treatment of my soon to be dead body were the result of sensitivities surrounding death. The thought had crossed my mind that none of them could or would be talked into such a scheme. Thankfully, it was their need to see me as mentally disturbed that won the day. The most obvious of all, my request that no autopsy be performed, was also the most outlandish, and in the end, the argument to the judge that proved successful was that the cause of death would be known thirty seconds after the fall from the gallows, accordingly, why would knives be necessary to determine more? Verifying my identity when dead never crossed their inadequate minds.

Holmes knew his escape hinged on the lack of an autopsy. For no matter how successful the substitution was, an autopsy would reveal the entire fiasco. He also realized that if the authorities ever determined the wrong man had been executed, a guard working for that same government no less, and allowed the foulest criminal in our history to escape, a manhunt of immense proportions would ensue. There would be no let up until he was found. His last days would be on the run. Under no circumstances could Holmes allow an autopsy to take place.

Money was the tool Holmes used to manage from the grave. He left considerable funds to a number of charities, but only on condition that his explicit instructions regarding his burial be followed. He hired a national detective agency, the Pinkertons, to manage and verify the entire goings-on and for an exorbitant sum. The Pinkerton guards were famous at the time for their monitoring of circumstances and the courtesy they demanded be afforded their clients. Law enforcement provided them with the highest measures of respect and acquiesced to any requests, reasonable or not, that the Pinkertons made. Holmes insisted that the agency only be paid if the procedures he outlined were followed to the letter verified by an independent auditor.

Holmes also insisted that his lawyers refuse all requests submitted by medical schools for access to his body following death. He was being offered large sums of money for his brain, as the organ was a highly coveted specimen by those seeking scientific knowledge. Holmes demanded that all official submissions be turned down by the Warden and he instructed his lawyers to arrange large donations to favorite charities if Holmes' wishes were honored after the end.

The 'sacredness' of the gravesite was just as important. Holmes knew his grave would be an attraction to seekers of fame and again to those willing to illegally possess the specimen his brain would provide science. He knew his body would be dug up and ravaged within weeks of the hanging. Holmes' was well aware of the ease with which cemetery guards could be paid off and made to look the other way at the opportune moment. To prevent this would be difficult and it took all of Holmes' now coveted powerful brain to devise a scheme to protect the burial site.

His instructions were elaborate in the extreme, including the clothes the body was to be dressed in, right down to the type of leather shoes and wool socks. Additionally, the body was to be enclosed within a burlap case before being lowered into the mahogany casket.

The actual sewing of the body into the burlap case was to be performed by the two jailors he had grown 'friendly' with during his incarceration. They were to be the only ones allowed to handle the body in order to place the cadaver properly. Or so Holmes said. Both of the jailors agreed to dutifully perform this service for Holmes. Both were handsomely compensated for their labors. They had no idea the acts they were performing were in any way part of an elaborate conspiracy.

The body was to be encased within a specially constructed coffin that would be filled to the brim with concrete and metallically locked before closing. Holmes arranged for a special undertaker to carry out the final placement and cementing of the body to ensure the dead 'floated' amidst the hardening concrete. The last step would be to lower the casket into a ten-foot hole at the gravesite. That hole would also be filled with concrete creating the amazing Holmes sarcophagus. His instructions went so far as to demand that a certain percentage of lye and water be used in the mixture of the concrete. When finished, the Pinkerton Agency was to file a final report concerning the burial, certifying that all orders were complied with. The administrator at Holmes' bank would then be permitted to release payment to the agency upon his own certification of compliance.

Once again, had any of these people realized Holmes' complete lack of interest in anything as ridiculous as the condition of his hydrocarbons following his death, more concern and care might have been taken to avoid not only his escape, but the murder of an innocent man.

In the history of man, has there ever been a more cerebral escape plan? Not one shovel full of dirt was to be lifted. No tunnels were to be dug. Not one gun was to be utilized. No fisticuffs. Despite my hatred for the man it was impossible not to appreciate his efforts. He seemed to have successfully engineered a scheme to escape in broad daylight and from maximum security on the day of his scheduled execution while the eyes of the entire nation would be watching.

***

The night before the hanging, Holmes slept like the proverbial log. He was confident everything had been accounted for.

The night guardsman was a congenial man but with a limited intellect and rather childish nature. He and I shared perhaps three or four talks the entire duration of my incarceration. Our having a relationship was not important to the success of the plan. At nine o'clock that last night I asked him if he could darken my cell and the hallway opposite my bunk. He was quite concerned by this request, but this being my last night, took pity upon me and agreed though only after my promise to tell no one. He entered the cell and extinguished the irritating illumination. Luxuriously dark, I slept wonderfully the entire night until I was awakened by the same guard re-igniting the light before the change of watch. I thanked him and we exchanged 'God be with you's.'

Early that morning, Holmes' lawyers returned with the clothes from the tailors— the clothes he was to be executed in. Holmes had begged the warden that he be allowed to wear his own clothes on the fateful day. The warden had allowed the request as just another of Holmes' idiosyncrasies. While at the tailor, the clothes were altered. He paid extra to ensure that not one wrinkle would be present or, heavens forbid, a stain. The suit was returned in pristine condition and with a perfect fit-- for Vince.

At the opposite end of the spectrum, Holmes instructed Vince to arrive the fateful morning with his uniform unkempt, looking as if he had slept the entire night in his work clothes.

The order for the guard to come as unkempt as Holmes was to be meticulous threw me for a loop. The obvious reaction would have been for all to notice the distinct difference-- just the kind of distinction one would believe a man switching places with another would be trying to avoid. Not so, at least according to the doctor. He explained that minor differences between Vince and he were to be avoided at all costs, while major ones welcomed. The human mind was triggered more so by minor changes than by the large ones everyone assumed gathered attention. Large changes were most often summarily dismissed. Small ones generated irritation, then the inevitable question. A second look could then prove fatal to Holmes.

The best way to avoid that kind of scrutiny was to engineer some larger device to draw attention. Hence the dramatic difference between his suit and the guard's uniform. Holmes knew the human eye would quickly register the smoothness and then the wrinkles, noticing the distinct difference between the two. Assessing the fault as an error in grooming, registering the guard's lack of respect in this situation and improper supervision by the warden, each would compartmentalize their dislike, locking the difference away as unimportant and quickly move on to something more substantial, and in the process skip over any other minor difference which might have alerted one to the fraud; like an obvious physical difference between the two men. Vince's distasteful appearance would serve to repulse any second look.

At six sharp that morning Vince came to the prison looking haggard in every way except that he was clean-shaven, just as he had been instructed to be by the doctor. Also as ordered, on his left cheek was the razor wound Vince had given himself that morning. The wound was deep and on the verge of needing stitches. Holmes was relieved to see that the scars' position correlated nicely with his own freshly reopened scar from that morning. The doctor noted the scope and location was perfect for the intended deception. Holmes suggested Vince have the prison nurse bandage the wound.

Holmes also played the religious card in order to gain the time he needed to perform the essential acts with the priest and Vince in the cell before the hanging. Obviously Holmes was not a religious man, yet by all reports on that final day pointed to his sudden devoutness in the face of his coming death. Truth be known, he 'converted,' not because of his often reported fear of death, but because he needed the extra time that morning seeing to the final details.

Then there was still the matter of the gallows hood.

My lawyer and I lobbied the superintendent extensively for the right to wear the hood from my cell to the gallows. The request was agreed to on one condition; the hood would need to be removed after I made my way up the steps so that the execution jury could attest to my identity and I could make final statement to the observers in the crowd. Only then could the hood be replaced. While this development presented problems, the fact that the gallows were significantly higher than where the jury was located, made an accurate identification near impossible, more so because of the suit the warden was allowing 'me' to wear.

Hours before the execution a huge crowd was already gathering to gain a better vantage point for the hanging. Extra squads of policemen were on hand to handle the crowds and quell a potential riot in the gallery. The *Philadelphia Inquirer* wrote of the pandemonium: "There was a good deal of fin de siècle brutality about the crowds. There was nothing that they could possibly see, but the high forbidding walls. There was nothing they could hear. Yet they all seemed drawn to the spot by some morbid fascination. Coarse jests were bandied from lip to lip as the crowd surged to and fro.

The number of tickets to the gallery had been oversold by double, but the total mass forced their way into the auditorium by sheer force."

Morbid fascination aside, the crowds sensed an immense energy being generated inside the prison. They began to feed upon that energy, hungry for anything even resembling death. Holmes had counted on this energy to cast his final spell over the proceedings.

Rather than be overwhelmed by the energy emanating from the crowd and right through the concrete walls of my cell, I disciplined myself to maintain focus. Lying on my cot I segregated those parts of my brain that were necessary for success. On the one side the plan was properly memorized. The other, my reactive side, would be needed to almost magically adapt to the altered circumstances I knew were going to evolve in rapid sequences, but only after my deliberate consideration of all factors involved.

All that last day Holmes directed, going so far as the placing of 'actors' in precise positions to ensure the proper shadow would play off each face optimally. Nothing was left to chance. Every word either he or Vince was to speak would be prompted by being a specific distance from a reference point or in proximity to a critical actor.

Holmes did not describe the actual substitution and change of clothing during the twenty-six minutes he allotted for this stage of the plan.

My best guess was that by then Vince was already subjugated to the extent that as soon as he walked into the cell, escorting the father, there was nothing more Holmes needed to do in order to ensure his cooperation.

Holmes then needed to concentrate on the priest. When he arrived, Holmes would have cast a hypnotic spell over the father to ensure that he followed every command. At that point, Vince and the doctor would have changed clothes and applied makeup.

Twenty-seven minutes after Vince opened the cell the second priest arrived under guard to offer Holmes communion and last rights. Eleven minutes later Mr. Rotan entered and offered last services to his client; wills, trusts, donations to charities, and the like. The hood was then adorned.

Immediately after, the assistant superintendent arrived and with all manner of tact insisted that the proceedings required some haste, as sorry as he was to be forced to require such at this time and place. Holmes' simple nod, instead of his usual glib remark would have seemed strange, but under these conditions no one took pause as the silence being anything other than acceptable.

The cell bars were then pushed back, and *he* calmly walked out between the two priests, two guards, the assistant superintendent and Holmes' lawyer. Once outside the procession formed up. Vince, now dressed in Holmes' tailored clothes, was positioned in between the two priests. The two prison guards were immediately behind them with the superintendent to the left and three strides behind. This gave the two guards enough room should violence break out. The prisoner was not handcuffed or restrained in any way. The various parties remained in these positions down the cell-block and up to the small door at the side of the gallows.

My position behind and away from the prisoner afforded me the best angle with which to orchestrate, as much as that was still possible, the journey to the gallows. I put to maximum use caution, patience, cunning, self-control and disguise. Three times questions were put to the prisoner by the fathers and superintendent and all three of them I warded off with the comment that the prisoner had asked that our final moments be graciously respectful of his request for privacy. The prisoner, wearing the hood, nodded each time I made the statement.

Twice on the way out the cellblock the prisoner, unable to see, stumbled but was caught by the two fathers who were walking alongside, arm in arm with Vince. The stumbles added nicely to the sensation of a man losing all coordination on his way to meet his maker. Before we arrived at the gallows the superintendent motioned for me to open the door to the gallows stairways. I did so and watched as the entire party made its way up the stairs while I held the rather poorly constructed door and then followed up in their wake.

This would be my first time viewing the means of 'my' death. I must admit, the device was quite intimidating. The scaffold stretched all the way across the corridor. The executioners were waiting at the top. They seemed genuinely surprised to see that the prisoner was wearing the hood, so much so in fact that the sheriff removed the garment at once, taking a long slow look at the prisoner. For that one terrifying instant my breath caught in my throat, but soon returned to normal as the sheriff ignored the face and instead, and quite expectedly, commented upon the state of the clothes the condemned man was wearing. He next turned to me and asked me to remove myself from the scaffolding and to wait below.

As Holmes looked up, from below the scaffolding, the superintendent stepped back to allow the prisoner time to address the gallery. There was a waist-level rail around the gallows and Vince rested his hands upon it as he appeared to calmly survey the crowd beyond. The crowd went deathly silent as their previously gathered courage faded before this hyperbole of evil. The condemned man looked down at the first layer of jury and observers behind them and began the speech that Holmes had implanted. Many would later remark that his pallor made him look dead already.

He talked in what seemed a monotone, which some in the press remarked made his words feel rehearsed a million times before. The speech was made without the slightest gesture, his hands holding the rail the entire time, his voice incredibly steady. His exact words were,

"Gentlemen, I have very few words to say. In fact, I would make no remarks at this time were it not for the feeling that if I did not speak it would imply that I acquiesced in my execution. I only wish to say that the extent of the wrongdoing I am guilty of in taking human life is the killing of two women. They died by my hands as the results of criminal operations. I wish also to state, so that no chance of misunderstanding may exist hereafter, that I am not guilty of taking the lives of any of the Pitezel family, either the three children or the father, Benjamin F. Pitezel, for whose death I am now to be hanged. I have never committed murder. That is all I have to say."

I couldn't understand why a man who had just admitted to murdering twenty-seven human beings in his memoirs would at the last moment change the story and only admit to killing two and none by murder. The press said this obvious fabrication was just another of Holmes' lies. I rather doubted so. There was a reason for the alteration, the motive just wasn't explained by the doctor.

Holmes mentioned Vince's time on the platform:

My position allowed me to maintain eye contact with Vince while he stated my last words. I was struck by the clever phenomenon of having orchestrated for another man to act my own last words while I carried on! I held my breath as he repeated his practiced lines, but my concern was unnecessary. He finished them with a marvelous demonstration of obedience precisely repeating the words I previously composed. After he finished, the sheriff pulled him back to shackle his legs, cuffing his hands behind his back. The father next talked with him in a slight tone that was indiscernible to all others. The prisoner shook his head, twice, and then hung it low, all the way down until his chin was resting on his chest. To the observers, he seemed to be peering directly into the abyss. While watching I became occupied with man's often repeated illusions of grandeur in valuing human life. Was there anything of intrinsic value in Vince's meager existence? Had his life offered anything to the totality of our knowledge, the tree, so to speak? Clearly he provided value to me, but to society as a whole? If so, I was oblivious to whatever that could have been, except to foresee the screams of injustice that would arise were the truth of this day's events ever to be discovered.

Setting all that aside, I watched as the noose was placed round his neck and adjusted in order to cause the accounted for delay upon the drop needed to break the neck. The officer's hands could be seen trembling while placing the noose. Then the hood was replaced over his head. What an abrupt, harsh way to expire, I thought. And they said I was cruel. How this modern civilization of ours so often relishes the sinking of its own teeth into vulnerable flesh, but of course only when suiting a given purpose or obscure rationalization.

During the adjustment of the noose, Holmes was reported by the national press to have said, "Take your time, old man."

While certainly good print, I doubted that these words were actually said, instead being some reporter's invention for drama, as I found the guard making such a remark, under the circumstances, hard to imagine.

At the appointed instant the floor beneath Vince opened into oblivion. He fell, as if a stone, slamming short as the rope reached its limits. His neck jerked over to one side, his legs swinging out, fulcrum-like, kicking violently, seemingly directed at me. Every muscle in his body contorting for what seemed an eternity.

But he didn't die, at least not right away.

Seconds later Vince was still alive, the so-called scientific method having failed, the hangman's talent and reputation for producing instantaneous death greatly exaggerated.

There were a number of written statements and eyewitness newspaper accounts regarding the death and actual handling of the body after the hanging. The official statement of death describes the abnormal amount of time it took for the body to cease movement after falling through the trap door. I fixated on the twisted thought that the substituted man had awoken from his trance and realized where he was-- at the end of that wrong rope. He would have begun fighting with every bit of strength he could muster as the weight of his body caused the rope to dig deeper and deeper into his esophagus and spinal column. Sound would have been impossible, at least sound that could have been understood as a plea of innocence. He was doomed. Because of continued twitches and jerks, twice the warden stopped the detail from cutting down the body. The movements continued on to such an extent he even considered lowering the man to the ground, restringing and then dropping him again.

Holmes' observations were more pointed:

Vince's condition of shock ensured he spent little time in pain. I was relieved to see this, not out of any sympathy for his condition, but rather because I was concerned he might call out to his mother or scream some other unexplainable thing, thereby canceling all my good efforts. None came forth. Two doctors checked for pulse and detecting something, decided to leave the body hanging from the rope for another quarter of an hour. Those fifteen minutes were most curious as the onlookers were allowed to march by the still twitching corpse, and proceeded to make many ribald and inappropriate comments about me. The most objectionable, along with the perpetrators face, I stored away for later use.

After some time the finally deceased's movement stopped and the attendants lowered the body to the floor. They placed the body into the temporary wooden coffin and delivered the box and contents to the professional processors Holmes had hired.

The body was lowered and the rope removed. The doctors next removed the hood to reveal the spectacle I had anticipated. At this, I had little to be concerned with. At the time of a hanging the human face nearly explodes from the instantaneous pressure the procedure creates. Afterwards there is little if any resemblance to a former self. I doubt his own wife would have recognized him in this condition.

The two Pinkerton detectives monitored the entire process ensuring that Holmes' orders were followed. The wagon was standing by. Mules, instead of horses, were needed to transport the unusually heavy cargo.

I moved back so as to not gather undo attention while doing my best to maintain appearances as the prison guard who had grown attached to the prisoner. The body was stretched out in an unpainted pine box. I tried to follow, but the crowd was too thick, too anxious, quite frankly, too violent, for their own up-close glance at evil. The superintendent called out to me from across the platform for me to assist with the cleaning detail, but I mumbled an excuse about sickness and insomnia, begging off any further duties. He sympathetically concurred and dismissed me for the day. When out of his sight I hurried to catch up with the procession.

In the wagon the mortician had already mixed the mortar and five barrels of cement needed to cover a quarter of the bottom of the larger permanent coffin. He had given the mixture sufficient time to partially harden so that the body would be suspended on top of a still softening layer of concrete. The body was then placed on top of that perfectly mixed concrete final resting place. Once the burlap encased body was transferred into the coffin, he poured the remaining three quarters of concrete over the remains, almost a ton, making it, once hard, near impossible for anyone to determine the true identity of the bones within, at least without extensive labor, and a century later, modern heavy equipment.

Hundreds of people lined up at the grave to witness the final placement. Twenty-five strong men on the end of lines connected to the coffin were required in order to move 'Holmes' from the wagon and lower him into the grave itself. Unlike at the prison, there was the utmost respect for the deceased, with none of the earlier catcalls.

After the coffin was placed into the ground, the double-sized hole was filled with an unheard of amount of concrete, surrounding and sealing shut.

The two detectives stood watch over the fresh grave the rest of the day and entire night. Holmes knew this watch was necessary in order to give the mixture time to harden. That night, Holmes himself visited the gravesite twice to assure himself of complete compliance. The second time, the detectives pulled a pistol and directed the strange man to stand down and exit the gravesite, or suffer grave consequences, unaware that the man was H. H. Holmes himself. He was quite pleased at this.

I tested them by approaching the site, closely monitoring their detective skills at such a late hour. Their reaction was exactly what I would have expected from such a fine organization, even to the extent of monitoring the actions of others outside the basic sphere of concern for which they were hired. Had they not followed my orders to the letter, I would have remedied their breach of contract in my own special way.

The following day, Holmes burned the prison uniform and notified prison supervisors in writing of Vince's intense stomach pains and present inability to perform his future duties. 'Vince' thereafter disappeared. The press, having already moved on, never mentioned his disappearance, which was understandable given the supposed finality of the real spectacle. Neither was Vince ever listed among the possible victims of the "Holmes Curse" that would soon capture the nation's imagination and hold a country spellbound. Instead, the papers were filled for the next three days with extolments of society's improvement following the murderer's execution.

Detective Frank Geyer, who had been instrumental in Holmes' capture, wrote, "Truth, like the sun, submits to be obscured but like the sun, only for a time."

The *Inter Ocean* declared, "A sigh of relief will go up from the whole country with the knowledge that Herman Mudgett, or Henry H. Holmes, man or monster, has been exterminated-- much the same as a plague to humanity would be stamped out."

How wrong they were.

CHAPTER 26

Holmes' death wasn't enough for a nation consumed with the notion of a supernatural evil being. The country had become addicted to the image of a real-life devil. Stories about Holmes continued in the press for weeks after the hanging. Prison officials gave interviews about a general feeling of something having "not been right" about the execution. The public's attention began to focus on the threats that Holmes had made before he was hung.

The media began reporting strange, awful experiences occurring to people who were associated with the arrest, incarceration and trial. Despite the obvious, they avoided connecting the dots-- after all, Holmes was dead and the country was far too sophisticated to believe in impossible to substantiate supernatural events. Yet one by one, relevant lawyers, jury members, witnesses and others began falling victim to what the press soon began referring to as the "Holmes Curse."

This portion of the Holmes legend was the hardest to comprehend. Most of the books written about the killer did what I assumed was their best detailing the curse and the many who suffered terrible fates supposedly because of this unexplained energy. Many explained it away as another strange coincidence, but in the same breath acknowledged that the sheer numbers involved were hard to swallow when coupled with explanations of numerical probabilities and chance within natural occurrence. There were too many to accept such a natural explanation; ten, twenty, even thirty times too many. Despite that, none took the next logical step and questioned the actual execution, choosing instead to wink and nod at years of spurious supernatural explanations.

None, that is, except for those visited by Holmes after this alleged execution.

One of the first to experience the 'curse' was the priest who attended to Holmes at the hanging. He was found beaten to a pulp, the obvious victim of a painful death. His face and head were covered in horrible wounds. Speculation was he'd been tortured for hours before expiring.

The next victim was the supervisor for Fidelity Mutual Life Insurance Company, O. Linford Perry, who played an essential role in the detection and eventual arrest of Holmes. The man was burned to death while restrained at his desk in his office. The entire office was consumed in flames. Everything, well, almost everything, was destroyed in the inferno. When investigators from the fire department walked through the ruins, attempting to determine the cause of the fire, they found, undamaged, the warrant for the arrest of Holmes and two wood framed cabinet photographs of the killer. These three items alone survived the intense heat of the blaze. The press, perhaps for the first time acknowledging a Curse, ran with this story for weeks.

Articles soon emerged about the dead Holmes' ability to draw upon metaphysical links. The once sceptics claiming his spirit could sap life energies from his victims at their moment of death. His hypnotic influence was even said to have possibly transcended his death and continued to act on those associated with his conviction and hanging. Most wrote these threats off as silly nonsense more appropriate for a comic strip or occult museum than the front pages of the nation's leading newspapers.

Throughout this all, reading everything he could get his hands on, Holmes thoroughly enjoyed the macabre speculation.

I loved the thought that I continued to live on in the public mind as a supernatural creature, periodically rising from my grave to wreak vengeance on those unwise enough to have applied their best efforts against me. The coroner, the attending physician, the prison superintendent, they all fell victim to the curse. The superintendent was perhaps the most interesting to watch die, for in his case I allowed suicide, while I stood back and directed. Prior to his making the decision of his life, I made him kneel down upon the floor while I rocked away in a chair, not three feet from him. Being a good catholic, he knew the horrific penalty he was going to face for taking his own life-- a penalty his Lord would impose no matter what the cause or reason for his choice.

As I again explained his options, the other being hours of my best torture followed by a terrible expiration, the man's mental distortions were amazing to observe, encompassing what I can only imagine to have been the doubts all men possess about the actual truth of religion. Ultimately, he sided with doubt and the elimination of pain, taking his own life, the whole time begging for forgiveness until the very end. His mysterious demise was ably surmised about and reported by the papers.

Holmes' visit to his 'old' judge was the most incredible to learn of.

His Honor, the judge met with my thirst for retribution next. We met late one night in the corner of his den with two logs on the fire. His wife and children had already retired for the night. The judge had been so engrossed reviewing the next day's case docket he failed to notice my entry and pleasure utilizing his wife's oak knitting chair.

"You're up late for a work night," I murmured, of course startling him.

Understandably, he took quite some time gathering his senses. In shock, he shifted closer in his chair as if to confirm what his senses were telling him. Watching him now, so vulnerable, he seemed so different, looking up at me, instead of down from his high bench in the courtroom. How the tables were now turned.

Finally able to talk, he caught his breath and exclaimed, "You!"

"You may close your mouth now, Your Honor. Who were you expecting, the jury foreman or perhaps the district attorney? If you were, let me assure you, they will not be attending tonight's proceedings."

"Are you real, or a figment of my imagination?" the judge asked, his fingers nervously strumming the pages of his brief.

"Come, come your Honor, for a man whose reputation was built upon logic, you seem strangely unable to assess the present situation. Perhaps if I

were to inform you, logically speaking that is, that your life were at stake, would your mind clear sufficiently enabling you to come to a conclusion?"

I owned every second of the time left allotted to him, just as he had previously mine.

"Holmes, while I have no idea how you have managed to do this impossible thing, I've little choice but to accept that you are real, and as unacceptable as this travesty is, I am now at your service. So... what it is you want?"

"What do I want? Why, I want to continue our arguments you so rudely ceased midway through the trial, of course. You do remember, don't you? The heated ones about circumstantial evidence, unbiased impartial juries, and reasonable doubt. You do remember don't you?"

"I must admit, that under the circumstances, I am having some difficulty functioning logically."

"While you recollect, let me begin by stating that from this moment onward you shall refer to me as 'Your Honor.' As for your title at these proceedings, I will refer to you as 'prisoner,' as you did me at my trial."

Holmes continued enjoying the obvious effect: "I have always considered 'prisoner' rather unfair in a country that prides itself upon 'innocent until proven guilty.' The word 'prisoner' raises all types of inaccurate characterizations in the mind of a jury about the man before them struggling for his life. Well, in any event, let us proceed."

The judge remained silent.

"In this, my courtroom, give me your best arguments. Keep them quiet, albeit powerful, as the consequences of awakening your family with an overly passionate legal argument are dire indeed. You may stand if you wish, but remain behind your desk and an appropriate distance from the door... your own prisoner's dock so to speak."

Reaching forward, I tapped his desk with my 'gavel'; a favorite stiletto.

"The basic issue before us is your life. Therefore, and under control, convince me, by artfully continuing our earlier arguments, that I should let you live. Begin."

"Holmes, this is ridiculous and I…"

"Order in my court! Prisoner, I will call the bailiff if you fail once more to address me properly. Now then, fully understanding the nuances involved, let me help you begin… I was thinking your arguments should be made with full regard to your Constitutional Bill of Rights. The Fourth Amendment, if I recall correctly, was the one you and I rather succinctly addressed. The same personal guarantees you, let me see if I can recall your exact words, oh yes! 'Holmes, your notoriety makes my application of the Fourth Amendment difficult.' Now without further delay, proceed!"

Those words apparently refreshed his memory for he jumped up saying, "But my words were true! Those guarantees were next too impossible to provide under the circumstances."*

"Ah, excellent rebuttal, but I believe guarantee is the word the founders selected, not 'best efforts under the circumstances.' You should have found other circumstances that enabled the proper application, no matter how terrible the suspect, including releasing me. Agreed?"

Imagining them both, I envisioned the judge struggling in the face of Holmes' thoughtful argument. I saw him slumped down in his desk chair, his mental wheels turning in slow recognition of obvious defeat. He knew he was guilty as charged.

"Holmes, ah excuse me, Your Honor, you are correct of course, except for one small matter. You did kill the victims you were charged with murdering and justice was served."

At this, Holmes would have rocked back and burst out in laughter, only to quickly catch myself, realizing what he would have to do if his outbursts were to wake his host's family upstairs.

"But of course I was guilty as charged, and where is the relevance in that fact, prisoner? We are considering the application of the law."

Silence descended over the office the same way it had the courtroom. Finally the judge responded, *"Sadly, there is none."* Realizing his wrong, he hung his no longer regal head. *"The matter should have been dismissed, suspended or remanded."*

"Exactly. Case closed."

He sat still, patiently awaiting my sentence for his legal error, now crime. For some reason that night death seemed less than appropriate for me to ensure the most retribution, as well as enjoyment for the rest of my long life. Power was what I was seeking, but the means was difficult to ascertain. How I could turn his honest recognition of error into my ability to control system logistics? Him being a judge, I asked him what remedy he would choose as I was considering some form of parole. He raised the possibility of me allowing him to right his wrong by establishing his court as one that would never again compromise individual rights. That was fine, I replied, but how would I maintain my privacy if he were allowed to live? His reply was quite startling. He promised obedience, which I considered, but told him I needed more than his word, so there that night, after deciding to allow him to live, I spent an hour or two educating him what would be in store for him should he breach our signed in blood contract. His taste for my brand of justice was evidently quite effective, for I was never required to visit either him or his family again.

My research established that the same judge that presided over Holmes' trial went on to indeed become one the hardiest champions of constitutional guarantees in the entire system. The rest of his career was dedicated to righting legal wrongs.

The research was revealing the 'coincidences' continued to mount.

The period that followed was one of the most enjoyable of my entire life. I visited the lead Detective, three of the witnesses who testified against me including the forensic specialist, one of the two fathers, one of the lawyers who deserted me and my favorite of them all… the jury foreman. He I saved for last so as to leave me with the most fulfilling sense of revenge. He deserved every single second of the misery I bestowed upon him. To him my life had been worth less than an hour of jury deliberation. Evidently, he had other more important things to do. His end, in terms of sheer agony, lasted much longer. In fact he lived for two and a half days, every minute of which was accounted for in pain. If I may say so myself, the actual implementation of my revenge turned out to be sheer genius. He was slowly executed by electrocution, perhaps the first ever.

Forced to admit there was more, the press began attempting to correlate the various incidents with the growing legend of the curse. One paper going so far as to state, "an influence malignant in the extreme and which not only pervades the very atmosphere about him, but, so it would seem, has actually the telepathic property of transmission." I was never quite sure exactly what they meant by that. But what I was sure of was they never took the logical step, as not one of the major media outlets that covered the numerous tragedies further investigated the possible real cause. None thought to exhume his grave proving identity. They might have been afraid too, for it seems two of the reporters that covered Holmes' time in prison also met with untimely and horrible deaths.

Holmes dead was more terrifying than Mudgett had been alive. As the murderous ghost, he lived on now in the minds of the American people as an eerie "creature of supernatural evil."

The diary went silent for almost a decade after Holmes cleaned up his trial and prison 'loose ends', as he liked to refer to them as. The next entry was from 1905, when he again returned to the United States from a trip to Berlin, Austria and Paris. Immediately upon departing the ship, he set off for the West Coast where he settled in San Francisco, purchasing a large house near the top of Nob Hill.

Just in time for chaos, unaccountable death and his favorite... anarchy.

CHAPTER 27

A t thirty-thousand feet, the steady drone of the jet's two big engines provided the first peace of mind I'd experienced since opening the boxes. *Not even he can follow me up here.* At least I hoped not.

Looking left, then right, I pondered if the passengers on either side of me had any idea what they were sitting next to. And what they would do if they did. As if to answer me, the middle-aged businessman to my right turned to me, caught my eye and nodded as if he understood... and approved.

God, I hope he doesn't say something that piques Herman's interest.

Thankfully, the man didn't say a word, just politely turned away. Relieved, I settled down into my chair letting him be my last concern before drifting away to enjoy the first sleep I'd enjoyed in a long while, the first one not tortured by him anyway.

At touchdown and for the first time in my life, I found myself wishing the flight were longer. Instead *it* returned with a vengeance, making every breath a struggle. *He* was demanding *his* own share of the oxygen. *We* were becoming one. He was also excited about returning to Chicago.

Home sweet home at last! I've waited far too long for this, Jeffrey. Thinking back, I should have insisted on Chicago from the first.

The thought had crossed my mind that my earlier actions were the result of my own volition-- apparently not.

Your own conscious decisions, Jeffrey, how could you be so foolish? I was there, right behind you, every step of the way. However, I will admit this visit was the most important. A man should always know where he comes from, so to speak.

"Let me be, asshole," I said out-loud, not caring if the people walking next to me through the terminal heard me. "I've given you everything you've insisted on. Tomorrow I'll walk through your doors and straight into hell, if for no other reason than to end your torture."

He was right of course. Truth be known, I was scared to death to visit the very site where so many of his atrocities were committed. The place he invented from the ground up to facilitate the production of terror. The place where God allowed evil to run amok. The place which wasn't of this world.

The know-it-alls had given the place a multitude of titles: Murder Castle, Murder Inc., The Factory, etc. While some came close to capturing the essence of what the place actually was, most of the names failed to accurately describe the horror, instead resembling an author's marketing ploy, or a studio's glossy trailer.

I rather liked the name Castle myself. The title fit. "Castle" was often repeated by the folk on the street. I used to peer down at them, lonely on their way home from work, calling out to those I was familiar with, asking them about their family's health and happiness. I often practiced medicine from that window, rather enjoying how all would stop, look up and smile at their good fortune for having such a giving physician in the neighborhood. My dream come true. The only things the Castle lacked was a real moat and drawbridge to keep out law enforcement.

No one knew, or probably ever would, how many beautiful young women met their fate deep within the Castle, in the dungeon, screaming in agony, tortured for hours, the subjects of the doctor's experiments. None could imagine the number of bereaved young ladies who took his hand and descended, believing that the sympathetic doctor possessed their last chance at regaining their normal lives and rectifying the innocent mistake they made. After all, he was the one, the good one they said, willing to perform abortions. He had been recommended by the ones they trusted. Being between the worst kind of rock and hard place, they would risk everything in taking his advice, placing themselves in his hands with no chance of outside assistance or rescue. How he must have enjoyed their trust after giving them the assurances only he could provide. Almost as much as he relished that first look of terror once they realized their ultimate mistake. Yes, the Castle provided the means for the doctor to fulfil all of his wildest expectations.

Despite the fact the Castle was long ago torn to the ground and replaced by, of all things, a United States Post Office, nothing, not even sixty years or more of government service, could erase the bloodstains splashed upon the walls while H. H. Holmes worked as owner and caretaker of the building. Evil still lived there.

Cursed by his words, I realized my trip to the Castle would delve into much more than brick and plaster. My visit to the Castle hung on the very questions that had haunted man from the beginnings of time. What happened to the tortured souls, the slaves of the devil, after their physical lives ended? How long did souls like these linger in the place where their bodies expired in the worst of ways? And would these deserving souls accept my intrusion with *his* blood amongst them again? Would they hold the genetic grudge I knew I would maintain if I were one of them? If I could find the courage to dare, I knew the Castle might hold the answers to some of these invisible eternal secrets.

Two or three miles from Lake Michigan and south of downtown Chicago, Englewood was the junction of three great railroads. Accordingly, the suburb was originally known as Junction Grove. Beautiful parks, tree lined avenues and museums dotted the landscape. Englewood was, in all respects, "up and coming," providing its citizens a fashionable growing environment.

The place overflowed with society! I was convinced that Englewood was to be mine the first time I spied its obvious potential, not to mention those innocents milling about completely oblivious to anything but the flowers and spring air. This was where life, in all its vitality, would be found.

Holmes moved right in. He obtained employment working at the sole pharmacy in the district. Shortly thereafter he took over for the proprietor who, mysteriously, grew quite ill. Before the man developed this precipitous illness Holmes acted as his physician.

After the man's death, Holmes 'borrowed' funds from his widow to purchase both the pharmacy and the vacant lot adjacent to the property. He had known the couple for only one or two years before he received the generous gift. Subsequently, the widow mysteriously disappeared, but not before amending her last will and testament to the Doctor's benefit.

The lot was perfect for what Holmes envisioned. Centered in the business district, it was located within a stone's throw from the Englewood stop of the Chicago rail line. Prior to purchasing the site Holmes learned of the future location for the upcoming World's Fair grounds. The stop for the Fair would be the Englewood station, within easy walking distance from his corner. He was informed the daily traffic through Englewood would number in the thousands for the two years the fair would be in operation... continuing even when the Fair stopped formal operations, for city officials had announced that the exhibits would remain open after the fair officially closed. Offering lodging to travel weary tourists eager to start the next day fresh and vibrant, ready to take in the many fascinations the fair would offer, was just what the doctor ordered and what he needed to produce the specimens his experiments required.

The young women who stepped off the trains would be strangers to the area. Perfectly suited for his wanton needs. They would be without family to provide care or even concern once they disappeared having fallen into Holmes' lair. If he was careful, no one would know their last whereabouts, no one would be able to point a finger at Holmes, and no one would be able to tear apart any of his carefully crafted alibis, leaving him free to carry on for years. The entire picture presented the sense of perfection that Holmes had dreamed of his entire life, causing him to decide right then and there that he would build his masterpiece from the bottom up. With sufficient funds on hand, he would be ready and waiting for them all! Planning his behemoth's function, he knew secrecy and disposal of waste were his two most critical issues. The Castle's architecture would concentrate on the elimination of forensic evidence enabling Holmes to escape detection and arrest. Knowing what was required, he began making plans to build his new murder factory at once.

Holmes promised himself that his Castle would be finished come 1893, just in time for the entire world to visit Chicago. The politicians were estimating the opening day crowds at over 500,000 people, perhaps the most heavily attended entertainment spectacle in the history of the world, further speculating at least half of them would be requiring lodging.

His rooms would be waiting, as would be the basement.

Today, Englewood couldn't be more different. Known locally as the 'Hood,' the neighborhood is an impoverished place infamous for drug abuse and violent crimes. Caucasians and Latinos are not seen on its streets. The police, afraid to be caught in the constant gang crossfire, leave their cars to buy cigarettes wearing full swat gear. Life in Englewood is every bit as dangerous as life on the streets of current day Mosul.

That morning, after meeting Kim the night before at Midway Airport, I asked the hotel concierge to hail us a cab for the trip to the post office. I'll never forget the man's reaction and we would come to find out for good reason. He had grown up in Englewood and spent the rest of his life getting out.

"What? The Hood, are you freaking nuts?" he said, before realizing where he was, who we were and what his job required. Quickly gathering himself. "Excuse me gentlemen, did I hear you correctly? You wish to proceed to Englewood? May I ask whether you are reporters covering another gang shooting?"

Even after having gained our assurances that we knew where it was we wanted to go, he remained hesitant to opening the first cab's door when the big yellow pulled up. He was that concerned for the safety of the hotel's customers. Finally, at our insistence, still shaking his head in disbelief, he opened the door and talked to the cabbie.

"Take these gentlemen to Englewood... 63rd and Wallace."

The first driver shook his head no, and without the slightest hesitation drove off, the car door swinging back and forth as he sped away.

Three tries later, the concierge finally obtained the services of a driver willing to take us. Brave as he was, even that driver refused our request, with a C-note to boot, to remain waiting at the curb while we toured the federal building. We decided to take our chances on finding a ride out after anyway and so took him up.

Kim loaded the sophisticated film equipment he'd borrowed from friends in Hollywood into the trunk, hoping to capture any extraordinary moments we might experience tracking Holmes down. I knew better than to doubt him. In the past I'd watched Kim record fabulous shots before having to change hats in order to extricate us from some rather dicey situations. I was glad he was along for the ride.

On the way there, we laughed the concierge's antics off, in that wide-eyed, false bravado expected of old male friends. After all, what could two hours in a suburb of Chicago, in broad daylight for crying out loud, threaten that we hadn't already seen somewhere else? We knew how local legends often turned out to be more barroom talk than actual tough. And what the hell could possibly happen inside a federal building, a United States Post Office too boot?

As we'd expected, and for most of the ride, Chicago was delightful. We traveled south along the lake, its bordering parks, Soldier Field and portions of the original World's Fair grounds. Today areas of the grounds are much the same way as they were in 1893. Closing my eyes, it was easy to visualize the millions of people who walked the grass that surrounded the collection of Greek columns and statues. Trying to stay focused, I reminded myself that Holmes had walked these same grounds, searching for that and those he treasured most.

Coming closer we both grew quieter as the surroundings changed. Kim hid his trepidation by meticulously and repeatedly preparing his film equipment, but despite his efforts there was no doubt - this place *was* different. Out the side windows of the cab, we noticed the housing becoming dilapidated, roads less cared for and the faces of the citizens more distinct, with that thousand mile stare so prevalent in atmospheres ruled by fear and raw power. Drawing attention to oneself was dangerous here, so the denizens did their best to fade away into obscurity. No one wanted to take the chance that a glance or inadvertent smile might attract the wrong kind of attention. No one dared look back, or, heaven forbid, stare.

At last there, we stepped out, unloaded, paid our fare and watched the cabbie speed off without one word in response to our continued attempts to convince him to wait. He was just gone. Standing out in broad daylight, my white skin began to feel like a neon sign advertising amusement park rides to young adults. Kim's proximity to my crime, for that's exactly what my being here was, made him just as much a target, maybe more so, for he was considered a traitor. Not one resident, in their "rides", passed without noticing me and staring down Kim. The initial response was shock, then disbelief, then downright anger. Isolated and all alone, we had no choice but to continue on with our original plans.

The Post Office was a large white rectangular building, with an architecture which seemed to scream out a pre-1940s construction. Outside, the post office was clean and well kept, but we couldn't help noticing that all the windows were barred. Multiple cameras pointed down from the roof to each place of possible entry, giving the building the look of a bank inside a war zone.

Trying to look cool, Kim walked up the front stairs to the entrance of the post office, loaded down with his equipment and turned back to me to rather nonchalantly ask, "What was all that garbage about? Looks fine to me, you sure we're in the right place?"

"I don't know, I'm not picking up anything strange, either."

Kim was right: there was nothing on the outside to suggest anything sinister had taken place deep inside these grounds. Images of murder and torture were washed away by the order and cleanliness that was the very essence of this building, leaving me wondering if perhaps all the talk and books were nothing but exaggerated lore, spun higher and higher with the passing of time.

At the front of the building there was a bronze plaque commemorating the construction of the post office under the New Deal and President Roosevelt. One of the braver Holmes authors had mentioned the same plaque. He had also questioned why anyone in our federal government would have knowingly selected this tainted ground to build the post office, when so many other, 'cleaner' places, were available close by.

"Kim, Check this out. Says right here and in bronze that this *is* the place."

Holmes had written about his having spent nights in the Lincoln Bedroom of the White House during the Depression. I couldn't help imagining his possible nighttime cocktails with FDR, discussing the President's handicap, the one he hid from the American people, and what Holmes could do to help the man walk again. What a fireside chat that would have been - the President's real deal with the devil! Now here we were in front of these two men's common post office, the same one the President had contemporaneously ordered built over the site of the Castle subsequent to those alleged meetings. In my bones I knew Holmes had been involved in that decision and the construction of this place was somehow connected with his secret medical advice and help.

Backing up, as Presidential politics and skullduggery was far too deep for me right then, I regained my immediate bearings, and just in time before the main event. I yelled ahead and up at Kim, "Let's walk around the perimeter before we go inside."

But the strange waves washing over me wouldn't stop. Looking across the street I was shocked to see a fully functional pharmacy. The business was contemporary, perhaps thirty-some years old and open for business. From the street signs on the immediate corner, I was convinced this pharmacy was in the same location as the one Holmes first operated here in Englewood, the one he stole from the widow of the man he murdered.

Would the coincidences never cease?

While I reminisced, Kim was working angles for the best shots, and not paying close attention, so I took it upon myself to warn him about the mail truck pulling up beside him. The carrier was a slightly overweight middle-aged woman who was immediately willing to chat. Seems chatting wasn't something Englewood was famous for.

"What you guys doing? You've been told about keeping an eye peeled around here, haven't you?"

"Yes, ma'am... but thanks for reminding us," Kim said drawing the woman into several minutes of small talk, putting her at ease, before finally coming to the point of our visit. "Have you ever seen or heard anything strange, you know... Twilight Zone stuff, X-Files things, around here?" he asked. "By here, I mean the post office, particularly inside and down in the basement."

She sat in the open-sided mail truck, sorting as she listened. Kim was leaning against the mail bin, his foot on the first step of the truck—they were friends already. I stayed back, out of the way, doing my best to fit in and failing miserably.

"No, can't say that I have. Not even once in all the time I've worked here. Eleven years last Tuesday."

Disappointed, we bid farewell and let her carry on with her duties. We circled the rather plain grounds of the building once, then twice, and finding nothing of interest, headed for the entrance, both beginning to feel somewhat cheated. What we once thought might be another hair-raising exploit was instead becoming a rather tame site inspection of an outdated post office.

Kim entered first, going through the big doors that swung effortlessly open, more evidence of the care applied here. I was right behind him, by now suspecting nothing. My lack of respect for the surroundings changed the instant I crossed the threshold to the building.

Right then and there, as if I'd crossed some kind of distinct line, I could sense that *he* was upset with my lack of respect.

It's hard to describe what happened next. Kim was ahead of me, already inside, immune to anything unusual. I was only three or four feet behind him. As I crossed the threshold, the air around me splashed in visible waves emanating from my center, spreading all the way across the room, exactly as if I jumped into the glass calm of an empty swimming pool and sent ripples all the way across to every corner. I'd never seen anything even remotely resembling this phenomena in my entire life. The waves went right through Kim, who, continuing with his set-up, appeared oblivious to them. He would later admit that goosebumps had risen over his entire body at that same instant.

Watching the waves, my body was pounded by an incredible force. As if I'd been struck across the chest with a two by four, the blow causing me to stagger and fall back a few steps. Fighting for air, no, not air, but life, I could feel the color draining from my face as my chest seemed to cave under the pressure. Taking a breath was impossible. Wheezing, my hands searched for support along the countertop, the same one used by customers eager to lick stamps for Christmas packages.

Great-great-grandpa had just reached out and touched me. *It was here, and he had just welcomed me home.*

Holding on to the counter with all my might, I remembered what he wrote about first time visitors. *I could often tell their potential by that first expression when they entered through the doors into my world. Some feeling the energy of that first strike, instantly comprehend what awaited them, but like the moth were unable to resist the flame. In that instant, I immediately knew if they would present the slightest problem should my later plans include them.* Holmes had accurately assessed my situation at that precise instant.

My weakness must have amused the voice as he felt me struggle to breathe, his laughter echoing about within my skull.

"Bud, are you okay?" Kim asked, shaking me by the shoulder.

I couldn't move, not even enough to answer him.

"You don't look so good. Go sit down over there by the door. Get some air," he suggested, giving me the space and privacy he knew I needed to gather myself.

An employee rushed over with water, helping me take another of the anti-seizure pills the neurologist recommended for times just like this.

Giving the dose time to work, I closed my eyes-- another huge mistake. Almost immediately, the original Murder Castle front doors, having somehow come back from the 1890s; the shimmering black and white tiled floors, spotless glass counters and ceiling-high shelves overflowing with drugs, emerged just the way they must have looked over a century ago. And there, behind it all, debonair and smiling, in full doctor's smock, stood Holmes, welcoming all new guests to his place of business.

And all that time, hell on earth was right below their and my feet.

"Jeffrey, are you beginning to feel at home?"

The thought that he might still be here, as ridiculous as that concept was, worked through my tortured psyche as I began regaining enough oxygen to function again. The voices were one thing, and all perfectly explainable in some neurological sort of way, but what I had just seen and felt was another. How could I argue with myself but that I'd just been given Herman's own personal touch?

I considered grabbing Kim by the lapels, dragging him back out those doors and getting the hell out of there as fast as we could. But I knew too many people's lives might depend upon the courage I needed to challenge the monster, so instead of running, as so many before me had, I hammered away at myself to regain control.

Feeling my buddy's hand on my shoulder, I opened my eyes and took a long deep breath. "Thanks. What do you think? Did you get any of that on… did you get any good footage?" I asked almost twice, trying to get back on track.

"Run of the mill. Nothing out of the ordinary, although, to tell you the truth, I felt something when we walked in, too. Don't know what it was, or if I can put a finger on it, but we'll have to check the machine later, there might be something on the video. The trigger was down on the camera the entire time."

He patted me on the back again, smiled and headed off to talk to the first employee he could find. As Kim worked away, chatting with the employees, I could see them shying away from all talk regarding the "building before." But Kim kept at them, not about to give up before he had what we needed: permission to inspect the basement.

The counter clerk told Kim that the boss was gone for the day and that getting permission to enter the basement without his okay would be impossible. She did tell us that the assistant super would be glad to talk to us, though. While we were waiting for her to come down from her office, the clerk whispered, "Every once in a while, I see things... out of the corner of my eye... things moving like shadows... but when I look up, they're gone."

Kim and I exchanged glances.

"Has anyone ever tried filming those things?" Kim asked her.

"Yeah, about two years ago there was a small film crew. They spent two nights in the basement even though they'd been given permission for three." She pointed to some doors across the huge expanse that I guessed led to the basement. "None of them would go back down that last night. They never showed us, or anyone, the movie."

She added that none of the permanent employees, except Terrance the custodian, ever set foot in the basement, despite all their fascinations with what might exist below their feet.

"Can you introduce us to him?" Kim inquired.

"Sure, let me go see if I can find him," she replied, and off she went.

Kim turned to me, "You doing better?"

"Yeah, actually I'm feeling pretty good, almost like whatever happened cleaned me out. I'm ready to go."

"Good. I need you tough."

After good naturedly telling him to get out of my face, another clerk came over, close, and whispered about the things she had heard, gossiped over, seen and even felt while working. But she was afraid to tell us more; they had all been instructed not to discuss the basement with the press which she assumed we were.

Before we could talk her into more, she saw the custodian coming down from the boss's office and hurried off.

He wasted no time at all, "Hey, I'm Terrance. I hear you guys are asking questions about the goings on in the basement?"

After twenty minutes of back of forth, he finally told us the assistant super was refusing to come out into the lobby after hearing the purpose of our visit and was ordering her employees to cease all communication about Holmes. She had told him to tell us we were free to tour the public sections of the building. But that was all.

Knowing we needed to back down a little, we stopped pushing, instead circling the lobby to let things settle down. Changing tact's, we 'set' up imaginary shooting platforms for when the film crews arrived to film the documentary. Given enough time and attitude, this tactic never failed-- everybody wants to be on film.

Surprisingly, the building was equipped with an extraordinary amount of surveillance equipment - as if Englewood would be on any terrorist's list. Something had happened here, something substantial enough to cause a person with influence to write a pretty big check to determine the why. Some areas were even equipped redundantly in case the primary gear failed. We would soon learn that these devices were all trained at the door leading to the staircase down to the basement below, the location of the majority of the unexplained detections the building had a history of.

According to Terrance, the companies that provided and installed the surveillance equipment were routinely called back to recalibrate to compensate for what was assumed to be numerous false alarms. Federal law required that each detection be investigated and explained. Time after time, rats, tremors, even flooding were used as explanations for the alarms, but instead of eliminating the problem, the alarms continued unabated and unexplained. The decision was finally made to turn all the downstairs detectors off so that work could be done upstairs. The basement was also ordered off-limits to anyone other than essential personnel.

My basement was the closest thing to home that I'd ever owned. There were times when I spent days down in the dark repeating failed experiments, sleeping on the cot I'd ordered installed. No one was allowed down unless they were needed. The bell next to the basement chute could be heard on the second floor and alerted my assistants when I needed food, water or material.

Before the alarms were silenced they'd been the source of gallows humor amongst the employees; that is except for the man who was required by regulation to go down into the basement to check each alarm. For that, only one man was qualified and also willing-- Terrance. He was also the longest serving employee at the office and had helped install the alarms in the basement as well as their elimination over two years ago. Terrance hadn't descended the stairs since.

We made note to request the records and dates associated with each alarm by F. O. I. A. There was no telling what this information might provide someone with an open mind about the nature of the detections.

***

Holmes began drawing plans for his castle a full year before construction began. He stayed at it modifying away until his masterpiece was finished. The design was a carefully crafted series of interlocking components, and not the haphazard mass of puzzles and dead ends the press and police would later describe the destroyed building to be. In fact, the Castle was a finely tuned machine for producing the hormones he needed to further his experiments, skeletons for sale, not to mention a life insurance proceeds conglomerate. The pharmacy business provided the essential smoke screen, also serving to make the necessary chemical deliveries less suspicious.

My design allowed for the clean consumption of twenty to thirty tons of waste per annum. When operating at full capacity there was no odor or residue that would reveal the building's true nature. AS further camouflage, forty percent of the design was dedicated to buttressing the cover stories involving the glass factory and drug design corporation.

He envisioned the building being known as the "hotel on the corner," with pharmacy and other assorted places of businesses on the first floor, lodgings on the second, and private accommodations on the third. The basement was ostensibly for his publicized inventions involving glass and chemicals. Holmes began advertising his newly invented anesthesia and wonder vitamins before construction even started.

When Holmes, the architect, was satisfied with the style and functionality of his design, he changed hats to become the general contractor. Doing so, he set out to obtain the best contractors in Illinois to construct their individual pieces of his masterpiece. None were allowed two pieces of the project. None were allowed to review his plans for the finished product, instead only limited to the individual drawings of their portions. In this manner, Holmes maintained the confusion that was necessary to conceal the whole, for he knew too much knowledge would result in suspicion. Any one contractor that stayed too long, or was involved with too much of the project, would endanger the scheme, thus the revolving door of contractors continued to furnish whatever labor and parts he deemed necessary. And so it went for two years.

At the end of a particular contractor's time line, Holmes would create a dispute that would allow him to fire the contractor from the project. The disputes ensured that fired contractors would not visit the site after their work was finished and any discussions with other builders would, by necessity, be centered on the disputes and money involved, and not the overall scheme… or the crazy doctor with the absurd building, the design of which made no sense. This method worked to the doctor's satisfaction with about nine out of ten contractors. Those that the scheme didn't take care of were handled in another fashion: they were done away with.

From my readings, there appears four builders who met with unfortunate accidents at other work sites after finishing their work with Holmes, each having been involved in contract disputes over final payments and having threatened legal proceedings. As far as I could determine, none caused the project to be shut-down or even stalled.

The most difficult components of the project, and also most critical, were those involving the disposal of waste. To accommodate this necessity Holmes designed a configuration that would employ a fireproof box heated by flames from a steam fed oil burner. The inner tomb-like compartment, built to human anatomical specifications was in essence an elongated kiln. Holmes' goal was for the burner to generate temperatures high enough to incinerate nearly anything that was placed inside. It was also important that the kiln's flame be thorough enough to destroy any odors that might emanate from the interior box.

When the kiln was finished, Holmes was pleased with the configuration. Only later did the kiln contractor recognize that the furnace's peculiar shape and extreme heat made what he'd constructed ideal for another completely different application from the one outlined on the plans.

The manager possesses far too much information concerning a critical component of the project. Accordingly, I shall invite him back next month to tour the basement with me alone.

The kiln contractor had indeed asked one too many questions while working on the box. Despite extensive research, I was unable to determine his whereabouts after the meeting Holmes mentioned took place. My guess is that he was done away with by the doctor in the same kiln that had generated their dispute.

The building cost many fortunes to construct. Rumor had it that the doctor expended all his considerable life's savings on the monstrosity. These rumors were indeed true. Capital requirements caused Holmes to intensify his nightly forays in search of the material to produce the funds needed to keep his builders satisfied.

The building began to loom taller and broader over the streets of Chicago. Church-like, the Castle's imposing turrets on its four corners towered above all that walked the rare rock sidewalk below. At first, the new building seemed washed in pure sunlight, a cheerful place that welcomed all. Early passersby strained their necks trying to see the rooftop, as the soon to be finished partial cobblestone street echoed with the sound of passing carriages and hand drawn vendor carts. Many, and fortunate for them, continued on only to fade into the distance, but a good number stopped at the corner to take in the new center of business in

Englewood, or they stopped simply to seek libations at the counter-top bar open for business through the wide and welcoming front doors. When Holmes' place was finished, the building became the joint to socialize, discuss neighborhood news, politics, or just to pass the time of day. And there was always the chance to chat with the personable young doctor who brought so much modern knowledge and a sympathetic ear that every woman in the area grew to love and appreciate. He was always gracious, offering time for everyone and, critically, kept their secrets close at heart.

When the police entered the Castle with a search warrant in the fall of 1895, what they would find would once again fill the nation's front pages for months... and shock the world for decades to come.

There were rooms lined with asbestos, floor to ceiling, in order to retard and contain any fire within, fire controlled by the doctor from the closet in his own stateroom with flammable gas. The asbestos, backed by iron, acting as a giant soundproof oven. Lines filled with sleeping gas ran from the same closet to individual bedrooms that could be sealed air-tight to prevent the smell of gas from escaping into hallways or adjoining rooms.

Hidden openings led to chutes that passed through the floors and emerged onto tables in the basement. The chutes diverged at the bottom, where victims could be directed to either the quick-lime pit or the softer landing spot next to the pit. These avenues were greased so that bodies would slide down by their own weight, the soft landing spot reserved for those victims that Holmes wished to operate on-- alive. Assistants waited at the bottom of the chutes to immediately restrain each arriving victim to a waiting gurney below.

In the basement racks were equipped with metal gears, very, oh so very medieval, for torture and experiment, including the stretching of the human body to determine if evolution could be sidetracked and a new race of giants created.

Unfortunately, her offspring did not demonstrate the increased size I hoped for.

Detention racks were situated in such a way as to allow victims the opportunity to observe the doctors' other operations while awaiting their own ordeal.

How the human brain fascinates me! There is so much to learn, especially what that mind is capable of under the influence of immense pain. Right, wrong, good, evil all disappear the instant the nerves are activated. Millions of years of evolution instantly evaporate and survival, no, that term would be too general, instead the lessening of such pain is foremost on the mind of the subject. Mothers will desert their children and strong men their greatest causes, for torture's pain answers all questions.

***

I walked across the cavernous main floor of the office, trying to imagine what the first floor of the Castle must have looked like before being torn to the ground by the Feds. The textures, sounds and smells that would have forever etched themselves upon the brains of those permitted to walk back out those front doors only to later find out the truth. I was interested in learning the nuances associated with this building while in operation. Those things the many literary pieces had missed describing, possibly because the only ones who had ever known suffered terrible demises. I also wanted to determine what this place that God looked the other way over must have been like to enter: unaware. Only Holmes could help me with this.

Each morning at daybreak I walked the Castle grounds. This was my most anticipated daily ritual. I wanted everything perfect so that first time visitors would feel welcome and safe thereby ensuring the attitudes I needed to foster what I craved. I was also concerned with the state of the surroundings from the last night's operation. Once or twice, my inspection revealed a failure of the system that would have been extremely embarrassing should the authorities have happened by. Most times the system and my assistants worked to perfection. When I was convinced we were ready, I would have my assistant open the front doors for business while I donned appropriate attire to begin another day.

Inside, colored glass, ornate and gathered in incredible design, surrounded the visitor on each wall of the pharmacy. The light, which filtered through the lower windows and wide open doors, seemed to dance in a kaleidoscope of bursting energy.

My studies had shown the change in attitude that colored light created in those exposed to its effects. Foremost was the blending of all edges, creating an eagerness to trust all offers of aid and authority. If done properly, this energy was as in the great cathedrals, and so I set out to make the entrance just that. From the initial facial expressions I would observe over the years as my customers walked through the front doors, my efforts in implementing this aspect were well worth the trouble and expense.

Far ahead of his time, Holmes utilized soothing blended colors to paint, much like todays scientifically designed modern medical offices, the interior of the Murder Castle. Everything blended, and nothing was out of place. Behind the counters were rows and rows of shelves, containing every drug known to man, and some only found here, having been invented in the offices below the alabaster floors at the customers' feet. Or so it was later said by eager reporters having heard of the doctor's horrible exploits.

At the Wallace Street side of the main floor, a spectacular staircase swept away from the apothecary commerce and proceeded past a roll top desk, where the manager of the lodgings worked placing the day's new tenants. A French crystal chandelier rose twenty feet above all heads, lighting the way on the imported hand-woven German carpeting, making transit up the staircase comfortable for all and most importantly, silent for the doctor late at night.

All second floor walls were thick enough to provide space for secret passageways. Some doors opened inward from the main hall, while others opened outward. There were sliding wood panels with hidden brass hinges enabling Holmes or his helpers to remove sections in an emergency. Many of the closets were equipped with an opening at the rear to permit Holmes to either enter or depart from whichever room he desired.

Down the hallway, one to the left and one to the right, two secret hiding places allowed Holmes to slide into and escape detection should he ever need to avoid arrest or the gun of a jealous husband. In those same secret rooms, early day alarm systems, the first of their kind, permitted Holmes to be cognizant of any door being opened in the entire building.

At the very end of the hallway was the mysterious "Darkroom." This room was the one most used by the press as evidence of Holmes' insanity. Once again the danger of assuming Holmes as anything less than genius raises its ugly head. The room was impervious to light, even at high noon. Holmes possessed incredible night vision which allowed him to observe the reactions of those blind inside the room. Holmes believed that all human secrets rose to the surface when faced with the most hideous of fears. The darkroom accomplished that goal best, and often immediately upon entry. I could only imagine the horrors that went on inside.

Built-in bookcases covered two walls of his combined living quarters and office space. His library included most medical, scientific, psychological, even spiritual authorities in the known and unknown world. The majority of his collection were eventually stolen, most quite coincidentally after the police and press first visited the Castle. The others were destroyed by the fire, including the material he often referenced as having been left to him by his grandfather.

The latest business machinery cluttered the two desks that faced each other in his third floor office. A walk-in safe was located directly across from his high backed leather chair. Holmes utilized the safe, among other things, to escape to his basement. To accomplish that feat, the back of the safe opened to a stairway that led to a no-entry intermediate room and then down to the basement, passing a tunnel which led to the alleyway behind the castle. The opening at the alley was hidden by false, made in plaster, garbage disposal units. Hence he could break through the plaster, should circumstances warrant, with his own strength. The perfect avenue of escape.

Then there was the basement, the same one that was the source of so much of the fascination about Holmes.

From my readings what became quickly obvious was that very few, if any, of the authors that wrote of the Castle actually ever ventured down into the basement. None accurately described his workshop in their works. The brick walled real-life dungeon was too cavernous and dark for all but the most courageous. Accordingly, descriptions of its actual makeup were suspect, especially those that claimed to have inspected the Castle before being destroyed.

Reporters described *touching* the brown sooty horrors that lay dormant following the fire 'accidentally' set by the policemen who first inspected the section below, again coincidentally while searching for any clues regarding missing persons after Holmes' arrest. The ones honestly attempting to describe the basement focused on the overpowering smells said to be so strong as to sicken anyone with the audacity to venture further down below. As a matter of fact, there was no smell. Holmes made certain of that from the first day he began operating the factory. Odor would have meant his immediate detection and downfall.

I was forced to punish him today, for yet again he failed miserably at his number one priority. The walls, the platforms and even the floors needed to be clean enough for me to take my dinner from.

Two brick-walled pits under the basement floor were a valuable aspect of his enterprise. These pits were filled with quicklime. This substance was one of the key components of his skeleton business.

The quicklime enabled the skeletons to be ready for shipment within two weeks. Its strength was tested every three days and replenished every thirty. Without quicklime we would have been lost.

Whether conducting experiments below or seducing beauty above, the doctor made sure he always stayed within a few short steps of an escape route. Holmes was invincible in his castle.

I was brought back to the present by Kim informing me that Terrance wanted to talk to us to clarify the many rumors about the post office and basement. He had worked here over twenty years. "There's really nothing down there but painted concrete and some boxes full of trash and unclaimed mail from over ten years ago."

His words had little effect on Kim and I. We weren't expecting much anyway, maybe just a feel or a touch, probably only a sense of something bigger.

"But I'll tell you one thing, the old brick tunnels from the original basement are still down there. The government used them for bomb shelters in the fifties, then compartments for extra water and secondary phone lines in the sixties. They've been empty the last forty years," he said.

Kim watched me, knowing the gears in my head were grinding away over Terrance's astounding off the cuff pronouncement.

The second diary mentioned the tunnels. The southernmost was said to contain a secret compartment, fronted by three loose bricks, which hid a rather sizable space. The three bricks were said to be deep in the tunnel, on the left side and about twelve inches down from the rather short ceiling. One of the bricks was reportedly engraved with "1861"-- the year Holmes was born.

We both knew it made no sense for the Feds to have built this structure around and over the original Holmes' tunnels unless someone had intended the architects and builders to do so - someone with influence.

Kim continued milking the man. Two minutes later the Terrance agreed to try one more time at getting his boss to change her mind.

Within earshot of their ongoing conversation Kim and I went loudly back and forth about how the focus of the film project would be centered on the basement and that we should consider using Terrance in the piece.

Or spin wasn't a complete lie, actual people, studio people, were interested in hearing about what we found - but we were close. Five minutes was all it took.

"She'll let you guys down into the basement, as long as you promise not to touch or disturb anything... personally I wouldn't worry much about that," humorously raising his eyebrows, "She'd never know a damn thing if you had."

Motioning for us to stay close, he unlocked the heavy steel doors protecting the secure area behind the counter. Kim and I barely containing our excitement, at the same time following Terrance's lead, while walking across a large tiled floor before ending up in front of a stack of dusty old boxes, piled haphazardly atop each other in front of a door. High overhead, we both noticed a motion detection device, pointed at the same door, obviously disconnected. The door to the basement looked to be painted over with four or five coats of regulation gray. Spider webs ran this way and that, proof - God's honest truth - no one went down into what my screaming mind was describing an abyss!

After clearing away the boxes we spent several minutes trying to pry open the door. Finally gaining some leverage, he got the beast of a door to give way, its high pitched protest echoing loudly across the entire main floor.

Seconds later you could have heard a pin drop on that same floor, as every one of the employees sorting mail stopped, as if to witness for posterity, our descent into hell. Not one of them made the slightest move to join us, even though it was apparent from the looks on their faces that at one time or another they had all contemplated crossing through this door and descending the stairs at our feet.

He forced the door open just enough, giving us space to squeeze through one at a time. The stairway was narrow and dropped down some twelve feet to the basement floor after midway turning 180 degrees. Worried about slipping and falling, and who wouldn't be, we took one slow step at a time. Looking down past the stairs into the darkness, I was reminded of a cavern. There was only one color, the concrete having been painted the same from top to bottom. What light there was fell in spooky wavering shadows. The only sound you could hear were our footsteps and Kim's camera whirring away.

Terrance led us further and further down until at the bottom we were cloaked in near total darkness. Then suddenly, and without warning he just stopped, Kim and I running into each other having been uninformed of his decision. Without a word of explanation, he turned, retreated a few steps, stopped again, then told us to wait while he went to get some fresh light bulbs.

Kim tried to laugh it all off, down here alone in the dark. His antics not working-- he was scared to death. I, however, and without appreciating why, was cool and calm as a cucumber. The deeper we'd gone the calmer I'd become. There was no doubt about it, I was comfortable down here.

When Terrance returned and installed high wattage fluorescent lights, the stairwell went brilliant allowing us to continue down. Close to the bottom, and once again without the slightest warning, we were struck by a terrible odor. The smell flooded upward, attacking us with a vengeance. It was the same smell that had burst out at me when having first opened my Grandfather's diary. I now knew the smell was somehow associated with evil spirits and violent death.

Kim said, "That smell actually hurts. Is it always like this down here?"

"No. First time ever, I mean it, really. Funny thing is, there's nothing down here capable of causing that stink," Terrance said.

As quickly as it had arisen, the foul odor began dissipating, then disappeared leaving nary a trace.

'Was it some kind of a warning, an indication of things to come?' I wrote down in my notes.

On the main floor, the painted walls' lack of contrast caused the entire place to meld together into some kind of weird film studio black room with no depth of field. Without depth perception, you had to focus on each step to maintain balance.

Kim and Terrance walked off away from me, down the long tunneling hallway that opened into what seemed a huge, borderless open space. They were soon across the basement, some two-hundred feet away.

Just like we'd been told, there were two, big, mostly empty separate rooms. Odd boxes cluttered the corners. In one a discarded Christmas tree stood with a full array of decorations. Looking further down the basement, I could see one of the old brick tunnels at eye level along the wall that bordered 63rd Street. The tunnels red-brick construction and condition made the entire space look old indeed.

Welcome home, my son! He'd given me just enough time to grow accustomed before interrupting. His voice as robust and clear as the sunny Chicago day twenty feet above my head.

He was happy I was finally here.

I turned to see if Kim had heard him. If so, he was doing a damn fine job not showing it.

Watch your friends. I do not want them to interfere. Send one away. You only need the assistance of one for right now. One hundred years of quiet waiting was growing impatient.

"Leave me alone and let me do this my way, old man. Give me time, after all, you've had over a century to get ready."

No one ventures into my laboratory without permission or purpose. The guard must go, but your friend can stay. If you don't get him to leave, he will die. His death will be on you.

My attention was pulled back by Kim's voice yelling from up ahead, "Jeff, I didn't catch what you said, once again?" He'd been keeping a close eye on me since my near seizure at the front doors. "The viewfinder is making you look different, not different the way you were upstairs, but really different. Your face seems out of this world. I can hardly recognize you."

To check, I ran my hand over my face, feeling my cheek, nose and both ears. If there was a change, I couldn't tell. "Don't know what you're talking about; I've never felt better." That part was true, I did feel great.

"Where's Terrance?"

"He was called up on the walkie-talkie. Said he'd be right back,"

Don't fret… he'll be gone long enough for us to proceed and you to collect everything you've come for.

The custodian must have walked right by me. I hadn't noticed him. As a result, Kim and I were alone… just the way Holmes wanted it.

Suddenly, as if activated by the voice, the cold drab painted concrete began coming to life, taking on a renewed vitality that hadn't been here when we first entered. I could feel the life's energy. Our basement was now a pulsing thing, as the old cracked red bricks began morphing into a flesh like liquid.

As my supervised imagination took charge, the reality of the Murder Factory became clear right in front of my eyes. To the left barely thirty feet away was a greased chute, situated so that rolling gurneys could be loaded with specimens to then be offloaded on the waist-high, cold, brass operating tables with drains below each to ease cleaning duties and do away with damaging evidence. After having been dropped, dead or the unluckiest ones - unconscious, each body was strapped in leather wrist and ankle bracelets making later movement and resistance impossible. Each table was equipped with a forehead strap and leather gag to eliminate bothersome noise and screams.

There were gleaming surgical instruments, macabre laboratory torture devices, and even an examination room for those whom Holmes decided to treat, for some hopefully less hideous reason, sympathetically as a real doctor.

A jumble of mechanical noises played throughout, right alongside the visions filling my mind, making my vision an orchestra of pain and torture. Clangs, whistles of steam, splashes from liquid puddles, the "yes, sir", and "no, sir" of subordinates following instructions and the moans and screams of those serving their last as the most horrible victims this earth could have created. The crescendo was rising to such a level that concentration was impossible, the room drowning in horror.

The basement, stretching half a city block, was lit by hanging candles, with a hallway wide and long enough to hold twenty gurneys in a row, with adequate space for the doctor and his assistants to move back and forth as operations required. Above each gurney were shelves stocked with food and water and hanging files for each patient with records of the doctor's musings and impressions. Despite my best efforts at accepting the former, the murderer's canvas before me was both amazing and horrible.

Across the hallway were wooden cabinets that stored the marketable items removed from bodies. Holmes established quite a business in confiscated gold and silver jewelry, to say nothing of stones, with a middleman who delivered the items to city jewelers. While taking the spectacle in I wondered if those businesses had ever wondered about the source of his seemingly never-ending supply, or had instead turned the other cheek as so many associated with 'the good doctor' had in the pursuit of capitalism.

Here was where Holmes experimented with and finalized the anesthesia he wrote about inventing. He hid the suspicious chloroform by patenting cleaning solutions for surfaces and laundry. Ammonia and benzene were just some of the chemicals he dealt with in order to confuse the authorities as to his true purpose. The number of his victims required that he use the most cost effective chemical blend. Holmes had little concern for whether a particular dose turned out to be too weak. Paraphrasing, he would muse, "Their pain was just a fact of death."

He was an expert in the use of corrosive substances and the disintegration of human tissue through chemical interaction, the acid vats being capable of devouring a human body within days. I imagined assistants wearing thick gloves to protect their own flesh while moving to and fro amongst the evil liquids in the performance of their duties.

A powerful incinerator sat at the center of all the activity. The furnace was set at such a tremendous temperature that it constantly hissed and wheezed as if alive, standing ready to take on whatever the chemicals could not handle. The horizontal iron gate-like device, complete with rollers, was used to feed the incinerator with produce. When finished, and cooled off enough to pull back out, nothing but ashes were left, and certainly not a scintilla of evidence.

Overcome by all around me, I sat down on the cold floor and popped another pill. Kim's shadow traversed the room and walls.

The walls that were moments ago all the way across the room were now much closer, almost in my face. When I extended my hand to touch them they retreated and were just as quickly miles away. All perspective was gone. Faces began to emerge from the walls, just faces, nothing below the neck. There was a sea of them all staring directly at me. Their features stretched and pulled and tugged at the concrete as if they were trying to escape from captivity.

They were! Their souls were trying to escape. I was sure of it.

Their complexion was rubbery, but still stony, the very same color as the paint on the walls. The sudden elasticity of the concrete allowed each face to pull away from the wall, pulling at their noses, chins and foreheads; even their eyes were concrete. Their agony was obvious as they tossed and turned, their mouths opening and closing as if either trying to scream or whisper obscene warnings to me.

I could sense their hatred of me, but also their fear. Why were they afraid of me? I didn't have to wait long before he told me.

They are my servants… they were then… they are now… and they will be forever. They can also be yours. They know this.

When they stared at me, I could see from the horrified look on their faces they recognized him, their eternal master back to reclaim still more of anything they had left to give.

These ghosts were somehow still afraid of pain. Was that possible? But this time they were afraid their agony would be delivered with new hands.

I looked over at Kim and observed him narrating into the recording device of his camera. One of the faces pushed out and was mere inches from Kim's visage. She was begging him for help. Unfortunately, or fortunately, depending upon perspective, Kim was oblivious to both her agony and her plea. He kept filming and walked right past her unaware. I walked towards her wanting to help, but as she turned away from Kim, she recognized me and quickly folded right back into the sea of concrete.

These lost souls' prolonged, perhaps eternal, agony was due to their permanent internment within the post office building. I knew it. The construction of this federal building in 1937 had prevented any from ever leaving and perhaps enjoying the eternal salvation they so richly deserved. Instead, locked into the concrete poured directly over the cursed bricks, they were forced to suffer the worst distress imaginable. They would never be allowed to leave, at least not until this building was destroyed and something far less sinister was erected in its place. Perhaps a park I thought or maybe a school.

No, never a school I quickly corrected myself.

Come back to me, Jeffrey. We have much to accomplish in so very little time.

His voice now more controlling than ever before, I fought with my body now instantly obeying his instructions, almost as if my own mind was suddenly irrelevant.

Relax, my son. His address was always "my son" or "Jeffrey" now. I hated this personification, but was powerless stop it.

Take a deep breath and accept your fate. I promise you will enjoy what I have planned for you. Relax and let me prove your destiny.

The vision of the two basements continued to phase in and out, from back then to now and then returning to the cold environment of the uncluttered concrete floors in the busy operating room of a hundred years ago. Each time the channel changed, back from the nothing of now, the floors returned to their slippery shade of red while Holmes' assistants worked away within.

Kim, the camera hanging in its harness, was now dead center within the old operating room.

"Watch out!" I yelled as he walked directly through one gurney carrying a moaning young female being pushed by a henchman. Kim turned in time only for me to watch them travel into, through and then out of his body without effect or any of them even appearing to notice.

Exasperated with my strange conduct, he held his arms out away from his sides, his hands up in the universal sign of, 'What's happening?'

Right then and there, in that instant, why I was here all came to me. He wanted me to kill my best friend Kim!

Your first is always the most difficult. I'll be right alongside you the entire time to walk you through. Just listen carefully and do everything I tell you

For the first time since I'd heard the voice, I could not argue with it.

You're worried they will know it was you, aren't you Jeffrey? Rest your mind at ease, for I was the master at concealing incriminating evidence. By the time we're finished, we'll be sure to make his death appear an accident.

My mind twisted into agonizing knots. My brain actually hurt. The thought of killing Kim filled my head.

He was twenty feet in front of me, alone in the basement of the Murder Castle. Kim was talking to me, talking to me right now, "Jeff, Jeff, snap out of it, man. You're still gone, and I need your help. You better keep close and pay attention," Kim said, turning and pointing in the direction of the operating room he couldn't see. "There's some interesting stuff down here. It's strange, I know, but twice already I could've sworn I was being touched. You?" Kim asked, moving closer so he could shake me if he needed to.

The act will come naturally to you. Before long you will come to enjoy the thrill even more than from sexual intercourse, Jeffrey.

Both of them were talking at the same time. I wanted to sit down, take my head in my hands and rub all this shit out.

Do you remember the first time you had sex, my boy? This is far better, more fulfilling, more enriching, more erotic even. Tomorrow, if you listen to me tonight, I will show you how to conduct both at the same time and, oh, yes, that is just too amazing for words!

Then for the first time, he touched me. He actually pushed me. I could feel his hand on my back. Had I a mirror to check, I would have sworn he'd left a mark.

You can do it. Just remember to follow my lead.

The air around me went mobile as the ghost whisked by me from behind and headed directly in Kim's direction.

I moved along with the evil wisp, closer and closer until almost at the last moment it seemed as if something were trying to stop me, pulling me back. Later I would see that each of my fingertips had been ground into bloody tips as I clawed at the concrete fighting myself, resisting the monster's demands.

"Give me time to think!" I yelled, loudly enough that Kim stopped, turned and dropped the camera to his hip, but as all good cameramen do under stress, he kept right on filming, oblivious to the entity right in front of his face, possibly measuring his elements to make his murder go down more smoothly.

Wake up, my son, for you were born to this. I have neither the time nor the patience to wait for you any longer. Accept your birthright and obligations! Follow your lessons and my guidance and finish him now.

Concrete faces flowed out the walls to place their moving liquid lips to Kim's ears. They were trying to warn Kim of his fate, that he would soon be the next. When they noticed me watching them they would instantly fade back into the wall, gone, but were quickly replaced by another. Don't ask me how, but this time Kim heard them.

"You're right... Let's get the hell out of here, I've seen enough." That wasn't like Kim at all.

Holmes' face materialized from thin air right next to Kim's. He looked back at me, saying, "*Every step of the way he has interfered with your lessons and my plans. He must be done away with. He sees things differently than you and I do. I have listened to him talking to others about you, Jeffrey, and they make plans to steal what is yours and yours alone. He is not your friend. These things need to be addressed.*"

Behind me, the furnace continued to hiss while I nodded in silent acquiescence and walked toward Kim, having made my mind up, and now lying flat my palms along the concrete wall in order to silence the faces that knew what was about to happen next. As soon as I did so, they re-treated back into the concrete, afraid of me, and giving up warning Kim of what was to come.

"*He will suffer a tragic accident by hitting his head on the concrete stair. Don't worry, I've used this same method countless times before. His head will burst open upon impact and he will die a painless death. I will make sure everything falls right into place. The authorities will suspect nothing.*"

He was behind me again, coaching, right at my ear.

"*We will cover you in blood, exactly the opposite of what the act should leave. You'll see firsthand how the reverse always works, then immediately afterwards, we will cry lament!*"

Possessed, I initially whispered, "I can do this now. I want to do this. I have wanted to do this since I can remember!" I practically yelled having forgotten the previous whisper.

Yes, yes you can, my son! I am proud of you. Watch and learn how I make this happen.

From what would have been out of the blue at any other time, Kim added, "Look at this, it looks like another tunnel of the original brick. Partner, watch my back, I'm gonna crawl in and take a few shots. You never know what we might find back there. Terrance told me he'd never had the guts to climb in and go through them."

Perfect. Do you see how smoothly that happened? We will fulfil your destiny and our duty when he comes back out.

Kim handed me the camera and bar-dipped over the edge, turned to take it back and the last thing I saw of him were the soles of his shoes as he crawled up into the darkness. Moving right along with him, the light from the camera shadowed the brick, casting the tunnel in a blood-like red.

Leaning forward against the concrete wall directly outside the opening to the tunnel, I rocked back and forth on my heels, actually hitting my forehead on the wall, once again hoping to knock him out of my head. It didn't work.

Kim's calls reached back out to me from the recesses, "I'll bet the tunnel goes all the way under Wallace. The deeper you go, the stronger the smell: the same one as on the staircase."

No one will ever know he was inside. Good! We've time for one more necessity. Go in with him, I want you to find the three bricks I told you about.

"Crawl in behind me to give the shot some perspective," Kim suggested almost interrupting the ghost.

I jumped in and crawled back away from the heat, but towards that awful smell again. Still ten feet behind Kim, having measured my depth, I looked for the inscribed brick. After wiping four or five free from years of accumulated dust, I found the one, and with some difficulty pulled the three bricks free. There was indeed a sizeable compartment behind them, but the entrance was only wide enough to stick one arm inside at a time.

Contemplating my next move, I felt Kim's floodlight on my face. I hadn't noticed him filming me.

"You have got to be an idiot reaching in there. Do you have any idea what might be inside?"

I didn't reply.

"All right, if you insist, dumb ass, but at least slow down so I can get the shot."

Completely blind to what was inside, images of metallic-bladed giant blenders played in my head. But as terrible as those horrors were, I wouldn't stop. Finally filling my hand, I pulled out what looked to be a leather bag of very old surgical equipment: forceps, scalpel, clamps and last, but certainly not least, ten folded over handwritten pages. The pages looked to be torn from a binding. Of course! These were pages torn from a book— maybe a diary. Maybe my diary! They were certainly old enough. Could they be the pages from the Holmes diary?

The voice answered. *You didn't really think Bert tore these from our books, did you?*

They were composed of scientific formulas, each page highlighting a conclusion of some sort. They were mathematically and medically far beyond anything within my comprehension. I'd need help interpreting them.

I backed out and shimmied down the opening onto the main floor.

The voice stayed on point.

Put those away until later. Wait right here and prepare yourself for when he comes back.

I fell to the floor, my back to the wall, hugging my knees, hoping to explode in seizure—knowing an episode was the only way I knew of to avoid what was coming. The tell-tale signs of a violent one were all around me: the pain in my gut, the voices, the visions, the lack of perspective.

The hallway, to the left and right of me, stretched all the way into what seemed oblivion, a thousand screaming faces now calling upon me to add another fresh face to their group. Were these, the ones now calling for Kim's death, the same ones who only minutes before tried to warn him of his fate?

What had happened to change their minds?

The two closest to me, both beautiful women, were whispering words of endearment, as if lovers, into my ears. They seemed long deprived, even depraved.

"I'm coming out. Where are you? I need some help. Grab my gear." Kim interrupted.

At his words the faces disappeared, as if afraid that their presence might alert him to the last few moments of his life. Right then, at that very moment, the channel clicked over into the present. Everything becoming crystal clear, each crack, spec of dirt, swirl of dust seemingly under my control. Fittingly enough, and except for the voice, the room was as silent as a tomb.

Stand right here, just so, my good boy.

I took the camera from Kim as he began to slide headfirst out the tunnel. Setting it aside, I grabbed him by both arms as he slid out chest-high. We were directly across and about five feet from the second stairwell.

The slow deliberate whisper at my ear commanded my every move; my body responding as if it were my own mind making the call instead of his voice.

Slide your hand under his left arm and hold the right out as you catch him. Very good. When his weight provides the proper momentum, block his first foot from moving forward, then let his energy flow towards the stairs.

It all happened so fast. As he fell out into my arms, my leg stopped his foot from gaining traction. My hold on him, as instructed, kept his hands from reaching out anywhere in front of himself. He was completely dependent upon me, just as Holmes said he would be. Kim's 200 pounds fell head first toward the second or third concrete step in the staircase, that step which was now the hardest thing on this planet.

You have him! Drive him now, Jeffrey! Drive him!

The concrete edge rose up sharply, ready to split Kim's scull wide open. I could already imagine, no, see, the blood spurting halfway up the staircase, covering me in its glory. Just as he had described the murder, the event would be an "accidental" killing.

My first would be perfection, the voice promised, and leave me hungry for more.

Except, and from a place I hardly recognized any longer, I instinctually rolled myself between Kim's head and the steps, screaming in agony as the impact tore at my knee and hip, both of us ending up in a confused heap. As I looked up, recoiling from the pain, the faces emerged one last time to ponder what just occurred, disappointed that they were cheated of feeling the intended's pain and seeing death after having only dreamed of it for so many decades. Then, *snap*, the channel changed and they all disappeared for good.

The voice went silent, obviously enraged by my refusal of his orders, refusing to utter another word.

"Jesus, what happened? I'm sorry, man, what a klutz I am. Here, sit down and let me go get you some help," Kim offered. He was completely unaware of how close he'd come.

"No, there's no way I'm staying down here alone. Help me up. I want out now, and I'm never coming back down here again."

As he dragged me out, supporting my bad side, the only thing that crossed my mind was the certainty had it been anyone else but Kim, I'd now be a murderer.

CHAPTER 28

The torn pages stayed folded in my jacket pocket for days, taking me that long to get over what had happened in order to gather the courage to take a look. But the time, instead of calming my nerves and solidifying my resolve, only gave my imagination the opportunity to run wild. That and the longitudinal bloodstains on the inside margin of each page. Best I could tell, the stains had been caused by someone having laid a bloody pen in the crease of the journal to keep his place and the diary wide open to facilitate the taking of bloody notes while conducting surgery-- the very same image I remembered seeing in the basement.

Slapping the pages against my thigh to rid them of the red brick dust they were covered in, I coughed out the foul air the act forced me to breathe. Considering they were at least a hundred years old, the paper and ink had stood the test of time rather well—as had the bloodstains. Before reading a word, I sat back, closed my eyes, took an almost painful deep breath and tried to settle my nerves before taking what I knew would be another huge step on my journey. What else could I do?

There were no introductory notes explaining the nature of the contents. They seemed to be a synopsis of some kind. Each page was cut off at just about the place a conclusion would have been disclosed. Was this just another tease? I would need expert help deciphering the content of the pages, but right now the important issue was determining how the pages had come to be in the tunnel in the first place. Voices and visions were one thing, brain lesions and tumor-like growths notwithstanding, but apparitions removing, transporting and placing pages in secret passages was quite another. With this direct evidence, my supposed mental illness could no longer serve as a crutch for my rapidly changing condition; someone, or something was behind all this.

Working backwards, I recalled Terrance telling us that no one except for the previously mentioned film crew had been down in the basement in over two years. I immediately crossed them off my list. Those college kids preparing their first documentary had been way over their heads already, besides they wouldn't have known which three bricks the opening was behind. If not them, the only logical assumption would be that the pages had been there from at least before 1960-- the date of the last diary entry and the year I was now certain Holmes died.

With this rough time table in place, I was on firmer ground, but the why they were in the tunnel and who was responsible were still way out there.

While possible, I seriously doubted Bert had visited the post office before having died. Such a trip would have been difficult for him to have concealed from the family. As well, knowing of the trip, someone would have mentioned it at that family dinner. No, Bert hadn't left those pages in the tunnels. There was only one choice left. The culprit could only have been Holmes. He had to have left them there. But why, when it would have been so much easier to have simply left them attached inside the books, especially if he intended for me to read them all anyway?

No matter how hard I tried to deny, I couldn't escape the conclusion that the pages were left as a treasure of sorts. A treasure for me, but only if I made the effort, going further than simply reading two old books. He wanted me to prove I was worthy of the content in these torn pages. That had to be it. The theory made even more sense when I went back and counted the total number of pages that were torn free: twenty-one pages from both of the books. I only had ten.

Where were the rest?

CHAPTER 29

The drugs they were giving me weren't working. The medical professionals were wrong-- they had to be. This thing in my head, this voice, was more than just my imagination. The pages I'd found in the tunnel proved that. Whatever was going on could no longer be 'medically 'explained away or denied any longer. Logic needed to be applied. I decided to take the pages to the one man I knew was qualified to provide answers, and keep them secret.

"When were these written?" Adam asked, holding the pages up, facing out the arched window of his offices with the bay serving as the perfect backdrop. I couldn't see his face when he asked his question. We both wanted it that way. He had spent the last hour buried in the material behind his desk at the hospital. Besides being a renowned brain surgeon, Adam was considered a source in neurology as well, having written a number of papers and given lectures worldwide.

Finally turning to face me, he looked me in the eye and pointedly asked, "And why are there redacted portions?"

With that tone, I knew this was going to be a lot tougher than I'd originally expected. "I don't know when they were written, but my best guess would be the forties or fifties. As to the other, it's probably better you don't know all the facts right now."

The last two days, I'd tried my best to pick these words apart before seeing him. I'd also copied every page from the diaries that contained medical information concerning the Doctor's experiments. While true that some of the words were obviously meant for someone with less than Holmes' scientific background, many were meant for a doctor and a brilliant one to boot. If anyone were to know what they meant, it was Adam.

Before I'd passed them on, I redacted anything that bordered on criminal. As a result, the pages looked like a congressional top-secret military budget proposal just released to the press.

Adam and I had developed a friendly relationship playing golf at the Country Club. Besides joining each other for rounds, we were both range junkies, spending hours hitting balls to better shape shots and pass the time shooting the shit surrounded by a good group of guys. Over time we'd come to recognize each other's swing flaws, and developed the ability to accept criticism from the other about that thing we treasured-- our golf swings. One day all that changed causing our friendship to move past golf into the realm of emotional aid.

I could tell something was wrong, something far removed from what was happening on the driving range, if for no other reason than the way he was lashing at the ground in rage after each swing. This conduct wasn't Adam. I certainly wasn't prepared for him to break down into tears. After necessary condolences, he came clean to me about an incident that occurred at the hospital that day. One of the other doctors in his surgery group negligently caused the death of one of their patients; at least that's what Adam told me. They covered up the incident and falsified the death report the hospital and legal authorities required, and Adam had been there to witness the negligence, fraud and crime. The other doctors, seeing him distressed, sat him down, explaining that it sometimes happens, and that at this late stage nothing could be done about the unfortunate accident, except to destroy all their promising futures. Being the youngest doctor of the group and the purest, he'd left that day in tatters, unsure of what to do. He needed someone to talk to. He selected me, his ex-lawyer friend. After coming completely clean, we discussed his various options, concluding with my promise to maintain the privacy of whatever decision he eventually made. I did. Our friendship grew. The right choice or not, he continued his practice.

He owed me this one now.

Settling down into his desk chair, Adam said, "Some of this genetic material was unheard of before the fifties. To be sure, the conditions the experiments were conducted within seem somewhat crude, and the anesthesia utilized was turn of the century, however…"

"Is it real? That's all I need from you!" my interruption stopping him cold. His medical analysis of the conditions Holmes had utilized wasn't what I was here for. I instantly regretted my outburst, "Adam, I'm sorry, it's just that this whole thing has started to wear on me."

Sensing my emotional overload, he just listened.

"The man writing about these experiments claimed to have harvested hormones from innocent victims in order to further his own longevity." I explained.

"Yeah, I can see that," he replied. "Were these patients ill or sick in any way before their ovaries were removed?"

Here we go, I thought. I couldn't imagine his reaction were I to tell him the whole story. I could hardly believe it myself and I'd been living this nightmare. Why should Adam now?

Keep it simple, stupid, I told myself, *just come out and say it.*

"No," I said, my eyes downcast, ashamed at what I was about to admit. "To the contrary, they were selected because of their perfect health."

His reaction was as if he were driving past an accident doing his best not to look, but failing. He rocked back in his chair, not able to help himself, and ran his hand through his hair before allowing it to drop and pointing one finger directly at me. "This is the thing you've been working on this past year, isn't it?"

I turned away, unable to answer.

"Why me?" he asked after a suitable pause.

With Adam I would be killing two birds with one stone, not only because he could diagnose and possibly remedy my condition, but also because he could decipher Holmes' data and outrageous conclusions from the torn pages.

"Besides the obvious, you owe me, and you're the only one I know who can help me while keeping this between us."

He shook his head as he withdrew a notepad from his desk. "I'll give you the names of three scientists who can get to the bottom of this for you."

"Not that kind of help, Adam," I said quickly. "This has to be from you, and kept a complete secret."

I could see his blood pressure rising as he considered the potential professional disaster his involvement might result in, not to mention the possible violation of hundreds of statutes. He was smart enough to know that the statute of limitations wasn't going to apply to any of these notes mentioning homicide.

"Have the authorities been notified about these possible homicides?" his words dripping with sarcasm. "You do know that's what's required, don't you, my lawyer friend?"

He immediately regretted the mistake he'd just made in bringing up the law, knowing right then and there, the same boat and all, that I had him instead of him having me. We were both on thin ice, and we both knew it. But forcing his participation wouldn't do me any good; I needed to ensure his enthusiasm. I needed him to want to help me. So instead of putting my foot in my mouth, I kept my mouth shut, watching him from the tops of both eyes, just as Holmes would have done.

Adam's eyes ducked down away from my stare for sure pondering the possibility that I was blackmailing him in some odd, old fashion sort of way, instead of the friendly request for aid this was first framed as.

He gave up.

"Okay, get to the point, Jeff." The deal was done, along with our friendship when this was over. His formal use of my name in his response signified that.

I gave him everything I had. Forty minutes later, having skimmed over the material, he left me alone in his office while he walked down the hall to schedule another MRI to check the pressure I told him I was feeling in my head.

I also told him about the voices.

When he returned, he resumed talking about the experiments.

"He's talking about four or five surgeries a day to obtain the material required for his needs. How many years was he involved with this stuff - two or three?" Despite his early reticence, Adam's sudden scientific curiosity had sparked an excitement that was clear in his voice.

"I'm not sure, perhaps a long time. Sixty, seventy years, maybe more."

He took a while calculating the mathematical horror of what I had just revealed. Who in his place wouldn't have? We might still be there, frozen in place, had my chair not creaked and his throat cleared at the same time, the stereo of sounds jolting us both.

"I need you to tell me, if you can, if this could have affected me genetically. He was my grandfather's grandfather."

"I understand. All right, give me a couple of hours to go over your file, and then let's finish up with a full physical, blood work, etc. I've got a hunch they may have missed something the first time around with you. I'll put some research into this material and we'll see if anything falls out. Right now, before all that, I couldn't give you an answer worth a damn."

The game was on.

"One more thing, that voice you keep hearing…."

"Yes?" I replied, expecting the worst, but hoping for the best.

"Well, they aren't that unusual. Many patients hear voices, especially those suffering from neural disorders. They can seem like echoes in the back of the mind. Schizophrenia often results in thought disorders, delusions, hallucinations and … voices. My guess is that your intense concentration on the contents of those boxes pushed you over an edge, so to speak. That edge left a gap that is either filled by your 'wobbles,' which are nothing more than partial seizures, or the voice, which right now I'd classify as a complex. Notice that the voice never tells you anything you don't already know, or couldn't create from existing knowledge. I'll bet you can almost guess what he says before it speaks, can't you?"

I nodded.

He continued, "Trust me, I *am* concerned with the existence of the voice, I just want you to know there's nothing supernatural going on, as in a demonic possession. And yes, there probably does contain a genetic component, but we might be able to fix your crossed-wires by surgery or medication, just give me a chance to diagnose the cause properly first."

This was the best news I'd heard in months.

Adam stood up and walked around behind my chair, patting me on the shoulder before going on. "You up for some rough medical leg work helping me out on this?"

"It's not like I have a choice, do I?"

"Nope," he said.

"Oh, one more thing, Adam, I need you to prescribe something strong that'll get me through the next few days, something a lot stronger than what I'm taking now."

He was writing the prescription down before I'd finished my request. He pushed the tablet across the desk at me. Even to a layman, the name of the drug was familiar. There was a time I would have doubted this drug even legal.

"Two hundred milligrams per day, no more, and one more thing," he said halfway out the office. "Bring me the un-redacted copies with you tomorrow."

He ran me through MRI two hours later.

Over the next two days and a dozen telephone calls, Adam explained, in terms I might understand, how Holmes had been preoccupied with cellular makeup, cell wall deterioration and the discovery of any substances or chemicals that could delay that deterioration.

Holmes was apparently in the forefront of stem cell research, seeking to determine how healthy cells replace damaged or aging ones. He'd been fascinated with the gene, that functional unit of heredity and the segment of DNA found on chromosomes in the nucleus of a cell.

From the pages I'd found, Adam was able to decipher that Holmes had identified a source of mature stem cells, well past the embryonic stage. He was then successful in differentiating those cells into the specialized ones that might prolong his longevity. He had developed a system to deliver those cells to the selected part of his body, fostering an environment there that encouraged the cells to integrate and function in concert with his body's natural cells. He was also able to suppress his body's immune system to minimize reaction to those transplanted cells. His success was tied to his isolation of cells from the ovaries in adult females and causing them to differentiate, and proliferate aggressively.

He continued that Holmes may have solved the mystery of pluripotent cells (the ability of a stem cell to develop into the various cell types that make up the body) and had been able to "order" them to become the precise cell in the body he desired. This allowed him to create cell lines and tissues identical to those that he wished to reproduce in his body, thereby retarding the aging process in order to prolong his longevity.

Adam also explained that modern medicine's quest for advanced stem cell research was centered around the belief that this science, once perfected, could cure almost all forms of cancer, or in the other extreme, to incite the disease.

While somewhat satisfying, I knew there was more to my future, or lack of one, than an explanation of the double helixes Holmes might have deposited in my brain, the ones awaiting my own gestation until I opened those damn boxes. I could beat this thing, I told myself, but only if I understood what he had done to interfere with nature, as well as the spirituals involved far down away from any books and scientific explanations.

Funny thing was, while Adam was explaining all this to me, the voice never once interrupted. His silence seemed approval of the knowledge the doctor was providing me.

That is until Adam called and gave me the results of the MRI: they were as negative as they could possibly be.

The small brain tumor the doctors identified months ago had progressed and was now not only malignant, but also in contact with my left temporal lobe. Its location made surgery difficult, if not impossible and chemo's effectiveness doubtful. Adam ended his explanation by first apologizing for his honesty, then telling me time was short.

My medical history had begun to mirror Bert's.

As I sat down to absorb what it all meant, and how fast this was happening, the voice stepped in for the first time in days, soothing me with an almost parent-like sympathetic concern.

Don't worry, Jeffrey. Your condition in not only treatable but completely reversible. We will handle your condition ourselves.

CHAPTER 30

Adam's new drug lessoned the pain but did little to kill the hideous things now more alive than ever within my psyche. In order to escape them, I had taken to hiding from life. The dark was my last refuge and the only place left to continue thinking things through. There in my room, the windows closed, then covered twice with extra bedclothes and towels at the base of the doors to seal out any light trying to leak in, I began understanding my Grandfather Bert— who had also locked himself away in the darkness before dying. Like him, entombed, I waited for the next episode to strike. They were happening ten to twenty times a day. Following a seizure, I would fall depressed, guilty of God knows everything and irritable at any and all for days, and praying to that same God that I'd not unknowing left this room only to inadvertently harm another innocent. Covering my anxieties in further research, or at least attempting to, my reading was now revealing Bert and I weren't the first. Apparently there were many others before us. Honest, sympathetic men who had without reason or regard suddenly been stricken. Dante, himself an epileptic, had written the Inferno about his own untreated seizures and the exact same places of the mind we shared. I had to agree; this *was* Hell.

No one in my presence was safe now, not my family, not my friends, none. Anyone too close was considered for that thing.

The finest medical mind in the world, besides diagnosing my condition as terminal, had explained away the visions and voices as common conditions for one suffering from temporal lobe epilepsy, but I had my doubts. Somehow I knew Adam was wrong. The ghost was behind it all, the same way I knew *he* had caused Bert's death. The accelerated growth of the tumor, no matter what the specialists said, was too closely aligned to my discovery of the books, my quest for knowledge, and refusal to accede to his demands.

The only answer I could come up with was there was a Holmes Curse.

Sensing my vulnerability, never relenting, the sickly sweet logical voice continued filling my head. He knew exactly what he was doing. He had me right where he wanted me: a near slave to his suggestions.

It was never madness, my boy, this thing you fear was our gift. Are you finally ready to accept who we really are?

All traces of the old me were being erased in a swirl of red liquid rotating slowly down time's drain.

I know where you are. I've been there myself. I've witnessed the same fears and emotions before. Three or four more days and your ordeal will all be over.

Choices, it was all coming down to choices about the rest of my, I was now convinced, short life. Unfortunately the knowledge I'd gained investigating Holmes was only serving to make the ultimate decision more difficult. As horrible as it was to admit, I had been born genetically evil. His genes had been passed on to me. I needed to accept the consequences of that fact. Then, and only then, could the choice I so feared be addressed. To be whom *I* was, or not to be at all-- perhaps the most horrible choice any man had ever been forced to make.

It was the same choice I'd been offered that first day I found the books, only now, instead of with that day's ignorant excitement, I carried the weight of knowledge on my shoulders. I knew my decisions mattered and innocent lives were at stake, people who didn't deserve to be the playthings of another Mudgett. The impossible choice between an instinctual need and a forever unrecognized good deed. Debating the choice over and over again, Goethe's words played simultaneously in my head: "I'd yield me to the devil instantly, did it not happen that myself am he!"

Ready to give up; I mean really give up, desperate and at the last all alone, I remembered something obscure, something I'd never fully understood. Maybe another glance offered the slightest chance. Bert's note, the one in the box, the one he had apparently written in sympathetic code to avoid the rest of the families' interest. Maybe these last words contained a clue:

"…Fishing allowed me the chance to avoid that which tormented me. When luck runs out, Port Costa, the spot closest to your school, always brought me fortune and peace of mind. Take the little I have to give and seek out your own sanctuary from that which pursues you…"

CHAPTER 31

I spilled the boxes over again— there was nothing else to do. Scattered in front of me, and except for the diaries, everything was the same; nothing had changed. The lines, lures, reels, his last note, even the map was still there.

This entire mess has something to do with the map, I told myself, at least I think it was myself, as now voices were impossible to differentiate. I was at the point of giving up trying to determine which one was which these days.

What had Bert been trying to tell me? The fact that the map was hidden with the diaries hadn't been an accident after all. That should have been obvious from the first, as nothing Bert did was accidental. Bert knew where everything belonged. The map was the key, the map and that strange semi-poetic note mentioning some spot on the river as the place that brought him peace of mind, and might one day turn into my own sanctuary.

Pulling the map out, what struck me of the maps many marked spots was there were only three some significant distance from the water's edge. One was at Eckley, another at Martinez and the last was located at Port Costa. These three landlocked spots, I was certain, represented something other than fishing success, and might just be the clues Bert had intended all along for me to track down. For the first time in my entire life, I forced myself to take direction from Bert, even if he *was* dead.

Port Costa was at the center of the map. The town was located directly across the river from Vallejo, and the academy where I'd gone to school in 1975. The last diary entry was in 1960.

The note emphasized the town's main street where it intersected the Southern Pacific Railway. Combing the history books in my den, I read that a hundred years or so ago the town had assisted suppling the railway workers and sailors to the surrounding industries. The main street was a mass of bordellos, bars and shops, servicing the vagabonds, pirates and day-to-days that used the town as their step off. After the thirties, and the Great Depression, the town slowly dwindled, eventually losing whatever significance the port once had. When the break bulk cargo business transferred one hundred percent of the river's cargo to the Ports of Oakland and San Francisco, Port Costa quietly died away. Now this small corner of a long-gone world was an antique.

The town was less than an hour from The City, as well as some of the most affluent neighborhoods in the entire United States. But that's where all similarities ended. Port Costa was as different from the Bay Area's other more modern small towns as different could be.

Port Costa was attached to the world by one road: a winding narrow thoroughfare, bordered by old oaks and cattle-less state and federally subsidized farms, all having seen the last of their more productive days, liberal politicians having long ago forbidden development, leaving an archaic "green-belt" and, in essence, a place time forgot.

Exiting off Highway 5, entering Port Costa, Rex riding shotgun, I found myself driving down a single lane road, the street looking like it hadn't been repaved in over fifty years. The road hard countered so as to drain the flooding winter rains straight to the river, which, along with the railroad, dominated the entire environment. Everything about the town was either parallel to the river and railroad tracks or at right angles to them both. As long as you avoided looking north across the channel to see the highly developed Benicia and Vallejo side, visualizing the way the town must have looked in the late nineteenth century was easy.

Once in town, two old buildings made up most of the northernmost riverside ending of this living historic postcard. My guess was that they were the first ones ever built in the town. The rest seemed nothing more than small shops and caretaker houses that must have slowly sprung up around the two. On the river, at the end of the main avenue, I looked for

the old mile long piers the books had depicted, the ones the historic pictures emphasized featuring the hundreds of ships waiting for cargo. They
were long gone. Closer observation revealed wrecked portions of those
same piers below the surface of the river.

The larger of the two buildings was the Burlington Hotel, which
looked to have been built sometime before the turn of the century. The
hotel was in severe disrepair, but still demonstrated traces of unique character the lodging had once broadcast as the leading bordello east of the
Mississippi River for over seventy-five years. Those days were too obviously long gone. 'For Sale' signs hung on each corner. Walking past, there
was something about the hotel I couldn't quite put my finger on; but
there was no doubt whatever it was pulled at me as I sauntered past down
Main Street.

For two hours I wandered the streets, searching for anything that
might clue me in as to why this spot was marked on Bert's map. I knew
that he wouldn't have been interested in the function of the hotel as the
old whorehouse; he just wasn't that way. Likewise, he wouldn't have been
interested in the small shops. The small graveyard beside the hotel offered potential, but after another two hours investigating the names of
those buried within, nothing jumped up and bit me.

I refused to give up. He wanted me here and I was determined to
know why.

From across the street, what looked to be a hard working middle-
aged man in jeans and baseball cap approached me asking, "Are you with
the railroad, mister?" Instead of answering, I stayed quiet. He continued,
"They told me last time they were here one of you was coming to survey
the joint to consider buying all the land close to the tracks. You know,
the plots next to my home. I was kind of hoping you were here to get on
with it."

"No," I said. "I don't work for the railroad. I've been hired to write a
documentary on the town. The old buildings fascinate me. Can you tell
me anything about them, especially the Burlington Hotel?" I pointed
back over his shoulder to the hotel looming directly behind him.

"They say back in the day The Burlington was the hottest place around. Nothing else even coming close, if you know what I mean." He was grinning from ear to ear.

I nodded in affirmation as we both stood there in the middle of the street gazing at the once grand old hotel. Three stories rose high above the street. The turreted corners angled off in old windowed stature and grace. The wide ground level entrance to the huge, cavernous first floor openly invited all those eager enough to enter and do business.

Then it hit me. Why of course! The Castle! The Burlington was the spitting image of Holmes's Murder Castle in Chicago.

Unable to believe I hadn't recognized the likeness the first time the place had crossed my line of sight, I looked for anything to differentiate the two, but after second and third looks there wasn't any doubt: the building was identical if not an exact replica, which had been brought back from the ashes just for me to see. I was dumbfounded!

Old quotes about the Castle from a myriad of sources flooded my mind. Descriptions of the corner store, the semi-hexagon entrance, everything, matched what was now right before my eyes. The shadows from the towering turrets seemed to watch me as I moved about trying to find any perspective that would provide some evidence of difference. There was none. The Castle was here now, right before my very eyes!

"How beautiful the hotel must have been in its heyday," I said out loud.

Seeing my reaction, "What's wrong, mister, was it something I said?" the man asked.

"What? Oh! No, uh... nothing, nothing at all, except that I just realized why I was supposed to be here in the first place, something from way, way back. Excuse me."

I walked over to the worn front doors. They were unlocked, although somewhat barricaded by four old barstools, probably put there for the locals to enjoy afternoon beers while watching the ship traffic heading downriver.

Cupping my hands to the dusty front door windows, I was able to make out the dramatic sweeping staircase that led upstairs, precisely as the one described in the books about its eastern counterpart. Little else was obvious, as the intense clutter and trash that filled the space made recognizing more detail impossible.

Walking around the side garden and onto the stone steps, I came across a bronze plaque the State of California erected to commemorate the building's historical significance. The tale the memorial told was fascinating, but most striking was the date the building was constructed—1883, some five years *before* the Castle was erected in Chicago. The gravity of that distinction shook me to the core. This meant, definitively, that Holmes was here, in Port Costa, before he returned to the Midwest and began his "career" in advanced medicine. He must have been, to have recreated this building so accurately and without the services of an architect. How strange that Holmes had never once mentioned Port Costa in his diary.

Perhaps his having overlooked Port Costa wasn't so strange. I remembered numerous historical pieces from 1883 detailing countless unresolved missing person cases around the Bay Area. The numbers, while intriguing, were so extreme that I'd been skeptical when I first learned of them. They no longer did, not with this proof that Holmes was here and at the same time.

Bert had wanted me to see the Burlington Hotel. He wanted me to know Herman was here.

The first piece of the puzzle was in place. Bert had known I'd recognize the twin to the Murder Castle. He knew I'd realize the significance, but only if I'd done my homework. Bert knew this could never be considered just another Holmes coincidence. But most of all, he knew this piece of dazzling evidence would forever stop me from taking his advice for granted any longer. He wanted my attention focused for the critical components to come.

And the Burlington did...like a laser.

The second location on the map was the one at the very city limits of Martinez. Bert's note indicated a place roughly four miles to the east of Port Costa. The site was centered high on the south bank of the Sacramento River straight across from Benicia. According to the map, there was a road that led right up to the spot.

Martinez was another one of those pioneer towns that sprang up after the Gold Rush to supply the streams of commerce that rode down the river and out the Golden Gate. Unlike the others, Martinez had evolved after the gold had run out and was now, for the most part, in the business of supplying labor to the major oil company refineries that dotted the area.

Studying the map, the second notation seemed to coincide with the old Alhambra Cemetery alongside the much newer Regional State Park. My money was on the graveyard as the park had been built after Bert died. The whole thing had that old cemetery feel to it anyway. Besides, there was an old family legend associated with the place.

One quick whistle and Rex jumped up into the bed of the Ford while I climbed into the cab at the same time wondering why I hadn't heard from the voice, not even once, since I'd picked up the map. Maybe he was bored with all this, or just busy planning a suitable ending.

The road to the cemetery, once out of Martinez, wound about, constantly changing elevation, up and back down, until the last mile or so when the road kept climbing until we leveled out about five hundred feet above the river. The land was covered in the old oaks and scrub pines the area was famous for. Quiet and peaceful, the entire area offered gorgeous views of the river and opposing banks. I could imagine us standing up to our knees in the river, side-by-side, casting lines in search of the next catch. Quite the place to settle down and fish with your grandson, I daydreamed. The thought was a fleeting one.

The split onto the unpaved road to the entrance of the cemetery came upon me so fast that I almost missed the tight turn, screeching to a halt on the loose stone and pine needle covered hardpan. Beyond the entrance, even at midday, the old graveyard was seriously eerie. Sitting high on a

flat, this barren, and, I had to admit, forsaken place, was well within sight
of Bert's decades ago solitary fishing expeditions on the river far below.
From the looks of things, there hadn't been anyone, dead or alive, visiting
here in quite some time, as the barbed wire fence that surrounded the
cemetery hung slack and loose in obvious disrepair. Peeking through, the
gravestones, at least those within sight, behind the fence were old, very
old. Dark shadows played across the graveyard beyond the entrance.

Sighing, I told Rex, "Another cemetery. How many has it been?
There has to be a better way for us to figure this thing out."

The gate amounted to old steel bars tied into a rusty fence that was
locked with a steel chain and padlock. Reading the barely legible sign
hanging from the fence on the gate, I was surprised to see, "No Trespass-
ing. Visitors are required to sign in at the Martinez Police Station where
a key may be obtained."

How strange and for what, I wondered-- vandals? Did anyone give a
damn about what was inside these old barbed wires? Puzzled, but without any other choice, I climbed back into the truck and drove down the
road to the station.

Some two hours later I was back with the key, having checked in and
been told that I was the first to request one in almost three years. They
wanted the key back before dark. I assured them I would follow their
wishes to the letter.

"A man would have to be a complete fool to hang out in an abandoned cemetery after dark." I told them, *almost* amusing myself.

Family legend was that Bert had buried an otherwise unknown relative here and all by himself. My father, then just a small boy, told me he
remembered, 1935-ish, sitting in the car parked outside a hardware store
while his Dad purchased a two dollar shovel and brand new wool blanket.
They had driven almost all day to Vallejo, picked up a package, turned
right around, crossed the river again and driven all the way back to Martinez, but before going home they had detoured into a cemetery. Bert refused, despite many query's, telling him what was in the trunk. Dad

remembered his Dad making two trips into the cemetery from the car while he waited, both times Bert making sure to close the trunk. When Dad turned to watch him open the trunk the second time, Bert ordered him to keep his eyes forward. After hearing the trunk slam shut that second time, Dad waited for over two hours. When Bert returned, he was dripping with sweat and covered in dirt. After brushing himself off, Bert climbed in, took the wheel of their old Chevy and said, "Let's go home." That was all there was to it. Not one word of explanation. Figures, I thought-- no casket, no ceremony, no stone, or even, heaven forbid, flowers. To be fair, the family was broke, struggling even eating and couldn't have come up with those extras for whomever had been buried here that day.

Those extras probably didn't matter in the long run.

The rusty old lock refused to give way even with the appropriate key. The strange collection of residue finally gave up when I used my weight, leaned in, and broke the entire locking mechanism. I made a note to buy a new one at the hardware store I'd noticed across the street from the police station.

Once inside, the cemetery was a series of concentric circles of hundreds of graves. Every single one of them were in serious disrepair, to the extent that some might be considered ruins. The closest grave to the entrance, not twenty feet away, was worded, "Died 1886. Unknown cause. The family says goodbye." That was all, not even a name, and hardly enough to pay respects. They probably had needed to move on and get back to work.

To the right, alongside the fence stood a large white sign, put up some twenty or thirty years ago by a ladies group, listing all known residents interred in the cemetery. Taking ten minutes to read the entire list, I was disappointed to see there was no Mudgett or Holmes noted. *No directions either*, I joked to myself. I hadn't really expected any, knowing Bert hadn't possibly purchased a plot, instead probably waiting until the grounds were closed, deserted, in order to deposit the body incognito.

I spent the next three hours walking the rows, amazed at some of the names I recognized, as well as the complete lack of care they were receiving. Some were downright historical: John Muir, one of the founders of California and the Sierra Club; John Walker, the first white man to have ever seen Yosemite Valley; and on and on the list went with important burials obviously forgotten, now as seemingly unimportant as the weekly residue. I wondered what would they have thought, these pioneers, were they witness to this, their final lack of respect?

Needing to keep an eye on available daylight, I set all that aside. Bert wanted me to see something here, for sure one of these plots, maybe a name, just as he had wanted me to find the Burlington. I couldn't let him down now.

The bottom trail closest to the railroad tracks contained the oldest sites. Two or three hundred yards from a turn to the right, in an explosion of brown flesh, a herd of perhaps twenty mule deer with two or three bucks in velvet, startled at my quiet approach, bound for thirty or forty yards before hurling themselves over the barbed wire. Rex, barking away just a few feet behind them chased the herd right up to the fence. Over the fence they quickly disappeared. The graveyard was the herd's priceless place of peace and quiet, tucked away, where no one hunted them--fitting really.

Enjoying the obvious peace all around me, I sat down at the herd's special spot where the ground still warm on my jeans, a strange earthy goodness flowing over my entire being for the first time in many a day. This was a good place to be.

There was a fallen head stone beside me. With what I thought at the time was nothing more than idle curiosity, I brushed the dirt off the stone to read the old worn granite prose. The strangely familiar words reminded me of the sentence fragments Bert had written on the on the map in the margin above the Southern Pacific tracks, so I pulled the map from my back pocket and re-read them: First, "Death loves a shining mark," then, "Like the sound of wind chimes." The identical words of those beside me on the stones!

My stomach somersaulted as the possibility of what I'd accidentally found hit me. The *shining mark* was the brilliant reflection off the river down below and the *wind chimes* were the breeze's music through the leaves of the trees that was playing even right then.

Knowing I was in the right place, I carefully read the entirety of the two beautiful headstones, but was disappointed to see that neither of the names on them was a Mudgett, nor even one of our distant relatives. More daunting, the dates of death predated Holmes' 'hanging.' What could Bert have possibly wanted me to see here? I will admit the thought that Bert might have buried Holmes here that day with my father had crossed my mind, but now, here, I knew that wasn't the case, he wouldn't have done that to these good people, making them share a grave for eternity with Holmes.

These sites had been dedicated, possibly even reserved for the finest, strongest and best people that had lived, worked and made Martinez a renowned place before the turn of the century. These citizens, buried here, were the leaders of a young and burgeoning California. *He* wouldn't have belonged here and Bert would have recognized that.

Baffled again and close to exhaustion, I lay down on this serene old earth and closed my eyes. Around me, the stones advertised the *big zero*, the one the tumor in my head was rapidly bringing to a climax. If I was going to give up, this *was* the place to do lay back and let the inevitable happen. Maybe this was what Bert was suggesting; that I couldn't win and should just give up.

In the same blink of that eye I chastised myself. The man had never quit on anything his entire life and he would have been ashamed to know I was considering such now. *No, not yet, keep going,* I told myself, *you need to find the final piece of the puzzle, and maybe beat this thing.*

Yelling for Rex to heel and watch my back, I studied the section of the map that contained the quotations. For the first time I recognized the numbered grid the map had been drawn on making returns to previously successful fishing holes easy. That grid used printed numbers to delineate locations on the map itself. There was also a printed compass rose located very close to the site of the cemetery. The set of numbers closest to the prose were 20/30, which was directly across from E/NE on the rose. Could these numbers and that compass setting be Bert's directions for me to the particular gravesite he wanted found? Was that possible? These numbers were printed on the paper before he purchased the map. If they were clues, I reasoned, he would've needed to have utilized them backwards, in other words, picked his location after determining these numbers would be my directions. Fascinating, and very Sherlock Holmes. The words he wrote down in the margins that matched those on the tombstones just might be my starting off point for this back-ass-ward search. The whole thing seemed rather farfetched, but what else was there and what choice did I have?

From a spot between the graves I paced off twenty steps to the W/SW, opposite that on the rose, then thirty steps to the ninety, the other direction. Nothing. Then thirty in the opposite direction. Again nothing. I repeated the same process using 30 steps as the initial distance, marking off each possible pivot point, then the same for the twenty steps. Still nothing. The possibilities were beginning to look endless.

Running my hand over my head, trying to stimulate any remaining intellect, I came up with one thing and one thing only: if I was to solve this riddle I'd have to think like an engineer not a lawyer. Bert would have applied mathematics and logic, not feeling. So, like he would have, I marked each spot with an oak twig and jammed the branch into the ground. When I was finished, there were eighteen new locations for me to consider.

Emptying my mind of anything preconceived, I looked at each spot again, not my way, but as he would have *predicted* I would have done so and on that day. Using that frame of mind, I eliminated ten of the spots immediately as they were too close to roots or because their views would have been blocked by trees alive at the time of the burial. Bert wouldn't have allowed that insult. Four others were eliminated due to their location on the trails themselves, leaving just four more. Of those, one was the most promising. The spot was situated between the family plots of two huge headstones with concrete borders that ran around the total of each plot. The local also had the best view of the river.

I knew it. This was the one.

With about an hour of sunlight left, I set Rex back at the front gate to stand guard and grabbed the shovel out of the truck before walking back. I began digging as fast as I could, without even considering whether digging here was really what Bert would have wanted me to do, or who, or what I would find. A couple of feet down, suddenly awash in doubt, I stopped. Dropping the shovel and collapsing onto the pile of fresh dirt around me, I took my customary deep breath. This was Bert's chosen place for whomever it was he rested here. This was a place of honor and worship, not exhumation. Except for the possibility Bert may have returned later, my visit today would be the first time whoever was here was ever paid respects by anyone in our family.

I had no right to disturb this sacred ground. Then what, what was this spot about? The frustration tore at my entire being.

Off in the distance, Rex's barking broke me out of my solitude. I hurried back to the gate in time to see him getting ready to launch at two Martinez police officers. Their patrol car was parked right behind my truck. They were both wielding batons and mace just in case.

"Down! Rex settle!" I commanded.

"That's a good dog," one of the cops commented while gesturing at Rex with his stick, "scared the hell out of us."

"You almost done?" the other, bigger, less patient of the two asked. "The chief wanted us to stop by and check up on you."

"Yeah, give me another hour and I'll lock up and have the key back."

"That reminds me, don't forget to buy a new lock to replace the one you broke and when you do, drop off two new keys," the big one said, then headed back to his patrol car without even looking back to see if I'd acknowledged. Very observant, I thought.

After they were gone, the cool breeze from the valley, signifying rain, swept over the oaks, singing their old song and washing away some of the clutter that had accumulated in my head. After replacing and smoothing

the earth I'd disturbed, I sat back on the same stone wall of the gravesite
facing the river and lit a cigarette to relax. I knew I'd found the place, but
what was I supposed to do with it now that I had it?

Scratching at my leg, I noticed a trail of California Red Ants, the ones
that bite hard, parading right up over my shoe, onto my sock and up my
pant leg. Brushing them away just in time I reached down to retie a shoe-
lace and found myself staring at some letters between my legs on the stone
I was sitting on. They were scratched into the base of the granite, in such
a way they faced the clearing between the two formal sites. Tracing their
rough texture with a finger, I could tell they were handmade, with a
screwdriver perhaps, so very out of place in this world of professionally
etched engravings. Clearing away the decades old moss that semi-ob-
scured the letters, I was able to make out four capitalized letters:

"C. L. M. P."

Nothing else, just those letters, not even a date. But none of that mattered anymore, for now I knew! No sir, I didn't need any more clues. My
mind as clear as a bell, nodding to myself, I knew whom they referred to.
I also knew why I wouldn't need the shovel, at least not here, for resting
right below me was my Great-Great-Grandmother: Clara Lovering
Mudgett Peverly-- Holmes' first and only legal wife.

As far as I knew, no one in the family had ever met Clara, none, that
is, except for Bert. However, by all accounts, she was the epitome of strong
womanhood, perhaps the only woman to have ever successfully stood up
to Holmes and lived to tell the tale. Apparently, at approximately sixty
years of age, and some forty years after having refused Holmes the divorce
he requested on her front doorstep in New Hampshire, Clara remarried,
believing Herman dead, and traveled cross country to settle in Vallejo, California. The proof below me, she passed on in her eighties after having
watched four generations of her family at work and play around her in San
Francisco-- incognito.

My guess was that Holmes had kept an eye on Clara her entire life,
unable to let go, her having been the only woman to say no. But why he let

her live when he could have easily done away with her, I had no idea. Herman probably just watched the only woman he ever reportedly loved from the shadows. Strangely enough, he never mentioned her in the diaries.

That day, the one my father told me about, had been his unknowing role in the burial of his great-grandmother. There was nothing here to indicate why Bert would have kept that matter a secret from his son, but there were a multitude of possibilities. Whatever the reason, it, I knew, was logical. Everything Bert had done was beginning to look like decisions which were decided upon in order to protect his family from the monster that cursed them... and had followed them across the country in order to monitor their entire lives, certainly Bert's and mine.

Sitting here now, her directly below me, I knew Clara was buried amongst good, honest folk. Bert knew what he was doing placing Clara here with these people, in this grove of honor and heritage. These residents were all pioneers of good character and this was here she belonged. He hadn't ever wanted me to disturb her, just to recognize the other side, the stronger side of what made Mudgetts good people; the dominant side that passed on the good blood to me, my good genes, and did battle, every day, with the evil ones. Bert was proud that Clara Mudgett was his grandmother and he wanted me to know that she deserved to be buried here, right here, over his and my cathedral, the river below, the place where we both fished.

Proud for the first time in as long as I could remember, my eyes softened, and contemplated the lightening split spruce tree that towered over both of us. Having grown back with time the tree remained horribly deformed, but in a breathtakingly beautiful way. It's at these moments that the strangest things come to mind for all of us. For me it was the realization that I had just been tested. Before the books I would have considered Clara without pity. As the one time wife of the devil, a woman who didn't deserve sympathy for the errors she'd made; but not anymore. Here and now my thoughts gathered momentum around the material she had been made of and how that strength firmed the soft ground around her. The same strength I could feel flowing up from the ground and into my soul. Bert knew I would be right here, thinking these very thoughts, over Clara, after seeing the Burlington House Hotel. He knew what was coming next and the strength I would need to survive. *How could he have known this?* He knew because forty years ago he had faced the same fight, the same terrible final ordeal I would soon have to endure in order to survive.

There was never a magic potion or secret verse, as I once believed, to erase the curse and give me the strength I'd need to beat Holmes. There was none of that here below me. But what *was* here was far more powerful than all that gibberish, for this was real. She was the one who had stood up to him and faced him down. Her life was proof that I could as well. Bert had known her proven strength was my last chance, that is, if I honored her with my recognition.

Based on what my father told me, she was buried in nothing more than a burlap sack and her last change of clothes. Lost away in obscurity, I doubted whether Clara had ever experienced the weight of flowers above her grave the decades she'd been here. Well that was about to change. With Rex at my heel, I walked over to the fence line and gathered a clump of beautiful wild flowers, tied them as best I could with the vine which grew woven through the barbed wire, walked back to kneel down and placed the flowers on her grave. As I did, the *voice*, quiet for so long, tried to interrupt my act with what I knew would be his usual trite ugliness, especially for Clara. Instead of allowing him the chance, with a strength I thought long gone, I closed my mind shut and sealed him out.

He couldn't say a word, only watch, as I paid my respects to a great woman.

With sunset's lingering light upon me, I drove to Eckley, the last of the three spots, across from the 1927 Carquinez Bridge. Eckley had served as the ferry landing for those crossing the river before the bridge was constructed. As the town's usefulness died, the small city dwindled and was slowly deserted then finally cleaned off by the state. The area now was a small park built into a hollow on the river about three hundred feet below the main road, and upriver from the C&H Sugar Plant directly across the river from Vallejo. The park paralleled the riverbank for about half a mile with railroad tracks cutting through the bottom of the park a stone's throw from the manmade riverbank.

The park was very familiar, for this was the place on the river across the bridge where the cadets used to drive to drink beer after classes. This was where we went to get away from it all. Now Eckley was a jogger's park, with manicured grounds and plush grasses perfect for dog walks and serenity along the river. Maybe even a romance or two. A pier had been added for those interested in fishing striped bass. None of this was here when Bert added the third spot to the map.

The old brick railroad 'track-changers house' represented on the map was still here. Had it not been, I would have never found Bert's third spot. Ten feet by ten feet in dimension, the shack was dead square between the westbound and eastbound tracks. Fifty years ago the house was manned around the clock by a railroad worker who would manually redirect the trains at the "Y" to the proper set of tracks, but not anymore; now the trains changed tracks automatically.

Wind-breaking eucalyptus trees swayed next to the tracks, the wind cold and crisp in the deceptive winter sun, the river flooding three or four knots only feet away. Pulling the map from my pocket, I was relieved to see that Bert had used the track-changer's shack as the baseline for his directions to the last spot. Give or take a couple hundred yards, the location was approximately one half mile up the tracks, the exact distance delineated by the number of railroad ties to the east and approximately twenty feet up the embankment, all clearly marked on the map and obvious to the eye. After walking off the ties I turned hard to my left onto a steeply sloped semi-clearing covered in the California barranca that I knew all too well would contain poison oak.

Unlike the first two, there was no mystery as to why this spot was on Bert's map. I knew exactly what was in the dirt below my feet. I could feel the bones in my bones. The culmination of my long journey was always

to be right here and for one and only one purpose—- him. Holmes was
on the side of this abandoned hill. Great-Great Grandpa was buried here.

Standing on this irreverent ground, under the red streaked sky, my
imagination raced with terrible visions of abomination and horror, unimaginable were I not so well educated with the subject. Just to stand this
close took an immense amount of fortitude and effort. Looking back, I
should have run away, but instead I made plans: the best laid plans of
mice and soon to be dead men.

The terrain made it easy to estimate roughly where the actual grave
was. Two hard rock ridges framed a small plateau of earth in what seemed
the only geologically possible setting. Kicking the dirt twice, I could feel
the soil was hard, but I hoped workable enough for my forty year-old
muscles, but then without warning, almost as if to remind me of the dif-
ficulties to come, a westbound train decided to screech, rumble and roar
by, much too close for comfort, creating a violent cacophony of sound and
raw energy. The beast of a machine overwhelmed everything around foolish enough to have remained close. The vibrations continued for over two
minutes as the countless railway cars passed by. After the last, I set about
facilitating my return in the dark, hopefully unseen, leaving two markers
pointing to the gravesite.

Now there was nothing but time.

Walking back to the truck, Rex jumped up front into the cab out of
the cold as we drove out the park north across the Benicia Bridge. Somehow a drive to nowhere contemplating the countryside and soft rolling
light brown hills was far easier than imagining my fast approaching date
with destiny. On the other side, unannounced, rain started coming down
in torrents, so hard the torrent made the car sound like a steel drum in a
Caribbean band. Actually, the sound was a blessing, allowing me a moment to forget everything, like in the old days. For an instant, I even considered wetting a lure when this was all over.

Then, about the time I was getting used to his silence, he said:

*He was never intended to be the one. He was only a caretaker while I
waited for you to declare yourself ready. Therefore, relax, my boy, and realize*

there is nothing he can have left you that changes anything about the choice you have to make. However, I will tell you one thing that I did find interesting today and that was... well... surprising. I never knew she followed me out here.

I knew what he was doing, and what he wanted. He was trying, talking about Clara, after today, to coax me into conversation and away from the strength my knowing about her had given me. To make what he knew we needed to do later go smoother. He could feel the apprehensive rumblings inside me too. This time his famous con wasn't going to work. I refused to answer him, letting him ramble on by himself until he grew bored and finished up by reminding me again to bring the books with me to the grave tonight. Then he gave up.

Twenty miles later, were it not for the new gristle Clara had provided me, I would have been shocked to see that the road I was driving on was named Lake Herman Road, 'Herman' standing out as if in neon.

The road meandered through old country before finally passing Blue Rock Springs Park, the site of the first Zodiac Killer slaying in 1970. Tonight the park was empty, as was usually the case when still early before the young lovers filled the secluded spots, the same young lovers who were unaware what horrors had occurred here. I wondered how long they would have stayed in the park had they known who I was when they pulled up next to me later that night.

Knowing I needed the rest, I reclined the seat all the way back to rest my head, but instead of sleep, my mind replayed images of Holmes being here, the voice, during the time of the Zodiac killings and what, if any, connection he might have had to those more modern horrors. The never ending Holmes' coincidences. But tonight there wasn't enough time for that. Someone else, someone alive tomorrow, would have to take up that possibility.

So with Rex curled up at my feet and me pacified by thoughts of certain eternity, I closed my eyes, set everything aside, and honest to God dozed off.

The sleep of the soon to be dead.

CHAPTER 32

Short hours later, who knows how many, I woke with a start. As deep slumber so often does to the exhausted, I forgot, in that mental fog, where I was. Minutes later, rational thought having returned, the first noticeable thing was the very real, very heavy Bay Area fog famous for obscuring everything. Tonight it was living up to its reputation.

Wiping the sleep from my eyes, I knew now was time to head back to the grave; it was certainly dark enough, with the fog providing that additional level of obscurity for grave-robbing. Gathering needed gumption, I drank the going cold liquor store coffee I'd bought earlier down the road. Rex amazed me by jumping up on the front seat to rest his head on my lap, the first time he'd ever done anything even remotely that friendly before. A dog's intuition, I guessed. He knew I needed something. Not quite knowing how, I stroked his ears, amazed how easy the simple gesture was and how much we both enjoyed the act.

"You all set for this, boy?" He raised his head and stared at me, his eyes as eager as ever. Fearing the worst for both of us, I patted him on the side, "Sorry, Rex."

Ten miles and twenty minutes later, we parked at the lot, nary another car or person anywhere to be seen. Two steps from the car, with a flash of lightening, the rain and breeze came up again and flushed away the fog. Now our horror was cold, wet, windy and soon to be muddy-- just perfect.

The park was pitch black, the only light, what little there was, coming from the dim cast from far across the river, and barely enough to function by. I remember wishing the horror-movie full moon would appear from between the clouds to shed more illumination on our precarious future path. Giving up, I reached into the box on the bed of the truck and grabbed the pick, shovel and hardware store flashlight. The backpack keeping the diaries dry. Once properly outfitted we trekked down to the tracks.

The crack and rumble of periodic thunder vibrated the night, the light and sound almost one on top of the other, heaven's way to warn of the possibility of being struck. Despite the natural terror of it all, to say nothing of the night's supernatural aspect, we moved on, scared to death, but undeterred.

Retracing my earlier steps to the track changers shack, I stepped off the rail ties, unable to hear a thing over the din of the rain and the thunder, which, knowing lightning's preference for metal, concerned me greatly walking on the steel tracks. That and the fact that should the westbound train come up behind us while we were on the tracks, I wasn't sure we'd hear a thing until much too late. The conditions were beginning to make it harder and harder for me to even show up, let alone win.

Fazed, I fumbled through the pockets of my jacket, but couldn't find the extra medication stocked away for just such a feeling of over-exposure. That twisting wrenched feeling was beginning to dominate my gut. I needed to fight the next seizure back.

Over the pounding rain, "Don't need the pill, damn thing wouldn't have worked anyway."

Except for Rex, I couldn't have been more alone in the entire world.

Five minutes later, and soaked to the bone, we were at the grave and just in time for the midnight train as the giant shook, rattled and rolled everything within a hundred feet of the lines. We were a lot closer than that. The incline of the hill made the train seem even closer, as the exhaust from the huge diesels spit out all covering me while roaring by. If the engineer had seen us in his bright-as-the-sun floodlight when they passed, I knew the police would be here within minutes.

Reacting to the train and heavy rain, a small landslide of mud soaked rocks fluttered down the embankment and clustered over the grave, only stopping long after the train disappeared around the bend-- just something else to scramble my nerves even more.

I needed to get back on top, so to speak.

"Been waiting for me long? Tell me, old man!" I yelled down into the earth. The sort of yell all of us give late at night after hearing a strange noise and fearing there might be a burglar in the house. That yell of false bravado you think just might convince them you're not really scared to death. But you are, as all of us are in the dark, shaking in our boots and just plain lucky when each such episode ends up that the yell hadn't been needed in the first place.

Welcome, Jeffrey, what took you so long?

Ah, there he was, dear old Herman.

I knew you'd put the silliness behind you to come set me free. You're too good a man to have forsaken family. Hurry now, for we have so much to do.

On my first swing the hairs on my arm stood on end as the pick slid into the earth much too easily, reminding me of a steak knife in soft butter left out overnight for French toast, or as if he'd been buried the night before. Shaking my head in disbelief, I mumbled that this didn't make any sense, not the way the earth looked and felt this afternoon.

Useless, I threw the pick up on the bank—the sharp end wouldn't be needed and began shoveling as fast as I could. As the hole gradually deepened the rain-wash began collecting around my boots making the entire pit a foul muddy mess. I would have to hurry or I'd be swimming in this thing before long. Within minutes the sweat began to roll down off my head into my eyes, overpowering even the heavy rain, flowing down my back and across my chest, as much from the terror as the exertion of the dig. To free my arms, I took off my overcoat and rolled up my sleeves, wishing for gloves, my hands already blistering.

The thought that he was crouched below ready to spring forth when enough of the earth was removed made each progressive lift of dirt heavier. Despite that, I kept digging, while our conversation escalated.

You have two or three more feet to go, be careful when you get close. You wouldn't want to harm your sweet grandpa now would you?

Shoveling, "How did you, old man, the supposed genius of all time, end up here, in this devil-forsaken place? Where did your plans go awry?"

He surprised me, that one, the man you called Uncle. I made the mistake of telling him my plans about you and demanding his assistance. After all, he was my grandson. You were three or four at the time, and just beginning to demonstrate an eagerness to learn. We made plans to meet here alongside the tracks, way out nowhere, to discuss your lessons, and instead, and out of the blue, he did this to me.

The more we talked the smaller the gap between reality and fantasy became. Unable to take much more, I stopped digging to take one last look for one of the pills Adam had given me and still couldn't find them. We kept up our chat.

I will admit, he really did surprise me.

Within two hours, the hole was deep enough to require tip toes to see over the high side of the grave. On the low side, the railroad tracks were within maybe two shovels' throw. Rex was nowhere to be seen, but I knew still up there, over me, someplace, keeping an eye out.

That's deep enough, my boy.

At that declaration, no longer needed, I heaved the shovel up and over the top.

Good! Now get down on your knees and search for me with your hands.

Covered in mud, I found them, the first of his remains, that is, after half digging, half swimming in the bottom of that pit for twenty more minutes. Not his entire body, mind you, but one hand, the hand that I could only assume he had reached up to the light with as he expired with his last breath. How I didn't know, the hand had remained extended, straight up, pinioned between rocks, for the past forty-some years. Clearing the dirt from around the arm bones, the cloud cover overhead decided at that moment to separate just enough to allow some of the moon to shine down on my work. The ring that ring the newspapers wrote about one hundred and twenty years ago at the trial, for the first time in decades washed by the rain, glistened in the light for the first time in decades.

Handcuffs hung from his wrist.

My discovery was accentuated by a sudden stillness, the wind going dead calm, and his sudden laughter ringing like a bell in my head. The devil himself was mocking my foolishness for having been so susceptible to have performed something so dangerous, or was Holmes just so excited by his coming freedom after all these years he couldn't contain himself any longer? The laughter soon died away to be replaced by his familiar whisper, accompanied now by the physical presence of his breath on my ear:

That's yours, my boy. Go ahead and take it. Take the ring. Don't worry; I won't feel a thing.

I couldn't breathe. Instead of doing what he said, I jumped up and out of the pit, sitting on the edge while looking down at the ring adorning the boney finger of his hand outstretched as if toward the moon.

Bones, long buried bones, didn't stay together like that, did they? Was this spectacle even possible, or just another figment of my diseased imagination?

He didn't give me time to consider this anomaly. *Don't dither. The remaining pages you and your friend were pondering are down there with me. They need to be rejoined with the others in the books. All you need to do in order to walk away from all this a free, immensely powerful man is to climb back down, find them, and allow me to instruct you in the proper way to apply they're secrets. Hurry, there's no time for delay, so let us continue.*

I closed my eyes and imagined Bert, forty years ago atop the grave, hurling shovels full of earth, as quickly as he could, and piling dirt upon the grandfather he never ever knew. Killing his own relative. Above it all, or more correctly, below, was Holmes, handcuffed, trying to talk him out of the courageous act, spinning the bald faced lies he was renowned for. Quite helpless, except, that is, for his famous tongue and powerful stares.

Bert, expiring from cancer, would have continued on, no matter what the monster said, with his duty and destiny. He knew he could stop and choose the other option, the one that would cure his curse, erasing his pain. All he had to do was pledge fealty and ask this evil thing, his grand-father, for help. But no, he refused to take the easy way out, instead continuing on doing what he knew in his heart he was right.

God, what a different man Bert had turned out to be from the one I grew up thinking he was.

At the very end, when dirt was replacing oxygen in Holmes' open mouth, Holmes applied his great Houdini-like talents, and removed the handcuff from one hand and forced his arm up through the heavy dirt. Never giving up. But it would have been too late. And there the arm and hand and ring had stayed waiting for the one.

All this time they'd waited for me.

Using the tactics I had learned reading his own horrible exploits, I asked the bones, "Bert put those handcuffs on you, didn't he Herman?"

Yes, while I was reading to him from the pages you shall soon possess, he rather cagily snuck up behind me and attached the devices. But enough about him, for he is long gone. Instead of wasting any more time, let's take a closer look at your new ring.

Instead of doing what he wanted, I paused.

To remind me who was in control, Holmes upped the ante by playing a different card. Pain, as with a knife, sliced through me, causing me to scream out in agony. This was now too much; I couldn't take anymore. I simply wasn't strong enough. His application of pain making my mind up for me. Agreeing to agree, I cocked my head back like a wolf to the moon and gave in, anything to stop the pain, screaming this time, "Yes," and jumped back down into the pit to find those pages to end this curse. I no longer cared which innocent would have to pay for my luxury. The agony was unbearable!

To hell with them all! We both laughed out together, liking the sound of genetic stereo. From his tone I knew the bastard was devilishly proud of his prodigy.

Sinking deeper and deeper into the mud at the bottom of the pit, seeing up over the edge of the grave was becoming more and more difficult. The visual perspective of it all began to flash in and out of focus almost replaying what had occurred at the post office basement. I couldn't help but thinking, Holmes had the remote control for the rest of my life in his hand.

With a crack and flash of lightning, the channel changed and I went from being the one doing the digging in the bottom of the pit to the one at the top observing the fool's labor. The top of the head beneath me was below the earth's surface, periodically lifting handfuls of mud over the top and onto a growing pile. The work was steady, disciplined and with purpose. The shifting rays from the moon were striking the heavy rain that disappeared into the pit, cloaking the work in a kaleidoscope of cinema. Whomever was below digging hadn't the slightest idea there was someone up above on the edge watching his work.

Without warning, and another crack, the channels switched back, and I was the one down in the pit. Curious, I lifted my head above ground level to see who the watcher was. There was no one there.

The mud at the bottom of the pit, now almost to my knees, was pulling hard at my feet and legs, each movement causing a loud suction sound above the noise of the storm. I was doubtful I'd be able to extract myself without help. To make matters worse, as if that were indeed possible, the ground below the mud began to shake and the air above my head pulsated as another roaring train streamed by, but in the opposite direction, making the entire pit feel like the center of an earthquake. One of the assist locomotives was running up-track to clear a scheduled train from a landslide, one of many affecting the area because of flooding. Had I been thinking clearly, I would have realized that the same locomotive would be coming right back at me down in my Poe's pit, followed by another bigger train close creating double the intensity.

But I wasn't-- thinking clearly that is.

The train's vibrations cleared the last of the earth around Holmes. His skeleton was disheveled, having been thrown in without the slightest care or concern for his eternal posture. Bert would have enjoyed that part, dumping him into the hole like a rat and then haphazardly shoveling dirt over him, later luxuriating in his eternal discomfort.

Bert had buried him alive.

Pieces of the skeleton came away easily in my hand. There was no perceptible odor. The upper torso remained fairly well clothed by a jacket of stiff leather, the cotton pants having long since disintegrated. Despite having been close to one hundred at the time of his death, and forty more in the dirt, the remains were remarkably well preserved.

"For such an old man, you took pretty good care of yourself."

As will you, once I show you how the science is applied. Now, keep going!

Before giving my muscles a chance to obey, I grabbed the skull, and, holding the heavy bone up with both hands, was amazed at the condition of his teeth: they were perfect! Thrusting the skull even higher up into the rain, I washed the dirt off his head, turning the skull this way and that, all the while the empty eye sockets staring back at me with a haunting taunt that chilled me to my already frozen bones.

There was no sign of arthritis, bone disease, joint inflammation or breaks of any kind. Where was the evidence of ninety nine years of life? What a specimen dead Holmes was! The only thing of any significance, other than the large size of his hands, was the ring he was wearing on the little finger of that extended hand. The ring appeared fused to the bone of his finger as if he were born with the jewelry.

The ring is yours. Take it to wear forever. The ring shall be recognized. Wear my gift to you with pride.

Without hesitating, I broke the finger off above the first joint. The ring was solid gold, except for the stone in the center. The dark red ruby was at least four carats. The facets were uncut and worn at the edges. At the center of the ruby was a brilliant white spot that dazzled each time the ring was turned in the moonlight. It looked to be a diamond. Removing the ring from the bone would require a chisel, and time. I didn't have any to spare, so the ring with bone went into my back pocket.

Then, *snap*, the channel switched and I was back on top leaning out over the edge looking down into the grave trying to see what was going on. I watched myself break the ring finger free from the hand. How eerie to replay that act! Strange sounds emerged from the hole as the bones were moved, clinking together like wind chimes. The dog barked and the 'me" below stopped his labors to lift himself to the edge, looking for what had alerted the dog, and, finding nothing, settling back down to his work searching for the pages. He'd looked directly through me as though I weren't even there.

Not understanding how, why or when, my hand was filled with the same shovel thrown out of the pit. I couldn't even remember having picked the damn thing up. Why did I need a shovel up here? The digging was being done down there.

I crawled back to the edge and was surprised to see there were now three men in the grave: Holmes, myself, and another, unrecognizable fellow. He was standing at the opposite side of the pit, as far away from Holmes as he could get while still in the hole. He wore round glasses and showed a quiet confident demeanor. The 'me' down there obviously didn't know either of them was in the hole with him. The grave was so crowded that any efforts removing mud or moving the skeleton caused arms and legs to pass right through the bodies of both men, but they didn't seem to mind. Holmes could be seen reading from one of the diaries, issuing orders from its contents. I reached around behind and searched the backpack where I had secured the books to keep them from getting wet-- sure enough they were both gone! I couldn't recall having ever removed them.

Back below, the two men were intensely interested in what my labors might result in.

Over them, I squeezed my eyes shut, put both hands to the sides of my head, and screamed as loud as I possibly could before collapsing in fear on my back in the tainted mud. Multiple personalities, visions, voices and rapidly changing visual perspectives; every one of the medical treatises on mental disorders mentioned these same phenomena. Could there be any doubt my mind was finally lost?

The channel changed again and back down into the pit I went. Turning full circle there was nothing but dirt and bones. The two extras were nowhere to be seen. "There's no one in this damn pit but me," I screamed.

Rifling through the inside top left pocket of Holmes's coat, I found a leather case, a dossier, which I hunched over to shield from the rain before reading. The dossier was full of bloodstained handwritten pages, torn from books, just like the ones in Chicago. The realization that these notes might contain be the cure to my condition shook me to my core.

I knew I would do what he wanted to get what I needed.

Of course you will, my son. I've already witnessed your willingness. These things happen every day, Jeffrey. Nature takes what's now yours every day, and with impunity. You are to be one of the few takers in a world full of beggars.

Heat overpowered me as the power in my hands became sensual, wicked even with a heady thrill that was impossible to refuse. I no longer needed to deny the actions my lineage demanded! Wicked fascination washed over me in a sheer wave of evil ecstasy.

I knew you were the one when I watched you with your mother. Three skips apart we are you and I, just as I was from the previous. You are the chosen one.

Here, there, when, or how, nothing then mattered, for in the bottom of that pit, my life had the clarity I'd always lacked. Herman's belief that death was the clearest of all life's mysteries had just come true. The evil that I'd fought off my entire life, never understanding my difference, was climbing up to rest on my shoulders like a pet. It was pulling me up leaving me weightless.

I remember the first time my eyes were opened. Rejoice for all that you will be has only just begun. Step out of this pit for these old bones were never important anyway, no, only the pages, that ring and your priceless awareness. You were the only one that could set me free from this prison. Thank you, my son.

I was teetering on the edge of eternity. None of the experiences from the past forty years mattered. They had all been worthless backdrop.

Chance had nothing to do with my ending up here in the bottom of this pit. My life had been according to script, directed by the most evil being who had ever existed.

There was no longer me.

My final transition to evil was interrupted by the other in the pit offering me his hand and asking, "Jeff, do you remember demanding answers to those questions you asked about long ago?"

Wait! I told myself. *That wasn't Holmes. Whose voice was this now?*

"Those answers you demanded from Him? I made the same demands once."

This voice sounded like Bert's.

"He will answer you Jeff, he will answer you if you remain strong, but he will also answer you if you continue to weaken, both ways you will be told. But let me warn you, his response may be different than you expect."

The voice *was* Bert's!

He was talking about those questions asking about God My demands for proof despite the monster he condoned in our midst.

Don't listen to him or the buffoon of which he speaks. Both are weak, what have they ever done, or did the one he worships do to me while I was alive, Holmes demanded. *Listen to me, He sat back and watched me torture thousands, thousands that were as innocent as a summer's sunrise. He did nothing, not even as I taunted and dared him over the screams and pleas of those he was said to love. He sat back and watched them bleed.*

There I was, between the two debaters, a crazy man at the bottom of a seven-foot pit filling with mud, bones floating upon the surface, mere feet from active railroad tracks, fighting schizophrenia, with both hands covering my ears screaming bloody murder over absolutely none of it, or positively all of it.

"He's right you know," Bert interrupted. "His response will only be understood by one of strength and devoutness," Bert proclaimed. "Faith can only come from within. Our blood, however horrible, was never to be the determining cause. Neither were the terrible natural instincts Herman did indeed bestow on you. Your solution begins and ends with your own will to defeat those impulses. Do you understand what I am trying to tell you? Remember, His only answer will be the one you make good on your own."

What could I do? A ghost was telling me God was only as real as the strength of my own convictions, regardless of the overwhelming evidence against his muddy sermon. I was lost and the medicine wasn't helping.

"Let me think, God damn you all!" I screamed at them both, intentionally taking His name in vain, almost hoping for a directed lightning bolt to end my misery. Time, I needed time, and this was about eternity for heaven's sake. I didn't know what to do. No one, and I do mean none, ever before me ever had.

Perhaps the fear of hell fire made my decision for me, but I doubt it. Maybe my all-embracing egoism or a final need for self-assertion. Or could have been my new found admiration for Clara and her incredible strength under similar circumstances. She no doubt played a part, but somehow the hatred in my gut for the one I now realized had controlled my entire life ruled the day. That knowledge burned through me like real flame.

Holmes knew my final decision before the deal was done, yelling, "No!"

Unbelievably powerful, his exclamation was no longer just a voice within my head, but a scream that seemed to stop the wind and rain cold.

My last image of his ghost were the soles of his shoes as he crawled up over the edge of the pit and took the shovel from my other hands. He never said another word, he just started laughing as hard as any man had ever laughed, but of course he wasn't a man.

Then he started shoveling dirt down on me the same way he had in all those nightmares. The ones after finding the books.

This hole in the earth, this culmination of everything that ever was, would be *my* grave unless I did something fast, but every time I tried scrambling up the side, the walls gave way, and splash, back down into the bottom I would go. And as if that wasn't enough for any one human being to endure, the earth was vibrating; which could only mean one thing-- another train was on its way!

While the locomotive's roar grew louder and louder, the side of the embankment started to slide down in hundreds of small rock and mud slides that funneled through the two ridges directly into the pit. The water was now to my waist as the rocks showered down on me, forcing me to turn away to keep them from knocking me unconscious. No such luck. The biggest hit me above the ear knocking me face down into the pit and barely conscious.

The train's pulse rippled across the pond at the bottom of the pit. Super-heated chaos ensued approximating hell on earth. Roaring by, the machine spewed heated rain water steam with such energy that my body was yanked as if a puppet on a string. That same force set off a landslide that buried me alive in a great avalanche of debris that re-filled my Great-Great-Grandfather's grave with fresh dirt. His bones, sharp and jagged, cut deeply into my back as hundreds of pounds of earth found their final resting place upon my chest.

With what strength was left, I grabbed his coat, clutching both sides as tightly as possible and circled the old leather over my head to shield me from the rocks and hopefully accumulate as much oxygen as was possible. The coat smelled musty and foul.

Within the bounds of normal human desperation, I considered yelling to him, telling him I had changed my mind! For him to give me another chance at life and death, but I didn't, for any number of reasons, not the least of which was knowing that opening my mouth to yell would only serve to fill the opening with mud. Besides, I knew he'd never listen to me again.

Coughing violently, fighting to breathe, I knew he was up there laughing, enjoying my final seconds, gleefully aware of what was occurring, him having gone through this same thing himself. But he was no longer concerned with me, having already moved on to the next-- the way nature works.

Then, as if on a switch, the shaking ceased, the train having stopped, stuck next to the grave in the landslide of its own making. What an instant before was so loud as to hurt, was now a deafening silence... quiet as a tomb. The train engineers standing six feet above and twenty feet away had no idea who or what they had helped bury.

Facing my end, Bert's written words flashed in my head, "The final moments are what define a man."

I had failed and would end up with *him* in hell.

"No," Bert said, "every man who is tested, truly tested, comes close to the edge of failure. Those we honor as the greatest often came the closest. We are, after all, just men."

His words soothed in that claustrophobic blackness, the coat going further and further into my mouth as starving lungs dragged out the last available remnants of air. I knew what he meant... those pages and the choice had been my test. Those pages, in one form or another, were the tool used to test all men with. Holmes, alive and dead, had been just a tool. Bert had forced this ordeal, the way he lived, insisting the condemned be given one last chance to choose. The first forty years of my life had been spent waiting. Now - laughing at the ridiculousness of the moment-- my life finally belonged to me.

So with my last gasp would come my final statement. Recalling the fascination I'd felt the moment I'd discovered that up-reached hand, I was forced to admit that whatever one thought of the monster, his final act of will was admirable. The same would be my statement of victory; proof of the slaying of my dragon. With this act, the world would know, if ever found, that good had won out over evil, and Holmes been defeated twice - a declaration my child could be proud of. So with every last bit of energy I was as a man, I forced my hand up in the dirt, through the rocks, gritting my teeth in pain, until my hand was straight up, out and away from me, towards the earth, the moon, the sky above.

There was only one thing left. The beating of my heart… bump, bump, bump, the oxygen gone, fed now only by remaining adrenaline, slowing in a depleted rhythm that was painfully perceptible, the muscle breaking down, unable to coordinate… bump… bump.. bump, the real beats and echoes confused, my lungs collapsing as the material over my mouth was involuntarily dragged down my throat… bump… then waiting for another, but none coming, never another, stopped, the black in my eyes becoming blacker.

After shedding one final tear knowing my body would be the one to never experience the weight of flowers, I let go, but before ending told myself that my death had served a purpose, and that given the chance to judge myself, I'd be proud.

Everything surrounding me then culminated in a strange sound, impossible to describe really, but certainly electrical in nature. The energy almost palpable in a physical sort of way. There was also a vibration of incredible intensity that I guessed was my body's tissue being broken down. Excruciating, the 'direction' seemed to gain strength while gathering me in its influence.

This new place was a nothing, a crushing and at the same time weightless nothing. An infinite nothing, of not even chaos, just zero. There was no place, no going to, no coming from, nothing to see, feel, hear or taste. There was no temperature. There was no cold, only a lack of heat. Could *nothing*, just empty, make noise and leave a sound? Impossible to even comprehend, it seemed to here, as a steady pounding began taking place and from far away from the inside of what used to be my eardrums. And wet, all was wet in a damp musty primeval sense, dripping down off nonexistent surfaces.

Crushing anxiety dunked in agony, one without limits or boundaries. There was no heat, no flames, no beings with horns on their heads. How I wished there were, for they would have been so much easier to accept. Instead, my hell was a compressed oblivion of fear. All good was gone.

Instants as eons and vice-versa, my entire being was snapped like a rubber band, as all matter was forced to catch up with my extreme movement and then slammed to a stop, restrained by what felt a great power. An incredibly bright light burned through me. Had I arms I would have lifted my hands to cover nonexistent eyes from the intensity of the torch. 'Bang, bang', a terrible pounding reverberated to every spot, repetitive, again and again, shaking what used to be my very soul with every beat.

Then faith happened.

The agony faded away and was replaced by hope-- a hope as limitless as the agony had been moments before. All my sorrow departed. All around me was still a nothing, but now a good nothing. By whom or what I have no idea, it just was, but only for the most instant of instants. Before I was given anytime to experience this heavenly nirvana, and assuredly wish never to leave, the same "sizzle and crack!" jolted me as electrical power surged through theoretical veins and burst open in a bath of what seemed fresh air. Sucking in with everything my newfound soul was, the old me gasped at life again. My lungs actually groaning desperately, pulling as much oxygen as they could get in as short a period of time as was possible, hacking, spitting and coughing all over myself. The pain was immense. There was no way to tell how long the gap between the two snaps had been. The duration could have been seconds or a million years, who knows, but when everything stopped I was allowed another indiscriminate period of time to relax in what I knew, could feel in my actual bones again, was another chance at life by someone or something who knew I deserved the opportunity, and by the slimmest of threads.

Coming to, the piercing light and immense pounding was still there. Opening my eyes and regaining focus I was shocked to see the huge horribly out of perspective face of a California Highway Patrolman staring down at me, his halogen flashlight blinding me, banging on my car's window inches from my face. Rex was barking at him, teeth bared, ready to fight to the death. The moon, as beautiful as I'd ever seen the orb, was shining down through the sunroof. Allowing me the thirty seconds he thought was needed to gather myself, the officer commenced to inform me that loitering was not permitted at Blue Rock Springs. "Move on, sir, or I'll be forced to issue a citation."

Looking about the car, I was shocked to see that there was no mud, no blood, nothing that could be associated with my earlier activities at Eckley. Reaching over to settle Rex, his coat was dry, when moments before he had been soaked to the bone. My watch read twenty minutes after midnight. Where was the time; where had the hours gone?

Had my journey all been a dream? Was this, no that, another seizure?

Outside the wind fluttered then went completely calm. Silence dominated the surroundings around the car. So quiet, I imagined hearing Sue sleeping, softly breathing in our bed at home. Then what I'd just been through became perfectly clear. Shaking my head, grinning even, I started the car waving goodbye to the patrolman. Real or imagined was of little consequence, I told myself. Either way, being *there* had defined who I was for the first time in my entire life.

At the exit from the park, I had one last choice to make. Left back to Eckley, and his grave, or right onto the freeway and home. I didn't even hesitate. There was no need going back.

Sue was waiting for me.

EPILOGUE

Looking back I really couldn't say how much was real and how much imagined-- or whether I actually *was* going insane. Over time, the seizures, gaps, even the wobbles slowed and finally stopped. My head cleared. Within a year the pain was gone. MRI revealed that the tumor had mysteriously disappeared. The closest the doctors could come to explaining my condition was by comparing my brain to a computer that had been rebooted. They surmised that when I experienced what they were sure had been a third grand mal in the car that night, and died again, my brain was defragged then reprogrammed clean minus the suspect virus. Without the tumor, my brain was relieved of the pressure that had caused the dementia, as the organ was again allowed to float free within my scull. During their examinations they took so much blood trying to isolate a natural anti-carcinogen in my body I thought they were going to drain me dry. Finally, I told them no more. Some things are better just left alone.

The family, looking out for my best interests and perhaps theirs as well, talked me into a year of therapy. Those days were spent with specialists attempting to teach me to recognize and control the self-created images and voices those same experts were sure the entire episode had been derived from. They went on and on, explaining that nothing had been real, that I had made it all up. Holmes had been executed, they said, just like the history books reported. Rather than debate the issue, and perhaps hoping they were correct, I went along with most everything they suggested.

When they were done, one warm sunny day, the dog and I returned and walked the tracks east of C&H Sugar. There was something still nagging at my brain. Remembering, I walked up close to the site and stood there resolute within my own being, my own mind, thinking about the journey that began when I opened those two old tackle boxes and ended at this very spot-- from my grandfather's fishing map. Looking about me, nothing was disturbed, or altered in any manner. The totality might as well have been make believe. That is except for two small matters-- as we neared the spot where I remembered the grave should be, Rex dug in and refused to come any closer, instead growling with an intensity that left little doubt in my mind. His obvious hatred of what was below our feet was all I needed to know in order to determine what was real and what was imagined. For you see, Rex hadn't needed therapy.

That and one other incongruity -- directly across and within a rock-slides' distance from where we were standing, the railroad ties had been repaired.

I think about him a lot now-- just the other day as a matter of fact. I was fly-fishing for Brook Trout in the Grand Tetons. The air was so clear that the mountains on both sides pressed over my face in that timeless sensation. There was a herd of elk a hundred yards away, fording the river, each animal watching my casts. Even though my creel was empty, I was enjoying the peace and quiet.

I flipped my fly forward into the stream with a practiced motion: the tight shoulder, delayed elbow and stiff wrist combination so out of reach for most. When done right, like a tango, the fly-cast can be watched for hours.

Dad was fifty yards downstream, his rod bent, fighting what looked to be a beauty. I knew I'd be hearing about his success and my lack of luck for hours unless I caught something fast. I was happy for him.

My fly was working closer and closer to a small hollow on the opposite side over a clean smooth boulder that broke the surface and progress of the flow, just the spot some lunker might prefer after fighting current all morning. On the fifth cast, the fly landed two feet in the hollow and was jumped by just the one I'd been told was there. Setting the barbless hook, I looked down at the glassy hip high waters and saw him, wearing his bowler, just where I knew Bert would be, at my shoulder, smiling, watching the entire episode.

"Thanks, Grandpa."

"Call me Pops."